PRAISE FOR JEREMY ROB

"[SecondWorld] is gripping, propelled by expe̶r̶t̶l̶y̶ ̶c̶o̶n̶t̶r̶o̶l̶l̶e̶d pacing and lively characters. Robinson's punchy prose style will appeal to fans of Matthew Reilly's fast-paced, bigger-than-life thrillers, but this is in no way a knockoff. It's a fresh and satisfying thriller that should bring its author plenty of new fans."

— Booklist

"A brisk thriller with neatly timed action sequences, snappy dialogue and the ultimate sympathetic figure in a badly burned little girl with a fighting spirit... The Nazis are determined to have the last gruesome laugh in this efficient doomsday thriller."

— Kirkus Reviews

"Relentless pacing and numerous plot twists drive this compelling stand-alone from Robinson... Thriller fans and apocalyptic fiction aficionados alike will find this audaciously plotted novel enormously satisfying."

— Publisher's Weekly

"A harrowing, edge of your seat thriller told by a master storyteller, Jeremy Robinson's Secondworld is an amazing, globetrotting tale that will truly leave you breathless."

— Richard Doestch, bestselling author of HALF-PAST DAWN

"Robinson blends myth, science and terminal velocity action like no one else."

— Scott Sigler, NY Times Bestselling author of NOCTURNAL

"Just when you think that 21st-century authors have come up with every possible way of destroying the world, along comes Jeremy Robinson."

— New Hampshire Magazine

"Threshold elevates Robinson to the highest tier of over-the-top action authors and it delivers beyond the expectations even of his fans. The next Chess Team adventure cannot come fast enough."

— Booklist Starred Review

ALSO BY JEREMY ROBINSON

Standalone Novels

SecondWorld
Project Nemesis
Island 731

The Jack Sigler Thrillers

Pulse
Instinct
Threshold
Ragnarok

The Chess Team Novellas
(Chesspocalypse Series)

Callsign: King - Book 1
Callsign: Queen - Book 1
Callsign: Rook - Book 1
Callsign: King - Book 2
Callsign: Bishop - Book 1
Callsign: Knight - Book 1
Callsign: Deep Blue - Book 1
Callsign: King - Book 3

The Last Hunter
(Antarktos Saga)

The Last Hunter - Descent
The Last Hunter - Pursuit
The Last Hunter - Ascent
The Last Hunter - Lament
The Last Hunter – Onslaught

The Origins Editions
(First five novels)

The Didymus Contingency
Raising The Past
Beneath
Antarktos Rising
Kronos

Writing as Jeremy Bishop

Torment
The Sentinel
The Raven

Humor Books

The Ninja's Path
The Zombie's Way

PROJECT NEMESIS

JEREMY ROBINSON

BREAKNECK MEDIA

ISBN 978-0-9886725-1-2

Printed in the United States of America

Visit Jeremy Robinson on the World Wide Web at:
www.jeremyrobinsononline.com

For WLVI Channel 56, for airing Creature Double Feature every Saturday morning of my childhood.

ACKNOWLEDGMENTS

Kaiju. It means "strange beast" in Japanese and describes a genre that includes Godzilla, King Kong, Gamera, Mothra and many more. I've been in love with the genre since I was a kid, and while my novels feature all manner of strange beasts, from aliens and stone golems to the mythological Hyrdra and half-human, half-demon Nephilim, I had never written a true homage to the genre that has fueled my imagination for the past thirty years. Well, now I have and it's one of my most fun stories to date, there are a few people I must thank, who made this book better than I could have on my own.

Kane Gilmour, my sometimes co-author, editor and constant supporter, you not only edited *Project Nemesis*, you single-handedly convinced me to pursue this long term dream. Thank you for that, but now you need to finish *your* Kaiju novel!

Jason Brodeur also lent a hand in editing Project Nemesis and did a fantastic job polishing the book until it gleamed like King Gidorah's golden scales.

The amazing Matt Frank, *Godzilla* artist extraordinaire, thank you so much for lending your formidable skills to *Project Nemesis* and designing a creature far cooler than what my imagination had conjured. I look forward to future collaborations!

I must also thank Thomas Dunne Books, my hardcover publisher, and Peter Wolverton, my editor there, for supporting this solo effort by offering opinions and running an advertisement for *Project Nemesis* in the paperback of *SecondWorld*. Your support of my self-publishing efforts is greatly appreciated.

No acknowledgements from this author can be complete without thanking the band of misfits who make writing about giant monsters so much more fun: Aquila, Solomon and Norah, my kids and fellow Kaiju fans, your imaginations inspire and intimidate me. And to my dear wife, you know what I'm going to say. I love you.

PROJECT
NEMESIS

"Νέμεσι πτερόεσσα βίου ῥοπά,
κυανῶπι θεά, θύγατερ Δίκας,
ἁ κοῦφα φρυάγματα θνατῶν,
ἐπέχεις ἀδάμαντι χαλινῷ."

"Nemesis, winged tilter of scales and lives,
Justice-spawned Goddess with sinister eyes!
Thou bridlest evil men who roil in vain
Against Thy harsh adamantine rein."
                    — Hymn to Nemesis, Mesomedes of Crete

PROLOGUE I

Five Years Ago

"Get down, stay quiet and don't move a muscle or we're stains," Master Sergeant Lenny Wilson whispered as he lay down, pushing his body deeper into the three-foot deep snow.

His partner's only reply was to shift his body farther out of sight. The white masks and full body BDUs they wore helped them to disappear, but the noon-day sun would reflect differently off their clothing. To the trained eye, they would stand out like a patch of matte finish on a glossy book cover.

And Wilson had no doubt the men searching for them would spot the aberration. There were fifty of them now, swarming through the mountainous pine forest. Packs of hungry wolves.

The ten men approaching their position were armed with an array of deadly high-tech weapons, but the hunt would end as soon as Wilson or his partner was spotted. Not just because they were outnumbered or unarmed but because that's the way the game was played.

They were being hunted.

Like animals.

Wilson pressed his face into the snow and remained still. He filled his mouth with snow and breathed around it, keeping his breath from condensing and giving away their position. He could only hope Endo was doing the same. Corporal Katsu Endo was on loan from the Japanese Self-Defense Force as part of a program that partnered seasoned American warriors with Japanese partners who'd never seen combat. The official spin on the program was that it built stronger ties between the two countries' militaries, but that didn't make much sense since the Japanese military had been limited to self-defense since the end of World War Two. It was bullshit, Wilson believed. The Japanese were being trained with the intention that they would one day see combat again, probably against the Chinese.

The Japanese Self-Defense Force was actually a vassal military for the U.S., should the need arise. That was Wilson's opinion at least, and he didn't disapprove. The Chinese would eventually be a problem. He felt sure of it. Still, he wasn't keen on being partnered with Endo. The man had never been in a situation like this. He lacked survival instincts, like a penguin in the desert. And Wilson had a reputation to protect. If Endo screwed this up...well, the man would get his first real lesson in how shitty his self-defense tactics really were.

"See anything?" someone asked. The voice was deep and gruff.

The question got four replies, all negative.

Boots crunched through the snow, some so loud and close that Wilson was sure the mound of snow and low hanging pine branches concealing him wouldn't be enough. But the men continued past and faded into the distance. When he could no longer hear them, Wilson counted to a minute, praying to God that Endo wouldn't move.

Ten men had come. Only nine had left. Someone stayed behind.

Another minute passed.

C'mon, you sonofabitch.

Crunch. The man shifted his weight, but the noise, in the silence of the woods, sounded like a rifle shot. Thirty seconds later, he gave up, double-timing his exit to catch up with the pack.

When the man's footfalls reduced to nothing, Wilson counted to sixty again before slowly lifting his head. He scanned the area, holding his breath. They were gone. He swallowed the icy glob of snow in his mouth, feeling the cold slip down his throat and land in his belly.

He looked to Endo and found the man starting to raise his head. "Not bad, Ketchup."

Endo frowned beneath his mask. "Katsu."

"Katsu. Catsup. Ketchup." Wilson spoke the words with conviction, as though his logic stream was enough justification for the nickname.

"My name is Katsu," Corporal Endo repeated, his barely detectable Japanese accent growing a little thicker.

Wilson shook his head. "Look. I'm a nice guy, so I'm going to give you a choice. You can be Ketchup or you can be Duck Sauce."

"Duck sauce is for Chinese food," Endo said.

Damnit, Wilson thought. "What do you use in Japan? What's the shit called? Worcestershire? No, that's not it. Soy sauce. That's the stuff. So what will it be? Soy Sauce or Ketchup?"

"They're coming back."

Endo said it so plainly and without trepidation that Wilson nearly missed it. He peeked up over the snow covered rise and saw several distant figures moving toward them. "Shit. They're not going to miss us on a second pass. We need to move."

"They'll see our tracks," Endo pointed out.

"That's why we're going to run."

"We'll be faster downhill."

"Uh-uh." Wilson motioned back toward the mountain rising behind them. "We'll head up." He cut off Endo's argument with a raised hand. "Listen, Ketchup, you're here to learn from me. You do what I say, when I say it. We're heading up because no one likes to. There's all kinds of hell in the mountains and these assholes aren't going to want to follow us."

Endo gave a nod, conceding the point. Without a sound, the pair crawled up the hillside until they were deep in the tangle of pine branches. Concealed for the moment, Wilson took a deep breath and mumbled, "Smells like Christmas." The scent conjured memories of his family. He tried to not think about his wife and two sons, but failed. He missed them terribly when he was deployed or training. He believed in the Marine Corps. Dedicated his life to it. But his family was his heart. Without them he wasn't whole. Not that he'd ever admit such a thing.

A sharp hiss snapped Wilson from his reverie. Endo stood higher on the hill, pointing to his ear.

The men seeking them out had arrived early, moving faster than Wilson anticipated. Wilson gave a curt hand signal that looked a little like he was chopping wood with his hand. They continued their ascent, moving as quickly and as silently as they could.

It had been six very cold hours since the exercise began and they were one of two teams still in the game. They'd begun as twenty-five two-man teams. The drill was basically a glorified version of Hide and Seek, but the men took it seriously, and winning gave you gloating rights—something Wilson enjoyed. Every time a team was spotted and laser sighted they joined the hunt. Since the men below had already been caught, they had no good reason to endure the cold. They were more motivated than ever.

"Here!" someone shouted.

Wilson plowed up the hill, forgoing any attempt at stealth. They needed to find someplace the others wouldn't want to follow and they needed it fast.

Shouting erupted below. The sound of pursuit followed.

Endo was a fast little shit; Wilson had to give him that. He ducked and weaved around and under branches that Wilson had to bulldoze his way through. Endo pulled ahead, disappearing into the dense foliage. A stab of fear coursed through Wilson. If he was the reason they were caught, he'd never live it down.

A shout of surprise rose up ahead of him. Had Endo injured himself? Maybe tripped or rolled his ankle? If so, they'd be done, but at least he could peg the loss on Ketchup and avoid some of the ridicule. Although they were one of the two final teams, he'd done enough trash talking to ensure anything other than first place would be humiliating.

Wilson pushed through a large tree branch and paused. Endo's footprints disappeared. He glanced up into the trees. "Ketchup! Where are you?"

No reply.

He took a step forward and the snow didn't give way. The snow here had melted and refrozen, forming a solid, inch-thick layer of lumpy ice. Knowing that Endo had most likely slid over the solid surface, Wilson lowered himself onto the ice and got down on his belly, dispersing his weight. He pushed himself forward, careful not to break or even scuff the surface.

But the voices of his pursuers grew louder, moving closer at a pace that far exceeded his flight. And they didn't have to worry about concealing their tracks. His only remote hope was to reach the next tree, duck behind it and hope they moved in a different direction.

The hunters were just out of sight, maybe thirty feet back.

Wilson slid beneath a pine branch weighted down by needles and snow, and he found himself facing a stone wall. Nowhere to go. He pulled his feet up close, held his breath and waited.

If asked, Wilson would have said he was a brave man. Perhaps one of the bravest. He'd seen action in Afghanistan twice. He'd killed and nearly been killed. It took a lot to ruffle his scarred feathers, but when Endo emerged from the base of the rock wall like some kind of giant gopher, Wilson nearly pissed himself.

Endo grabbed hold of Wilson's jacket and hauled him back. Despite being seventy-five pounds heavier than Endo, Wilson slipped up over the ice. Darkness enveloped him, and he felt a strange pressure that told him he was underground. Gravity helped him complete the second leg of his five second journey, dropping him onto a solid slab of stone. It took all he had for Wilson to not shout in surprise or cough in pain, but he completed his passage into the darkness without a peep.

Wilson listened to the men outside. They stopped at the frozen snow. Some punched their way through, some searched the trees and two were sent back to make sure it wasn't a false trail.

Five minutes later, everything was quiet again.

Wilson knew he should thank Endo. Maybe even use his real name. He'd not only kept Wilson from being discovered, but also ensured they would win the hunt. Although they weren't armed, they did carry food and water. Properly rationed, they could make it a week, though he doubted they'd even need to spend the night.

A sharp crack made Wilson jump. Then a bright red glow lit Endo's face. The white mask made him look like ghost. A chill rose up Wilson's back. He fought against it showing on his face, but Endo chuckled and shook his head.

Wilson was about to chew the man out—so what if Endo had saved them, no one mocked Lenny Wilson—but then Endo held the glow stick up, lighting the space around them, and this time, there was no stopping Wilson's shout of horror.

Less than twenty-four hours after Wilson hauled himself out of the cave and lost the exercise, he stood outside the entrance once more with Endo by his side. They were joined by General Lance Gordon and no one else. The report of what they'd found had been fast-tracked up the chain of command until it landed on Gordon's desk and stopped. He'd flown out of Washington D.C. within the hour and made his way to the frozen North.

"This is it?" Gordon asked with a huff that sent a cloud of steam from his mouth.

Gordon didn't look like a general. He didn't have the same rigid poise or clean cut look, especially for a man out of the Pentagon. What he did have was a commanding presence that said he'd lay into you like a Howitzer if you crossed him. Wilson answered quickly. "Yes, sir."

"Who found it?" Gordon asked.

"Corporal Endo, sir," Wilson replied.

The General turned his gaze to Endo, sizing him up. As men, they were opposites. The pale white Gordon stood at six-three, weighed two hundred fifty pounds, had rough skin on his face and was dressed in black thermal BDUs. Endo, dressed in his white BDUs from the previous day, was five-five, weighed one sixty-five and had a tan smooth-skinned face that Gordon doubted had ever felt a razor's edge.

"Lead the way," Gordon said to Endo, motioning to the sliver of black in the wall of stone.

Endo gave a curt nod and without a word, dropped to the ground and slid into the hole.

"You're sure about this, General?" Wilson said. "You don't need to go in there."

Gordon craned his head around toward Wilson, a single eyebrow perched high on his forehead like a pterodactyl swooping in for the kill. "I didn't fly over the whole damned country of Canada to stare at a hole in the ground."

Wilson snapped to attention, gave a nod and followed after Endo, landing on his feet. Gordon entered behind him.

A light bloomed. Endo aimed the powerful beam at the floor, letting the reflected light illuminate the area around them. Wilson did the same with his flashlight, as did Gordon.

"Where is it?" Gordon asked.

Endo stepped to the side and raised his flashlight. The beam penetrated the darkness and lit up a wall of what looked like mottled brown marble. He raised the beam higher, stopping when it reached what looked like a hooked stalactite taller than Gordon.

With a sigh, Wilson added his light. "Know what it is?"

Gordon aimed his flashlight at the ceiling. It was fifty feet up. He found the top of the object and followed it down to the floor. Thirty feet tall. He played the light to the right, stopping when the beam's reach faded, more than two hundred feet away.

"Did anyone else see this?" Gordon asked.

"No sir," Wilson said. "Just the two of us. And not for long. The few details we saw before leaving are in our reports."

"Your reports no longer exist," the General said as he stared up at the empty eye socket big enough to drive a Humvee through. "As of right now, we are the only three people with any real knowledge of...this. And I would like it to stay that way. Do either of you have a problem with that?"

"No," Endo said.

"No, sir," Wilson added.

"Good," Gordon said. "As of right now, you both work for me."

Wilson managed to take his eyes off their discovery and looked at Gordon. "Endo's Japanese, sir."

The pterodactyl rose on the General's forehead. He didn't miss much, especially the plainly obvious. "I can see that."

Wilson wilted a little and diverted his eyes back to the thing.

"I'll need both of you here for the next few years before—"

"Next few years?" Wilson said in surprise, though he never took his eyes off the monster.

"You have a problem with that?" Gordon asked.

"Not if my family can join me," Wilson said. "I'm scheduled to head home in a month."

"Family." Gordon said the word like it tasted bad coming out of his mouth. He turned to Endo. "You have family?"

Endo shook his head. "I am yours."

The declaration was more intimate sounding than Gordon would have preferred, but when Endo turned his gaze back to the creature's remains and the man's eyes glowed with excitement, he realized the words had more to do with the beast than they did with him.

When Endo looked back at Gordon, the General waved him closer, but spoke to Wilson. "How many kids, Master Sergeant?"

"Two, sir," Wilson replied. "Boys. Five and seven."

While Wilson replied, the General drew his side arm. He turned it around and handed it to Endo, who looked at the weapon with wide eyes before casting his gaze on the General.

Gordon motioned to the back of Wilson's head. Gave a nod and a smile like he was welcoming Endo to a theme park, which wasn't too far from the truth. Endo looked down at the weapon in his hand. It was a sound-suppressed M9 9mm handgun. Not the world's most powerful gun, but more than enough to do the job.

Endo frowned.

Then shrugged.

He raised the pistol, pointed it at the back of Wilson's head and pulled the trigger.

PROLOGUE II

Two Weeks Ago

Maigo Tilly dropped her bright pink Hello Kitty backpack onto the kitchen's cold, tan slate floor. It glowed with innocence. Her high forehead pinched together at the midline, eyebrows twisting up. Her lips trembled in time with her fingers. She stared at the red.

The growing pool found the floor's grout and flowed down the straight track, heading for Maigo's stocking toes. She stepped away from it, keeping to the center of a single tile while her mother's blood flowed around her, following the grout like the channels of a sacrificial altar.

But the blood couldn't hold her attention. The frozen scene beyond it called to her. Her eyes rose slowly, first seeing the bare foot of her mother, twitching as her life faded. Then the twitching stopped. Maigo could tell her mother was dead by her skin. Normally tan, it was now sickly pale. Her mother's designer dress was stained with red from below, the fluid pulled up through the cotton fabric.

The shaking in Maigo's lips grew severe as her eyes skipped past her mother's hands and the horror there, and looked at her face. Whatever the woman had been feeling at the time her life ended had been erased. The face revealed nothing. Her skull, however—everything. Her head, once a smooth curve, was now a crescent. Most of it was missing.

Not missing.

Scattered.

Maigo looked higher. The 33rd-floor penthouse of the Clarendon Back Bay building provided stunning views of downtown Boston and the harbor. It was a castle in the sky—the kind reserved for Boston's elite. It came with every amenity the seven-million-dollar price tag could fetch, including a Jacuzzi hot tub big enough to swim in, remote controlled everything and massive windows lining every outside wall. But the view of downtown was marred by streaks of maroon and clumps of pink. When a particularly weighty dollop of brain matter slipped free and struck the floor with a wet slap, Maigo finally gasped.

And then again. And again. She'd been holding her breath.

"It's okay, Maigo," her father said.

He was a stark contrast to her mother—plump, balding, pale and unkind. Maigo didn't like her father much, but he was around so rarely that she was able to bear his moods. Also, her mother insisted. Told her to be thankful. To look at the view. To enjoy their many blessings.

Maigo said nothing. She was incapable.

"It was an accident," he said. "No, it was—"

While her father decided what had happened, Maigo looked back to her mother's hands. Her left arm and hand, perfectly manicured, lay to the side. Tears filled Maigo's eyes as she remembered the feeling of those long, red, fingernails on her back, scratching her gently to sleep. The sadness faded when she looked at her mother's right hand, interlocked with her father's hands and a gun. A pistol. It was the kind a woman might own. Small. But Maigo knew everything about her mother. They had no secrets.

Not about school. Or boys. Or the bruises her mother hid.

She didn't own a gun. She loathed them.

Maigo's trembling hands became fists when she saw that her father was wearing white plastic gloves, the kind that doctors wear.

"You did this," she said, before she could realize she shouldn't.

"No," he said, "No! I found her like this. She did it to herself."

Maigo watched her father carefully loop her mother's finger around the gun's trigger.

"She killed herself, Maigo."

"She wouldn't."

"She did."

Fueled by anger, Maigo shouted, "You killed her!"

Her father frowned, but just a little. He picked up her mother's hand, moving it again.

"Leave her alone," Maigo said.

"Your mother killed herself, Maigo," her father said, "but she killed you first."

Maigo looked at the gun and noticed it was now leveled at her core. The last thing she saw was a small grin on her father's face. Then—nothing.

STAGE 1

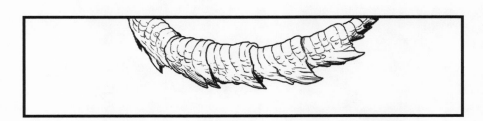

1

Now

"You have got to be kidding me!" I shout to myself when Def Leppard's Pour Some Sugar on Me blares from my pickup truck's feeble speakers. If the flashback to my childhood wasn't bad enough, every thump of the bass drum releases a grating rattle. Whoever owned the beat up, faded red Chevy S-10 before me blew nearly every speaker. Probably some teenager. Man, I'd like to punch that kid in the face. Of course, right now I'd like to punch every radio DJ within a hundred miles, too.

I tap the radio's "seek" button. Boston. More than a Feeling.

Again. Jane's Addiction. Pets.

One more time. Aerosmith. Love in an Elevator.

I punch, literally punch, the radio's power button, but all I manage to do is spin the volume up. Steven Tyler howls in my ear. The vibrating speakers make him sound like a smoker with an artificial voice box. I tap the button more carefully, despite the racket, and silence fills the cab once more.

My neck cracks as I roll it, releasing my music-induced tension. "Welcome to Maine," I say, doing my best DJ impression, "home of the seventies, eighties, nineties, and...that's it."

I should probably invest in a new stereo system someday. Hell, I should probably buy a car with anti-lock brakes, eighteen airbags and all the other things most people care about. But that would require an effort beyond my actual desire to replace Betty.

Yeah, I named my truck. Betty was the name of my first girlfriend. Like this truck, she had a grating voice and a high maintenance personality. Despite girlfriend-Betty being easier on the eyes, I stayed with her for only six months. Pickup truck-Betty talks less. And doesn't complain when I turn her on. We've been together for going on five years now, and even though she's rough around the edges, she's just about the only thing in my life that makes any sense.

I glance in the rearview. The road behind me is as empty as the road ahead. I catch a glimpse of my face in the mirror and shake my head. I don't look like a DHS agent. DHS—Department of Homeland Security. Most of the people working for the DHS are straight-shooting, tight-ass suits. An inordinate percentage of the men have mustaches, like they're 70s porn stars or 1900s Englishmen ready to engage in some old fashioned fisticuffs.

Of course, I am sporting the beginning of a beard myself, but that's less of a style choice and more of a result of my ancient shaver, pilfered from my father when I moved out ten years ago, crapping out a week ago. I think it looks good, but if any of my superiors saw it, I'd probably get a good talking to. Proper dress. Appearances matter. That kind of stuff. It's a good thing my superiors don't give a rat's ass about me or my department. I don't think I've seen or heard from someone with a higher pay scale than mine in the last six months.

I adjust the maroon beanie cap covering my crew-cut brown hair. The tight-fitting knit hat has become a staple of my wardrobe, and it is a style choice, mostly because it disguises the fact that my hair is slowly retreating like soldiers from my muddy battlefield. I think it makes me look like The Edge, from U2, a band of the eighties, nineties, and today that I actually wouldn't mind hearing on the radio.

My smartphone—which is really a company phone—cuts through the silence, saying, "Turn right," in a far from sexy, yet feminine voice that is the closest thing I've had to a girlfriend in a year. Other than Betty, I mean. I spot the dirt road up ahead and turn onto the uneven surface. The road is covered in half buried stones the size of grape-fruits and rows of hardened ridges formed by water, which, in combination with Betty's rigid suspension, bounces me around like I'm on a grocery-store horsey ride, having a seizure.

Twenty minutes and a headache later, I arrive at my destination. I pull the truck into the lone parking space, put it in park and kill the engine. The car door creaks as it opens, allowing the outside world to wash over me. Warm summer air chases away the chill of Betty's air conditioning, which works like a champ. The smell of pine and earth and, I think, water, fills my nose.

It's been too long.

Once upon a time, I'd been a real salt of the Earth type. I camped, fished, hunted, slept under the stars and smoked a doobie or two. It's been at least ten years of indoor and pot-free living since then. Thank God I'm not in drug enforcement. I'd be horrible at it, mostly because I think I'd let all of the potheads walk.

The small cabin is on loan to me from Ted Watson, one of two people I actually oversee. I'm supposed to hire two more team members out of whatever law enforcement branch I can entice them from, but I haven't really bothered. Seeing as how every case I have is like a bad episode of The X-Files, but without the actual monsters, aliens and government conspiracies, I just don't see the need to deal with more personalities.

Not that Ted is hard to deal with. He's kind of like a grown up version of Chunk, from The Goonies—chubby, funny and he occasionally breaks into a jiggly dance. He's also brilliant with computers and electronics. I'm pretty sure he got posted to my team because, like me, he doesn't exactly fit the company profile. Anne Cooper, on the other hand, does. Cooper, who I call Coop, mostly because it bothers her, is a straight-laced administrator who does things by the book, even though so little of our mandate is in any book not written by a fiction author, a lunatic or both.

They've been with me for three years now, manning the home front—a house perched atop Prospect Hill in Beverly, Massachusetts.

From the top floor you can see the ocean and, on a clear day, Boston. It's a nice place to live and work, but it's not the great outdoors.

Believe it or not, I'm not on vacation. I'm working. Watson's family just happened to have a cabin in the area, and I felt like being nostalgic for a night before beginning my "investigation."

With a shake of my head, I push away thoughts of the ridiculous day I'll have tomorrow and hop up the steps to the front door. Despite the apparent disuse of the cabin, the porch wood feels firm beneath my feet. Maybe it's faux worn, I wonder, like those beat-up looking hutches made for rich old ladies who want to have rustic kitchens without the actual rust.

I dig into my pocket for the key while scanning the area. Most of the trees are pines, though a few maples line the dirt road, their leaves glowing lime green in the afternoon sun. There's no mailbox or even a number on the cabin. As I pull the key from my pocket, I lean back and peer down the road. Nothing. And there wasn't a single house on the way here, which suits me, because while I don't have any doobies, I do have a twelve-pack buried in a cooler full of ice.

I'm not supposed to drink on the job, but I'm not technically working right now and I'm pretty good at warding off hangovers. Besides, I'm pretty sure that even drunk off my ass, I'll be able to figure out the mystery of Sasquatch.

Yeah, Sasquatch.

Fucking Sasquatch.

I work for the Department of Homeland Security, and I'm investigating a rash of squatch sightings in the northern woods of Boonie-town, Maine. When the DHS was created in 2002, in the wake of 9-11, the bill was loaded with "riders," tacked-on provisions that wouldn't normally pass if they weren't attached to something guaranteed to pass, like the creation of the DHS. Riders usually have nothing to do with the actual bill, but the one that created my division did. The DHS has seventy Fusion Centers around the country. They're hubs where intel and resources from federal and local law enforcement agencies can be pooled in an effort to openly share information between departments—

something that might have helped avoid the events of 9-11. Each hub has its own lead investigator tasked with investigations that affect multiple law enforcement agencies, and that are a threat to national security. That's me, lead investigator, except my Fusion Center has yet to be involved in any serious investigation. Fusion Centers are most commonly identified by the city they're in, such as Fusion Center – Boston, my closest neighbor in the DHS, otherwise known as "those assholes in Beantown".

The Fusion Center I head up is known as Fusion Center – P. The P is for "paranormal". Seriously. The supernatural paranoid who added the rider believed the end of the world was nigh and that it would be a supernatural event. That's also why we're located in Beverly, Mass, next door neighbor to Salem, Mass. Salem being the apparent gateway to hell and home to the gruesome Salem witch trials, as well as scores of modern witches like Susan Beacon, who claimed she caused the "perfect storm" with a curse. There isn't a day that goes by that I don't praise the good Lord she made that claim before my stint at the FC-P began or I would have had to investigate it as a threat against the United States.

FC-P is the seventy-first Fusion Center and it doesn't technically exist. You won't find us in any public documentation. Despite its creation, the FC-P is pretty much an embarrassment. That's why the 'Paranormal' on our IDs was reduced to the letter P.

The deadbolt unlocks smoothly, barely making a sound. I push the door open and step in. The dim room holds two comfortable looking rocking chairs, a dining room table, a wood stove and what appears to be a large, black bean bag. I try the lights, but nothing happens.

The breakers, I think, vaguely remembering Ted saying something about them being shut off. I move to take a step into the cabin, and freeze before I leave the doorframe.

The bean bag moved.

I reach for my gun, but find it missing. It's in the truck. Haven't worn it in two years. Imaginary creatures and specters don't normally pose a threat.

Before I can think of what to do next, the screen door finally decides to slam shut behind me. The bean bag explodes with motion, rearing up a round head the size of a large pumpkin. Two large black eyes fix on me with unwavering focus.

Moving with slow, measured movements, the bear stands. It's just about the same height as me, but is probably upwards of seven hundred pounds. I raise my hand in an "its okay" posture, like the bear will understand it, and I back away, but I don't get far. My back smacks into the closed screen door, which makes a loud snapping sound.

The spooked bear huffs angrily, throws itself forward and charges.

2

Dr. Kendra Elliot threw a manila folder across her office and let loose a string of curses that would make a sailor squirm. The fifty-seven sheets of data-laden paper exploded from the folder like confetti, half en route to the wall, half when the folder hit it. By the time the last sheet slipped onto the dull gray industrial carpet, Elliot's anger had been replaced by regret. The pages weren't numbered, and though the pages declared her failure, careful study of what went wrong would help her find her mistake, and correct it.

Hopefully before I die, Elliot thought.

She stood from behind the executive desk that she neither liked nor had gotten accustomed to in the four years she'd sat behind it. Her hip somehow found the desk's corner as she rounded the cherry wood behemoth. She grunted in pain and clenched her teeth against her returning anger. She wanted to scream out a curse, but held her tongue. She was one of the lead researchers at BioLance, a government-funded laboratory working on a slew of different projects ranging from gene-splicing to tissue regenerating foam and to the cure for cancer, and she did her best to act the part. Elliot's current focus was Project: ROG (Rapid Organ Growth). The lab operated like many others around the country with one glaring difference. BioLance didn't exist. It was a code name.

And despite the fact that the facility appeared to be run like any other high-tech firm, Elliot was under no illusions; she worked for the Man. She didn't mind. The money was great, the resources essentially unlimited and the staff beyond comparison. More than that, since the lab didn't officially exist, and no one's real names appeared on any documents, she could bend, or break, any laws she needed to with two exceptions. The two strictly enforced rules were:

1. Never do anything to endanger the public.

2. Never do anything to reveal BioLance, its resources, experiments, data and personnel identities to the public.

She suspected that rule number one was actually an extension of rule number two, rather than genuine concern for public welfare. As a result, the facility and the staff that worked and lived there were guarded closely. She didn't even know where the lab was located, though she suspected the Northeast, based on the trees and terrain she could see through her office window, though it could have easily been Canada.

Elliot glanced down at the corner of the desk that had jabbed her hip. The finish was actually worn from the number of times she'd run into it. And it wasn't because she had childbearing hips. Just the opposite. Her body was tall and rail-like. Not even the tight-fitting power suit she wore could accentuate her curves. There was nothing to accentuate.

It wasn't the desk's fault, either. At seven feet long, the desk was large, but the office was far larger, accommodating several bookcases, cabinets and an executive table with ten chairs, with room to spare. It was her eyes that betrayed her. She wore thick glasses that might have been in style thirty years previous. They shrunk her blue eyes to the size of almonds and ruined her depth perception.

With a sigh, Elliot bent down and picked at the fresh carpet of strewn pages. She put them in order by memory, scanning each page as she picked it up. When she reached the final page, her knees were sore, but she didn't stand. She just looked at the ten numbered lines of text and the word "Failed" next to each one.

She hated that word with a passion. Failed. She'd heard it over and over again during her first twenty years of life, as her father, who wanted sons and got one girl, pushed her into sports. She had the body for it, strong, fast and agile, but not the mind. Despite being fiercely competitive, her intellect rarely focused on the field, court or rink.

His death, and the money left to his failure of a daughter, finally freed her to pursue her dreams. Eight years and four degrees later, her past caught up with her. Someone figured out that dear old Dad hadn't died of entirely natural causes and she was the only suspect. But she wasn't arrested. She was offered a job.

But she was still failing.

She crumpled the page into a tight ball and tossed it into the barrel across the room.

"You should have played basketball," General Lance Gordon said from the doorway.

Had it been anyone else, she would have exploded with a torrent of verbal abuse. But Gordon was her employer, as well as the man who recruited her, and as such, he knew she was a murderer. Which might be why he stayed by the door.

She stood, straightened her dress and placed the folder on the desk. "What can I do for you, General?"

"For starters, be honest."

"About?"

"Is the pressure too much? Can you handle it?"

Yes and no, she thought. "No and yes. I'm fine." But she knew she wasn't. A year ago, Gordon had asked the impossible. Find a way to grow viable, adult, human organs in under a month. He'd given her an eighteen-month deadline. She was no closer to success than she had been a year ago.

"Uh-huh," he said.

He doesn't believe me, she thought. He's going to fire me right now. Not that people were ever fired from BioLance. They were disappeared.

"Tell about the results," he said.

"You've seen the report?"

"You know how I feel about those reports," he said. "Until one of you eggheads starts writing them in plain English, I'm not going to know what's being said." He motioned to the trash can containing the crumpled list of failures. "Though the last page sums up everything pretty well, I'd say."

She cleared her throat. "In layman's terms, we've successfully increased subject growth rate. Through a combination of genetic tinkering, steroids, electrical impulses, and raw materials provided by the umbilical, we can grow a twenty year old male inside of a month."

"But?" Gordon asked.

"But once it's removed from the amniotic fluid, it loses viscosity. Organs become sludge. Bones powder. The body just falls apart."

"But before that happens," Gordon said, "the body is...alive?"

"Physically," she said, "not mentally. We've engineered the bodies to grow with only a cerebellum, which controls bodily functions such as respiration, digestion and the heart. But there are no higher brain functions. No soul, if that's your concern."

"Hardly," he said, and then reached into his leather jacket—no one wore uniforms—causing Elliot to flinch. Gordon paused, a smile on his face. "Don't worry, Kendra, you're still too valuable to let go."

Still, she thought. She swallowed and determined always to be valuable.

Gordon took a glass vial from his jacket's inside pocket. It contained a clear liquid. He held the vial out to her slowly. "Treat this like it's your child." He paused and corrected himself, "Unless you would treat your child like you did your—"

"I get the idea," she said, and took the vial. A hand-written label had been stuck on the side, and up over the top, keeping the cap in place. She read the words aloud. "Kyodaina".

"Endo's name," he explained. "Not sure what it means. Don't really care."

Elliot was not a fan of Katsu Endo. She stood nearly five inches taller than him, but his eyes burned with a passion that made her uncomfortable. His unflinching loyalty to Gordon, and the gun worn on his hip, left few questions about the fate of the few people who'd lost their jobs during her time with BioLance. She'd share their fate, too, if she didn't start producing results. She closed her eyes, imagining her end—staring in the burning brown eyes of Katsu Endo.

She wouldn't allow it to happen. She would do anything—anything—to avoid it.

"What is it?" she asked, stepping closer to the General.

"DNA," he said.

"From what?" she asked.

"You don't need to know."

She didn't like that answer, but hid her aggravation behind a smile. "The computer is going to tell me what it is the moment it's analyzed."

"No. It's not."

Elliot stood so close that she felt his breath on her face and smelled the coffee he'd been drinking. French Vanilla, artificially sweetened. She looked in his eyes. Tired and bloodshot. Decaf.

"Just add this to your stew and see what happens."

"That's not very scientific," she replied, her face just inches from his. She tilted her head and opened her lips slightly, the invitation as easy to read as a billboard.

"You're not my type," Gordon said, nonplussed by her blatant advance.

"You're a man," she replied. "Does it matter?"

He looked down briefly, his tongue flicking between his lips for just a moment.

It didn't matter, she knew. Something else was stopping him.

She connected the dots.

"Our chances of success might increase if we focused on a single organ," she said. It was a lie, but his answer told her everything she needed to know.

"The heart," he said without missing a beat.

She stepped back and nodded. "Heart it is. I'll get the team—"

"Not the team," he said. "Just you."

"W—what?"

"You're on your own, Kendra. Your team has already been dismissed."

She blanched, which drew a laugh from Gordon.

"They're confined to quarters."

"Confined to quarters?" It didn't make sense. What he was asking would take the entire team months of trial and error. That he was simply confining the staff to their quarters meant she had a very limited amount of time. "How long do I have?"

"Two days," he said.

She flinched at this and dropped the vial. A gasp slipped from her lips as she bent down and tried to catch it. She missed.

But Gordon didn't. He snatched the glass vial from the air just inches above the floor. She looked up into his angry brown eyes. "That is the last mistake you'll make. Understood?"

She nodded quickly, her eyes locked on his for just a moment, before she snatched the vial from his hand and made for the door. The clock was ticking. Her life, and she suspected Gordon's, depended on her success.

"Try not to worry, Kendra," he called after her. "I think you'll be surprised by the results."

She held up the vial and looked at the clear liquid. What the hell is this?

3

My body and the screen door behind it are no match for the bear. It lowers its head like a bull, plows into my gut and shoves. As my insides shift and the air bursts from my lungs, I feel the door's crossbeam flex and crack across my back. Pain lances through my arms and legs, and for a fraction of a second I worry that I've broken my spine. But then I feel the tug of the metal screen on my body as I pass through it and catapult to the ground, my landing cushioned only by my ass and the layer of brown pine needles covering the forest floor like wall-to-wall carpeting.

Wheezing for air, I scramble back from the cabin until my head whacks Betty's side. My head spins from the impact and from lack of air, but I notice my arms and legs are working just fine.

Not paralyzed, I think. Yet.

The bear steps out of the cabin's front door with all the grim intent of a father who's just found his teenage daughter in bed with a boy. It stands again, looking at me, trying to intimidate me and succeeding.

I find my breath and shout at the bear, "Hiyah!" But it comes out as a pitiful wheezy thing. If I ever do come up against a Sasquatch, I'm screwed.

My legs shake beneath me, but I manage to get to my feet. Now the bear thinks I'm trying to intimidate it. I'm not, but if I was, I'd be failing. The bear grunts again, taking two steps toward me before dropping to all four paws and pounding down the steps.

I grab the driver's side door and yank. My hand painfully rips away from the handle. Locked.

Why the hell did I lock my truck out here? Even in Beverly, Betty wouldn't be a blip on a car thief's radar.

The gun, I remember. I left my gun in the cab. That's why I locked it. Unfortunately, that's also why I'm trying to get in the cab.

The bear grunts as it reaches the bottom of the steps and makes a beeline for me.

An involuntary shout rises from deep inside me, fueling my flight. I turn around, plant my hands on the side of Betty's flatbed and leap over and in. I land hard on my back, coughing for air and wincing in pain. But I'm hidden.

For about half a second.

The bear rises up, grabbing on to the side of the truck. Its long black claws squeak against the metal, grating on my ears. I roll to the far side of the flatbed, out of reach. As the truck rocks and more screeching fills the air, I realize the bear is actually trying to claw its way inside.

Black bears are rarely this aggressive, though there are plenty of accounts of people being mauled. And there is always the chance that this bear is rabid.

I reach into my right pants pocket, fumbling for my keys, but don't find them. I'm momentarily confused, as though I've looked up and found the sky had turned red. I always keep my keys in my right pocket. I check the left anyway and as I suspected, find nothing.

That's when I remember.

I unlocked the door.

When the bear charged, the keys were still in my hand. And since they're not now... I sit up fast, which makes the bear flinch and fall, landing hard on its side.

I look over the side and can't help but smile at the suddenly silly looking bear. "Looks like we're both kind of screw-ups," I tell it.

The bear gets back to its feet with a quickness that surprises me, lunging up and swiping at my face, missing by inches. I stumble back, catching myself on the cab before falling out of the flatbed with less grace than the bear.

"Keys," I tell myself. "Find the keys." Without them, I could be playing tag until the bear either gets bored or I get dead.

I glance toward the cabin, but have trouble focusing as my eyes keep flicking back to the black ball of death beating the shit out of my darling Betty's paint job. I scour the porch. Nothing. No key.

I look into the dark doorway, but the cabin's interior is deep in shadow. I strain my eyes, looking for the keychain, which holds five keys, a pocket jackknife and a mini-flashlight. A breeze tickles my skin and sifts through the trees. The pines creak. The maples sound like a librarian quieting some unruly patrons with a serious "Shhhhh". Light dances across the pine floor of the forest, then up the stairs and into the doorway.

It's just a flash of light, but hallelujah, my path has been revealed. The keys are a foot inside the door, on the floor.

Now I just need to get past the bear, snatch the keys, get back to Betty, unlock the door, hop inside and not get mauled. *No problem*, I tell myself, *for Chuck Norris.*

The plan evolves in my subconscious and spurs me into action long before I can realize how stupid it is. Some people might say this is instinct—acting quickly, without thought, to stay alive. As I hit the ground on the far side of the truck, I just think it's nuts.

But I'm committed.

As is the bear.

The moment my feet hit the ground, the bear disappears from view. I know it's running toward me, but I'm not sure if it's going around the front or back of the truck. So circling the truck is out of the question. Going under the truck is too. Betty rides low to the ground and it would take a good minute to shuffle all the way to the other side. Over the top, I decide and hop back up into the cab.

The bear is faster than expected and nearly catches my foot in its jaws.

The bear took just two seconds to round the truck. That will give me about a three second lead if you figure in my speed and its reaction time. Not much. But I'll work with what I've got.

Without pausing to look at the bear, I jump from the flatbed, land in a roll that springs me back to my feet and sprint to the cabin door. I can't see the bear, but a loud grunt lets me know it's in hot pursuit. I take the stairs in one leap, scoop up the keys as I pass through the door, and then remember the deadbolt.

I grip the heavy wooden door and fling it shut behind me, still heading toward the back of the cabin.

The door slams shut, the spring loaded deadbolt snapping loudly into place. A second slam shakes the entire cabin, but the door holds. I stop in the center of the living/dining room and look back. The door vibrates under a second attack, but holds. The bear can't get through.

I plant my hands on my knees, catching my breath.

The bear has given up.

I twirl the keys around on my finger and laugh. At least I'll have a story to tell this time.

A raspy mewl spins me around like an ice skater. My leg kicks out, connecting with an end table and knocking a vase full of fake flowers crashing to the floor.

The mewling grows frantic and I see the source.

Two baby bears.

Several things occur to me at once.

One: the bear is a mama protecting her young, which explains a lot, but kind of sucks, since this is pretty much the only scenario in which a bear will kill a human being.

Two: the door, which I have just locked behind me, was already locked when I arrived, which means mama bear has another way in. I've just locked myself in the bear's den.

Three: I'm fairly screwed.

I back toward the front door, preparing to unlock it and bolt, but it's suddenly slammed again. I jump away with a shout that scares the cubs. Their mewl becomes a frantic cry for help. A rectangle of light beyond the cubs catches my attention. The kitchen has a back door. It's wide open.

The view beyond it catches me off guard. The cabin sits atop a small hill. Below that hill is the most pristine lake I've laid eyes on, outside of a National Geographic documentary, in ten years. Sparkles of sunlight flicker on the windswept waves, shifting across the surface like a flock of birds. The trees fringing the lake sway hypnotically, holding my attention.

That is, until the view is blotted out by seven hundred pounds of hungry mamma. If not for pausing to sniff her crying cubs, I'd be dead. In that two second pause I manage to unlock the front door, fling it open and throw myself down from the porch. By the time I hit the ground I hear the bear's loud huffing and know she's coming again.

I run into the car, crashing against the door and fumbling with the keys until I find the right one. Luckily, Betty and I have been together for a while—we're simpatico, like long-time lovers—so slipping the key in and unlocking the door takes no thought. I slide behind the wheel, take hold of the door handle and pull. It crashes shut with such force that I think I've just transformed into Captain Marvel, though I don't recall shouting "Shazam!" That, or the bear rammed the door. I look to the left.

It's the bear. Which is too bad. I used to really like Captain Marvel.

I stick my tongue out at the bear and hold it just long enough to get it covered in glass cubes when the bear stands and brings its paws down on the window. I shout again and slide over to the passenger's seat while Smokey the psychotic bear claws the crap out of Betty's fake leather upholstery. Using the keychain's smallest key, I unlock the glove compartment and grab hold of the holstered gun inside.

That's when the rope holding the passenger side door shut since I was T-boned two months ago decides to give way. I spill out backwards, landing hard on my back. I groan and slowly open my eyes. They snap the rest of the way open when I see four clawed paws rounding the front of the truck.

I feel the holstered gun in my hand and with a practiced familiarity, unbutton the clasp and free the weapon with one smooth move. I turn the muzzle skyward and without looking, fire two shots in the air before pointing the weapon at the approaching jaws.

But I don't fire.

There's no need.

Even mamma bears can be spooked. With a cry that sounds like a deeper version of the cubs' call, the bear backpedals and runs away, heading toward the lake. It calls out again as it passes the cabin and is joined by the two cubs, who scurry along behind. The trio run until I can't see them. With any luck, they'll keep going until they're miles away.

Gun in hand, I feel safer than I did inside the truck's cab. Speaking of which... I lean my head up, and look at Betty. "I put up with a lot. You know I do. But you almost got me killed here."

I lean my head back, catching my breath. "It's just not working out, Betty."

It's a joke. For myself. Fueled by the elation of not being gored. But it actually makes me a little sad. I get to my feet, leaning my battered body on the truck's hood. I pat the dull red metal. "I don't mean it. I should have got the door fixed months ago."

But I didn't. Because that's the way I am. I make a mental note to change my lax ways before they get me killed. Then I grab the twelve pack and head into the cabin.

4

"Dr. Elliot, wake up."

Dr. Kendra Elliot had never been a graceful sleeper. She snored. She drooled. And she always, always woke up grumpy. But today, her fury at being woken was quickly consumed by confusion. She wasn't in bed. She was in the lab. And it was a voice that had woken her, not her alarm.

General Gordon's voice.

He stood next to her, a grin on his face.

She mistook the smile as mockery and quickly checked herself over. Some of her hair had come loose, but most of it was still tied back. She wiped away the crust from her eyes and was happy to find her cheek free of moisture. All in all, she didn't seem too out of sorts.

So why was Gordon smiling at her so queerly?

When she couldn't take it anymore, she asked, "What?"

He raised an eyebrow at her. His signature expression. No one really understood how he got the eyebrow so high on his forehead, but everyone knew what it meant. You missed something obvious, which wasn't always true. Sometimes what Gordon considered obvious was a mystery to the rest of the world.

She looked behind her, half expecting to see Endo there, leveling a gun at her forehead, but all she saw was the curved back wall of the white lab. A row of computer stations and hardware lined the wall of the round room. Centrifuges, nucleic acid extraction systems, a fluorescent spectrophotometer, incubators, DNA hybridization ovens, heat and cooling baths, electron and florescent microscopes and a long freezer—everything required for a multitude of biological sciences. The long countertop stopped at a line of refrigerators with glass doors. The first five held carefully labeled samples. The sixth, lunch, though that fridge was nearly empty today.

I'm alone, she remembered.

And then she remembered why, and whipped her head around toward the lab's centerpiece. She gasped, nearly falling from her chair.

"Yes," Gordon said. "Magnificent."

It wasn't the word she would have chosen. Impossible came to mind first, and she was in the impossible business.

The center of the room was an artificial womb. While spherical in appearance, the top and bottom didn't complete the eight-foot-diameter sphere. The bottom led to a filtration system that constantly sterilized the embryonic fluid that filled the womb, running it beneath a powerful UV light. The top of the sphere, which could only be reached from the floor above the lab, was the only way to access the inside. A black umbilical hung from the ceiling, coiling and twisting in the clear fluid, attached to the body that floated at the center of the womb. It served the same function as a normal umbilical cord, supplying the fetus with the nutrients and raw materials it needed to grow.

"How did you do it?" Gordon asked.

Elliot stood slowly and placed her hand against the glass. The fetus inside the womb was at least fifteen inches from head to toe. She glanced down to the touch-screen controls and tapped the black screen twice, waking it. The weight, measured by fluid displacement, showed 3.5 pounds. She shook her head.

Impossible.

"Kendra," Gordon said, his voice insistent. "How?"

Her eyes flicked to him, back to the baby girl she'd created, then back to Gordon. "I attached the DNA you supplied to a retroviral vector, which wasn't as hard as it sounds, because we're making a systemic change rather than targeting specific organs. The vector was injected into an embryo already in progress, to speed things along. It's fast acting and has few side effects, so there was no danger to the embryo, but the end result was that all of the DNA, in every cell, was altered inside an hour. I had no idea what the effect would be, but I would have never guessed... Gordon, this—she—was barely four weeks along."

"And now?"

She huffed, unable to believe the words coming out of her mouth. "Seven months, at least. It might survive if it was born."

"If it doesn't turn to sludge, you mean?"

She nodded.

"How long until we can extract the heart?"

"What time is it?"

Gordon looked at his wristwatch. "Five-twenty. A.M."

Her eyes widened and this time she said it aloud. "Impossible."

"What?"

"Gordon, I—"

"Stop calling me Gordon."

She barely heard him, but spoke again, "General. I put the embryo in the womb at four-thirty." She'd been sleeping for just over thirty minutes, but she'd never felt more awake. She opened the calculator via the touch screen and tapped furiously, speaking her equations as she worked them out. "It's only been growing for fifty minutes. If we assume that it's roughly thirty-two weeks along, minus the four weeks it had grown prior to the DNA insertion, that's twenty-eight weeks of growth in fifty minutes. To make it easy, lets round up to one hour."

General Gordon spoke, but she didn't hear him.

"Twenty eight weeks is seven months. Divide sixty minutes by seven. The fetus is growing a month every eight point—let's round to nine minutes. A year's growth takes one hundred eight minutes, or one hour and forty-eight minutes."

"Going to round that to two hours?" Gordon asked.

"Actually, yes." She glanced up and saw the dubious look in his eyes. "This is hardly science at this point. Best I can offer is a guess, but by the time I figure out exact numbers, the growth rate might have changed."

He nodded. The answer was acceptable.

"Two hours for every year of growth," she said. "If we take this out to twenty-one years, just to be sure that the organs have fully matured...we'll have a fully grown fetus—a woman—in forty two hours."

Elliot plopped down in her chair like she'd just finished running a marathon. She smiled wide and looked up at Gordon feeling true excitement for the first time since she ended her father's life. "This changes everything."

"Yes," Gordon said. "Yes, it does."

Elliot turned back to the fetus. She felt if she watched closely enough she should be able to see it actually growing.

"But," Gordon said.

She turned back toward him.

"Why did you use a female embryo?"

She knew the reason for the question. "Don't worry, General. Female hearts are generally smaller than male hearts, but I chose the fetus genetically predisposed to have the strongest heart. It just turned out to be female."

"Who is she?"

"The DNA donor?"

He nodded.

"A girl, sir. From Mass General Hospital in Boston. Strange name. Maigo. Japanese, I think." BioLance had been using DNA gathered from transplantation waiting lists around the country. The moment they managed to grow a viable organ, one of those people would get a brand new kidney, liver, heart, lung, whatever. And since the new organ, made healthy through genetic tinkering, would be grown from the recipient's own DNA, there would be no risk of rejection. No drugs required. No side effects. Elliot saw it as a chance for redemption. She didn't really regret killing her father, but if there was a God, maybe He could forgive the act if she managed to save millions of lives. Of course, she might also piss Him off by keeping Him from claiming people when He wanted to. "Maigo," she said again, pronouncing the name my-go. "She was waiting for a liver."

"Was?" he asked.

"She died last week. Gunshot wound. Blood loss, and a concussion from falling onto a tile floor, left her in a coma and needing a transplant. Her...father is a suspect, but hasn't been arrested because of lack of evid—"

"I don't need the details," Gordon said. He pursed his lips for a moment, staring at the floor. Then he clucked his tongue and turned around, heading for the door.

"Sir?" she called after him.

He paused, but didn't turn around. "You should know. I also modified the DNA...with your own."

This spun him around.

"You did what?" Both eyebrows were raised. This was a new expression—genuine surprise.

"The heart," she said, squeezing her hands together. "It's for you?"

He just stared at her.

"Your body won't reject it. By this time next week, you'll feel twenty years younger. You won't need to take any meds."

He regarded her for another moment, then spoke. "Kendra, if this works out, you won't have to look over your shoulder for Endo ever again. And I might just take you up on your earlier offer."

She grinned, hoping the General was just joking. But he never joked, which made his departing words so much more horrible.

"If it doesn't work out, better that you don't look over your shoulder. It'll be easier for you that way."

5

I wake with a groan. My head throbs with pain. I think my eyes have been plucked out until I reach up and rub them. Moving sucks. My body aches, every inch of it. I think I'm feeling pain in places I didn't know existed. What the hell happened?

My eyes manage to open for a moment, before the pain doubles and I close them again. But I saw enough to remember where I am. The cabin's faded blue, painted wood ceiling is hard to forget. The previous day's adventures come back to me like a flip book in honey, which is to say, slowly. The long drive. The awful music. The bear. A stab of pain lances from my feet, up through my body and explodes out of my forehead. That sonuvabitch bear!

That's why my body hurts. But it doesn't explain the headache. Then I remember the rest of my day. With the bear gone, I got the power on and assessed the damage. They'd probably been staying in the cabin for just a few days, but they're bears. Wild animals tend to be less tidy than people, even me. Although the bedroom and bathroom were unmolested, the bear family did a number on the living room and kitchen. Most of the damage was cosmetic, but there was enough baby bear shit on the floor to ruin my night, and the braided rug in the middle of the living room smelled like bear piss. I picked up the poop, broken glass, scattered pots and pans, and a deck of cards the cubs had been chewing on. I rolled up the braided rug, wincing at the smell, and dragged it outside. The backdoor, through which the bears had entered, hadn't been damaged. Not by the bears, anyway. Judging by the rot setting in, whoever closed this place up for the winter, forgot to shut the back door. I closed the door, which had warped, but managed to get the deadbolt locked. By the time I finished, the place looked respectable again, but it was also 10 pm and the pain from the abuse I'd taken was starting to stiffen my joints.

The only source of entertainment in the cabin was an old radio, and I wasn't about to turn that on. I'd had all the 80s jams I could take. So I sat back in one of the living room's cushy rocking chairs, propped up my feet and cracked open a beer.

Then another.

And another.

And that's pretty much where my memory ends. I somehow made it to the bed. Must have been nearly midnight at that point. And now, here I am, swimming in pain.

Three loud knocks ricochet through the inside of my head like bullets. I clutch my head and whine incoherently into the pillow. It's not the bear. Bears don't knock. Whoever it is can wait.

Three more booming knocks and I swear I'm in a war zone. I squeeze a pillow over my head lest I end up with post traumatic stress disorder. The knock comes again, louder, more persistent. I'm about to shout, "Go away," when the person at the door beats me to the punch.

"Willowdale Police," a woman says. Her voice is like a foghorn. "Is anyone there?"

No, I think. I'm not here.

Boom. Boom. Boom. "I know you're there, and I don't have a whole lot to do today, so please, open the door."

My eyes open against the pain. It's dull in comparison to the agony this woman's voice is causing me. I spin out of bed, onto my feet and nearly fall over. I catch myself in the doorframe. Am I still buzzed? I looked up into the living room. The morning light streaming through the windows feels like hot pokers in my eyes. I let them adjust for a moment, then notice the beer cans littering the floor by the rocking chair. I count them quickly. Eight empties.

Geez.

"Willowdale Police!" the woman shouts, punctuating the words with another volley of cannon fire. "Please open the door."

"Willowdale," I whisper to myself. Watson never gave me the name of the town, just directions. Willowdale is where the Sasquatch sightings have been reported. Lucky for me, I already have a mamma bear suspect. Maybe two suspects if the woman at the door is as brutish as she sounds.

I stumble to the door, pausing with a hand against the wall, trying to steady myself and clear my head. My arm feels weighted by a concrete block, but I manage to raise it and look at my watch. 5:30 A.M. Sonofa— . Through the curtained window, I see a clenched fist rise up, ready to slam the door. I don't think I could take a point-blank knock without toppling over in agony.

"I'm here!" I shout, grumpily unlocking the door and throwing it open. "Isn't there a raccoon in a fence somewhere that you should be deal—"

My eyes clear and I get a good look at the police officer standing on the front porch. "Holy." I say it aloud, but manage not to voice the thought that accompanied the word. Did Watson send me a strip-o-cop? I quickly decide that's not the case. This woman isn't wearing make-up. She's just naturally stunning. Her wavy orange hair is pulled back in a ponytail. Freckles fringe her high cheeks. And her eyes—they're technically brown, but they're so close to the color of her hair that they seem to glow.

Before I can ogle her tightly fitting uniform, and the curves beneath it, she says, "Looks like I have my Sasquatch suspect."

I look for the bear, but don't see it. She's talking about me. I look down and find myself dressed only in black boxer-briefs. How did I not notice I wasn't dressed? And why am I covered in streaks of mud and pine needles?

"We had some complaints. Lots of hooting and hollering in the woods last night. People around here are on a Sasquatch kick, but I don't buy that, do you?"

All I can do is laugh, but that hurts, so it turns into a wince.

"You just pass gas?" the woman asks.

She catches me off guard. "What? No!"

"Made kind of a funny face," she says. I look for a hidden grin, but she's deadpan. "Been drinking, chief?"

"Chief?"

"Answer the question."

I lean forward and read the name tag, careful not to glance below it more than once. "Listen, Officer Collins."

"Sheriff Collins," she corrects.

"Huh," I say, a bit surprised. "Sheriff Collins, drinking in the privacy of your own home isn't illegal. Nor is getting shit-faced." Probably shouldn't have said that last bit, but too late now.

"No," she agrees with a snarky smile. "But running around the woods in your underwear, singing Dude Looks Like a Lady isn't exactly in the privacy of your own home, is it? Neither is discharging a firearm."

Damnit.

"I wasn't drinking when—"

Double damnit. I just confirmed that I'm the one with the gun. That I was drinking isn't really up for debate.

Her hand moves slowly toward the gun holstered on her hip. Most hung-over, still buzzed people wouldn't notice, but I'm not your average drunk. Details like this are what I'm good at. But she needs to know I'm not a threat. "I'm DHS," I say.

Her hand pauses, but doesn't retreat. "You're Department of Homeland Security? Didn't know they were having trouble recruiting people."

I'm confused for a moment, but then I read between the lines and hear the unspoken jab about lowering standards.

"Ha. Ha," I say. "I can get my badge."

"Please do."

As I turn to find my shorts, I catch sight of her hand unclip the sidearm. For a small town cop, she's not taking any chances. Suppose that
makes sense though, drunks with guns are never a good combination.
And I'm a stranger. She probably knows everyone in town by name. Her
next question confirms this.

"You a friend of the Watsons?"

"I work with Ted," I say.

"Haven't met him."

"He's Bill and Diane's son," I say from the bedroom where I find
my cargo shorts. Bending over to pick up the shorts is agony, but I
manage to grab them, slip them over my ankles and pull them up. I
find my yellow T-shirt on the bed and pull it on, too. My maroon cap
is on the nightstand. I feel momentarily embarrassed that super-babe
officer saw my receding hairline, but then again, she saw me shirt-
less, which I'm pretty sure isn't a bad thing. Despite my casual
disposition, I keep in good shape.

"I said I hadn't met him," she says from the living room. "Not that
I didn't know who he was."

I shake my head. I can't decide if I like her smart-ass commentary
or hate it. She's still in the doorway when I return. I dig into my
pocket, fish out my badge and flip it open like an old pro. She's not
impressed.

While inspecting the badge, she asks, "Why did you discharge
your firearm Mister..." She reads my name from the badge.
"...Hudson?"

"There was a bear," I say.

"You realize this is not bear hunting season?"

"I didn't shoot the bear. The back door was open. She was in
here with a pair of cubs when I opened the door."

I see a flicker of understanding in her eyes. If she lives out here,
she knows how mamma bear reacted.

I point to the ruined screen door. "She knocked me through the
door. Nearly took my head off. Scratched the hell out of Betty."

She stiffens. "You have a woman with you? Is she hurt?"

"No," I say and then realize I really don't want to tell this woman who Betty is, but I've got no choice. "Betty...is my truck."

She steps back and turns to the truck. The claw marks are easy to see. "You named your truck, Betty?"

"I'm adorable, I know."

"You're weird is what you are."

"How come you don't have a Maine accent," I ask, suddenly noticing she lacks the laconic drawl prevalent in Northern Maine.

She ignores the question. "What's the P stand for?" She holds up my ID, which reads, Fusion Center – P beneath the big blocky DHS. "Fusion Centers are designated by cities, not letters."

Triple damnit. Why does a backwoods cop know anything about the DHS? I consider making something up, but she's probably wondering if the ID is a fake, so anything other than the ridiculous truth might land me in a jail cell, and I do not want my superiors bailing me out.

Still, I can't quite bring myself to say the exact word. "Preternatural," I say, hoping she has no idea what it means.

No such luck.

An honest grin emerges on her face. "Please tell me DHS isn't investigating Sasquatch sightings."

The depth of my frown matches her smile, but upside down. She laughs, but quickly squelches it by covering her mouth with her hand. "Well, Special Investigator Jon Hudson, you've arrived just in time. The Johnsons are my next stop and you're going to want to talk to them."

"I am?"

"Most of the sightings are reported by them."

"I'm not really feeling up to it right now, thanks."

"Look," she says, a serious tone creeping back into her voice. "They're just up the road, and I fielded at least five calls from them last night. Near as I can tell, you were the cause for all of them."

"Last night?" I say. "Kind of a slow response time."

"They call a lot," she admits.

"The boy who called Sasquatch," I say.

She nods, but corrects me. "Old man who called Sasquatch. Look, I'm going to give you two choices, come with me and talk to Mr. Johnson, or I'm going to book you for public drunkenness."

I smile. It's screwy, but I kind of like that she's playing hardball, and that she wants me to come with her. But my head and body would rather I spend the next few hours in a fetal position.

"I have coffee," she says. "And ibuprofen."

"Sold."

6

Ten seconds after sitting in the passenger's seat of Collins's tricked out Sheriff's SUV, I'm ready to ditch Betty and find me a new girl. Whether that's a new car or Collins, I have yet to decide. The seats are cushy, the engine roars when she turns the key just once—Betty takes some coaxing—and her badass stereo has an MP3 player port. I look around, counting eight speakers. "How's the sound system?"

"We're not car shopping," she says, and picks up a thermos from between the seats. She pops off the red cap and unscrews the cover, releasing a rich coffee aroma that distracts me from my pounding headache.

She pours a cup. "It's sugared, but no cream."

"Perfect," I say, reaching for the cup. She hands it to me, and I test the temperature with a sip. Hot enough, but not too hot to chug. I drain the cup in three large gulps. "You mentioned ibuprofen?" I hold the cup out and make a face that begs for more.

She hands the thermos to me. "You need it more than I do."

I pour another cup and drain it. When I put the cup down, she's got three maroon pills in her hand. "Figured a big guy like you might need three."

"Figured right," I say, taking the pills and popping them in my mouth. I pour a third cup, and swallow it down with the pills. I breathe a sigh of relief as the caffeine flows through my system, chasing away the cobwebs. The hot liquid will dissolve the pain meds fast and the caffeine will speed its delivery to my system. I'll be feeling peachy in about thirty minutes. "Thank y—" The flavor of the coffee finally registers. "This is French roast?"

She thinks for a moment and then nods. "Sounds right."

"Sounds right?" I take a sip. "Starbucks French roast. Sugar, but no cream."

"So?" she asks.

"So," I say, "your teeth are whiter than any coffee drinker's should be. You'd also know exactly what your thermos held, and you wouldn't be so willing to let a stranger drink your wake-up juice." I thrust a finger in the air, hitting the SUV's ceiling. "And, Starbucks French roast with sugar, no cream, is what I have been drinking every morning for the past four years." I take another drink, straight from the thermos, and wipe the moisture from my lip. "You lied to me."

"Watson, I think you've got it," she says.

"Watson indeed. How long have you known Ted?"

"About ten years," she says. "Don't know him well, but he called me a few days back. Told me you'd be in the area, what you were doing, and asked me to bring this to you." She motions to the coffee.

"So that's why you came to the cabin?"

"At five thirty in the morning? I don't know Ted that well. I'm here at the crack of dawn because you spooked the neighbors."

I look up the road. Nothing but trees. "I don't see any neighbors."

She puts the truck in gear and speeds over the rough road. I barely feel it.

Betty, your days are numbered.

We only drive thirty seconds before I see a large log cabin with a sculpted yard, perfectly managed flower beds and a tall U.S. flag snapping in the breeze. Retirees for sure. Possibly ex-military. The gravel driveway crunches under the SUV's tires.

"That's Mr. Johnson," Collins says.

I see the old codger sitting in a rocking chair on the wraparound porch and take note of the U.S. Marines cap he's wearing. If there is anything I respect, its folks in the armed services who are braver than I am and who risk everything in service to their country. Technically, my job is similar, but I hardly think Sasquatch is a threat to national security, though given the number of calls Mr. Johnson has made, he might disagree. But I won't give him a hard time. He looks down at us, staring over his aviator glasses and takes a long drag from a bright orange can of Moxie soda. Not ribbing this guy is going to be tough.

I pull down the sun guard and flip open the mirror.

"Don't bother," Collins says. "There isn't anything you can do that will make you look like a DHS agent."

There are rings under my eyes, a twig in my cap and dirt smudged on my cheek. I pluck the twig from the cap and then use it to rub the dirt from my face. I lick my thumb and finish the job with my own spit. I slap my face, three times on each side, adding a little color and helping the coffee wake me up. I look at Collins. "Better than nothing, right?"

"S'pose." The word carries just a hint of an accent.

"Georgia."

"What?"

"You were raised in Georgia."

She just looks at me for a moment, twisting her full lips.

"I'm good with accents and local dialects," I explain. "Kind of a hobby."

She just opens her door and hops out.

I follow quickly, nearly falling out of the SUV as I open and close the door. Mr. Johnson is already on his feet, standing at the top of the porch. He waggles his hand at me. "What's wrong with this one?" he says to Collins. "Looked like he was having a seizure in the car there."

The accent is thick and slow. A Mainer through and through.

I straighten myself up and put on a grin. "Mr. Johnson."

The man's eyes widen slightly and his white caterpillar eyebrows rise. "You told him my name?"

"Mr. Johnson," Collins says. "This is Jon Hudson. He's an investigator with the—"

"U.S. Fish and Wildlife Service," I say, climbing the steps. I hold my hand out to shake his.

He looks at my hand, then back up at me. "Jeezum Crow, boy, you look shot at and missed, shit on an' hit."

I nod. "Had a run in with a rack a poundahs."

He returns my smile and shakes my hand. "Ayah." We're speaking the same language now.

"How ya doin' this mornin'?" I ask him.

"Oh, fair t' middlin'," he says. "Be a lot better if not for that shoot'n an hollr'n last night."

"Won't happen again," I say.

Johnson gives me a one-eyed squint. "How's that?"

I nod to Collins. "Officer Collins here was just telling me about it. Couple of kids up to no good. She ran them out of town."

"That right?" he asks.

Collins clears her throat uncomfortably. "Won't be bothering you again, Mr. Johnson. Made it clear I'd throw them in jail next time."

"But that's not why we're really here," I say. "Is it Mr. Johnson?"

He walks along the porch, aided by a cane. "Follow me."

Collins pulls me back and lets Mr. Johnson get a few feet ahead of us. "What's a rack of pounders?"

"Six pack," I say. "I was being honest."

"Over here," Johnson says. He stops at the side of the porch, leaning on the railing. He points out at the woods. "Seen 'em walking out there. At night mostly. Sometimes during the day, though they keep to the shadows. Just shapes. Sounds."

"Sure it's not a bear?" I ask.

He whips around toward me and hitches a thumb at Collins. "You already sound like her!"

"Just trying to consider all possibilities."

"Ain't no bear. I've seen bear. Hunted bear. Whatever it is out there, it walks on two legs. Comes 'round least twice a day. Usually dawn and dusk. Maybe in the night, but me and Sally—that's my wife—turn in 'round nine, so I wouldn't know."

The man's testimony is plain and simple. He's not claiming to have seen brown fur, a large head or any other traditional Sasquatch feature. He just knows that something is walking in his woods, and that it's a biped.

"Served in Vietnam, sir?" I ask.

"Walked the Ho Chi Min Trail. Yes, sir."

"Then I believe you," I say.

"Well, damn," he says. "It's 'bout time someone did."

"But," I say quickly. "There is one other possibility I'm not sure you've considered."

"What's that?" he says.

"Only other biped out here, aside from ol' Squatch, that I can think of."

He thinks for just a moment, but then shakes his head. "Damn, son, you're right. People."

I can see that this idea bothers the man even more than Sasquatch. To him, Bigfoot is probably just another denizen of the forest. Like a bear. Or a cougar. But people, in his woods? Those are trespassers. And now that I've put the idea in his head, he's probably going to spend the night on the porch with a shotgun. And since I don't want to be the reason Mr. Johnson spends the rest of his life in jail for murder, I turn to Collins and ask, "Feel up to a hike?"

7

After getting some basic information from Mr. Johnson, we strike out into the woods. I put on a good tough guy show for the old vet, but once Collins and I are concealed by the forest, I lean my head against the rough bark of a pine and groan.

"You going to puke?" she asks.

"Just hoping the pain killers kick in soon."

"Probably should eat something.

I load my voice with sarcasm and say, "You think?"

A granola bar hits the side of my head and falls at my feet. It's one of those super healthy kinds. Flax seeds. Agave and honey. Almonds. Cherries. I would have preferred the chewy chocolate-chip variety, but food is food and this is healthier. Bending over to pick it up hurts like hell, but I unwrap it and wolf it down in four bites. Without moving from my position by the tree, I unzip my pants.

"Oh God," Collins says. I can hear her feet crunching away through the leaf litter. "You know I could fine you for indecent exposure."

"I drank at least eight beers last night and a pint of coffee twenty minutes ago. What did you think was going to happen?" I sigh with relief as my bladder drains. My headache fades too, and I feel myself return to some semblance of normalcy, though I'm going to need something to drink soon or that headache is going to come back with a vengeance.

After putting myself together, I turn and find Collins just twenty feet away, atop a small rise, her back to me. I stand and stare for a moment. Stay professional, I tell myself. Don't do anything stupid. I turn my eyes to the ground and clear my throat so she knows I'm coming.

"Feel better?" she asks.

"Dandy," I say.

"Something interesting on the ground?"

I don't look up. Stay professional. "Thinking," I reply. "Let's go over what we know so far."

"You're taking this seriously?" she asks. "Kind of figured you were putting on a show for Mr. Johnson."

"As much as I would like to go back to bed, I believe him. Sure, he's a little paranoid. All old people are. And he's probably more than a little bored. But there's a nugget of truth in there somewhere, and he's a nice guy, so it's worth checking out. My good deed for the day."

She smiles at me as I climb up the hill behind her and manage to keep my eyes from wandering. "You don't get to do this much, do you? Look for clues. An actual investigation."

"About as much as you do, I'd guess."

"Touché" she says. "So. Investigator. What do we know?"

"Johnson heard something walking around on two legs. Probably a person. But he also hears the sound fairly regularly and around the same times of day. Which hints at a routine. But his hunting days were already over when he and his wife had the place built, so he's never actually explored the woods, or hunted them. I'm willing to bet he hasn't even driven farther down the road, for fear of getting stuck." I turn to Collins. "And you've never been past their house, either?"

"Never had a reason," she admits.

I reach for my smartphone, thinking I might be able to find a satellite view of the area, but it's missing. It's still in the truck. "Have a phone with Internet access?"

She pulls an iPhone from her pocket, waggles it like it's a piece of junk and puts it back. "Have the phone, but not the coverage."

I would never admit it, but the fact that we've got a little bit of a mystery here excites me. "Well, let's have a look around."

We meander through the woods for ten minutes. The forest is fairly young, like it was clear cut fifty years ago. As a result, the area is congested with brush, ferns and several smaller trees that make walking in a straight line impossible. Despite the challenging terrain, we blaze our trail in silence. And as we do, I feel something change between us. Nothing romantic or some kind of sexual tension. Just the opposite. We relax. All of the morning's awkwardness and tension just melts away. Then I realize what it is. I'm comfortable. And despite my relaxed persona, I find true relaxation elusive. People unnerve me until I really get to know them. Cooper and Watson are pretty much the only people that know the real Jon Hudson, but Collins is already worming her way past my defenses, though not intentionally.

I pull a maple branch aside so that Collins can pass, but then I see something on the ground and let it go. The branch snaps against her legs and elicits a shout, but then she's by my side, looking down at my discovery.

"It's a path," she says. "Could be a game trail."

I shake my head. "No. Animals don't disguise their paths." The worn center of the path has been covered with leaves, but the slight depression is impossible to conceal. "Which way did Mr. Johnson say he heard the footsteps heading?"

Collins points to the right.

I stand and look back, trying to see any hint of the log cabin. It's hidden. "Mr. Johnson has good ears." I step over the path, careful not to disturb the leafy disguise and walk twenty feet beyond it. Collins follows my lead and we follow the path without walking on it. If someone is up to no good out here, it might require a longer investigation, and there's no sense in tipping off the bad guys that someone has found their path.

The path ends a half mile farther when it merges with the dirt road. But it continues on the other side. The road here is in even worse disrepair. Foot-deep potholes. Large rocks uncovered by years of unchecked erosion. Even Collins's SUV couldn't get through here.

"This isn't right," Collins says.

"A little pavement wouldn't hurt," I say.

"No, look at the rocks. They're too big."

She's right, the rocks are pretty big, impossible to drive over, but I'm not exactly a dirt road expert.

"A lot of the dirt roads in town need to be graded every year. Some get new dirt. If it's a busy road, I get to sit and watch. There are a lot of stones in the dirt they use, but nothing bigger than my fist. She holds up a clenched fist. Callused skin covers all of her knuckles. Interesting. "Some of these are more than a foot tall. That means the original layer of dirt was even higher. Makes no sense."

She's right. "Someone put rocks here, which means—" We both turn to the left, looking down the dirt road. "—we're going thataway."

We make good time on the road. The large rocks disappear after fifty feet. Definitely a manmade deterrent. But why? Are some hillbillies out here making moonshine? We're not even in the right part of the country for that. We've barely gone a half mile when the road ends at a chain link gate overgrown with vines. A fallen tree has come down in front of gate, its roots pulled from the ground as though toppled by the wind.

Collins kicks the tree with her boot toe. "Convenient."

"Dirt bikes could get past the boulders," I say. "Not this."

"So what's the big secret?"

The gate is eight feet tall and nearly impossible to see through. A spiral of razor wire tops the gate, which is connected on either side to a ten-foot-tall chain link fence—also topped with razor wire. Big secret is right. "Have any militias in the area? Cults?"

"Not that I know of."

I slide over the tree for a closer look at the gate. There's a sign under the vines. My keys are still in my pocket, so I take out the small jackknife, which I keep sharp, and I cut vegetation away. The white, metal sign is splotched with rust, but I have no trouble reading the text. At the top is a bright red message that would unnerve just about anyone:

U.S. ARMY

RESTRICTED AREA

USE OF DEADLY FORCE

IS AUTHORIZED

WARNING

It's followed by a paragraph of text:

This site has been declared a restricted area by the authority of the Commanding General, in accordance with the provisions of the directive issued by the Secretary of Defense on 20 August 1954, pursuant to the provisions of Section 21, Internal Security Act of 1950. Unauthorized entry is prohibited. All persons and vehicles entering hereon are liable to search. Photographing, making notes, drawings, maps, or graphic representation of this site or its activities, is prohibited unless specifically authorized by the Commanding Officer. Any such material found in the possession of unauthorized persons will be confiscated.

The dates are a dead giveaway. "It's a Nike site."

"A what?"

"In the wake of World War II, the U.S. Army wanted an air defense network so something like Pearl Harbor couldn't happen again. Nike was a line-of-site anti-aircraft missile system deployed around the United States, especially in coastal and high population areas during the early '50s. There were hundreds of sites, all with signs just like this one. But the missiles were never used and when the Russians built ICBMs, Nike was officially obsolete. They were decommissioned and the sites were abandoned by the mid seventies. But—"

The tone in my voice catches Collins's attention.

I meet her fiery eyes. "—this was not a Nike site."

"What? How do you know?"

"I grew up with a Nike site in the woods behind my house. I played up there with my cousins when I was a kid. Drank up there with my friends when I was older. Never did figure out how to get inside the bunker, but the site was surrounded by a six-foot-high chain link fence. No razor wire. I think the signs and armed guards were deterrent enough."

"Other sites in higher risk areas could have had more of a barrier," she says.

"Sure, but they would have been topped with barbed wire. Razor wire wasn't developed until the '80s and this style wasn't used until at least the '90s. Also, why have a Nike site way the hell out here? They defended coasts and population areas. Willowdale is neither of those things." I reach up and rub one of the blades between my fingers, a thin layer of rust coating my fingertips. I slide my rusty index finger over my tongue. Tastes chemical, not metallic. I spit. "The rust is fake. Someone doesn't want visitors."

"Ahem," comes a deep voice that spins both Collins and me around. Her hand goes to her hip, but she doesn't draw, which is probably a good thing considering the shotgun leveled at her chest.

8

"Mind telling me what you're doing on my land?" the man asks. He's dressed like a local—blue jeans, flannel shirt, Red Sox cap—but it feels too local, like a costume rather than genuine attire. And it's far too warm for flannel. It's only 6 in the morning and the temp has to be pushing mid-eighties. Going to be a scorcher today, but this guy is dressed for Fall. I give a quick up and down glance. He's lanky, maybe a buck eighty, but he's got an unnaturally thick torso. The flannel is hiding body armor, I'm sure of it. Definitely militia material.

"Just in case you missed the uniform," I say, "you're pointing that thing at the Sheriff."

He turns the barrel toward me.

Better.

Then I realize I'm not armed, unless you count the one and a half inch keychain blade still in my hand. But that's like bringing— well, a one and a half inch knife to a shotgun fight.

"Sir," Collins says sounding just as calm as ever, "I'd appreciate it if you lowered your weapon."

"Not until y'all tell me what you're doing on my land."

Y'all. Not a Yankee.

"Doesn't look like your land," I say, motioning to the sign.

"Bought the site in ninety-five," he says. As he speaks, he puts a hand to his cheek and scratches twice, with all four fingers. I know a hand signal when I see one, even if it's cleverly disguised. He's just invited some friends to the party. Things are going to go from bad to worse fairly quickly unless we can disarm this guy—mentally, not physically. Without knowing what we're up against, I'm not about to start a shootout.

"Cool beans," I say. I've always hated the phrase, but it's ridiculous, non-threatening and shows a good degree of disinterest. "Listen, we don't want any trouble. I'm with the U.S. Fish and Wildlife Service. A bear in the area has ransacked a cabin nearby. Nearly mauled the old guy down the road."

"Mr. Johnson," the guy says, catching me off guard.

"You know him?"

"We've met," he says. "In town. He the one that called you out?"

"Yeah," I say, but then regret it. If these people are as dangerous as I think, I don't want them anywhere near the Johnsons.

"Look, sir," Collins says, and I note that she's not doing any normal cop stuff, like asking for a name. "We just need to know if you've seen the bear. Big black bear."

"Maybe seven hundred pounds," I say. If he's patrolling these woods, he's likely seen the bear I encountered and the more accurately I describe it, the more likely he is to believe our story. "Has two cubs."

The man's doing a great job of hiding his thoughts and emotions, but I see a glimmer of recognition in his eyes. He's seen the bear.

"Yeah," he says. "I've seen her, but not for a few days."

The guy has just unknowingly admitted to patrolling the woods.

"Well, give us a call if you do," Collins says and puts on a crafty smile. "I'd tell you to be careful, but I can see you know to handle yourself."

Militia or not, killer or not, Collins's smile and radiant eyes are enough to bring peace to the Middle East. The man rubs his cheek again, this time with a flat hand. He taps his skin twice. Another hand signal, telling his buddies to hold off.

While this is a relief, it's also disconcerting. Whoever he's motioning to is close enough to see his signals, through the gate. Even worse, if the people on the other side of the gate were obeying his hand signals, and I have no reason to believe they weren't, then they're pros. Like Mr. Johnson, I've got pretty good ears, but I didn't hear a thing. Not a rustle of leaves, a snap of a twig or a shift in the breeze. I'm still leaning toward a militia, but these guys aren't just backwoods conspiracy theorists. They're ex-military, possibly even ex-Special Forces.

He lowers the shotgun and my blood pressure lowers a tad. I give him a nod and a smile. "Thanks."

"I'm going to assume you have a permit for that," Collins says, motioning to the shotgun. "Just make sure I don't get called out here for any kind of nonsense."

She's smart. Leaving without a warning would be decidedly too easy and the guy might think we're just trying get away so we can come back with reinforcements, which is actually true. We can't come back here without a small army. Maybe a large one. Thankfully, despite being the team leader of Fusion Center – P, I am still a fairly high ranking DHS agent, just not a very respected one. But I can easily find out if these guys are on anyone's radar, and if not, put them there.

"In the meantime," she says. "Put up some actual no trespassing signs. If it's not posted, it's not illegal for us or anyone else to be out here."

She's pushing it now, but he just nods and says, "Will do."

Collins turns her back to him and starts away. I stay rooted in place for a moment, waiting to see if the guy will make any kind of threatening move. He turns toward me, clearly annoyed that I haven't followed her. He motions toward Collins with the shotgun. "Go on, git."

Git.

Kansas, I think, but keep the deduction to myself. Where he's from has no bearing on who he is now or what's going on out here. It just confirms that everything about him is a sham. No way a man from Kansas is an honest to goodness Sox fan. "You're a baseball fan, who's your pick this year? I'm partial to the Angels." That last bit was just to let him know that I'm not a Red Sox fan, which is a lie, I am, but it gives him the freedom to answer honestly.

"Royals," he says.

Thought so. "Huh," I say.

He stares at me with eyes that say he's losing his patience. I turn away with a wave and say, "Watch out for that bear. She's a testy one."

He doesn't say a word as we make a casual retreat along the dirt road. Neither of us looks back. Neither of us speaks. She knows as well as I do that we were lucky to get away in one piece.

Five minutes into our walk, when I'm sure we can't be seen, or heard, I speak softly. "What's your assessment?"

"At least three of them," she says. "One behind the fence, one behind us."

This surprises me. I pride myself on my powers of observation, but that's a detail I missed.

"The hand signals were for the guy behind the fence. Never saw him, but I'm sure he was there," she explains. "Never saw the second guy, either, but he kept glancing past you like someone was there."

"Anything else?"

"Best guess? Maybe a marijuana farm."

"Good thinking." And it was. I jumped right to militia, but there were probably a good number of other possibilities, none of them legal.

"Can you dig up the records on the land?" I ask. "Find out who owns it?"

"Already planning to," she says.

"I'll make some calls, see if there are any ongoing investigations, try to get some updated satellite images, and see about getting us some backup."

"What about the whole Preternatural thing?" she asks. "Won't they yank you from the case?"

"Paranormal," I admit. "I was hoping you wouldn't know what Preternatural meant. And yeah, they probably would try to yank me from the case, but the nearest Fusion Center is Boston, so it will take

some time for them to get here and I intend on being so fully en-
trenched in this case by then that they won't have any choice but to
keep me on."

"I can request it too, if it will help," she says.

This gets a big fat grin from me. "Thanks."

She shrugs like its nothing. But it's something. Or maybe I just
hope it's something. I remind myself that I've only known Collins for
about an hour. If I apply Occam's Razor—the simplest explanation is
usually the right one—then it's most definitely nothing.

"Fuck you, Occam," I mutter.

"What was that?" she says.

"Nothing," I say quickly, then point up ahead. "Look, there's Mr.
Johnson."

She turns forward and offers a wave to the man.

He doesn't respond.

The hairs on the back of my neck spring up. Something's off.

I look closer, taking in all the details. He's sitting in his rocking
chair, facing toward us, not rocking. His eyes are open, but he hasn't
acknowledged our approach, despite the fact that he's eager to find
out what's going on in his woods. The bright orange can of Moxie is
on the porch next to him, but it's on its side. Brown fluid drips from
the deck floor to the staircase's top step. No way an old guy would let
a spill like that go. It'd get sticky. Attract ants.

That's when I see the hole in his forehead. It's small. 9mm probably.
Hard to see. But it's there and Mr. Johnson is very dead. Probably his
wife, too. And since we never heard a gunshot, that means the hit was
sound-suppressed.

Definitely pros. Given how fast they got to Mr. Johnson, the
shooter must have been sent the moment I uttered the man's name.
The Royals fan was wearing a mic. These guys are organized and
deadly, and we're about to be next.

I do my best to hide my fury, slide up closer to Collins and wrap
my arm around her waist. She tenses and I know I'm a second away
from getting pummeled, so I speak fast and serious, "Johnson's dead."

She starts to look, but I stop her with a growled, "Don't look!" I force myself to calm and say, "Put your arm around me. Lean your head on my shoulder."

She listens and I whisper through a big phony smile. "In ten seconds, I'm going to shove you into the woods to our left. Run like hell until you can't see the road, then turn a sharp right and make for the Watson's cabin."

She nuzzles into me. "What are you going to do?"

"I'll be right behind you. Your car is compromised. We need to get to Betty. Ready?"

I feel her body tense under my hand. "Go."

I thrust her to the left and she hits full speed by the time she reaches the side of the road. I'm on her heels, picking up speed fast.

The bullets start flying before I make it five steps.

9

My hand goes to the side of my head as a flash of pain nearly knocks me to the ground. I'm sure my hand will come away bloody, but it doesn't. Not shot, just still hungover. The coffee and painkiller quick fix works well if you're kicking back and taking it easy, not so much if you're sprinting through the woods while unknown assailants are trying to blow your head off. Of course, those things also make the pain easier to ignore. Despite the white hot agony ping-ponging through my head, I do not want to die.

I run flat out, as fast as I can, bunny-hopping bushes, rocks and fallen trees. When there isn't an obstacle to leap, I zigzag like a slalom skier. I probably look ridiculous, but the idea is to not get shot. Moving unpredictably is my best bet at throwing off their aim. Even with all the chaotic movements, I'm pretty damn fast. But Collins—the woman must be part greyhound. Not only am I not gaining on her, but she's actually leaving me in the dust.

Bullets tear through a tree as I pass. I duck my head instinctively, but don't slow and don't look back. Any delay and I'm screwed. Which means that making a quick getaway in Betty is out of the question. Even if the truck started on the first try, it would be close. The driver's side door faces the road and contrary to what is seen in movies, bullets make short work of car doors. More than that, Betty takes a good minute to get going. These guys could casually stroll up to the truck and tap on the glass before popping me in the face.

"Collins!" I shout. "No time for Betty. Just get the backpack out of the flatbed and keep on going."

She doesn't nod or reply in any way, but I'm sure she's heard me.

I hear a coughing sound behind me. Bullets tear into the earth around my feet. Pain, like a bee sting, flares in my right thigh. I've been shot, but I don't fall to the ground, so it's not bad. But their improving aim and the fact that I can now hear the sound-suppressed gunfire means they're closing in.

The cabin emerges through the thick forest. Collins forks right, heading for Betty. I watch as she clears the trees, picks up even more speed—which seems impossible—and leaps into Betty's flatbed. Without missing a beat, Collins leans over, snags the backpack and hurtles out the far side. A string of holes appear in the truck's side, each punctuated by a metallic punching sound.

Sorry, Betty.

I maintain my course, heading for the cabin's bedroom window. Blocking my path is a wood pile, cut and stacked for the stove inside. I leap the pile as bullets tear into the wood, falling gracelessly on the far side. But I don't slow as I roll back to my feet and come up with a ten-pound log. I heave the thing ahead of me.

The bedroom window shatters a moment before I arrive. I throw myself through while the glass is still falling. My feet hit the floor, but forward momentum pulls me onto the bed. I roll over the corner, grasping the thick, black wool blanket in one hand and snatching my gun from the nightstand with the other. Then I'm out the bedroom door and charging across the living room.

The back door is locked and barricaded to keep the bear from returning. And the front door will make me an easy target. So I whip the blanket around my arm twice, hold it above my head and leap through the window on the opposite end of the living room. I curl into a tight ball and let the blanket shield me from the broken glass.

As I hit the ground atop the blanket, I feel a pinch in my arm, but ignore it. I get to my feet and keep running. The blanket billows out behind me, which makes me easier to see, for the moment, but also disguises my body.

I half expect a barrage of bullets to turn the blanket into a Light Bright page in the hands of a maniacal child, but nothing happens. The house is blocking their view, or maybe they don't know I exited the far side, though that seems doubtful considering the amount of noise I made. Still, I don't seem to be a target for the moment, so I reel in the blanket and ball it around my right arm.

I round a tree and come face-to-barrel with a handgun. I try to stop, but the downward slope and leaf litter keep my feet in motion while my top half tries to stop. I fall on my ass, while raising my weapon, but neither gun goes off.

"Fuck," Collins says, lowering her weapon.

I climb to my feet. No time for sharing apologies. "Let's go."

She pauses, looking uphill. "I see three of them."

I take her arm and yank her back. "Now!"

The slope makes our flight a little faster, but we're forced to slow down when the forest grows thicker or else we risk taking a fall. The bullets have stopped flying for the moment, but any delay on our part might change that. When we reach the base of the hill, I turn right. There's no real logic behind it, there just isn't time to think about a direction.

Turns out, it was the wrong choice. The woods end abruptly at the site of an old landslide. The wide arc of land curves for a hundred feet in either direction and the trees are sparse around the rim. We stop at the edge and look down. The grade isn't too bad. We could make it. But we'd be easy targets on the way down and the forest doesn't start again for another few hundred feet.

A branch cracks in the woods behind us. Without discussing our options, Collins and I both leap over the edge. But we don't run. We duck. A tangle of roots dangle from the overhang of earth, and we use them to keep from tumbling down the slope. I place my handgun to my lips, "shhh."

She nods.

Fast approaching footsteps slow as they approach the edge.

"Think I saw them go over," a man says.

A second man, sounding a little winded, says, "Me too."

"Careful," says a third voice I recognize as the man from Kansas. "The cop was carrying."

Dirt trickles over the edge as just one of the men approaches. "Not seeing them."

"No way they made the woods," Kansas says.

I see a forehead slide into view. Another inch and he'll see me. More dirt falls from above. The earth flexes. The idea must strike Collins at the same time it does me because we both grab hold of the roots hanging from the flexing ledge of soil and pull. The ground bows forward and with a shout, the man falls over the edge.

I don't watch him land. Instead, I spring up and level my weapon at Kansas's surprised face. Then I erase it. A second, louder gunshot makes me flinch, but its good news. The second man hunting us spins away, a hole punched in the center of his chest.

I'm about to congratulate Collins when a hand grips my shoulder and spins me around. A fist like a concrete block finds the side of my head and spills me to the ground. I flip head over heels, tumbling down the slope. I strike a number of large rocks and scraggly bushes on the way down, but nothing slows me. The hillside is content to beat the shit out of me. I stop at the bottom and groan when I lift my head.

Collins tumbles to a stop a few feet away. She doesn't move, but she's breathing. I look for our guns. They're both gone.

The good news is that the man pursuing us has lost his weapon, too. The bad news is that he's built like a steroid addict. He's got the seething rage to boot.

I cough and collect my beanie cap from the ground, dusting it off before putting it back on my head like I haven't got a care in the world. It's an act, of course. The living freight train looks like he could tear my head clean off. I just don't want him to expect a fight.

I add a stagger to my step, moving slowly away from him. I place a hand on my arm like its hurt and am momentarily surprised to find it warm with blood. As he closes the distance, I realize that a lot of my act is easy to pull off because it's not an act at all. I'm shot, cut and beaten.

Shit.

As he winds up for a punch, I shake off my weariness and step forward, kicking out hard, aiming for his nuts. I connect hard, but not with the soft flesh between his legs. I look down and find his hand wrapped around my foot. He caught my kick.

As he raises his other hand, I see his eyes go to my knee. He's going to break my freaking leg. Unable to do anything else, I try to duplicate a move I saw in a kung-fu movie once. I jump up and kick with my other leg, aiming for his head. The kick misses, but the sudden twist frees me from his grasp.

I stagger quickly to my feet, but then he's on me, throwing hammer punches. I do my best to block the blows, but he connects with my shoulder, numbing the arm. As my defense falls, he does the opposite of what I expect. Instead of bashing in my face, he sweep kicks my legs out from under me, sending me hard to my back. My fall is broken by a twisted root that digs into my ribs and further pushes the air from my lungs.

This guy is big, fast and knows how to fight. At my best, I might not be able to take him, and right now I am so far from my best, it's silly.

But I am not alone.

Shickt.

I recognize the sound a moment before the big man does, and I grin.

Collins strikes before the man can turn around, bringing the telescopic steel baton hard against his left arm. The strike would have broken most people's arms, but the meat surrounding this guy's bones protects him. Doesn't stop it from hurting, though.

"Argh!" the man shouts, spinning around and swinging a punch that would knock out a horse.

Collins avoids the strike, leaning just out of range—the mark of a confident fighter.

I remember the calluses on her knuckles and see the look of loathing in her eyes. Whatever happened in Collins's past to make her train in hand-to-hand combat to the point where her fingers tell the tale, it's coming to the surface. Then she lets it loose.

Collins swings twice, striking the man's arm in the same spot, and then a little higher up, on the clavicle, which breaks, audibly. The man howls, but lets out a punch of his own. Collins leans back, dulling the blow, but it still connects with her shoulder. She moves with the strike, spinning away. But the man presses forward, swinging again. Using the momentum of her spin, Collins brings the club around and whips it into the man's wrist.

The combined force of both strikes shatters the man's forearm, but it also knocks the club out of Collins's hands.

She's far from weaponless. While the man staggers away, she pulls a can of mace from her belt and sharp-shoots the liquid fire into his eyes. Then she's on top of him, throwing punches, elbows and knees to every part of his body. He's on the ropes, but this man is hardcore. Despite all the injuries, he kicks out hard and fast, catching Collins in the side of the head. She goes down hard.

The man stumbles over to her prone body. After balancing himself, he lifts up his leg. One good stomp could shatter her skull. But the man has made the same mistake twice.

Collins is not alone.

I bring the metal baton against the back of the man's neck as hard as I can. He crumples in on himself, spine shattered, control removed.

He falls next to Collins who wakes and rolls away, getting back to her feet, ready to fight. When she sees the man on the ground, she lets her pain show. She holds her head and winces. I'd like to hold her. Take a look. Tell her she'll be okay. But I can't. There isn't time. These three were definitely not acting on their own. There will be more and we need to be long gone by the time they arrive.

I look back to the slope and see my backpack at the base. "Get the pack. I'll try to find the guns." She grunts her agreement and we separate. It takes a minute for me to scale the slope, but once I'm at the top I quickly find our weapons, and the big man's—a sound suppressed M9 Beretta, preferred sidearm of the U.S. Army. If these guys are Special Ops, they're probably Rangers. That doesn't really mean the man is a Ranger—no way he could 'roid up while on the job—but it's possible he used to be in the Army's employ.

Distant voices echo through the forest. They're looking for us.

I hobble down the hill, feeling like an old man, and pause at the big guy's body.

"No I.D. on him," Collins says. "Couldn't find any tattoos, either."

I reach my hand out to her. "iPhone."

She pulls it out and after swiping it on, hands it to me. "Still no service."

"Don't need the phone," I say, starting the phone's photo app. I take a quick picture of the man's full prone body, and then a close up of his face. Voices get louder, rolling down from the top of the hill. They've spotted the bodies. "Time to go."

10

Ten Hours Later

Dr. Kendra Elliot's eyes looked small behind her thick glasses, despite the fact that they were open wide. The bloodshot orbs stung, because she refused to blink for as long as she could stand. She didn't want to miss a second.

The subject—Maigo—was exceptional.

Elliot had stayed in the lab for the past ten hours, just watching. She'd left just twice, both times to use the bathroom. She hadn't eaten. Hadn't drunk anything. Hadn't slept. And she'd never felt better.

The rate of growth seemed to be following some kind of Moore's law, which observes that computers double in power and speed every two years. Except instead of doubling every two years, Maigo's growth doubled every two hours. The girl had far exceeded Elliot's calculations, and further calculations became impossible to predict. She guessed the girl was eighteen, based on muscle tone (which looked like an Olympian's), height, weight and development of her more feminine features.

And she was feminine. For the most part. Her breasts were full. Her hips wide. A cloud of black hair billowed around Maigo's face, obscuring her smooth jaw, lush lips and long-lashed eyes. Elliot felt pangs of jealousy mixed with surges of revolt. A week ago, Maigo had been a real girl, though she hadn't lived to see any of these features develop. That she had possibly been murdered by her father filled Elliot with an anger born from her own past.

Elliot shook her head. The life this girl could have lived...

Envy crept into her thoughts once again, but then she reminded herself that the girl, the real Maigo, was dead and buried. The picture-perfect thing of beauty would never exist in the world outside this laboratory, and within the day, this Maigo would be dead.

Again.

"My God," General Gordon said. "Look at her."

Elliot yelped and spun around. Gordon stood right behind her. "I—I didn't hear you come in."

"You were too busy ogling her," he said, pointing to Maigo.

Elliot blushed despite the accusation not being entirely true. Admiring was a more accurate word, though she didn't bother correcting the man.

"Not that I can blame you," he said, walking around the spherical womb, looking at Maigo from every angle. The curved glass distorted the view like a fish bowl, magnifying the portion of her body directly in front of the viewer. "I might have you make me another one when—" He stopped walking. "What's that?"

Elliot stood and walked around the womb, stopping beside the General. He was pointing to the dimpled area where the girl's back met her butt. Elliot fought her rising jealousy again and said, "Did you call me over her to admire her—"

"Base of the spine," Gordon said. "Just above her ass."

Elliot leaned in closer, squinting. There was a small bump at the base of her spine. "Could be the subject's tail bone. Some people have oversized tailbones. Would be her single flaw."

"I'd like a closer look," he said.

"It's really not a big—"

"Now."

Elliot rolled her eyes and stomped back to her chair. She double-tapped the touch screen and began accessing the camera controls.

"How long until she's ready?" Gordon asked.

Elliot released a single submersible camera into the womb. The small device operated like a baseball-sized ROV, complete with sample-taking abilities and robotic arms. "Best guess, two more hours."

"My team is on standby," he said.

"Your team?"

"Surgeons." He stepped around the womb, eyes still on Maigo. "They're in the med-lab, awaiting delivery."

Using the touch-screen controls, Elliot manually steered the ROV toward the anomaly at the base of Maigo's spine. "Delivery of what?"

"The girl," he said. "And me."

The display showed the view from the ROV's camera as it lowered through the womb. Curves of tan flesh passed by like the polished wall of some deep sea discovery. "You're really going through with it?"

"Either that or I drop dead sometime in the next six months."

The aberration came into view. Elliot pushed the ROV nearer for a close up look. "That soon?"

"Was that hope I heard in your voice?"

Elliot glanced up at him, terrified that he was serious. He was smiling, which in its own way, was just as frightening.

"Cardiomyopathy," he said. "Weak heart. Barely moving enough oxygen to my brain as it is. Can't run. Can't get too angry. Can't screw. The pleasures of life have been stolen from me. You're going to give them back."

Elliot cringed, wondering if he was alluding to her previous offer. It seemed like a good idea at the time, but she was fairly certain she would regret it in the coming weeks, if the General survived the operation.

"Here we go," she said, focusing on the touch-screen image. The bump came into view. It was nondescript. A lump. "Could be excess bone growth. Could be a tumor. A side effect of the rapid growth. I still have no idea what was in that DNA sample you gave me. It's hard to say, but I think we'll be fine as long we don't see any other strange growths in the next few hours." Then an idea came to her. "It could be a vestigial tail."

Gordon remained calm, as though this idea didn't concern him at all. "A tail?"

"It's rare, only twenty-three cases reported since the eighteen hundreds, but we're screwing with nature here. We all have tails in the womb, as embryos, but they usually get absorbed into the rest of the body after the first thirty-five days. It's a dormant trait, weeded out by evolution, and typically reduced to a normal coccyx. Your tailbone." Elliot moved the camera a little closer. The ROV's small light seemed to reflect off the surface of the girl's skin. "But it's not a problem. Think of it like wisdom teeth. People don't need them anymore, so we sometimes have them removed. It's cosmetic. Not functional. It's a—huh."

"What?" Gordon asked, leaning over the touch screen.

"The skin over the bump," she said. "Watch." Elliot turned the ROV light side to side. The skin around the bump glowed in the light, but the skin covering the aberration shimmered.

"The skin is reflective?" Gordon asked.

Elliot didn't reply. Instead she worked the controls, getting even closer with the ROV. The view screen showed a needle-tipped limb stretching out toward the lump.

"What are you doing?"

"Getting a biopsy," Elliot said. The camera zoomed in closer, blurred and then focused.

"Looks like goose bumps," the general said.

Elliot guided the needle closer to the skin. "I would have said scales."

"Too lumpy," Gordon said.

The needle struck the skin and stopped.

"The hell?" Elliot said. "The needle couldn't break the skin. Should have slipped right through."

"That a problem?" Gordon asked.

Elliot ignored the general, focusing on the task at hand. She put the ROV in reverse, pulled back a foot and then pushed it forward again, charging forward like a knight with a javelin. The needle struck and this time punched through the skin.

Maigo flinched violently.

The sudden movement from inside the tank made Elliot jump so bad that she spilled out of her chair. When she recovered, she found Gordon standing a few feet back, one hand over his chest, the other fumbling with a pill bottle. But his eyes never left the tank.

"She doesn't have a brain," Gordon said. "Just what she needs to maintain basic functions?"

"Yes," Elliot said. All of their subjects were designed that way. Helped to get past the moral loophole of the bodies they grew being actual people. No brain. No soul. "She shouldn't feel a thing."

Gordon got the pill bottle open, dropped two blue ovals into his hand and dry swallowed them. "Then what the fuck was that?"

Elliot picked herself up off the floor and got back into the chair. She looked back at the screen and frowned. The lump wiggled.

Vestigial tails in humans were functionless. There were no muscles to control them. They just hung. Useless flesh.

This was not vestigial. This was the real thing.

Maigo had a tail.

"Keep a close eye on it," Gordon said. He looked strong and collected again. "If you see any changes to her skin anywhere else on her body we will go forward with the procedure right away. Otherwise, prep to have her moved to medical in two hours."

"I'm not sure that's a good idea," Elliot said. "We don't know what changes are taking place inside her body."

"That's why we're going to cut her open and take a look before it's my turn."

Elliot frowned. It was a stupid idea. And while she didn't have strong feelings about whether or not Gordon died, she wanted him to live simply because Endo would pay her a visit soon after the General closed his eyes for good. Endo might very well liquidate everyone on site.

As though on cue, Endo's voice came over a two way radio clipped to the General's belt. "Longhorn, this is Hound, come in." The sentence was followed by a chirp that let Gordon know Endo was done speaking.

Gordon lifted the radio to his mouth and spoke, "I hear you, Hound. Give me a sit-rep."

"Sheriff Collins and the man with her have not yet been eliminated."

Gordon grumbled to himself before replying. "Why the hell not? You've been at it an entire day."

"They have proven to be...resourceful," Endo said. "Elusive."

More grumbling. Elliot could tell the General was working hard at not getting upset.

"We have a perimeter set up," Endo continued. "The roads are being patrolled. And if they keep heading on their current course they will have to cross seventy-five miles of rough terrain before reaching civilization."

Gordon rolled his neck and said, "Hound, I need you back here."

"But we're close."

"Keep your men on it. Patrol the roads. Scour the woods. But I need you back here. Now."

"Longhorn, sir," Endo said, "is it...time?"

"Yes, Hound." Gordon looked at his wristwatch. "1800 hours."

"I'll be back in thirty," Endo said, his voice quick now. "Out."

Gordon lowered the radio and leveled his eyes at Elliot. "You get that? 1800 hours." He started toward the door, but paused. "Kendra, live or die, well done. This is your finest work."

He stomped away with a determined stride. If the heart was compatible, Elliot had no doubt the General would pull through just fine. But she couldn't shake the feeling that his compliment, unusually sincere, was really a goodbye.

Live or die, goodbye.

She shook off the feeling. Gordon's ambitions exceeded his desire to live. Besides, once he had Maigo's heart in his chest, she would no longer have anything to fear from General Lance Gordon. The DNA kill switch she built into the organ guaranteed it.

"Live or die," she said, and then grinned. "Goodbye."

11

The cat and mouse game lasted for most of the day. There were a few close calls early on as Collins and I pushed our beaten bodies to the limits, and then beyond. Doubling back toward the compound is what finally did it. They just didn't see the move coming and walked right past any trail we left. A skilled tracker like my friend Mark Hawkins would have seen it, but these guys were trained for combat, not search and rescue...or search and destroy as the case may be.

They know Collins is the sheriff, but they don't know anything about me other than my U.S. Fish and Wildlife Service story. They have no reason to think we'd do anything more than head for the hills. We're severely outnumbered and outgunned. We have no idea what's really going on. And yeah, we probably should try to find some way to get help.

But here's the thing.

They killed Mr. and Mrs. Johnson.

They tried to kill Collins and me.

And damn it all, they shot Betty.

I'm not leaving before I get some answers, in part because I really want to put a bullet in the guy who killed the Johnsons. I'm certain that was a sniper and not the goons who chased us into the woods.

We're only a few miles from the compound now, where the woods are thick and full of rocky outcrops, caves and crisscrossing streams. Hobbling like a phony panhandler in Manhattan, I lean against a tree, breathing hard. "I think we're good."

Collins stops next to me and drops my backpack on the ground. She leans over, hands on knees. Her chest presses against her uniform with each breath. My pain and exhaustion are momentarily forgotten. Her voice pulls my attention higher. "You sure?"

"Sun will be down in two hours." I hold up the wool blanket I've been lugging around all day. "Will be impossible to find us in the dark."

"And here I thought you were trying to save your blankie."

"Har har," I say, and honestly, I'm having fun, which is ridiculous. I'm either far too bored in general, which is possible, or I'm just digging the good Sheriff's vibe, which is also possible. Probably both.

I lean over the edge of the shallow ravine that made me stop in the first place. It's not much, just ten feet deep and maybe eight across. One side slopes up to level ground and the other ends in an earthy overhang. It's actually kind of a shallow cave, maybe six feet deep. "This is perfect. We can rest here. Head out at first light. If they spend the night looking for us, they'll be exhausted by morning. If not, we can get a look inside that fence before they're out of bed."

Collins looks over the edge. She's not impressed. "If they see us in there, we're dead."

"They're not going to see us."

"Right, your blankie."

"And the storm," I say.

Collins looks to the bright blue sky above us.

"Listen," I say.

She does. The trees bend in the wind, creaking and swooshing. It's not much, but a few hours ago, there was no breeze at all. "Now smell the air. Deep breath."

I take a deep breath through my nose with her. Pine. Earth. Rot. And then a mix of water and ozone. The storm.

The look on her face says she can't smell a thing.

"Trust me," I say. "It's coming."

"Okay, Mr. Nature," Collins says, "but we're not going to get much rest if we're soaked. Maybe we should—"

"Ye of little faith," I say.

She raises a skeptical eyebrow.

"Help me get some sticks. I'll take care of the rest."

She does, and twenty hurried minutes later, we're done. As the first drops of rain tickle my exposed skin, I toss the last handful of dry leaves into the small ravine. The air is thick with humidity now and I'm soaked with sweat. I could really go for a swim, or a shower, but I'd also rather not be shot. We've spent too much time out in the open as it is.

I step back and inspect our handiwork.

"Can't even see it," Collins says.

The large wool blanket is pinned to the ground over the highest point of the ravine. It then comes down at a forty-five degree angle, supported by several long branches wedged into place, which also gives it a natural shape. The whole structure is covered with layers of leaves that camouflage the shelter and will help repel the water.

"Shall I carry you over the threshold?" I ask with a grin.

She laughs at me. Really laughs. "You don't look like you could pick me up if I said yes." She heads down the slope.

I manage to keep myself from pointing out that she did not, in fact, say no. Then I pick up the backpack and follow her into the valley. At the base of our structure, the wool blanket hangs down. It's just a foot high and fringed by sticks and debris. The only way in is to shimmy under it, which Collins does quickly. I take one last look at the sky. The clouds overhead are dark gray, but they're black in the distance. Thunder rumbles through the forest. Sleep is going to be hard to come by, shelter or no shelter.

At least I'll have good company, I think.

I duck down and shove my backpack through before following after it.

Collins is sitting against the back wall where the ceiling is earth rather than leaf covered blanket. Her head is lolled to the side. Her eyes closed.

Asleep.

"Fantastic," I say and sit down next to her. It's dark inside the shelter, and warm. I nearly fall asleep too, but the pain in my arm and legs keep me focused. I drag my backpack close, open up the largest pocket and pull out a large green poncho. I throw it over Collins like a blanket, just in case water makes it through. Next comes a first aid kit. Yeah, I carry a first aid kit among other things like a compass, a map of the area, a flashlight, measuring tape, string for setting up a search grid, sample bags and even a magnifying glass. I'd like to say it's all for show, to make people think I'm really investigating their Chupacabra sighting, but the truth is, I like to be prepared...just in case the easily spooked senator who added the FC-P to the DHS bill wasn't actually nuts.

I flick on the LED flashlight and inspect the wounds on my arm and leg. The one on my arm hurts worse. It's a puncture, and not very wide, but the soreness comes from the muscle beneath. Luckily, the bleeding has stopped, but the arm is going to hurt for a while. I clean it with alcohol, gritting my teeth against the pain, and then coat the area with antibiotic cream before applying a bandage thick enough to absorb any blood that might flow if it reopens. The leg is next. There's a lot of dry blood, so I have to clean the area first, but I can tell it's not too bad when the alcohol barely makes me flinch. The bullet just grazed my skin, leaving an inch-long slice. After applying more antibiotic ointment, I cover the gash with a really tough looking band-aid. Going to hurt a lot more when I pull that son-of-a-bitch off.

How Michael Phelps keeps himself hairless, I will never know. Nor do I really want to know.

I could probably use some ice on a dozen different places, but the rest of my wounds are going to have to wait. My day is catching up with me. I shift to get comfortable, and I find the best spot is half leaning against Collins. She doesn't seem to mind, so I tip my head back onto her shoulder and close my eyes.

As I drift to sleep, I pull my handgun from my waist, check that the safety is on and place the weapon by my hip.

I dream of thunder. And revenge.

12

Maigo was on her back. Elliot had prepped the rapidly growing woman herself, dragging her up out of the womb. It was a wet and clumsy affair, but Gordon wanted the surgeons, who had been flown in and knew nothing about the nature of their research, to remain unaware of Maigo's...special features.

The girl's tail had grown three feet. The skin at her feet and the tip of the tail had grown dark and thick with hard, nearly black nodules. If she'd been allowed to continue growing, Elliot thought the condition would eventually expand to the rest of her body, which was a shame considering the girl's beauty. But it was Maigo's toenails that disturbed Elliot the most. They'd grown thick and rough at first, like the skin, but then they grew out and hooked into talons, like polished obsidian.

Maigo currently measured nearly six feet tall and though slender, weighed in at nearly two hundred pounds. Despite the weight, Elliot had managed to hoist her onto a gurney. After giving the girl more sedatives, she tucked the long tail beneath one of Maigo's legs and taped it in place. She then covered the nude lower body with several white sheets. A thick leather restraint went over everything ensuring that the girl and sheet couldn't move. Elliot bound her ankles and wrists, just to be safe. The doctors had questioned the restraints at first, but Elliot wrote them off as a precaution and showed them the paperwork that declared Maigo brain dead and authorized the transplantation of her heart to Gordon.

Elliot scrubbed her hands for the tenth time in the past hour. She knew Maigo had no transferable diseases, but knowing the girl was only part human repulsed her. She slipped on a pair of blue rubber gloves, straightened her plastic face shield and turned back to join the doctors. There were six of them—two surgeons, a perfusionist, an anesthetist and two nurses. She knew none of their names, didn't care to and would likely never see them again. Her job was to observe the operation and make sure Maigo stayed sedated.

Gordon sat on his operating table, prepared for surgery. The doctors had wanted to sedate him so the transplant could happen quickly, but Gordon demanded to see the heart that was being put in his chest. Elliot knew that Gordon really wanted to see if the heart would turn to sludge. If she had failed to grow him a viable heart, the surgery was off.

Endo was also present. He stood in the corner of the room, arms crossed. He watched the surgeons prep Maigo's chest, smearing it with brown iodine. His presence bothered her far more than Maigo's, because she knew what it meant. Endo was there in case the surgery failed and Gordon died. If that happened, she doubted anyone, including her, would leave the room alive.

"Making incision," declared one of the surgeons. He drew a scalpel quickly across the skin.

Elliot thought the man was being a little careless, but decided it was simply because he knew Maigo would not need to be stitched up afterwards. He cut two more incisions, making a capital "I" shape on her chest. When the man shoved his fingers beneath Maigo's skin and began to lift, Elliot looked away. They were handling the girl like a pig in a slaughter house. Although Elliot felt unnerved by Maigo, she was still the girl's creator. She winced at the wet sound of separating flesh. When the shick, shick of scissors followed, she nearly gagged.

"Clamp this," one of the surgeons said.

Elliot looked back up. Her view was mostly blocked by three of the doctors and a tray of surgical tools, but she could see Maigo's white ribs through a gap. A sharp whine filled the air. She saw the circular bone saw just before it was placed against Maigo's sternum. As the saw chewed through bone, the sound became grating, like nails on a chalkboard. Elliot was about to stand and leave when the saw was lifted away and shut off.

"Splitting the ribs," one of the surgeons said. "What are the vitals?"

"Elevated heart rate and blood pressure," the anesthetist said, looking at the silent heart monitor. She turned to the EEG display showing Maigo's brain activity, which showed very little since Maigo had no real brain. "No change in brain activity."

"Good," the surgeon said before placing a rib splitter in the sternum's incision. He turned the crank, quickly separating the flexible ribs and exposing the lungs and heart below.

Elliot stood and walked closer. The scene was horrible, but this was the moment of truth. She needed to see. Gordon leaned in closer too, eager to see whether he would live or die.

"Deflating the lungs," the surgeon said, then rather callously poked each lung with a scalpel. Air hissed from the puncture wounds and the lungs sagged away, revealing the heart.

Elliot held her breath.

The surgeon roughly probed the fist-sized heart with his fingers. Then, as though holding a newborn baby, he declared, "Looks like we have a healthy heart." He turned to Gordon. "Congratulations, sir."

Gordon didn't reply. Instead he looked at Elliot and gave her a smile. An earnest smile. It felt so strange, coming from the gruff General, but she had come through for him in a big way. If the surgeons were any good—and she was sure they were—then Gordon would have a new, fully compatible heart beating in his chest in the next few hours.

She returned the smile, thinking, you're welcome.

The anesthetist laid Gordon back on the operating table and directed the bright lights above him toward his chest. "Just lie back and relax," she said while checking the IV already in his arm. "Time for a nap." She took a rubber stopper off the end of a previously prepared syringe and injected the sedative into his IV line.

The wrinkles in Gordon's forehead smoothed out as he relaxed. He turned his head lazily toward Endo. "She's okay."

Was he talking about Maigo? Or were the drugs already making him silly?

But Endo nodded as though he knew what this meant.

The anesthetist slipped a mask over the General's nose and mouth. "Count back from ten."

He made it to "four" before losing consciousness.

"We're good to go," the anesthetist said.

While the nurse began shaving Gordon's chest, one of the surgeons lifted Maigo's freshly severed heart from her chest. The organ should have captivated Elliot, but she couldn't look at it. Instead, she gazed at Maigo's still form.

She's dead.

A deep sense of sadness confused Elliot. Researchers sometimes became attached to their specimens. Rooted for them. Secretly wished they would live. But Maigo had been around for such a short amount of time. Then again, in that time, she'd become a fully grown and stunning woman. And now, she was a bloody, torn-open corpse.

Ignoring the doctors prepping for the real surgery, Elliot stepped up to Maigo and looked down. She cringed at the sight of the girl's spread ribs and the open cavity between them, where her heart and inflated lungs had been. She shook her head slowly. Moving on autopilot, Elliot disengaged the rib separator and placed it on the medical tray. The ribs flexed back together at a jagged angle. It was then that Elliot noticed a few of the ribs had broken. The surgeon had been unnecessarily rough.

A sudden burst of anger gave her clarity. She was identifying with Maigo, who'd been just a girl not long ago and had just undergone a gross abuse. Elliot wanted to be angry at Gordon and the doctors, but she was really to blame. She created Maigo to save her own life.

You had to die, she thought. I'm sorry.

With tears in her eyes, she lifted the skin back in place. She pushed everything back together and kept her eyes on Maigo's face.

A hand on her shoulder made her flinch.

She turned.

Endo.

Her pulse quickened, but she saw no threat in his eyes.

"She was beautiful," he said.

What was this? Endo had never spoken to her. Not once.

He turned to Elliot. "We are aligned, you and I."

Aligned?

Then she understood. When Gordon said, "She's okay," he was talking about her!

"You two really don't need to be here now," said one of the masked surgeons. "In fact, it would be great if you could remove the body."

Endo lifted a sheet up over Maigo's body, covering her torso and head. He turned to Elliot again. "You can take her. I'll remain here."

The way he spoke those last three words churned up old fears. There was a threat in his tone, but it wasn't directed toward her. It's the doctors, she realized. I'm okay, but the doctors...

She decided that it didn't matter what happened to the doctors. Elliot let out a sigh and smiled. "Thank you, Endo."

He gave a nod and stepped back to the door, opening it for her. She unlocked the gurney's wheels and turned the mobile bed toward the door. As she passed by Endo, he stopped her with a hand on her arm. "Thank you, Dr. Elliot. The General is a good friend. To both of us."

Before she could reply, he stepped back inside the room and let the door close.

Endo's transformation from silent killer to kind ally felt so strange, but she wasn't about to debate it with the man. She rolled the gurney down the long white hall, took the elevator down two flights to the basement and then headed for the morgue, where she would later oversee a post-mortem dissection to learn what she could about Maigo's altered physiology. She wasn't sure she could figure out exactly what the foreign DNA had done to Maigo, but if she was now in the General's good graces, he might well tell her.

She stopped the gurney next to a large refrigeration unit where the body would be kept until the rest of the BioLance staff returned.

But who knew how long that would be?

Elliot decided she couldn't wait to learn more. Although she wasn't qualified to perform a post-mortem examination, she had five more Maigo embryos ready to go. She could have another adolescent and still-living subject to examine by the time Gordon woke up. Feeling invigorated, she pushed the corpse quickly inside the refrigeration unit. As the gurney passed through the open door, the sheet covering Maigo's body caught on the door's lock and slid away, exposing the body.

With an annoyed groan, Elliot turned toward the falling sheet. She caught just a glimpse of Maigo's body as she turned, but it was enough. With a shout, she jumped back and slammed into a wall of chilled supplies. A bottle, filled with some kind of horrible smelling chemical fell to the floor and shattered. But Elliot barely noticed. Her eyes were locked on Maigo's chest.

The I-shaped wound was now covered in a dark crust that resembled the skin on the girl's feet and tail.

"What the hell?" she whispered and leaned down for a closer look. She touched the hard growth with her finger, but had forgotten she was still wearing gloves. She stood up and removed the gloves one by one. She placed them on the shelf from where the bottle had fallen and turned back to the body.

In the split second it took to discard the gloves, everything changed.

Maigo's eyes were open.

Elliot's muscles locked with fear and a scream built in her throat, but it never got the chance to escape. The last thing Dr. Kendra Elliot saw was Maigo's now six-foot-long tail rising up from beneath the sheets.

13

I sit up with a gasp, clutching my chest and rolling my eyes around in confusion. The strange scent of earth and a glowing ceiling make the transition from dream to wakefulness a surreal experience, because the dream seemed more real than what I'm seeing. When my eyes finally land on Collins's worried face, I remember where I am.

"You okay, chief?" Collins asks.

I groan and push myself up against the earthen wall behind me. "Nothing like waking up from a dream about being eaten by a bear and finding yourself inside a giant glowing stomach." I look up at my hastily built shelter. It survived the night, and the storm, keeping us concealed and dry. With the morning sun on it, the wool blanket shimmers.

I smack my lips and clear my throat. I hate mornings. So little about them is good, but this morning is worse than usual. My morning breath is usually enough to sour my mood, but today's aches and pains make waking exquisitely revolting in a way that only the Devil could appreciate.

"Here," Collins says, before tossing a water bottle to me.

The bottle strikes my chest and falls to the ground beside me. I turn my head down and look at it, barely registering what has just happened.

"Nice catch," Collins says, shaking her head.

I slowly reach for the bottle, pop the top and take a swig. Then another. And another. By the time the water is half drained, I'm feeling a little more awake. I flinch as something strikes my chest and falls in my lap.

An oatmeal cream pie from my backpack.

Collins laughs lightly. "Cat-like reflexes."

I have no witty retort, so I unwrap the hydrogenated corn syrup foodstuff and shove it into my mouth. I mumble a "thanks" between chews, and then chase my breakfast with the remaining water.

"So much for rationing," Collins says.

"I don't plan on staying out here much longer." When I wipe my mouth with the back of my hand, I see that Collins isn't planning on sitting still either. Just the opposite. She's made herself at home and rummaged through my pack. My clothes are stacked in a neat pile next to her, along with a half empty bottle of water and a Chocodile wrapper.

My map is spread open across the poncho that I'd given her last night. She has two areas circled in red pen. With a fresh groan, I push away from the wall and kneel beside her.

She taps the bigger of the two circles with her pen. "This is where they are. You can see the road here, ending just after the Johnsons' house. The land is just empty. It doesn't show a Nike site or any other roads into the area."

I look over the map, nodding.

Collins taps on the second red circle. "This is where I think we are, give or take a half mile in any direction." She measures out the distance with her pen and compares it to the scale on the map's legend. "About two miles. If you're up for it, we can be there in under thirty minutes."

I flex my spine side to side a little, testing my body. I'm sore, head to toe, but not seriously injured. After a good stretch, I should be okay to go. "No problem. What time is it?"

"Bout five thirty in the morning," she says.

I shake my head. "Two days in a row. You're going to be the death of me."

"Please, you slept like a baby," she says. "Snored like a monster, though."

"Shut up," I say, as I stand and start stretching.

"Louder than the thunder," she says and begins packing my clothes.

"You don't need to do that," I tell her. "We'll take the map and the weapons. Move fast and quiet. If we need to, we can come back, but I needed new clothes anyway."

"I noticed." She holds up one of my favorite T-shirts and turns it so I can see the big holes in the arm pits.

"Ventilation," I say. I'm tempted to throw the shirt on and take it with me, but it's bright orange. Done stretching, I tuck my handgun into the back of my pants and step toward the exit.

"You look sad," she says. "Did you name your shirt, too?"

I stop in my tracks and tilt my head up. The air smells funny. I lean closer to the wool blanket and sniff.

"What is it?" she asks.

The smell registers. "Smoke." I take hold of the blanket roof and yank it down. A dark gray cloud begins to settle into the pit. "C'mon," I say and charge out of the small gorge, drawing my weapon just in case we're being smoked out. I scan the area and find nothing. The forest is covered in a waist-high layer of floating soot.

Collins joins me, eyes wide. "Where's it coming from? Is it a forest fire?"

I take a sniff and cough. There are a lot of chemicals in the air. Probably toxic. A mix of burning plastic, rubber, wood and various other modern building materials. Not a forest fire. "They must be cutting their losses. Burning evidence."

"Damnit!" Collins bites her lips, looking pissed. The bad guys are getting away on her watch.

And on my watch. Remembering that this could have been my ticket out of paranormal investigations, I charge back into the pit, whip out my pocket knife and cut two long swaths of the still-wet wool blanket. I toss one to Collins while wrapping the other around my nose and mouth, tying it tight. The damp wool should help filter the air, but running the two miles is still going to be rough.

When Collins cinches her wool face mask tight, I say, "Let's go," and start jogging in the general direction of the fake Nike site.

Twenty minutes later, I'm out of breath and wheezing like a ninety-year-old asthmatic. I stop and lean against a tree, rubbing my burning eyes. The smoke now reaches high into the trees. We're getting close, but if the wind doesn't push this shit away soon, Collins and I could be in real trouble.

She stops next to me. "We should keep moving."

Woman puts me to shame.

I nod wearily and prepare to continue my charge through the woods when a loud crack fills the air. I stop mid-step and throw myself against the tree, pulling Collins with me.

We stand in silence. Listening.

Leaves shuffle to our left. But the sound is distant. Maybe fifty feet.

We both turn toward the sound and watch. Smoke billows past in silent wisps of gray.

Crack! The sound makes us jump, not because it's closer, but because it's so damn loud. The tell tale "shh" of a falling tree follows. Then a dull thud. The tree couldn't have been too large, but smoke billows away from the impact, clearing the air briefly. That's when I see it.

It's just a shape. Dark and large. Far too big to be a human being. It passes through the haze, oblivious to our presence.

"Do you see it?" I whisper into Collins's ear.

She nods, and leans her head back to whisper in my ear. "The bear?"

I turn to her and find our faces just inches apart. If it weren't for the double thick wool blankets covering our faces, kissing her would be as easy as puckering my lips. With a jolt, I forget all about the bear and realize that I've got my arms around her waist. The back of her body is pressed against the front of mine.

"Bear?" I say dumbly.

"This is why I don't think women should serve on the front lines," she says.

My brain slowly registers the joke, but I forget all about it when the creature plows through some brush. The sound is distant. The bear is moving away. It's a good thing, too. Having a run-in with momma bear would likely give our position away. Not that I expect to find anyone left when we reach the Nike site. Setting fire to the evil lair is usually the last step of a bad guy evacuation.

I casually slip my hands away from Collins's waist and she steps away. I can see a joke forming in her eyes, and I decide my ego is assaulting itself just fine already. I step past her. "Let's pick up the pace. We need to get out of this smoke."

Five minutes later, the wind finally shifts and the heavy smoke is lifted up and away. My body still feels coated in the stuff, and I'm sure I'll be smelling it for a week, but at least we can breathe freely. I unwrap the wool from my face and throw it to the ground. As I scratch my stubbly cheeks, I take a deep breath through my nose. The scent of smoke is still there, but mixed with the scent of pine and earth and... "Damnit."

It's just a whisper, but combined with my suddenly raised pistol and sweeping aim, my fear is obvious. Collins raises her weapon too and follows my lead, searching for danger.

After a minute and no immediate danger detected, I motion to her and then point to my nose. I watch her take a deep breath through her nose. Once. Twice. And then she's got the scent.

She mouths the word, "Blood?"

I nod and then point in the direction we were already headed. Moving more slowly, and with our weapons raised, we proceed forward like a couple of TV cops patrolling an apartment building.

The trees thin ahead as the terrain becomes more rocky.

Then I see it. The trail. The disguised path winds its way through the rocks. I scan the trail from left to right, looking for any signs of passage.

I find a boot.

Most of it is hidden behind a half buried boulder. I approach slowly, wary of a trap. The boot is a black, military style, steel-toed affair. The top looks wet. As I round the boot, I get a look inside.

"My God."

There's a foot inside the boot.

Collins lets out a gasp when she sees it. We lean in closer, and I use a stick to lift it up. Leaves cling to the boot, saturated with drying blood. I drop the boot back down and step back when I see a flash of bone.

"A bear wouldn't have done this," Collins said.

I correct her, saying, "A black bear wouldn't have done this." I lift my hand and point ahead. "Or that."

Bits and pieces of clothing and flesh litter the forest floor.

"Not sure if this needs to be said, but you have my permission to shoot anything that moves."

She nods. "Likewise."

"Ready to follow the breadcrumbs?" I ask.

Part of me hopes she'll say we should go while the getting is good. A man has been torn to shreds and discarded through the forest like he was nothing more than the petals of a "love me, love me not" flower. But my revolt and fear are matched by my curiosity and ambition. And it seems the lovely Sheriff Collins has equal parts of both as well.

She frowns. "After you, Hansel."

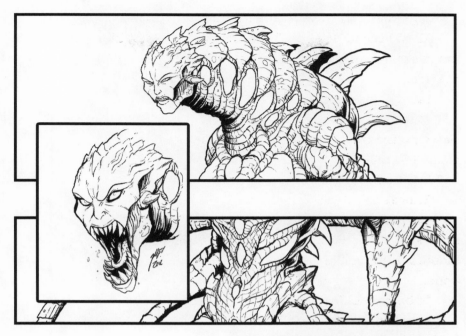

STAGE 2

14

The razor wire chain-link fence is no longer an issue. A twenty foot section has been bent over and flattened into the ground. The chunks of flesh led us right to it. Whatever left the trail also took out the fence. But how?

"What could have done this?" Collins asks.

"Aside from a Humvee?" I ask.

"There aren't any tracks," she says, missing my sarcasm. There's no room for a Humvee, and the terrain is far too rough for anything smaller.

I walk next to the rolls of razor wire, searching for some sign of what happened, but it's hard to focus on the details while my eyes keep shifting up, wary of danger. I've been holding my weapon at the ready so long that it feels slick in my perspiring hands. Better to put it away, I decide, than have it flung from my sweaty hands when I need it most. I tuck the gun into my waist and focus on a portion of the razor wire that has been pulled away from the fence.

"You smell that?" Collins asks.

Smoke still permeates the air, but there's something fleshy mixed in with it. Like raw hamburger mixed with vinegar, which is very different from the scent of the human flesh scattered about. It's more musky. More animal. "Yeah," I say. "I smell it," but I'm not really giving it much thought.

There's something caught in the razor wire. I reach into my cargo shorts pocket and take out one of three Ziploc bags I carry, just in case something like this happens. I invert the bag over my hand and carefully reach down. Avoiding the razor wire is like playing a game of operation, except here, if I hit the metal, I might need stitches.

The swatch of black dangling from the wire looks like fabric, but as soon as my bagged fingers close around it, I know its skin. It's squishy, but firm, and the bottom side feels slick. I pull the three inch long specimen slowly out of the razor wire and turn it over, finding bright pink flesh crisscrossed with lines of blood.

Definitely skin.

But of what? The bear? I look at the destroyed fence. Could a bear do this?

Maybe a stampede of bears? Was this some kind of illegal breeding program for exotic pets?

I hold the sample up to my nose and take a quick sniff. "Ugh," I moan. Hamburger and vinegar. Delightful. Whatever this skin came from is also the source of the smell. But why is it so strong here?

"Over here," Collins says.

"I found something, too," I say, as I stand. I pull the sample inside the bag and zip it shut. My eyes are on the sample as I walk. The skin side is dark. Nearly black. And it's covered in small lumps that reflect the sun. I rub my hand over the surface. Feels like a novel written in Braille.

I see Collins through the bag. "Check this out, it's—" The distorted view through the Ziploc bag resolves, and I see what she's standing next to. I lower the bag and see it for myself. "Holy shit."

It's a pine tree with a wound that would have been fatal to a human being. Five deep gouges stretch across the trunk, reaching all the way down to the pale wood beneath the armor-like bark. Bears can sometimes scratch up trees, but this... I place my hand against the tree and spread my fingers wide. Whatever made this mark had a hand, or paw, twice the width of my hand.

"It's at least a foot from top to bottom," she says. "Before you ask, no, I don't know what could have done this, and neither do you."

She's right about that. "But I have this," I say, holding up the bag.

She leans in and squints at my disgusting find. "And that's?"

"I have no idea. But a lab can tell us exactly what it—"

There's a snap in the forest. It's gentle, like a dry twig, but it's followed by a loud crack that's more like an explosion. I jump back as the top of a pine tree slams to the ground between us. Pine needles scratch across my face, stinging my skin, but I barely notice. The tree could have pulverized us, so I'm pretty psyched to still be breathing.

Collins and I stare at each other in shock, and then slowly crane our heads along the path of the fallen tree. The hundred foot pine isn't broken, as I expected. It's uprooted. A circular patch of earth rises from the ground like a crashed UFO, held in place by a network of roots. Ten feet from the base, the bark is scratched up.

A guttural grunt sends a chill through my body.

That tree didn't just fall over.

It was pushed.

Whatever flattened the fence, left a trail of human bits and gouged the tree is still here. Or rather, returned. I'm fairly certain it's what we passed in the woods. It must have caught our scent, or found our trail, and followed us. That's why the scent is so strong, we're downwind of it.

I silently flag down Collins, which takes a few seconds, because she's watching the base of the tree like a deer that's spotted a lion. When she finally looks in my direction, I point to myself, then her and then past the fallen fence, indicating that I want to go inside. She looks unsure, but we have no other options. If this giant bear, or whatever, is hunting us, our only chance at finding someplace to hide, or making some kind of sheltered last stand, is on the other side of this fence. Out here, it's just trees for miles in every direction, and I don't think Collins's hand-to-hand combat skills are going to help much against something that can shove a tree over.

I repeat my silent message, this time pointing to the fallen fence a bit more forcefully. When she nods her agreement, I put my fingers to my lips. She nods again, and we both tiptoe back toward the fence.

I can hear the thing moving, shifting through the leaf litter a hundred feet behind me. But I don't look back. I'm careful to keep a tree between me and the base of the fallen tree so that I won't be seen as I make my snail's pace retreat, but then I think this is a waste of time. If the tree really was meant for Collins and me, then it already knows we're here. Stealth might be the wrong approach.

A roar rips through the air. It's like nothing I've heard, and as I cup my hands to my ears, motion above draws my eyes upward.

The trees are bending away from the sound.

The fucking trees.

Collins meets my eyes again, and this time I mouth the word, "Run," and neither of us wastes time debating it. Like Olympic runners off the starting line, we sprint forward, hurtling the fallen razor wire and passing the downed fence. We're officially in enemy territory now, but I'll take a hundred shotgun-wielding Special Ops guys over King Kong back there any day.

As we leave the fence behind, I take a quick look back.

On the one hand, I wish I hadn't; the image of something dark and monstrous rearing up behind and above the ten foot tall circle of roots is going to be impossible to forget. On the other hand, I'm glad I did, because when orange light starts glowing out of the sides of its head, I run faster than I ever have in my life.

The forest gives way to tall grass and then a winding, uphill, paved road that's cracked and in disrepair. I head up it. If this place was actually built like a Nike site, the access hatches will be on top. If not, at least we'll have a better view of our surroundings, and the high ground—not that I believe that's going to help us much. 9mm bullets work wonders on people, but they aren't the ammo of choice against elephant-sized animals.

The ground shakes.

Another tree cracks.

If we don't find someplace to hide, we're screwed. As we reach the crest of the hill and get a look at what's on top, I say it out loud. "Yup, we're screwed."

There are bodies—half eaten bodies—everywhere. A helicopter, burning, lies on its side. What remains of the pilot is smeared against the windshield. Beyond the dead is a large building—easy to see by satellite—but it's ruined. Smoke billows from the second and third floors. And a wall on the bottom floor has been blown out, I suspect from where our large friend made its exit.

The pavement beneath my feet shudders.

What choice do we have? I grab Collins's wrist and yank her toward the building. A second roar pursues us, sending my hands to my ears and blowing out the burning building's remaining windows.

So screwed.

15

Ceaseless hunger gnawed at her gut. It was all she knew. All she could think about.

Hunt.

Kill.

Feast.

Repeat.

But there was something beneath it all. An emotion, more than a thought. Hate. A seething caldron of loathing that fueled her hunger. She didn't know why. Couldn't remember—anything. There was only hate and hunger. So she embraced both, consuming and destroying in equal parts.

When she could no longer find prey, she moved into the woods where she caught a fleeing man, but she hadn't seen more than small animals since. Then came the man and woman. She caught their scent and the hunt began again. Tracking them was made difficult because of the smoke, but the air soon cleared and she closed the distance.

Nearly upon them, a fit of rage tore through her body. Pain raced through her nervous system. She could feel her insides growing, her bones shifting, her skin stretching and tearing in an effort to keep up. All that pain and hate was vented on a tree that nearly crushed her prey.

But it missed.

And they fled.

After the growth spurt, the hunger returned with its own brand of stomach-gnawing pain. With a roar, she gave chase.

The power of her own body intoxicated her. The ground flattened beneath her clawed hands and feet. Trees fell away from her and compressed beneath her grasp. Pavement crumbled to dust beneath her heavy, black feet. Despite being able to stand upright, she ran on all fours with cat-like hind legs and long, powerful forelimbs to match. Her long tail, tipped with three trident-like spines, spun as she ran, providing balance, though the razor-pronged tips worked just as well for skewering prey.

As she charged up the paved hill, she stomped her feet down harder than she needed to, pleased with how the hard surface crumbled beneath her. But when she reached the top and saw the man and woman running toward the building she had only just escaped from, she let out a roar of anger.

She remembered little about the building. Just pain and helplessness.

And food.

A lot of food.

When she left, it was because she couldn't find anything else to hunt, kill and consume. But now there were two more meals waiting inside. From experience, she knew they would be simple to catch inside the straight hallways and nearly empty rooms.

But her hunger commanded her to attack now. End the hunt. Eat!

She charged across the clearing in front of the three-story tall, dull gray building. She paid little attention to the burning husk of the helicopter—it wasn't food—and even less attention to the corpses oozing up between her digits as she stomped forward. She was locked on target, aiming to take the man and woman together. One in each hand, two quick bites to remove the heads and their fight, and then she would eat until the blood cooled. Then she would discard the husks with the rest and start the hunt anew.

But the man and woman were fast. They entered the building through the front double doors and slammed them shut just before she reached her prey. She lunged, claws extended, but she found only the metal door. Her momentum carried her forward and she instinctively flipped over so that her shielded back would take the brunt of the impact. The segmented carapace covering her back stretched down to where her tail began, each section hosting two curved, boney plates jutting out at angles on either side.

The doors and front wall of the building exploded inward, leaving a ten foot hole. She rolled away from the building, snapped back to her feet and looked through the opening. Swirling dust filled the hall, but her sharp eyesight pierced through, and she saw the man and woman running down the hall.

Nowhere to go now, she felt more than thought.

She pushed into the hall and found her back scraping against the ceiling. When she'd left the building she could maneuver the hallways with ease. Now she had to push her way through, leaving a trail of rectangular ceiling panels in her wake.

She roared again, frustrated that the constricting hallway slowed her pursuit. The sound shook the walls, burst lights and knocked ceiling panels down. It also knocked the man and woman to the ground.

The ceiling shattered as she lunged forward, sensing the kill. But her prey got back up and ran, this time to the side, leaving the hallway through an open door. She remembered the building's rooms. They would be stuck. They would be... She slammed her head through the open door—gone.

A stairwell leading down. A door two flights down opened and closed.

After rearing back, she thrust herself forward, smashing into the doorframe and the wall, both of which gave way to her strength and caved in. She thrashed and tore, ripping through wood, steel and drywall. Then she was in the stairwell, leaping over the edge. Her feet found the next flight down before she'd fully dropped away from the floor above.

The tight, claustrophobic space enraged her. She flexed her body, pushing out with her arms, legs and spiked back. When the building resisted, she roared with primal rage and flexed again. The walls crumbled around her. Sunlight flooded the stairwell and a warm breeze tickled her skin.

Twisting around the stairs, she squeezed her body down one more flight, pushing the weakened walls away from her back. When she reached the bottom, she simply flung herself at the door, taking it and most of the wall into the adjoining, subterranean hallway.

She remembered this space. The long white hall, smeared with blood. But it looked different when she was here last. Bigger. Now it seemed barely large enough contain her. She shoved her way through, ruining walls, ceiling and floor with each step.

The air was a mix of blood and chemicals, but she had no trouble picking out the man and woman's scent. They were close by.

Two doors to her left looked familiar. One of them swung back and forth. A sign of passage.

She pushed through the double swinging doors slowly, searching for her prey. The room was cool and the walls were lined with square metal hatches. A large, open door at the back of the room drew her forward. The doorframe resisted, but eventually it cracked and came free, as the walls crumbled. Debris fell away from her back as she stopped in front of the open door and looked inside.

Her prey was gone.

But there was someone else inside.

Someone familiar.

A woman. Dead. And only partially consumed. But her blood had long since run cold and the corpse held no further interest.

But there was a memory. It tickled her mind. She had spoken to the woman in a language she no longer remembered. Her thoughts, once clear, had clouded with rage and hunger. She looked at the blood smearing the walls. Did the shapes mean something?

Pain lanced through her gut.

Her muscles quaked and expanded.

The ceiling pushed down on her.

With a roar, she twisted around, ruining the ceiling, and charging out of the room. The man and woman were gone.

She nearly tore the building down as she worked her way back out of the basement, through the building and back into the clearing. By the time the sun warmed her back again, long strands of saliva hung from her open jaws. She breathed deep, hoping for a scent.

But she found something else.

Direction.

She didn't know how. Or why. Or even what it meant. But the rage she felt usurped her hunger and told her where to go.

South.

And she obeyed.

16

It's ten minutes before I work up the courage to move, and even then it's just to scratch an itch on the tip of my nose that has been growing in intensity since I climbed into the morgue's body cooler. The power is out, so I'm not being chilled, but the smell grows worse by the minute, despite me being the only body inside. Of course, the odor could be coming from one of the neighboring units. My next door neighbor is Collins, but what do the other twenty-odd drawers hold?

I decide I don't need to know. Between the bits of human flesh scattered in the forest, the field of gnawed bodies and that...thing, I've seen enough nightmare material for a lifetime.

But as hard as I try, I can't get the image of the creature out of my mind. I got a clear view of it when it chased us inside the building. At least fifteen feet tall, while on all fours. Maybe twice that if it stood on its hind legs. Its rough skin, which would probably be better described as armor, was a mix of black and dark gray, perfect nighttime camouflage, if you ignore the twenty-something glowing orange membranes lining the sides of its neck and ribs, and stretching down the center of its torso. And the face—all angles and full of rage, but somehow feminine. And the eyes... The eyes looked human. Deep brown. The kind of eyes romantics write songs about.

Despite its size, the thing was fast. It moved with speed and grace, like a cat. A long tail that looked more like a weapon than a biological requirement snapped around the creature like an angry snake. I didn't get a good look at its back, but I think there were overlapping shells, like an armadillo's carapace, but thicker and covered with what looked like hardened shark fins.

I would love to be able to say it was like something I've seen before—a bear, a tiger, a fucking dragon even, but it was like nothing I've seen before. It wasn't human. Wasn't animal.

What then?

Alien?

What else could it be?

A chuckle escapes from my mouth as I'm struck by a realization. I clamp my hand over my mouth and wait to be devoured. Nothing happens.

I hear Collins's drawer slide open.

A moment later, my square metal door opens and Collins is looking down at me. "You just figure out a joke or something?" She pulls out the long metal drawer.

I swing my legs around and sit up. "Actually, yeah. This case is now officially my jurisdiction, which means the full resources of the DHS are at my disposal."

"Assuming anyone believes you," she says.

"There is plenty of evidence here."

"Yeah," she says. "But you saw it. Who's going to believe us?"

The answer that comes to mind makes me frown. "Sooner or later, that thing is going to find civilization. When that happens—"

"We can't let that happen," Collins says, her sunset eyes burning with determination.

I'm not sure exactly how we can stop it—my personal armament doesn't include Hellfire missiles—but I agree. I pull out my cell phone. No signal. "Let's get to higher ground."

As we head for the exit, I glance right and see the large open fridge. There's a body in there. I saw it when we ran into the morgue. I slow and alter course. It's a woman. She has brown hair pulled back in a way that makes me think she's mid-thirties, but there's no way to be sure. Her face is missing. She's wearing professional clothes and a lab coat stained dark brown by her own blood. One of her legs looks gnawed on, and there's a hole through her chest.

I stop at the door, looking at the poor woman. Then my cop side kicks in. Who are you? It doesn't take me long to find a pair of vinyl gloves. I pull them on and carefully inspect the body while doing my best not to breathe through my nose.

Collins steps past me, deeper into the freezer, while I pick the woman's pockets. No money. No wallet. No I.D. "I've got nothing."

"Hudson," she says like I've just uttered the most ridiculous words a human being has ever conjured. "Have you seen this?"

I look up. My legs flex and I spring up like a stunned jack-in-the-box. I want to curse. Or run. Or scream. But all I can do is look.

The chrome side-wall across from the dead woman is covered in text. I can't read a word of it, but I recognize the ink as blood. Most likely the woman's blood. "You don't think she—"

"No," Collins says. "There's too much. She'd have died while writing it."

While most of the text is smeared and illegible, there is one word, at the top, that is larger than the rest.

Νέμεσις

"Any ideas?" Collins asks.

I shake my head, no, but say, "Greek maybe. Get a picture. We need to go."

Collins uses her iPhone to snap several photos of the bloody text. After quickly reviewing the photos she says, "Good."

There's no sign of the creature other than the destruction it left in its wake. We're two stories underground, yet I see sunlight at the end of the hall. Must be how it got out, I think. It takes us a minute to find a second staircase that hasn't been destroyed, but once we do, our ascent to the building's third floor (five stories up) is slowed only by our own exhaustion. We're both walking by the time we reach the top of the stairs.

Leaning against the wall, propped up by my left forearm, I fish into my pocket and find my phone. No bars.

Shit.

When I put the phone away, Collins holds hers out to me. "Time to join the modern world." I take the phone and look at the bright display. Three bars.

Without another word, I dial. The call is answered on the second ring.

"Ashley, hey!" says Ted Watson. I can't see him, but I know he's sitting behind his computer-laden desk, Mountain Dew in hand or nearby, surrounded by monitor screens that can hold his attention far easier than the ocean view just beyond them. Before I can get a word in, he keeps talking. "How'd it go with Jon this morning? He's a little rough around the edges, but I thought you two might hit it off. I mean, I'm no match-maker. Bad luck with those kinds of things, actually. My parents got divorced. Twice each. And—oh, I'm sorry. I didn't mean—I know that's a touchy subject."

I hear him making breathy noises at himself. It's not uncommon for him to get flustered by his inability to stop talking. Takes work to stop himself sometimes. He frequently has to stick his foot in his mouth after he's insulted someone. Luckily for him, and this is probably why we're pals, my feathers are hard to ruffle.

"Sorry, Ash," he says, sounding like a normal person. "What did you call for?"

"You need to lay off the caffeine, Watson," I say.

"H—Hudson?" He sounds confused for just a moment, then starts to get excited again. "No way! You didn't—"

"Ted, listen," I say loudly. I hardly ever interrupt his rants. That I did tells him this isn't a social call.

"Did you find something?" He asks. "Is Sasquatch—"

"If this were Sasquatch, I'd be thrilled. We've got twenty to thirty dead."

"People?"

"Yes, Ted. People."

"Who killed them?"

"Not who. What."

That takes all of the talk out of him and gives me time to lay out the entire story, from our visit to the Johnsons', to the gun-toting goon squad, to the orange-glowing creature. I finish by recalling the bloody text.

"Any way I can get a look at the text?" he asks. All of the Ted Watson mania is gone. He's either gone pale with fright or realizes the gravity of the situation.

"Hold on," I say. Despite not owning a newfangled phone, we usually have a lot of time to kill in the office and Watson lets me play Angry Birds on his phone. I open the Web browser, connect to the DHS webmail server and log in. "Almost there," I say. After attaching several different images to the blank e-mail, I hit send. "On the way. Included a photo of one of the shooters. I.D. him if you can, but the creature is our biggest problem."

"Gotcha," he says.

"Put Coop on."

"Hudson," Cooper says in greeting as she takes the phone.

"You heard?"

"Everything."

Conversations with Cooper are barebones and to the point. After speaking with Watson, her brevity is refreshing.

"You're sure this is an FC-P threat?"

"Wouldn't be calling if it wasn't."

"Understood. Protocol says I need to send a threat assessment to Deputy Secretary Stephens; shall I do that?"

I inwardly cringe at the idea of involving DHS bureaucracy in this, but not following protocol will only give them a reason to pull me, once they realize a huge wad of shit is airborne and en route toward the fan. "Yes. The threat is imminent and could affect thousands."

"Thousands?"

It's a big number, I know, but if this thing got loose in a downtown somewhere... I shake my head. "Better to overestimate than underestimate it."

"Agreed."

"Coop," I say, "I need you to get in touch with Maine authorities. Local P.D. within a thirty mile radius of Willowdale. State Police. Any National Guard in the area. We're going to need some heavy hitters. SWAT. Maybe more. Have them carrying high caliber rounds."

"Where do you want them?" she asks.

"I don't know yet. Just have them on standby."

"Will do."

"Thanks," I say. "Put Watson back on."

"Hey," Watson says. He sounds out of breath.

"Can you trace this phone's GPS?"

"Hold on." I hear his keyboard clacking. "Yeah, got you."

"Got a satellite view?"

"Archived, yeah."

"What do you see?"

"Trees," he says. "Lots of trees. Wait, you're not far from the cabin."

"How old are the images?" I ask.

"Timestamps say they're just a few months old."

Damnit, that means that whoever is running this place has some serious resources. "Can you get some real time satellite coverage?"

"Going to take some time. Need approval. Might be hard to get."

"Why's that?" I ask, growing annoyed, but then I realize why. FC-P is requesting a spy satellite be repositioned over the state of Maine to track a giant man-eating monster. This is going to blow up in our faces until the bodies start piling up. "Put Coop back on."

"Here," Coop says.

"Lie," I tell her. "Tell Stephens there's a biological terror threat, but do not elaborate. Let him draw his own conclusions."

"Makes sense," she says and then Ted is back on.

"Anything else?" he asks.

"Send a helicopter to my position," I say. "Something with a big gun."

"I'll try," he says, sounding agitated. Watson is amazing in so many ways, but he's easily distracted and oversensitive. It's also been a really long time since FC-P had a threat level higher than what I call RPSC—Rastafarian Pot-Smoking Chill. We're out of practice. If he can't stay calm and get his job done, people could die.

"Ted," I say, "you and I both know there is no try."

He chuckles. "There is only do. I'll get it done."

"Thank you, Ted. Call me back when you have an ETA on the chopper."

"Will do," he says, and I hang up.

I hand the phone back to Collins. "Keep that on. They might need to track the GPS." I don't say, "in case something happens to us," but I can see she understands.

I push open the door and enter the third floor hallway. The walls are splattered with blood. The bodies of five doctors, dressed for surgery, litter the floor. They're mangled, like the woman in the morgue fridge, but not mostly consumed like the people outside.

I step over the bodies, working hard to not let them distract me. We need to figure out where the creature is heading and make sure an army is waiting when it gets there. "Let's try to find the roof access."

Collins has her hand over her mouth as she steps around the bodies. Without looking away from the corpses, she nods.

The distinct sound of a gun being racked stops us in our tracks. "Put your hands on top of your heads and turn around slowly." The accent is subtle, but easy for me to place. The man with a gun aimed at my back is Japanese.

17

When a bullet doesn't punch through the back of my head, I take that as a cue to turn around. If he's going to kill me, I'd like to look him in the eye first. I move slowly and keep my fingers locked behind my head. I see the gun first. It's a Ruger Mark II .22 semiautomatic pistol with a sound suppressor. The low caliber and the sound suppressor say a lot about the man holding the weapon.

That combination means that this gun will barely make a sound when he fires it. My body hitting the floor would be much louder. The bullet, aimed at the head, will lack the power to punch through a skull twice, meaning the bullet will ricochet inside the target's skull and shred gray matter. The victim will be very dead, but there will be very little mess. When this man kills, I doubt anyone finds the bodies.

The men we faced before were soldiers. Big guns and muscles with minds for tactics. This man kills up close and personal, and rather than simple tactics, he must have a mind for strategy, which is probably why I'm not dead.

The man himself defies a label. He looks at me with the same cold stare of the soldiers, but I can see his mind working, too. His black hair is slicked back, though some of it is out of place, probably from hiding. He's wearing a black suit coat and a white shirt—partially unbuttoned, but no tie. Best guess is that he's some kind of assassin, but his presence here makes no sense.

Not that anything has made sense since we ran into the shotgun-wielding Royals fan.

Collins follows my cue and turns around.

"Sheriff Collins," the man says with a nod. Then he looks at me. "Your resourcefulness is impressive for U.S. Fish and Wildlife Service."

I shrug. "It's a gift."

He smiles a little. "Why are you here?"

"Honestly," I say, matching his smile, "and I shit you not, we're here because Mr. Johnson, the Vet you assholes murdered, called in a report about a Sasquatch."

"Sasquatch?"

"Your patrols were noisy," I explain. "Went too close to his house. Freaked the old man out."

"It's the truth," Collins said. "He's been calling for months."

The man's eyes cut back and forth between Collins and me. He's trying to figure out if we're telling the truth. "Then we are not enemies."

The hell we're not, I think, and I know Collins is on the same page, but she's smart and stays quiet.

The man lowers his weapon to a downward angle, which isn't supposed to be as threatening, but makes me just as uncomfortable. "Could you point that to the side a little. Maybe aim for my leg? I'd rather you keep it pointed at my head than at my boys."

I see Collins smile a little.

At first, I'm not sure the man has understood the request, but then his aim adjusts slightly to the right. "Now place your weapons on the floor. Slowly. One at a time."

"Thought we weren't enemies," I say. When he doesn't reply, Collins complies, drawing her pistol between two fingers and placing it on the floor.

"Now you," the man says, adjusting the Ruger back to my crotch.

I follow orders, and when my weapon is on the floor, the man waves for us to step toward him and says, "I need your help."

"Feeding time at the mad science circus?" I say.

He ignores me and points to a pair of double doors. "There is a wounded man. I need to get him to a hospital."

This is about the last thing I expected the man to say. And if it's true, I will help. But not until I have some answers. "Tell us what happened here," I say. "And then we'll help."

"You will be better off not knowing," he says. "There are some things that cannot be forgiven."

Exactly what I was thinking.

I look at Collins to make sure she's on board. I don't want to risk her life without consent. She grants it, verbally. "We'll take the chance."

He bows slightly. "Very well. This is a research facility working on medical advancements in gene therapy, bio-engineering and accelerated organ growth for transplantation. A recent experiment has had...unforeseen consequences."

"You mean that creature," I say. "That's kind of a big unforeseen consequence. How did it happen?"

"I am not a scientist," the man says, and there is no doubt he's telling the truth.

"Then who are you?" Collins asked.

"Katsu Endo," he says. "I am the personal bodyguard of the man in the next room."

"And he is?" I ask.

"General Lance Gordon."

"General?" I say. "So this is a military facility?"

"The General was here to receive an experimental heart transplant," he says. "The...creature—"

The way he says this reveals he's just as confused about the creature's appearance as they are. Could it really have been created accidentally? Something that large would take time to grow, unless... I recall the man's words, accelerated organ growth. But how quickly could something the size of an elephant grow?

"—did not appear until after the operation was complete."

"How did you survive?" Collins asked.

"I barred the doors," Endo says. "Shut off the lights. Stayed quiet. It passed us by several times."

That I'm dubious is an understatement. "It killed everyone else here. Everyone. And just you and the General survived?"

"Actually," he says. "Two other people managed to survive." He raises his eyebrows at me.

"Right," I say. Touché. It's hard to say if everything this man has said is the truth, but he's showing no telltale signs of lying. That said, I'm positive we're not getting the whole truth. And if this man really is a bodyguard for a U.S. general, then maybe he wasn't involved in the decision to kill the Johnsons, Collins and me. "All right, look, we'll help you get your boss out of here, but once he's safe, I need your guarantee that you're going to let us go."

He stares at us. I can see the idea bothers him. His instinct is to probably kill us both where we stand.

"Look," I say. "Someone needs to clean up the mess that was made here. That thing is headed toward civilization and when it gets there, a whole shit-storm of trouble is going to come your way. General or not, you two are screwed. The only chance of avoiding that scenario is letting us get the word out to organize a response."

I can see him strategizing, working through the possibilities. He raises the gun back to my head. "I agree with everything you've said, but do not believe they are the words of a Fish and Wildlife Service officer. Show me your I.D."

I sigh, but comply, slowly taking out my I.D. and tossing it to him. He catches it in his hand, flips it open and looks a little surprised. "DHS?"

"That's me," I say.

For a moment he looks like he doesn't believe me. Who can blame him, really? With my cargo shorts, t-shirt and beanie cap, I look like the average Mainer out for a hike in the woods. Of course, Collins and I also evaded an armed search party, killed three soldiers and survived the creature's assault.

He throws the badge back to me. "The General is your direct superior. You have a duty to save his life."

I hear a hint of a question in his words and answer truthfully. "Yes."

He holsters his weapon and turns toward the door. "Come with me."

Collins and I look at each other, quickly pick up our weapons, and follow the man. I keep my weapon still drawn but aimed at the floor. I don't think the man is going to ambush us. He could have killed us already, but I still don't trust him.

I push open the door and enter a surgical suite. The operating table flood-lights have been extinguished, and the room is dimly lit by a single lamp. There are surgical instruments covering trays, some bloody, some clean.

But the unconscious general isn't lying on the operating table, or on a gurney or even sitting on a chair. He's standing on the far side of the room, stark naked, with a hand against the empty wall and staring at it like he's looking through a window.

Endo has stopped just inside the door. He looks as confused as I am.

"General," he says, confirming at least part of his story—this man is a general. "General Gordon."

The General flinches, hearing Endo for the first time, and turns his head around. "Endo?" His voice sounds dry and scratchy.

"I'm here, sir." Endo says.

"I can feel her," the General says.

Endo steps toward the naked man. "Feel who?"

"Maigo." When the General turns around, Collins and I both take quick breaths. A long cut over his sternum has been sewn shut, but isn't bandaged in any kind of way. A trickle of blood runs over his belly to his leg and all the way to the floor.

"General!" Endo says, sounding genuinely concerned. He takes a step forward, but the older man holds up his hand in a way that commands authority.

The open hand becomes a pointed finger. It lands on me. "Who—" And then on Collins. "—are they?"

Endo looks at both of us and then says, "Sheriff Collins and Jon Hudson from DHS."

"DHS?" the General says, looking confused. "This is our couple from the woods?"

Oh shit. They were aware of what went down in the woods. Doesn't mean they ordered it, but they didn't disapprove.

"Yes," Endo says. "But they're going to help you—"

"I'm fine." The General levels his eyes at Endo. "Kill them."

18

"Don't even think about it, Endo," I say. Before the General even finished giving the order to have us killed, Collins and I raised our weapons and sighted Endo's head.

Endo, his back still to us, holds his hands out where we can see them, but he doesn't give up his weapon, and since he strikes me as the kind of guy who never surrenders, I think the death count is about to go up a notch. Maybe two.

"Endo," the General says.

I'm not sure why Gordon is pressuring Endo to make a move. He must realize he'll be dead before he can turn all the way around.

"Sir," Endo says apologetically. "I—can't."

Can't, I think, not won't. Whatever truce we had with the man is now over. If he could, he would kill us without hesitation or an ounce of guilt.

Gordon rolls his eyes and sighs. He steps boldly around Endo and I adjust my aim to cover the older man while Collins keeps Endo in her sights. The General steps between me and Endo. "Use me for cover."

"What?" Endo says. "You'll be killed."

"I don't think so," Gordon says.

"Sir, if you think the fact that you're a general will keep me from popping a cap in your naked ass, you're wrong. Endo, don't fucking move."

To his credit, Endo doesn't move. He knows the score. He might not worry about harm coming to himself, but the General is his responsibility and he seems to take his job very seriously.

The General squints at me and smirks. "Think you have a pair, don't you?"

"Who is Maigo?" I ask, hoping a change of subject will calm things down.

Gordon looks back over his shoulder, toward the empty wall. "She..."

What direction is the wall facing? I try to picture where I am in relation to the building's exterior. South, I think, he's looking south.

"Is Maigo the monster?" Collins asks.

The General whips toward her, offended. "Monster?" His eyes turn to me. "Monster!"

He takes a step forward. How this man is walking after open heart surgery, I have no idea, but it would be great if whatever painkiller they gave him wore off soon.

My finger tenses over the trigger. "Not one more step, General."

He steps. I hold my fire. I really do not want to kill a U.S. general.

His next step cuts the distance between us in half.

My finger begins to pull on the trigger, but in the time it takes to fire the gun, Gordon closes the distance. He moves like a striking snake, faster than a blink, and twists the gun in my hand. The weapon is wrenched from my grasp before I can fully understand what's happening. I catch up around the same time Gordon flings the gun to the side with such force that it embeds in the wall.

Collins opens fire as Endo takes action, diving behind the operating table. She fires a constant stream, but he's covered and in a moment, he's going to return fire and we've got no place to hide.

I throw a punch and put everything I have into it. As my fist covers the distance toward Gordon's stitched chest, I picture my fist punching through to his heart. I cringe as my fist strikes flesh, but the impact is solid. Like punching a wall. I flinch back from the blow. Did they put a metal plate in his chest?

Click, click, click.

Collins is out of ammo.

"Hudson, run!" she shouts, turning for the door.

But I don't have to run. Gordon retaliates with his own punch, also aimed for my sternum. I lean away from the punch, dulling the power, but the strike is still powerful enough to throw me back. As I stumble back toward the doors, Collins goes airborne and tackles me the rest of the way through. Between Gordon's punch, Collins's tackle and the impact with the doors, and then the floor, I'm fairly well dazed.

But when bullets tear into the wall just above us, a flood of adrenaline helps return some clarity. The double doors swing shut, blocking Endo's barrage. Collins gets to her feet and yanks me up with her. Man, she's tough.

As bullets punch the double doors, we sprint down the blood-stained hallway, leaping mangled bodies. I point to a sign of a man walking on a staircase, halfway down the hall. "There!"

The doors to the operating room slam open just as we reach the stairwell door and lunge inside. Bullets rake the metal door as I slam it shut behind us. The stairs below us are in ruins, as are most of the walls, giving us a clear view of the outside. I scan the sky for incoming help, but find nothing but early morning blue sky, the rising mist of a humid day and a column of thick smoke cutting through the middle of it all.

"Can't go down," Collins says, noting the ruined staircase.

I yank a ruined chunk of concrete-encrusted rebar from the wall and wedge it between the door handle and the frame. With a quick shake, I confirm that the door won't be opening any time soon. "We were headed up already. Let's go."

I only make it one step as my foot lands on something squishy. I flinch back, thinking I've stepped on a body. And in a sense, I have.

The mound of skin looks human. As does the black hair. But it's just skin. There's no body. I see arms and legs, but no skeletal structure. No muscles. It's like someone slipped out of a human suit.

"Look," Collins says. "What's that?"

The skin flops over easily as I push it with my foot. The first thing I make out is a leg. The inside of the thigh has been torn open. But above where the two legs come together...that's something different. "A tail?"

I follow the four foot long tapering tube of skin down to the end, where it turns rough and black. Definitely a tail. My eyes land on another patch of dark skin and I kick it away from the body.

A foot. A black, clawed, inhuman foot.

The door shakes and then rattles from an impact. Endo is trying to force his way through. "Head up," I tell Collins. "Make sure we have roof access. I'm going to get a sample." She vaults up the stairs without question or hesitation.

As a volley of bullets strike the outside of the door, I pull out a Ziploc bag and my small knife. I quickly locate one of the hollow fingers and slice it free, catching it in the inverted baggie before zipping it shut and charging up the stairs.

Endo's banging stops when I reach the top of the first set of stairs. I glance back. The rebar is still firmly in place.

Then the door explodes inward as though blown apart by C4. I flinch back, instincts telling me to flee, but my curiosity holds me in place long enough to see General Gordon through the cloud of dust—lowering his foot.

Never mind how a man just out of open heart surgery can walk, how the fuck can he kick in a steel door locked with rebar and attached to a concrete wall? Not even Lou Ferrigno could pull that off.

Question for another day. I bolt up the stairs before Endo can put a bullet in my head. I'm thrilled to find an open doorway waiting for me at the top of the stairs. Not so thrilled when I step out and find the pummeled door lying on the gravel rooftop. Smoke roils up around the building, but the pocket of air atop the roof is still breathable.

"What happened down there?" Collins asks.

"Gordon kicked in the door," I say.

She's surprised by the answer, but doesn't question it. Footsteps echo from the stairwell as they approach.

I step to the side of the roof exit, motioning for her to do the same. She goes to the opposite side, a little farther away with her reloaded pistol aimed at the open door.

We wait.

And wait.

A full minute passes. Maybe the footsteps were headed away? Endo and Gordon could be long gone by now, leaving through an exit I don't know about, but I didn't get the impression they wanted us to survive. Still, how long are we going to stand guard by an empty door?

Collins must be thinking the same thing because she inches close to the door leading with her weapon.

And then, in a blink, her weapon is gone.

A black-shoed foot kicks up fast and high, striking Collins's hands. The gun arcs away, disappearing over the side of the building. As Collins stumbles back from the blow, Endo emerges from the doorway, swiveling his weapon toward Collins.

I dive over his back, grasping his gun hand as he pulls the trigger. The round blasts a hole in the roof, just missing Collins's foot. The gun barrel grows hot in my hand, but I don't let go. Instead, I twist.

But my effort comes at a cost. Endo strikes hard and with precision, striking my left shoulder until the arm goes numb.

The gun comes free and I twist it toward Endo, but he's too fast. A perfectly placed roundhouse kick knocks the gun from my hand.

As my left arm tingles back to life, I turn to face Endo. "Seriously? Kung-fu?"

He bounces around, light on his feet. "Kung-fu is Chinese. I am Japanese."

"Okay, so ninjutsu," I say, looking for some kind of weakness to exploit, but he's in constant motion. "You realize how stereo—"

In no mood for banter, he kicks again forcing me to bend back. The sole of his shoe passes just an inch from my nose. Before I can recover, he sends another kick into my gut, pitching me forward. He's a blur of motion as he spins again. I'm in slow motion, bending forward like I want to be kicked into oblivion, my face red, my lips forming an O and the air escaping my lungs with an "oof!" As I see his leg, I know that unconsciousness will come next, and then if Collins can't take him on her own, death.

But Collins, it seems, knows exactly how to handle Endo. She charges past me and tackles the smaller man hard, pulling him away and saving my face from a shoe-shaped bruise. The pair fall together, and before they hit the roof, Collins hammers Endo's kidneys with three solid punches.

It's a hardcore move and the pain shows on Endo's face. Why does she know how to fight like this?

When they hit, Endo uses their momentum to roll and winds up on top of Collins, straddling her waist. He might be in pain, but he's a pro, and doesn't have a problem hitting girls. He sends a flurry of punches toward Collins, but she gets her arms up in time to block most of them.

I'm still doubled over and could spend a few minutes in an oxygen bar, but the sight of Collins being punched sends me into a rage. Half stumbling, I charge. My attack isn't graceful, but I'm pretty heavy. My intention is to use my body as a battering ram and hope the blow knocks Endo for a loop long enough for Collins and I to both recover.

I lower my shoulder and dive.

But Collins beats me to the punch. Endo sees me coming and delays a punch for just a moment while he glances in my direction. It's all the opening Collins needs. She lifts her legs, wraps them around Endo's head and yanks him back, smashing the smaller man to the ground.

While this is great—kudos to Collins for being a badass—I sail through the air, striking nothing. Instead, I soar over Collins and slam into the roof, sliding to a stop like a seal on an iceberg. The gravel scores my skin and burrows into my palms.

With embarrassment now fueling my anger, I push quickly to my feet and find Collins and Endo already facing off. Collins has her fists clenched, but carries herself with the easy gait of someone who knows how to deliver physical punishment. Endo remains mostly motionless, like a coiled snake, but he's standing awkwardly, in pain from the blows to his side.

Endo's hand goes to his ear. It's a reflex that many people do when they're wearing an ear bud and the audio is breaking up. He's receiving orders. Probably from Gordon.

A distant chop fills the air. Back-up is on the way, and it's actually a little sooner than I expected. For a moment, I worry that the approaching helicopter isn't for me, but I see Endo's eyes look to the sky in surprise.

Before Collins or I can continue the fight, Endo gives a little nod as though to say, "good fight," and then he bolts.

Collins starts after him, but I stop her saying, "Let him go." He's too quick to catch and he's not our first priority.

She turns to face me, and I'm surprised to see blood flowing from her nose. Before I can voice my concern, she says, "He hits like a girl." She wipes the blood away with her sleeve and pinches the top of her nose. "Not even broken."

The chop of the helicopter turns us around. It's a red Bell 407 helicopter, which is a popular multi-use chopper used for everything from medevac to air tours, but this is the first time I've seen one outfitted for battle. A large FN MAG machine gun is mounted in the open side door, though no one is manning the weapon. In fact, the only person I can see is the pilot. Regardless, this chopper is our ticket out of here.

I head across the roof, waving my arms. The pilot gives me a nod and brings the chopper down, descending slowly. As it lowers, rotor wash kicks up the gravel and grit on the roof, stinging my exposed skin. The chop of the blades is deafening, but evenly spaced. So when

I hear a loud whump between chops, I know it's not the helicopter. I turn around, toward the sound and see the far end of the building fall away. A plume of dust billows up.

Collins and I glance at each other. Is it the creature, or—

Whump! Whump! Whump-whump-whump-whump!

Ten-foot sections of the building fall away, one at a time, as a series of detonations demolish the structure. I bolt for the chopper, which is just a foot off the ground, but slowly rising and moving away. The pilot can see what's happening too, and he probably doesn't want to be above the explosion when it arrives.

The roof shakes beneath my feet.

The helicopter is out past the front of the building now, maybe five feet up. The pilot waves us on, his shock visible on his face despite the mustache, aviator glasses and headphones hiding most of it.

Whump! Whump! WHUMP!

As I hit the edge of the building, the roof falls away beneath me. My foot hits the small wall at the edge of the roof—

—and I leap.

19

The helicopter skids slap hard against my hands, sending a vibration through my arms that nearly knocks me loose. My left arm, still numb from Endo's beating, falls away first, but my right hand closes down like a vice. As I twist around, I find Collins hanging next to me, two hands on the skid. She shouts something to me, but I can't hear her over the thunderous helicopter. I can read her lips, though. Hold on.

No shit, I think, but I don't say anything.

My hand is starting to slip.

I try to raise my left arm, but half way up, something cramps, and the pain nearly throws me free. So I focus on holding tight. I stare at my hand, willing it to hold. I watch as my hand slowly but surely slides over the metal, which I'm only now realizing is coated in condensation created by the combination of cool metal and humid air.

When my thumb comes away and I'm hanging by just four fingers, I know I'm screwed. Gravity finishes the job. A shout bursts from my mouth as I fall.

I hit the ground just a moment later, landing on my feet. In shock, I look down. I'm standing in the clearing at the front of the building. I feel like an idiot. I was so preoccupied with not falling that I failed to notice the helicopter was descending, which also reveals the skill of the pilot. Wouldn't have taken much to shake me lose, but he kept the descent smooth and stable while two people clung to a skid and a building collapsed. The helicopter is now just seven feet off the ground. Collins looks down and sees me standing. She lets go and lands next to me.

As we move back, the chopper lands, swirling smoke and dust down around us. The research facility is a pancake, demolished with precision. If there was any evidence to be found in the building, it is no doubt pulverized. And anything still worth finding isn't going to give up its secrets easily. A round-the-clock search crew would probably take months to sift through the debris.

And we don't have months. We have days. Maybe hours. Hell, that thing could have already reached civilization.

The rotors slow, but don't stop, which is a good thing, because we need to get back in the air.

I point to the open side door and the large machine gun mounted there. "You know how to use that?" I shout to Collins.

She nods. Of course she does.

Without further discussion she climbs into the helicopter, gets behind the big gun and yanks back the charging handle, prepping it for action. Seeing the fiery-haired, bloodied but beautiful sheriff comfortable behind the weapon manages to bring a small grin to my face. She sees me and smiles back before nodding toward the front of the chopper, telling me to get inside.

I run around and climb into the passenger's seat. As soon as I close the door and turn around to face the pilot, I know, without a doubt, that this guy is a civilian. He's got gray hair, a bushy gray mustache with matching eyebrows and tan weathered skin. Like me, he's dressed for summer, but instead of boots, he's wearing flip-flops.

"Who the hell are you?" I shout.

He points to his headphones and hands a set to me. I slip them on while he hands a second set to Collins.

"Who the hell are you?" I repeat.

"Rich Woodall," he says. "Friends call me Woodstock."

"That's your name," I say. "But you're not military. Or police. Who called you?"

His eyes widen. "Ohh. Chief Warrant Officer Five, U.S. Marine Corp...retired. But don't let that fool you. I flew for twenty-five years and in three different wars. I can fly better than any of them hipsters they got flying these days."

"Doesn't exactly explain the big gun, does it?" I say.

He glances back at the machine gun with a grin. "I host...retreats. For weekend warrior types. Mostly Vets, like myself, who get their rocks off shooting big guns at wrecked cars and store dummies. Look, I heard the call for a chopper on the police band and responded. Spoke to your buddy, Watson. He wasn't too keen on using my services, but I was closest. Point is, I'll get you where you need to go, and honestly, I'm all you've got. Unless you want to hang around here for fifteen more minutes."

I just stare at him. I'm sure he's breaking laws. Probably a bunch of them. But he is clearly here to help and he might just end up saving some lives.

"Should consider yourself lucky I listen to the police bands," he says.

"Okay, okay," I say, "Take us up, Weekend Warrior."

He gives me a snarky grin and we lift into the sky so fast that my stomach lurches. As we clear the tree line, we circle the clearing. The destruction is mind numbing. The flattened rectangle of a building looks more like a basketball court from above. Dead bodies litter the area around the building, many surrounded by brown-stained grass.

"Holy Mongolian clusterfuck, what happened out here?" the gruff pilot says.

"Wouldn't believe me if I told you," I say.

"Was Sasquatch, wasn't it?"

My head snaps toward the man. "Everyone around here believe in Sasquatch?"

"You don't?"

I think about everything I've just seen and experienced. Sasquatch would be normal in comparison. "Look, something is on the loose down in those woods and it's a whole lot worse than Bigfoot. We need to find it and stop it before it reaches a human population."

He gives a nod, accepting my ridiculous and vague explanation. "Which way you want me to head?"

"Not sure yet," I say. "Just take us up."

"What should I be looking for?"

"Fallen trees," I tell him before taking out my phone. I check the bars. Three solid. I select Watson's name from the list and put the phone to my ear, under the headphone.

He answers. "Boss."

"What you got for me, Ted?"

"Just got off the phone with State Police. They can have a helicopter to you in thirty minutes."

"Forget the chopper," I say. "I'm already airborne and armed. Guy named Woodstock."

"Yeah, I spoke to him," Watson says. "Wasn't sure he was going to be reliable. He working out?"

"So far," I say. "But have the State Police still come. Just have them bring a full crew. We might need the firepower and boots on the ground. Anything else?"

"Still working on translating the text, but we I.D'd the shooter," Watson says. "First Sergeant Steve Thompson, U.S. Army. Retired five years ago. Been off the grid since. No known last address. No family."

No surprises there, but it confirms my suspicion that the General is recruiting his crew from previous commands. "Ted, find everything you can on General Lance Gordon. And a man named Endo."

"Endo?"

"That's all I've got. General Gordon was here. Endo is his bodyguard."

"What did the General tell you?" he asked.

"Nothing," I say. "The General is a hostile. Tried to kill Collins and me. Red flag him in case he pops up on someone's radar."

"Is Ashley okay?" Watson asks.

I glance back a Collins. She's scanning the forest below, aiming with the machine gun. "She's tough as nails," I say, but think that won't be specific enough for Ted. "She's fine. Oh, one last name. See if you get any pings. Maigo."

"What?"

I shout the name over the loud rotor chop. "Maigo!"

"How is that spelled?"

"No idea."

"Okay," he says. "Coop wants me to tell you that Stephens is in the loop. Said we're all fired if this turns out to be a goose chase, but gave us temporary clearance to coordinate a local response."

"Temporary?"

"FC-Boston is en route."

"Fuck." Ted can't hear me. It's just a whisper. But the headset mic picks it up, and I see both Collins and Woodstock turn toward me. I ignore them and say, "We'll deal with them when they arrive. What's the word on satellite coverage?"

"Couldn't request it until Stephens gave the green light," Watson says. "Should be available in thirty minutes."

"Copy that," I say, reverting to radio language. "Call me the second anything changes or you find out something. If you can't get through on my phone, call Collins."

"Jon," Watson says. "Be careful."

When I hang up, Woodstock is staring at me. He didn't hear everything, but he heard my side of the conversation including the fact that a U.S. general is a hostile. "You going to have a problem if we face off with a general?"

He shakes his head, no. "Nah, every general I ever met was a dick. Now, which way?"

I look out the window. Trees for as far as I can see in every direction. I was hoping for a path of fallen trees or something else equally obvious, but the forest is thick. A fallen tree would simply disappear.

Then I remember the General, hand against the wall. I can feel her, he said.

Maigo.

I turn to my right, looking for any sign of the monster's passage. Nothing. But it's the only clue I've got. I point out the window and say, "That way. South."

20

"I don't know if this is the best place, Nick," Jenny Hester said, as she stood on the side of a nameless dirt road.

"Its fine," Nick replied. "I come up here to go hunting with the guys all the time. Never seen anyone else. It's an old logging road. No one knows about it."

"The guys know about it."

"They're all working."

Jenny put her hands on her curvy hips that her father used to say would get her in trouble. Truth was, they got her spoiled rotten by every guy she dated. Her hips had power. While Nick rummaged through the flatbed of his truck, Jenny bent over and pretended to look at a rock. "I just don't know."

In addition to being young and attractive, Jenny was also smart. She knew she was messing with Nick, giving him mixed signals. But she enjoyed reducing men to a state of blubbering desperation.

When she looked back and found Nick's eyes locked on target, she grinned. Then she saw the blanket in his hands and decided to go light on him. Unlike most of her conquests, Nick was a good guy. He was still a horny bastard, like all the rest, but she felt safe with him. She found this less arousing, but at the same time she had begun to wonder if she could settle down with Nick. He had a good job with the electric company. A small, but nice, house. At twenty-five, he was five years older than she was, but probably the youngest she had dated.

She found herself staring back at him when their eyes connected. Her stomach swirled. Yeah, there's something else there, she thought.

He lifted up the blanket with a sheepish grin. "So you don't get sap on your ass."

She laughed. Considerate and funny. If she were still living, her mother would have said that Nick was a keeper. She'd heard her say that once, about a boy. But Jenny was just fourteen at the time and wasn't yet thinking about keeping anything or anyone.

Nick walked past, toward the side of the road. "We'll just go back a ways. Anyone comes down the road, we'll hear them." He held a stand of ferns aside and motioned to the pine woods with his free hand. "After you?"

Jenny just smiled and walked into the forest. While this was a first for her, like most people in the area, she grew up around and in the woods. She was as comfortable in the outdoors as she was in her living room, or in this case, her bedroom.

The woods rose up a casual hill, which she walked with long strides, knowing it would pull her already tight jeans a little bit tighter. She looked back and found Nick staring at her butt, a permanent smile locked on his face. His eyes shot up to meet hers when he finally noticed her looking at him.

"Sorry," he said. "I'm just the luckiest son-of-a-bitch in Maine."

And he's romantic, she thought.

She paused in a section of forest between a group of tall pine trees. The ground was covered in a thick carpet of brown pine needles. With a blanket on top, it might actually be comfortable. "This will work," she said, keeping her back to him while unbuttoning her shirt.

She glanced back and saw Nick unfolding the blanket and unfurling it over the ground like a waiter at a fancy restaurant. "It's a little warm," he said. "Took it out of the dryer before I left the house."

She paused unbuttoning, "You washed the blanket?"

"Course," he said. "Used two dryer sheets, too."

Definitely a keeper.

She could hear him undoing his belt. "Slow down, cowboy. Let me do that." She turned to face him, smiling wide. Her breasts weren't quite as impressive as her backside, but her too-tight bra did a good job accentuating what she had. Problem was, Nick didn't seem to notice.

In fact, he wasn't looking at her at all. His hands were frozen on his belt buckle, but his eyes quickly scanned the forest above them. His smile slowly faded away.

Sensing something wasn't right, Jenny pulled her shirt closed and moved closer to Nick. "What is it? What's wrong?"

"Can you smell it?" he asked.

She took a sniff. Pine needles. She sniffed again, deeper. "Vinegar?"

He gave a nod. "And something else. Like steak."

She smelled it then, and put her hand over her nose. "Ugh, it's awful." She noticed that he was only looking uphill. "How do you know it's coming from up there?"

"Air moves downhill," he said. "So whatever it is, we're downwind of it."

"What do you mean, it?"

"Probably a bear that got into someone's lunch, or kitchen even."

It made sense. Black bears had no qualms going where the smell of food led them, and Jenny had heard more than a few stories of ransacked kitchens, cars and trash barrels. "Are we safe?"

"I won't be dropping trou if that's what you mean," he said with a grin. "Not until I know it's gone, at least."

She laughed and said, "Okay, so how do we know if it's gone?"

"Bears are afraid of people," he said. "If it knows we're here, it will bolt. So we just need to let it know we're here." A mischievous look filled his eyes and he ran up the hill, hooting loudly and shouting. "Lookout bear, here I come!"

A bit more apprehensive, Jenny followed Nick up the hill, buttoning her shirt as she scanned the area for any sign of a bear—fleeing or otherwise.

But she saw nothing.

Nick's voice suddenly changed from a hoot to a higher pitched scream of surprise. Despite having no idea what had happened, Jenny joined in, screaming loudly and stopping in her tracks. She screamed again when Nick dove to the side and a large black bear charged over the crest of the hill and bolted past them.

She watched it sprint down the hill, it's fur bouncing wildly. She could hear it breathing heavily, huffing with each step. And then it was gone, across the dirt road and out of sight.

"Holy shit," Nick said, picking himself up and brushing pine needles from his clothes.

"Have you ever seen a bear run like that?" Jenny asked.

"During bear hunting season, yeah," he said. "But it's not hunting season, and that's when they're running away from people. I was making a lot of noise. It should have steered clear."

A tingling ran up the skin of Jenny's exposed arms. "We should leave."

The tingle spread over her body when Nick nodded quickly, his eyes starting to show uncommon fear. She turned down the hill and hurried toward the truck. Nick was a hunter. He knew the woods—these woods—maybe better than anyone in town. If he was spooked, then something was—

Nick shouted again, but this time it was like he'd been muffled by a pillow half way through. As Jenny spun around, the now high pitched wail was cut short. Her eyes went wide as she saw the impossible. Nick stood ten feet back, but half of him was missing.

His entire torso, head and arms were gone.

Nick's knees collapsed and the lower part of his body toppled over, spilling out severed intestines and blood.

Jenny shook uncontrollably as her mind struggled to make sense of what she was seeing.

A wet smack drew her eyes up. There was the rest of Nick, clutched in the jaws of something massive. It was as black as the bear, but bigger. It tossed Nick's body up and caught it again, the way a lizard or a bird repositions a meal before swallowing it whole. Then it repeated the move, each time biting down hard, stabbing its long curved teeth into the body, shredding bits of meat and clothing with each bite. Blood rained down on the forest floor, staining the still laid-out blanket red.

Jenny was too scared to scream. She simply turned around slowly, and then quickly walked down the hill on shaking legs. She mumbled incoherently to herself, and she viewed the world through blurred vision as tears streamed over her face. When a sickening slurp behind her was followed by an audible swallow, she lost control of her bladder. And when the ground shook beneath her, she began to weep.

When it shook again, she ran.

The third impact tore a scream from her lungs.

And just as she was sure she would be cut in half, she reached the dirt road and Nick's pickup truck. She whipped open the door and was bathed in Nick's scent. She missed him already, and the memory of his body filled her with something new—rage.

She reached into the truck, grabbed the shotgun from the rack in the back window and turned around to face the creature.

It slid out of the forest. The small trees lining the road bent and broke. Its massive, strangely feminine head, loomed forty feet above her. Brown, almost human-like eyes gazed down at her, focused like a predator. A forearm came out of the forest and pressed into the dirt road just a few feet away. The limb was as thick as a tree. The five black claw-tipped digits were the size of her arm. The creature's chest emerged next, broad and powerful, while at the same time, beautiful.

A large portion of each breast glowed with swirling orange light, like it contained phosphorescent liquid. The same light flickered all across the creature's torso and the sides of its neck. The sight nearly mesmerized her.

A deep resonating growl drew her watering eyes back up to the monster's head. Its jaws opened, revealing railroad-spike sized teeth and bits of Nick's body stuck between them.

Jenny matched the growl with a battle cry of her own, gave the shotgun a firm pump and aimed it at the creature's glowing chest. "Fuck you," she grumbled, and pulled the trigger.

The last thing Jenny heard was the creature's impossibly loud howl of pain. She would have clutched her hands to her ears if not for the sudden explosion of heat and light that washed over her just a second after she pulled the trigger.

When the light faded, all that remained was a charred husk, standing like a statue, holding a melted shotgun.

21

The view from the helicopter is split into two colors—blue and green. The sky is thick with haze rising from the damp forest, but last night's storm has fled and the smoke from the burning lab is far behind us. The forest below stretches to the horizon, the hilly ground rising and falling into the distance like an ocean of pine, frozen in place. The stillness of it all infuriates me.

I look back to Collins. "See anything?"

"Would have told you if I had," she says, and I can tell she's equally frustrated.

"Want me to start flying a pattern?" Woodstock asks. He turns his head away from me, looking to the left, and I notice for the first time that he's got a ponytail. Maybe the nickname has nothing to do with his last name? When I don't answer, he adds, "The trees are thick in these parts and stand upwards of a hundred feet. We could have flown over King Kong and not seen him."

"Actually, that's not a bad description," I say.

He cocks his head toward me. "No shit?"

"Imagine a hairless, armor-plated Kong with a tail and more feline, yeah." It's actually a very crude description of the creature I saw, but the size and color match close enough.

My phone rings. I put it to my ear. "Please have something for me."

"General Lance Gordon," Watson says. "Retired—"

"Let me guess, five years ago."

"Yep," he says. "And First Sergeant Steve Thompson retired about a month later."

"Hold on, Ted," I say, and lower the phone. "Hey Woodstock, when did you retire?"

He scrunches his forehead. "Going on seven years, why?"

"Nothing." I put the phone back to my ear. "Keep going, Ted."

"Gordon went private sector. Tax records show him as a consultant to Zoomb."

"The search engine?"

"Yeah, but they're a lot more than a search engine company. Five years ago, they were valued at ten million, today they're competitors with Google, snatching up high-tech companies in all fields, not just Web tech. They've got their fingers in space research, deep-sea exploration, weapons development, robotics and loads of bio-tech."

"Tell me about the bio-tech," I say.

"Not much to tell. It's all pretty hush-hush. They own five bio-tech companies. Nearest to your location is—" Paper rustles in my ear. "—BioLance. Their main office is in Boston. The Prudential building."

"But if they were pushing ethical boundaries, it's possible they had some unlisted locations, right?"

"Exactly what I thought," Watson says. "I looked up the land records for the phony Nike site. Looks like it was bought from the town four years ago by a company named Pruitt Resources, which turned out to be a shell company of a shell company owned by—"

"—Zoomb," I say. "So somehow Gordon is involved with BioLance."

"Or running the show," Watson says. "Guys like him know well enough not to have their name directly associated with anything questionable."

"Right," I say. "Anything on Endo?"

"Nothing yet and I've checked the Army and Zoomb personnel records, but it would be a simple thing to hide someone. The only reason Gordon is listed is because hiding someone so high profile would be nearly impossible. Oh, Maigo. It's a name for sure. Japanese. Means, lost child."

"Okay," I say. "Do a search for the name. Army. Zoomb. Current news and archived news. Keep it to a U.S. search for now, but if that doesn't get any pings, check Japan and then everywhere else."

"Will do," Watson says and then reads my mind. "Still fifteen minutes on real-time sat coverage. They're repositioning one just for us, which Coop says is burning Stephens's ass."

"Anything else?" I ask, feeling just as confused as before, but also annoyed that none of it helps us locate the creature.

"Umm." More rustling papers. Watson is a techie, but organizes his thoughts on paper. He's got three large flat screens side by side, but his desk is stacked high with pages, and that's when we're looking into phony basilisk sightings or swamp gas specters, never mind an honest-to-goodness threat to U.S. citizens. "Oh! Yeah, one more thing. Most of the text on the fridge wall is impossible to make out, but the larger word at the top, Némesis—" He pronounces it *Nemesees*, "—translates to exactly what it sounds like: Nemesis."

"Which tells me...what exactly?"

"No idea," he says, "but I'm about to run a search on the word, see if there is any connection to bio-research."

"Let me know what you find. And have someone from the FBI keep a watch on the BioLance offices in Boston."

"Might step on a few toes," he says.

"I don't give a damn if we stomp the shit out of some toes, Ted," I say, probably a little angrier than necessary. "This is a paranormal event, Ted. It's our jurisdiction. Don't pussyfoot."

"Sorry," he says, and I can tell I've hurt his feelings.

Watson is a gentle soul. Easy to take advantage of and makes an easy target. But that's not me, and that's not our relationship.

"Ted, sorry, I'm not upset with you," I say. It's a shitty apology, but I don't have time for more. "We good?"

"Nothing a little Ben and Jerry's can't fix," he says with a little of his normal jovial self coming through.

"Chunky Monkey heals all wounds," I say, and I get a laugh out of him. "Later, Ted."

When I hang up, Woodstock looks like he's tasted something sour. He turns to me and says, "So, you two supposed to be like Mulder and Scully or something? Heard what you said. Paranormal."

I just stare back, unsure whether I feel like explaining or if I want to lay some sarcasm on him. He doesn't deserve it, but my monster-fueled vitriol needs a release. Collins interrupts before I can decide.

"Over there," she says, pointing through the open side door. I look past her and see a road, barely visible through the pine canopy, snaking through the forest.

Woodstock circles the chopper around so I can get a look out of my window.

"Some of the trees are knocked over," Collins says. "Thought I saw a pick-up."

"I see it," I say. A portion of the forest on one side of the road is wider. As we pass over, I see several smaller trees lying across the road and a pick-up. And then, just before the trees block my view again, I see a person. "I saw someone! We need to get down there!"

"Ain't no way I can put her down there," Woodstock says. He brings the chopper into a hover and we head up.

I see a break in the trees and point to it. "How 'bout over there?"

We cruise over the forest and find a marsh beside the road, free of trees. It's about a half mile from the truck.

"I don't know," Woodstock says.

"That person could be in trouble," I say.

"All right, listen," he says. "I'm gonna bring us down, but I'm not going to land. I'll keep her a few feet off the ground."

"You can do that?" I ask.

"You pick up a trick or two when you've been flying long as I have." He starts the descent. "Just haul ass to that truck, find that person and haul ass back. If you're in decent shape, we can be back in the air inside what, ten minutes?"

I nod, but then remember how crappy my body feels. "Make it fifteen. If we're not back in twenty head back up and come check on us."

He gives a nod and slowly adjusts the controls so that we stop just three feet above the ground. "Last stop."

Collins and I leap from the chopper and duck-run away from it as the rotor wash kicks up dirt and sprays marsh water. We run for a quarter mile and then slow to a jog. Fifteen minutes might not have been long enough, I think. Then I spot the truck up ahead.

I reach for my gun and find it missing. Crap. Collins is unarmed, too.

Collins sees me reach for my non-existent gun and says, "Probably should have stayed in the chopper and covered you from above."

Damn. She's right. If we don't switch from reactionary thinking to strategic thinking soon, it could cause problems.

"If it makes you feel better," she says, unclipping something from her belt and tossing it to me.

I catch the small bottle in my hands and look down at it. Pepper spray. For a moment, I smile. Then I see the truck, or rather, what's left of it.

The right side of the black pick-up is shiny and new. The left is scarred with mottled gray streaks and is tilted down, its tires missing. No, not missing. Melted.

I see the person standing beside the truck, partially concealed by a fallen tree and shadow. "Hey!" I shout. "We're here to help."

When the figure doesn't turn or even acknowledge the sound of my voice, I know something is wrong, but I'm not prepared for how wrong. Collins beats me by a few steps, but backs away just as quickly, hands going to her mouth. "Oh my God!"

I stop, see the body for what it really is—a well done, charred human being—and I do my own back-step. Whoever this was, he or she—it's impossible to tell—has been cooked through and frozen in place. "How is it still standing?"

"Look at the shotgun," Collins says.

I hadn't even realized the elephant trunk-like object clutched in the black hands was a gun. But now that I'm looking, I see it for what it is, a 12 gauge semi-automatic shotgun.

"Whatever burned the victim was hot enough to melt the gun, the tires and parts of the truck," Collins said. "I think the body was burned fast enough that the victim was dead and charred in place."

I look at the bent and broken trees. "So our creature comes out of the woods, finds the truck, cooks the owner and then—" I turn to the opposite side of the road and find more broken trees leading into the forest on the other side. "—and keeps on going."

An idea strikes me and I pull out my phone. No signal. I hold my hand out to Collins. "Phone."

She hands her phone to me. It has just a single bar. But I'm not about to watch ten hours of Nayan Cat, so it will do. I call Watson. When he picks up, I start speaking before he can greet me. "Ted, get my GPS location. Draw a straight line between the BioLance lab and where I am now, then extend that out in a straight line and tell me what's there."

He doesn't reply, but I can hear him working. He comes back on the line a moment later and says, "Looks like Ashton, a small town fifteen miles out, and then its nothing but trees all the way to Portland and the ocean."

Portland. Shit. It's the largest and most densely populated city in the state. It has something like 63,000 residents, but on a nice summer day like this, that number might be double.

I hang up. "We need to—"

The ground shakes. It's subtle, but I can feel it in my legs, and I can see by the look on Collins's face that she can too.

A roar follows, and it's nowhere near subtle.

I don't know if it has our scent or if it hears the nearby chop of the helicopter, but the creature is nearby.

The ground shakes again, more violently.

Correction, it's not just nearby, it's coming back.

22

I'd like to say that Collins and I are having some kind of simpatico moment that reveals we're like-minded and destined to be soul mates, but I'm pretty sure that sprinting away from the man-eating monster like a pair of terrified ostriches is what most everyone on the planet would do. We're neck and neck down the dirt road, neither of us speaking, all wounds and weariness forgotten.

The booming footfalls of the charging creature grow louder. Closer.

Trees crack and swoosh through the forest, impacting the ground with a rattle. A plume of pine scent washes over the road, pushed by the force of the falling trees.

A loud snap draws my eyes to the forest on my left. Through the maze of conifers, I see another tree fall, as a massive black shape moves past. The tree drops parallel to the road, not toward it.

"It's not coming after us," I say between quick breaths. "It's heading for the helicopter!"

As we round a bend in the road, I see the chopper just a hundred yards ahead, hovering ten feet off the ground. When Woodstock sees us coming, he begins to descend. But that's not what I want. There's no way we can beat the creature to the chopper.

Knowing Woodstock is watching us, and probably wondering why we're running, I stop in the road. I shake my head no and wave my arms. The helicopter pauses, five feet from the ground, the chop of its blades drowning out the booming steps of the oncoming behemoth.

Fighting the urge to pitch forward and catch my breath, I put my arms out to my sides, palm up, and then flap them like a bird. The helicopter hand signal translates to pull up. The frantic way I am performing the signal should translate to something like, "Pull the frig up, right now!"

The helicopter rises, but not as fast as I would like.

But then, it's too late.

Trees at the end of the road explode into the watery clearing. A smaller pine shoots across the clearing like an ICBM, just missing the helicopter's skids. Seeing all this, Woodstock pulls up fast. It saves his life.

The creature explodes from the forest, savagery incarnate. It roars up at the rising chopper, drowning out the chopping blades. It looks just about the same as I remember—sleek and black, long tail, protective carapace on its back, thick armored skin, orange glowing membranes on its neck and body and scythe-like teeth—with one exception: it's doubled in size. The creature now stands an easy forty feet tall and its boney trident-tipped tail adds another twenty to thirty feet. Despite it now being large enough to actually give Kong a run for his money, it's still fast and agile, like a cat.

I'm pretty sure Kong wouldn't stand a chance.

The monster leaps into the clearing, landing on all fours. I see its hind legs tense, and then it leaps up, reaching for the rising chopper. A quick maneuver to the side, while rising, saves Woodstock's life again, though I suspect the wet, squishy earth below the beast also kept it from leaping higher.

The swampy ground all but explodes when the giant crashes back down, water spraying everywhere. But the creature is unfazed. It just watches the helicopter, now out of reach, as it turns toward us and hovers.

Woodstock is probably freaking out, but he hasn't fled, and that he's turned toward us is a good sign. He's not going to leave us behind. Good man, I think. He's looking for a signal from me, so I come up with a plan that's borderline stupid and do my best to hand signal it to him. I point in the distance, make a circle and then point to the ground at my feet. I'm trying to say, "Lead it away, circle around and come back for us," but there's no way to know if he understands.

When the helicopter peels away and takes off low over the trees, I suspect the message might have been received. And then, as I'd hoped, the creature obeys, too. It watches the helicopter until it disappears over the trees, then the creature climbs out of the marsh and storms into the forest, giving chase. Its tail whips back and forth as it picks up speed. The tail-tip, which looks like a black, three-pronged spear tip, strikes a tree—probably unintentionally—and splits it in two.

Collins and I watch the top half of the tree fall into the swamp, and then turn to each other. I'm still out of breath when I say, "I don't...have any good...one liners, do you?"

"How about...we're screwed," she says, equally winded.

"Good enough."

"What's the plan?" she asks.

I point to the trees. "We climb."

"I'm not sure I want to look that thing in the eyes," she says.

"He's not going to be able to land that chopper again." I look to the top of the trees. "We need to meet him half way."

She looks up. "All the way to the top, then?"

"All the way."

"Let's go," she says and enters the woods.

It takes us just thirty seconds to find a tree that is both tall enough, but also has enough branches to climb to the top.

Collins stops at the tree's base. "Those branches don't look strong enough to hold us."

She's right. As pine trees grow taller, the lower branches die and jut out from the trunk like old bones. They're dry and brittle, but they're still wood. Unless they're rotting, we should be okay. "Keep your hands and feet close to the trunk, where the branch meets the tree. That's where the branch will be strongest. And always keep three contact points, so if a branch breaks, your weight is still distributed over three branches."

"That a fat joke?" she says

I'm absolutely terrified, but Collins manages to get a smile out me. "Seriously," I say, "If we don't get eaten today, I might just ask you to marry me."

Now it's her turn to smile, but the laugh that goes with it is a little too loud. She clamps her hand over her mouth.

I shake my head and say, "You first," I give her a boost onto the lowest branch. Once she's twenty feet above me, I leap up, catch a branch and pull myself up. It's not pretty, and I'm glad Collins is too busy climbing to watch me dangling like a drunk monkey, but I manage to get the branch beneath me. The rest of the climb goes swiftly. Sticking to the branch-bases and the three-contact-points rule, we head high fairly swiftly.

As we near the top, we slow down. The branches are fresh, stronger and less likely to break, but also smaller and more flexible. Nearer the top, we give up on holding the branches in our hands and opt for holding onto the trunk itself, which is only the thickness of a telephone pole.

Ten feet from the top, just five feet from clearing the canopy, Collins stops. "The tree is bending," she says.

I look up and see the tree top listing to the side. "Don't move. I'm coming."

"I'm not sure that's a good idea," she says.

"Nothing a little physics can't fix." I work my way up and around the tree so that I'm on the opposite side of the trunk from her. It's slow going because the top of the tree is thick with smaller branches, but when I get closer to Collins, the bend starts to straighten out. I stop a few feet short of her. If I get any closer, the tree will bend too far in my direction, and then our combined weight will pull it down.

The chop of the helicopter grows louder. I search the sky, but I'm still about a foot below most of the trees, so I can't see to the horizon. "Can you see him?"

Collins searches the area and points into the distance. "Coming from the East. He's never going to see us."

"Get your iPhone," I tell her.

"I don't think he can answer his phone while he's flying."

"The back of the phone is reflective," I say.

Understanding, she digs into her pocket, takes out the phone, tears off the plastic case and holds it up in the sun, wiggling it back and forth. The strobing reflection won't be big, but in a sea of pine green, it should be the only thing different.

"He's coming this way," she says. "But...I think he's still being chased."

"What do you see?" I ask her.

"The trees behind the helicopter—they're moving." She looks down at me. "This is going to be close."

I inch a little higher in the tree. "Can you get any closer to the top?"

She climbs up another foot, but then stops. "It's not much thicker than a broom handle up here."

The sound of the helicopter grows louder. Woodstock is just seconds away, which means the creature is, too.

"Here he comes!" Collins says, pocketing the phone and inching higher still.

The tree tops fill with thunder as the helicopter makes a rapid stop just above us. The top of our tree hits the bottom of the chopper and bends. Collins is close enough to the skids that she's able to pull herself up and into the side of the chopper, but when her weight leaves the tree, the top of it bends in my direction.

The strong treetop isn't going to break from my weight, but in a moment, I'm going to be dangling out over the forest like a cat-toy. Before this can happen, I slide down the trunk, stopping once I reach the more rigid old growth. The tree straightens out above me, but our distinguished guest has arrived below.

The roar, which sounds like a thousand cellos and violins mixed by a dubstep DJ, shakes a flurry of pine needles from the trees. I feel the thing's warm breath wash over me, and I get a nose full of its fishy breath. God damn, I do not want to be eaten by this thing!

The tree shakes and I'm propelled into action. I climb the tree fast, lunging up and around the thinning trunk, never giving any one side long enough to bend. Then, with a crack, the tree falls away beneath me. With one last thrust, I reach up and catch the helicopter's skid.

Collins's hand instantly clutches my wrist, locking me in place as the helicopter ascends slowly, hovering when it's far from the creature's reach. Once we're level and stable, Collins helps me climb into the helicopter. Exhausted, I slump into one of two back seats and put on a headset.

Woodstock looks back from the cockpit. "Where to?" That he seems to be unruffled by everything that's just happened is amazing.

"Lead it back to the road," I say.

He looks dubious.

"We have a chance to stop it, here and now," I say. "And G.I. Jane over here is just itching to fire your gun."

He looks at Collins. She's already behind the big machine gun, finger on the trigger. "Hot damn, you're my kind a lady."

We bank hard and head toward the road. I look down and see the dark shape of the giant still giving chase. Trees sway as it passes through. Then we're above the open dirt road. Woodstock keeps us about two hundred feet from the ground, swivels the chopper so the machine gun is facing the forest and shouts, "Give'm hell!"

And then, when the trees bow down as though in reverence to a primal force, and the monster steps into the road, Collins pulls the trigger.

23

Brilliant orange tracer-fire streaks down toward the creature, revealing the path of the stream of bullets unleashed by Collins. Her arms shake as she holds the machine gun, but not much, since most of the kick is absorbed by the gun's mount.

Following the tracer rounds, I see that Collins is aiming for the thing's snout. And by the way it's twitching and snapping, it's clear that her aim is true. But, I'm not so certain that she's actually hurting the monster. Its skin must be inches thick, and the rough surface could be dense hide, impervious to even the high caliber machine-gun rounds. A lack of blood on the snout confirms it.

Although the creature isn't being seriously injured, it is getting annoyed. The thing lets out a roar that rattles the chopper enough to knock Collins's finger off the trigger. The gun falls silent and Woodstock reacts to the turbulence by bringing us around the creature.

I stand behind Collins, looking over her shoulder, gripping two of the many handle bars on the roof and walls of the chopper. I lose sight of the creature for a moment as we cut over the forest, but when we arrive back over the road, it spins and leaps.

Open jaws reach up for the helicopter. I lean away from the sword-filled maw with a shout, but Collins remains calm and crushes her finger down on the trigger. Hot metal spews from the gun.

Mammoth teeth shatter.

Rounds strike the thing's softer throat.

The jaws snap shut and the monster makes a pathetic sounding yelp, like a dog...or a person. It falls back, landing clumsily on its side. A cloud of dirt billows from the dirt road, and several trees fall as the whipping tail shreds the wood. The ruined pines topple over, landing on the creature, obscuring it from view.

Can't be that easy, I think. But maybe a few of the machine gun rounds made it through the roof of its mouth and into its brain? The bullets could have performed like Endo's .22 rounds, bouncing around the inside of the skull and shredding brain matter.

The tail stops twitching.

Collins takes her hand off the trigger and looks over the gun. "Is it dead?"

No one replies, but Woodstock brings us a little bit lower.

"Too many trees in the way," I say. When I notice we're still descending, I add, "Woodstock, don't get any—"

The fallen trees burst upward.

The creature rolls to its feet.

"Up, up, up!" I scream, and I immediately feel the G-force of rapid ascent pushing me toward the helicopter's floor.

The monster rises from the ground and leaps again, this time reaching up with its hands. Sonuvabitch, we might be too close!

As the creature rises, the glowing patches on its neck flare bright orange. I point to the light, where the skin is translucent and maybe not as tough, and shout. "Fire!"

Machine gun fire tears through the air as the giant's two hands, each with five black-clawed digits, close in on the chopper.

The tracer rounds stitch a path across the thing's face, throwing up bits of dark skin, but nothing more. Then, as Collins adjusts her aim downward, and the creature continues up, a single round strikes the bright orange membrane.

A bright explosion fills the air between the chopper and the monster. A ball of fire roils toward us, but the shockwave hits first, and it hits hard. The helicopter tips to a forty-five degree angle that carries us away from the burning flames, but knocks Collins away from the machine gun.

With one hand gripping a handle bar, I get my other arm around Collins's back and hold her while Woodstock levels us out and heads for high ground.

"The hell was that?" Woodstock shouts. "A missile strike?"

While I would be thrilled to have some heavy hitting support right now, I didn't hear the sound of an incoming missile or the boom an exploding missile would make. I search the sky for signs of a jet or attack helicopter, but find nothing. "I don't know what it was!"

Once we're level, I put Collins in one of the seats, and I discover that she's actually unconscious. Blood covers her face. The machine gun must have smacked her forehead. I quickly buckle her in place and look for the monster again.

It's three hundred feet below now and shrinking as we rise higher. It stands in the dirt road, unharmed, and just stares up at us. At me. Then, with a single whip of its tail, it turns to the forest, slips into the trees and disappears.

I note its direction.

South.

Why is it heading south? I'm under the impression that this thing was created in a BioLance laboratory, so why would it head in any direction? Why wouldn't it just stay put? Or wander aimlessly? Or mark its territory like any other predator? Of course, it doesn't really resemble anything on Earth, predator or otherwise. But why south? Is it some kind of instinctual migration? Maybe it's part bird? I could ask these questions endlessly and go mad from never having the answer, so I'm glad when Woodstock interrupts my thoughts—until I hear what he has to say.

"That explosion did a number on my bird. Everything's gone screwy. Probably something electrical. Melted wires, maybe. I'm flying manually right now, but I got no altimeter, compass, fuel gauge—nothing."

None of this sounds good, but we have a mission to complete. "What are you trying to say?"

"I gotta put her down someplace where I can fix what's wrong," he explains.

"We need to get to Ashton," I say. "The helicopter can wait."

"Not sure you're understanding the situation," he says. "Either I put her down, someplace nearby, or we're eventually going to crash, probably sooner than later."

"The police station isn't far," Collins says. "You can land in the parking lot."

I'm about to object, but Collins puts her hand on my arm. "My car is there."

"Helicopter will be faster."

"Not if we crash," Woodstock says.

"And you haven't seen my car," Collins adds.

My first real investigation is falling to crap all around me and FC-Boston is on their way, hoping to take it away. If they beat me to the punch and manage to stop this creature, I'll be out of a job along with Watson and Coop. Then again, the odds of them handling this situation without having any idea of what they're up against is as unlikely as Michael Jackson making another comeback. And that means people's lives are at stake—the morons from FC-B and thousands of locals.

I turn to Collins. "How fast is your car?"

Fifteen minutes later, I have my answer as Collins pegs the gas pedal to the floor and all 440 horses propel us down the main street of town, which is lined by the police station, post office and general store. Not a soul in sight. The cop-blue Mustang belongs to Collins, but she's installed some upgrades—a siren and LED police flashers on the dash—in case she needs to respond to an emergency from home. Despite moving down the road like a rocket, people will see and hear us coming more than a mile away.

We made it to the station in one piece, though the landing was a little rougher than usual. Woodstock borrowed the station's second, currently unused cruiser and was headed home for parts. He promised to meet us in Ashton just as soon as he finished with repairs, which I think is good of the man considering he's not in law enforcement and he knows there's a chance he might die horribly as a result. I respect that kind of bravery and sense of duty. I just hope I don't get him killed.

After raiding the police station's armory for body armor, a couple of high caliber magnums, two shotguns and plenty of ammo, we leapt in the car like a couple of Duke boys on the run and left a cloud of dust behind us.

And now, once again, I'm terrified.

Collins drives like a maniac and Maine's back roads aren't exactly straight. One wrong move and we're going to pancake into a tree at seventy miles per hour. So I keep my mouth shut and let her focus on driving.

She glances over at me.

"Road please," I say.

She turns back to the road, but just long enough to see that the next turn is still a few hundred feet off. She looks back. "You're missing something."

"What? I—"

She puts her hand to her head. I duplicate the move, realizing what she's telling me. When I feel my short prickly hair, it's confirmed. My beanie cap is gone. The thing is so much a part of my head that I can still feel it there, like an amputee's ghost limb.

"You shouldn't worry about it," she says. "Look better without it."

Was that a compliment? Before I can blush, I catch a glimpse of fast approaching trees. My head snaps forward. "Turn!"

Collins downshifts and drifts around the curve like a pro before straightening out and accelerating.

After I catch my breath, I loosen my grip on the "oh shit" handle and say, "Can I ask you a serious question?"

She glances at me, but doesn't speak. I take it as permission. "What the hell are you doing out here in Podunk country?"

"What do you mean?" she asks.

"Well, for starters you drive like you were raised in a Fast and the Furious movie. You can shoot as well as anyone I've ever seen, including big-ass machine guns. You've got solid investigative skills, killer instincts and you can fight like a son-of-a-bitch. I would normally say that you're just a Daddy's girl that didn't want to venture too far from town, but you're not from Maine. Or even New England. You are from Georgia right?"

No reply.

"So the real question is, who are you hiding from?"

We take another corner, a little faster than the last. When we straighten out, my head clunks against the door window. Looks like I struck a nerve, though that was not my intention.

"I have a question for you," she says, a little snippy.

Thinking that she's going to ask something tough, maybe about FC-P or my relaxed nature, or maybe make fun of my receding hairline, in exchange for her reply, I say, "Shoot."

"It's twenty minutes to Ashton." She glances at me, eyes dead serious. "Can you try not to talk to me until we get there?"

Really struck a nerve. As I fall silent, we pick up speed, and I think I've just doubled my chances of not surviving the next hour.

24

Trevor Reed didn't much like parades. The average pomp of the town's 4th of July parade was bad enough, but this farmer's nonsense, which had begun long before he became mayor, also smelled like warm shit. And that wasn't an insult to the farmers, because many of them actually carted warm shit through the center of town to sell at the farmer's market as manure.

Reed catered to the town's farmers. They were a part of the economy for now and were well-liked. So he put on a smile, joined the motorcade along with the town's three police officers and waved to his constituents like he cared. But he didn't. Not really. What he cared about was zoning, land laws and minimum lot sizes for new development.

By the time he retired, he planned to have turned the town into the place in Northern Maine to buy a modern, affordable home. Times were tough for the farmers, and as they went out of business, he bought up the land and leased it back to "ease the burden." By the time his current term was up, he would own half the land in town, and most of it was already clear-cut, level farmland. He would save a bundle on deforestation, and the fertile soil would grow grass so green that commuters to Portland or Lewiston wouldn't be able to resist.

Reed cringed in the back seat of the convertible he rode in as the marching band leading the way reached a crescendo that made his spine compress. He never stopped smiling, though. He could hold the practiced expression for hours.

Between beats of the bass drum, he heard a shrill chirp. What kind of an instrument is that, he wondered. Then it repeated, and he saw the police chief, an overweight man named Mitchell Schwartz, pick up his phone and answer it.

The man's face contorted with confusion for a moment as he blocked his other ear with his finger. "What's that, Josie? I can't make out a word!" He listened again, shaking his head in frustration.

The police chief made it just one step away from the car when Reed leaned out and grabbed his arm. "Whatever it is," the mayor said, "it can wait."

"It might be important," Schwartz replied, speaking loudly over the band.

"If I have to endure this hell, so do you," Reed said. "No one is going to like the new zoning laws, which you'll be supporting. We both need to make a good impression or things are going to get difficult."

Reed had made sure that every person in town who held a position of actual power would benefit from the changes he was making. He called it "oiling the gears," but he knew it was closer to bribery. And once someone was complicit, they were his. The police chief would get a new house out of the deal and a good sized chunk of change. All technically legal, but shady enough to scare him. Reed sometimes thought he could probably murder someone and get away with it.

He winced as the crowds lining the sidewalks cheered. Kids screamed as clowns tossed candy. Horses brayed. Some moron was honking an air horn. And far ahead, at the front of the parade, the fire department let their single engine's siren wail. It was sensory chaos.

His smile wavered.

Schwartz saw it and knew what it meant. He shouted into the phone, "I'll call you back, Josie!" Then he hung up.

Reed sat back down on the slippery white leather seat and twisted his lips back up. Schwartz, who was walking next to the car, tried to smile, too, but it wasn't nearly as convincing.

All of a sudden, the marching band's horns stopped. Tension flowed from Reed's shoulders. The drums continued to beat out a rhythm, but he didn't mind that nearly as much as the rest. But then, the drums faded, too, except for a single bass drum that kept time with a boom—boom, boom-boom-boom.

The repetitive beat helped Reed center his thoughts even more. If only the whole parade could be like this. It made all the shouting people and distant chaos bearable. He closed his eyes for a moment, focusing on the drum.

Boom—boom, boom-boom-boom.

Boom—boom, boom-boom-BOOM!

He jumped in his seat with a shout of surprise. He sat up, looking ahead at the bass drum player, but even he was looking around in confusion.

"Sounded like an explosion," Schwartz said, then he looked angry. "Might have been what Josie was calling about." He took out his phone and started dialing.

BOOM!

The sound came from behind the parade. Reed twisted around. The neighborhood just outside of town was a craphole full of old houses he would have liked to tear down. Beyond it, at the crest of the hill was a neighborhood he had built through a development company no one in town knew was owned by him. At least most of the neighborhood at the bottom of the hill was blocked by trees. He looked for an explosion, thinking someone's propane tank must have exploded, but saw nothing. Just trees.

BOOM!

The trees shook.

Then one broke and fell away.

Screams rose in the distance.

Cars were stopped at the edge of the neighborhood as they waited for the parade to pass, but the owners were getting out and running.

What the hell was happening?

BOOM! A foot, or a hand, or...something...dropped down from within the trees and crushed the car at the edge of town.

Reed was only partially aware that the parade and gathered crowd were slowly starting to move away while he remained transfixed. As a result, he saw every detail.

The trees parted and a massive black face, full of malice, pushed through. A pair of eyes that looked almost human, locked onto him. A squeak rose in his throat as the monster pushed through the trees, revealing long, powerful arms and an armored back. The squeak rose in volume, becoming an ear splitting scream.

The shrill cry acted as a catalyst. The monster exploded out of the trees and charged down Main Street.

"Go!" Reed shouted to the driver.

The creature leaned over, biting some people in half as they fled, devouring others whole and crushing many more under its limbs, as it ran on all fours. A long tail whipped back and forth, destroying buildings like they were made from Lego blocks.

"What are you waiting for?" Reed screamed. As he spun around, the first thing he noticed was that the sidewalk had emptied. The second was that Schwartz was gone. And the third was that his driver had taken off on foot. The road was littered with fleeing people, discarded instruments, cars and mobile farm stands.

He stood to leap out of the convertible and flee on foot, but his feet never reached the ground. A sudden numbness spread through his legs, then a pain so intense that he knew the limbs were no longer attached. He screamed, but the sound was muffled, like that time his brothers locked him in the front closet. He couldn't see, either. He felt humid air on his face and smelled something horrible, but the details were lost on his shocked mind.

Then he moved.

He was pushed.

An undulating motion flipped him over.

Then, he fell.

He was only half conscious when he landed. Blood loss and fear had claimed much of his mind. But the jolt of landing mixed with the sharp scent of bile snapped him back to consciousness.

A voice cried out, "Hello? Is someone there?"

It was a woman. He didn't recognize the voice. But it grew sharp a moment later. "It's burning!"

He opened his mouth to reply, but then he felt it too, a sharp, hot sting covering the lower portion of his body. He put his hands down and felt a sludgy goo between his fingers. A moment later, his hands began to burn too.

The woman sloshed and whimpered and then—light.

A small beam of light cut through the dark. The woman had a flashlight. She scanned back and forth, aiming up, revealing moving walls of white and pink. Then she brought it down and Reed wished she hadn't. Bodies—human and animal in various stages of decomposition—were everywhere, heaped up in a pool of white, viscous fluid.

He shouted in fear and the flashlight cut toward him.

"Mayor Reed?" the woman said. "Where—where are we?"

He wasn't entirely sure, but he was beginning to suspect. A sound above them drew the woman's attention and the flashlight beam up. The light arrived just in time to reveal the ceiling of their wet cage opening up. Then, a headless horse fell through.

The large animal slammed on top of Reed, crushing him beneath the murky liquid, which found its way into his lungs and gut, mercifully drowning him before slowly digesting him.

The woman survived for another three hours.

25

In my mind, I know that Woodstock's helicopter moved faster in the air than Collins's Mustang can on the ground, but holy Hell, I feel like I've been strapped to a bullet. Trees whip past in a blur. Street signs with town names come and go before I can fully read them. I have no idea if we're going the right way, but I trust that Evel Knievel Collins know where's she's going.

"Jim, this is Ashley, do you read?" For the past five minutes, Collins has been trying to raise Ashton's small, but efficient police force. So far, they're not answering. She puts the radio down and pushes the gas pedal a little closer to the floor.

When I catch enough letters of a "Welcome to Ashton" sign to piece together the message, I say, "Any other reason they might not be replying?"

She mumbles her answer through grinding teeth.

"What?" I say.

Her teeth are still clenched, but she enunciates the word, "Parade."

Shit.

"Seriously? For what?"

"Summer-Fest Farmer Parade," she says. "Lots of tractors, horses, things like that. Ends in a field where the parade becomes a farmers' market. And there's a corn maze for the kids."

Kids.

The tires squeal as we take a ninety degree turn like it's a broad curve. The front end bursts through the brush on the left hand side of the turn. If there had been anyone coming the opposite way, I don't think anyone would have survived.

Despite what she's just told me about the parade, I say, "Ease up. We're almost there and it would be good if we didn't kill anyone on the way."

We take a sudden right turn, but she slows down enough to stay on the right side of the road, which is good because we've entered a residential neighborhood of identical, megalithic homes. The McMansions have invaded the far north, I think, and then I note all the people standing outside their homes.

"Does the parade come through here?" I ask.

"Uh-uh."

What the hell are they all doing outside?

"Okay, listen," I say, intending to come up with some kind of action plan—defensive perimeter working with whatever local police are in town, evacuation plans, things like that—but then the people outside their homes hear the siren and turn around to face us. They're panic stricken. As though rehearsed, each and every one of them then points down the road, which crests ahead before leading downhill.

I squint in the sunlight streaming through the windshield, but see smoke rising into the air, thick and black. "What's ahead?"

"Downtown," she says and punches the steering wheel three times.

We're too late.

Collins slams the gas pedal to the floor and we launch a few feet in the air as we crest the hill. The car slams back down on the downhill slope. The tires squeal as they catch, and I'm pinned against my seat as we accelerate rapidly. Whoever built the new neighborhood clear-cut the old trees and planted new ones, so our view of what's below is clear, though part of me wishes it wasn't.

Downtown looks to be mostly brick buildings—the kind scattered throughout all of New England—but it's mired in smoke. The sun shines off lines of parked cars, but I can't see any movement. The road is littered with debris. Still, it's clear we won't be speeding through town. As we close the distance, passing through older neighborhoods with tall trees and smaller homes, I lose sight of the town, but it's not long before we see the first signs of damage.

Collins brakes hard and swerves, barely avoiding a collision with an old station wagon that's been crushed in the middle. I look for bodies when we pass, but see none. They either got out and away, or—

Another car. A small one. It's so flat that I can't make out what it used to be, but the red-smeared window tells me that the owner was still inside when it was compressed.

Collins slows.

"Keep going," I say. "No way they survived."

She shakes her head in anger and continues past the car. Then fifteen more. Then thirty. And they're all like the first two—empty or bloodied. But not all of them are crushed. Some are on their roofs. Some have been peeled open, and judging by the blood splatter, their occupants plucked out.

"Why are there so many?" I wonder aloud.

"They were waiting for the parade to pass," Collins explains.

For the creature, it must have been like finding a buffet.

The last few cars are unharmed. The doors are open. The occupants gone. The monster didn't waste time with them. Why not?

I roll down my window, hoping to hear signs of life, battle or the creature's whereabouts. But I don't hear anything. Instead, I get a pungent waft of farm—hay, manure and horse shit—mixed with blood, smoke and vinegar. My stomach turns and I quickly roll up the window.

Collins drives with one hand on the wheel, the other covering her nose and mouth. But the smell isn't the worst of it; the sight we find upon reaching downtown Ashton is something I will never be able to forget.

The first thing I notice are the bodies. Not one of them is whole. There are legs, arms, torsos, heads and unrecognizable heaps of guts. I realize I'm trying to count the dead, but there are too many of them and they're...all mixed up. But there must be hundreds. And it's not just people. Bits and pieces of horses, cows, goats and assorted other farm animals are scattered around, mixed with human remains and strewn fruit and vegetable crops.

When I feel my stomach tensing and taste bile in my mouth, I divert my attention away from the dead and look at the structural damage. A few of the buildings have been destroyed, blown out into the street. That's where it entered town, I think. Almost all of the rest are in a partial state of destruction. They'll have to be demolished before the town can be rebuilt, but it's possible they could contain survivors. At the center of town, just a block ahead where a small traffic circle wraps around a park and gazebo, is a stark white church engulfed in flames. If anyone sought refuge in God's house, they were dying horribly now if they weren't dead already.

And there isn't a thing we can do about it. I would like nothing more than to rush out of the car and save some lives, but there isn't a single sign of life anywhere, and there's no way for Collins or me to put out a fire, stabilize the buildings or—if it's still nearby—combat the creature. Besides, I don't think I'd make it five steps before collapsing and puking my guts out.

When my eyes come back to the carnage, details leap out at me. An array of shiny metal is mixed in with the dead. A tuba. A trumpet. Red and white uniforms. A marching band. I turn to the side and find a ruined food stand. Its still-standing sign reads "Fried Dough! Yum!" The corpses on the sidewalks are mixed with balloons, popcorn boxes and blood-soaked cotton candy.

In a flash, I picture this classic scene of small town Americana— the smiles, the laughs, the families. Then the horrible slaughter that followed—the screams and the horror of seeing parents, or children, killed. Eaten. Tears fill my eyes.

My vision is blurred when I see movement in the distance.

"What is that?" I ask, wiping my eyes.

Collins is wiping her own eyes when she says, "I'm not sure."

Blinking away the last of my tears, I see a girl, no older than ten, limping down the center of Main Street. She's injured, but neither the wound, nor the destruction, nor even the layers of dead covering the street are slowing her down.

"It's still here," I say.

Collins sucks in a quick breath, adrenaline sharpening her eyes.

"Turn the car around," I say.

"What are you going to do?"

"I'll be right back." I throw open the door and sprint toward the girl. My first step lands in a slick of blood that nearly topples me to the ground, so I look down and pick my steps, trying to see the bodies as obstacles. It doesn't really work, but watching my feet helps me avoid some missteps that would have destroyed my psyche and left me in a fetal position for a few months.

I find the girl by colliding with her. We both spill to the ground—she to the bare pavement, me against the back of a half eaten horse. She screams as we fall, but stops when I say, "It's okay. I'm here to help you."

Her head snaps up toward me. Her big blue eyes glimmer with tears and her soot-coated cheeks are covered with clean streaks from crying. She's out of breath, but already getting to her feet. The blue and white checkered dress she's wearing is covered in blood, which from what I can see, is not hers. With her two braids, she looks a little like Laura Ingalls from Little House on the Prairie.

"You can't help," she says. "You can't—you'll just—you can't."

She's hysterical, and really, who can blame her? I'm almost there, too.

Then her face screws up with fear and her eyes drift high above my head.

Fuck. My. Ass.

I turn around and face the big white church on the opposite side of the traffic circle. A shape, as black as the smoke, cuts through the rising cloud. A massive hand reaches forward and claws at the building's roof, which peels apart like it's made of gingerbread and frosting. Orange light glows through the smoke, getting brighter until the head slips through and bites down on the tall steeple, shattering it.

The beast is bigger now. It's impossible to tell just how much, but the church isn't small, and the creature is making short work of the building. But it hasn't seen us, yet, so that's—

The shrill scream tenses all of my muscles. I freeze in place, half standing and watching as the giant stops its assault on the church and cranes its head toward the girl.

And me.

Stand still, I tell myself. Stand still and you'll just blend in with the dead and it won't be able to see you.

But this girl is not Collins, and we are decidedly not on the same page.

She turns and runs.

The church explodes outwards as the creature roars and fights its way through the building.

The roar is so loud that I'm momentarily stunned, but then I'm sprinting and bunny-hopping over the dead. I reach the girl quickly. She screams as I scoop her up. And even though she must realize that I'm trying to save her, she continues to scream as I run through town like a wide receiver being pursued by an opposing team armed with assault rifles. Of course, the truth is much worse than that.

A loud crack and rumble behind me signifies the destruction of the church. The girl's scream rises another octave. The ground shakes. A roar weakens my limbs. As I approach the far side of town, I look up for the car and feel all hope drain away.

The car is missing.

Collins is gone.

26

By the time I reach the far edge of town, my legs, lungs and just about every other part of me is burning with the kind of tired I know is going to hurt worse in two days than it does right now. But I'm pretty sure I've got about ten seconds until I feel a crushing pain and then nothing at all.

In my darker moments, usually when I'm bored, I have imagined what it would be like to be on death row, or a POW before a firing squad or diagnosed with something terminal. It's morbid, but what does it feel like to know you have just seconds, minutes, hours or days left to live? Granted, anyone can kick the bucket at any time for a million different reasons, but to know, without a doubt, that death looms just over the horizon is different. I know that now. I can feel death thundering up behind me, brazen in its approach.

It moves in for the kill with a squeal.

From the side?

As I turn to face my end, I see a flash of blue slide up next to me.

The Mustang!

Collins throws the door open from the inside. She doesn't say anything. Doesn't have to. I throw myself and the girl into the car and before I've had a chance to right myself or close the door, Collins hits the gas.

The car's acceleration combined with a hard thump from behind that pushes the car forward, knocks the door shut—on my legs. I shout, thinking I've been bit, but then realize the pain isn't that bad. The girl moves herself off of me, giving me space to pull my legs in and right myself in the seat. Once upright, I slam the door closed and pull the girl into my lap, quickly adjusting the seat to accommodate both of us. In the few seconds it's taken me to do all this, Collins has accelerated to 50 mph.

I close my eyes and sigh with relief.

"Hudson!" Collins shouts. "Snap out of it!"

I sit up fast, my relief shattered, and bump my head into the girl's elbow. I turn to Collins to ask what's wrong when I see a flash of movement in my periphery. I glance back in time to see a large, clawed leg land just behind the car.

My head twists to the speedometer. 55 mph. Collins shifts and gives the engine all the fuel it can handle. 60mph.

I look back and the creature has only fallen behind enough that I can see its whole body. It's definitely bigger now, but no less agile. It runs on four legs, just like the first time I saw it outside the secret BioLance lab. The spines on its back are longer now, and the carapace they're attached to is thick and looks harder than tank armor. With every step it takes, the membranes on the sides of its neck and body glow brighter.

The whine of the Mustang's gears grows higher. Collins takes her foot off the gas for just a moment to push in the clutch and slam into the next gear, but in that momentary lag, the monster strikes.

Its jaws drop open to reveal monstrous, scimitar teeth, a thick wriggling tongue and a throat that's glowing orange, though more dully than the membranes on the neck. A roar vibrates the entire car, along with my teeth, and the creature lunges forward. As the giant jaws snap shut, the Mustang's gears catch and we surge out of reach.

I watch the speedometer climb.

70 mph.

The angry monster leaps after us, keeping pace.

We hit the hill leading toward the McMansions and their unharmed occupants.

75 mph, fighting gravity.

We seem to find a momentary equilibrium with the creature. Is 75 mph its top speed? How is that even possible? But then I look at the speedometer again.

80 mph.

It's keeping pace. Does it think the car will grow tired? Does it know the car will eventually run out of gas? Or has it detected the homes full of people up ahead and it's happy to just follow us?

85 mph.

"We need to get off this road," I say.

"There aren't any side roads," Collins points out, but I already know this.

"We need to run," I say. "On foot. Through the woods. Three different directions."

The girl whimpers at this idea. Collins balks. "Why the hell would we—"

She figures it out. "Damnit." We passed somewhere between fifty and a hundred people in the jam-packed family neighborhood. By continuing any further we are sentencing each and every one of them to death.

"Kid," I say. "I saw you run. You're fast. Just keep to the trees. Find a cave, or some fallen trees to hide beneath. If it comes your way, I'll distract it."

It's not exactly a wonderful pep-talk, but I've just offered to take the fall for her if it comes to it. So when she says, "Are you stupid?" I'm a little surprised, but then she explains by pointing at the speedometer.

90 mph.

Yeah, it's a stupid plan. But I can't very well lead this thing into a neighborhood to save my own skin. Odds are, I'll be eaten anyway and then have one more thing to answer for upon reaching the Pearly Gates. I'm still not sure how I'm going to explain breaking into my neighbor's house to look at Juggs magazines when I was sixteen.

"Collins," I say. It's just a name, but she knows what it means. It's time.

She lifts her foot from the gas.

Before she can hit the brakes, a large shape comes over the top of the hill. At first I think it's a giant grasshopper head, but then the rest comes into view. Woodstock! The helicopter pulls up hard and swivels to the side just in time to miss being crushed in the monster's jaws.

As the chopper circles fast, the monster spins around and roars before lunging and missing again.

Collins's foot finds the gas pedal again, and we race up the hill while the creature pounds after the chopper, which is now well out of reach.

It must remember the helicopter, I think. I didn't think we hurt it much, but given how fast it went for the chopper, we must have made an impression. That doesn't give me any kind of satisfaction. It's far larger now and the helicopter's machine gun will be even more useless.

When we reach the top of the long hill, Collins pulls over in front of a three-story home with a three-car garage. The owner stands by the garage, waving us over. Collins pulls into the driveway and rolls down her window.

"Looked like that thing wanted your car bad," the man says. His eyes are wide and his skin probably far whiter than usual, but he's speaking clearly. "Pull into the garage. We can close the door and hide you."

Collins gives the man a nod and accepts his offer.

"We have a bomb shelter in the back if you want to hide," he says. "Been gathering the neighbors."

I climb out of the car with the girl and look down the street. Where there were rows of families lining the streets, there are now just a few stragglers rushing this way, led by a woman in a nightgown.

"That's Deb," the man says. "My wife. She's a lot faster than me on account of the arthritis."

I nearly make a sarcastic remark about not needing the man's medical history, but if that creature had reached the top of the hill, a lot of lives might have been saved because of this man. Still might be. "Thanks," I say. "For what you're doing."

"Who's this?" he asks, looking at the girl in my arms.

Before I can answer, the girl turns to face him and I see a flash of recognition. "Joy?"

"You know her?" I ask.

He nods. "I'm her softball coach."

"Found her in town," I say. The message and my tone carry the weight of what this means. "She's going to need help finding her family when this is all over."

The man looks grim. "All right." He reaches his hands out to the girl and she slides over to him. "I gotcha, Joy." With a nod, he departs. As they head for the back of the garage, I see the girl bury her face into the shoulder of a man she clearly trusts. Her body shakes with deep, heart-breaking sobs.

I storm back into the street, looking toward town and wishing I could grow into a giant version of myself, like in one of those Japanese kids shows, and beat the living shit out of this thing. Collins joins me, watching in silence as the helicopter becomes a speck in the distance.

I can't see the creature past the ruins of the town, but its frustrated roar pierces the air one last time.

When my phone rings, Collins and I both jump. I answer it quickly. "What?"

"Just got the live satellite feed," Watson says.

"Little too late," I growl.

"The request was delayed by the Deputy Director's office. They wanted to confirm the legitimacy of your request. Why? What happened?" he asks.

My face turns red with anger. Having satellite coverage might not have done much to save lives, but any future delays might. Of course, there is another question along these lines. "I asked for you to warn all law enforcement in the area. Why wasn't anyone in town notified to evacuate? Half the town was there for a damn farmer's parade!"

"We called," Watson says, sounding upset. "Three times. Got the same secretary each time. Said she was trying to get the call out, but no one was answering on account of the parade."

I sigh. It's not Watson's fault, but he needs to know what's at stake. "Still tracking Collins's phone?"

"Yeah."

"Ashton is about one mile south of our current location," I say. "Take a look."

Five seconds pass and then I hear him curse, again and again as he scrolls through the town.

There's a click and I can tell by the switch in audio quality that I'm on speaker. "What happened?" It's Cooper. She must have been standing beside him when he zoomed in.

"Short version," I say, "is that our big problem is a hell of a lot bigger now. Ted, scan south and zoom out a bit. See anything?"

Watson's voice has a quiver to it as he replies. The top view of the town's destruction and gore is probably shocking. "Just lots of trees and—wait, there's a helicopter. It's pretty high, though. Headed in your direction."

"There's nothing behind it?" I ask.

"Like in the air?" he says. "No."

"Or on the ground?" I say.

"No, nothing," he says. "Should there be?"

Part of me thinks, God no, but the rest of me realizes that if the monster isn't coming back, it has continued its rampage toward Maine's most dense population.

I ignore the question. "Coop, please inform Director Stephens that Ashton, Maine has been destroyed. Hundreds, possibly thousands are dead. Tell him that if he delays a request from me again I will personally put a bullet in his head."

"That's not going to help," she says plainly.

"Then translate it into whatever kind of threat will help."

"Done," she says, all business, no emotion. It's cold, but it helps me focus.

"What kind of response do we have available?" I ask.

"National Guard is on stand-by, as are SWAT teams in Portland and Northern New Hampshire. Heavier hitters are farther out."

"What about Air Force?"

"You want an airstrike on U.S. soil?" Coop asks, sounding a little surprised.

"Might save a few thousand people," I say. "So, yeah. I do."

"I'll look into it."

"No, Coop," I say, nearly shouting. "You will God damn do it and right this fucking minute."

Silence.

I continue. "Pick out a strategic location where we can defend the Northern area of the city; the nearest forested area and as far away from the population as possible. Have everyone available rendezvous there. Ted, once this location has been chosen, forward the satellite feed to Collins's phone and mark the LZ. By the time I get there I better see an army waiting for me and A-10 Thunderbolts circling the city, understood?"

More silence. I've been working with both for years, and they've gotten accustomed to my lax temperament, so my spitfire is probably throwing them for a loop. The loudest they've ever heard me shout before was when I lost a game of ping pong and fifty bucks, against Watson. I make an effort to lower my voice. "Guys," I say. "I can't do this without you. You can hate me later."

"Done," Cooper says, and I hear her heels clacking away.

"Yeah," Ted says. "And boss, next time I'll just take the satellite."

"You can do that?" I ask, surprised and a little confused.

"I can do a lot," he says, and the way he says it makes me wonder if there is another reason Watson got posted to the ass-end of the DHS.

The helicopter thunders overhead and descends toward the street.

"Thanks, Ted," I say and hang up.

Collins heads for her car while I rush toward the helicopter as it sets down. I take my seat in the front of the chopper and put on the headset. Woodstock looks to me, his face grim. "Where we heading?"

The side door slides open. Collins climbs in with weapons, ammo and a spare tactical vest for Woodstock. She slams the door closed and shouts, "Let's go!"

As the helicopter lifts into the air, I answer Woodstock's question. "Take us south to Portland. Exact coordinates are incoming."

"We going to kill that sonuvabitch?" he asks.

Despite my advice to Watson, and Yoda's advice to Luke, I say, "We're going to try."

27

General Lance Gordon had rarely, if ever, felt so good in his life. The new heart had returned him to the energy of his youth and beyond. He felt sharper, more focused and had a sense of purpose that went far beyond anything he had done for the U.S. military and his covert employment with Zoomb since. The enemies destroyed, the lives saved and the technology developed, all of it seemed trivial now.

His mind was awake for the first time in his life. He wondered if his heart had just been shitty from the get-go and this is what other people felt like. But when he looked around and saw the sluggish look in the day-to-dayers passing by the car, he knew that wasn't true. If anything, he'd already lived a fuller life than most.

"How much longer?" he asked.

Endo looked back from the front seat of the black BMW. "We're five minutes out."

They'd been driving for most of the day, taking a maze of Maine back roads until they reached Route 95 and sped south through Maine, New Hampshire and Massachusetts, where they connected with Route 1 to finish the journey to Boston. They'd just crossed the utilitarian looking, pale green Tobin Memorial Bridge, and were headed downtown to the Prudential Tower where Zoomb had offices and the resources Gordon needed—computers, Internet connection, a secure location and a private locker to which only Gordon had access.

He didn't exactly know why he needed those things yet, it was just a gut feeling, a burning desire to find out...something...and then what? He wasn't sure. He just knew he had to look.

In Boston.

He could feel her still. Maigo. But distant, like an old memory. At first he thought it might have something to do with the girl. She was from Boston and he felt drawn here, but he suspected it had more to do with her other half—the portion of her unearthed from the Alaskan mountainside after his "retirement." They'd given him everything he wanted—a staggering finder's fee and control of BioLance—after verifying the find, purchasing the land and extracting the body, in pieces, to a location that even he didn't know.

Finding out where that was and what Zoomb knew about the creature were his next steps. After that—his gut would guide him. And Endo, ever faithful, would follow. Or drive.

Despite the lack of mid-day traffic, Endo slowed the car far short of the Prudential Tower parking garage. Gordon knew the man well enough to intuit something was amiss. "What is it?"

"Black suburban," Endo said. "One o'clock."

Gordon easily spotted the big black SUV parked a block ahead, just across the street from the parking garage.

"Looks like FBI," Endo added.

Gordon nodded. "You think they'd switch to pink hybrids eventually. Might as well have a bright yellow FBI stenciled on the sides."

"Think they're here for us?" Endo asked.

"Only one way to find out," the general replied.

Endo gave a nod and pulled back out into the street. Gordon rolled down his tinted window and looked out, pretending to gaze at the tall buildings. They rolled past the Suburban slowly, long enough for everyone inside to get a good long look at his face. After they passed, he sat back and rolled up the window.

"Here they come," Endo said, looking in the rearview mirror. "What's our engagement protocol?"

The engagement protocol was typically put in place by Zoomb's head of covert security. Every site operated under different protocols, numbered one through ten. Level one was cheery and friendly—wide open to the public. The BioLance facility was rated an eight, which meant they could engage with deadly force if the facility was in danger of being revealed to the public. Had the facility been rated a seven, the Sheriff and the DHS agent would have simply been monitored until a solid threat was confirmed. Had it been set to nine, they would have been shot long before ever reaching the perimeter fence.

"Ten," Gordon answered.

Endo nodded and pulled into the garage, slowing to take a ticket and then driving casually inside and taking the ramp up. They rounded the corner and drove up again, reaching a section of the garage with numbered, reserved spaces. Gordon's space was number 576. It was a normal parking space, half way up the long ramp, no different than all the rest with one exception—it was dead center in a thirty-foot-long security camera blind spot.

Before the SUV made it around the first turn, Endo exited the car and dashed to the far side of the garage. While he did, Gordon stood and got into the driver's seat. As he closed the door, the Suburban roared up the ramp and screeched to a halt behind the BMW, blocking it in.

Four agents poured out of the big vehicle. Two took up defensive positions behind the hood of the SUV, aiming their handguns at random spots on the car. Two others quickly approached the BMW, weapons drawn. One man aimed at Gordon's head, the other at the empty back seat.

Gordon knew the drill and kept his hands on the steering wheel.

"General Lance Gordon!" the nearest man shouted. "FBI! Keep your hands where I can see them!"

Gordon turned slowly, facing the man with a smirk.

"I thought you said he was in the rear passenger's seat?" the man said to no one in particular.

"He was," one of the men back by the SUV shouted back.

When the nearest FBI man saw Gordon's grin widen, he realized the truth. He started to shout a warning, but Gordon pulled the handle on his door and kicked it open. The heavy door struck the man's leg with a crack. The man dropped to the concrete floor, screaming and clutching his shattered knee.

As the second, very surprised man jumped back and adjusted his aim toward Gordon, the old general lunged out with shocking speed and clutched the weapon, and the man's hand, crushing both. The man started to scream, but Gordon yanked him in close and delivered a punch to the man's chest. Beneath his knuckles, he felt ribs bend, separate and then break. He felt muscle and sinew tearing away. He felt the man's raw heart, flex inward, and burst.

When he drew his fist back, the man was dead, his chest caved in like he'd been on the receiving end of a cannon ball.

Gordon looked up and saw Endo grappling with the fourth FBI agent, a dead man already at their feet. When he looked away, he heard a crack and knew the agent was dead. He closed the door to his car and stood over the FBI agent whose knee he'd turned to powder.

The man watched as Gordon picked up the dropped handgun.

"Glock 23," Gordon said. "Standard issue. Not really a man's gun, is it, though?"

The agent didn't reply.

"Still, I suppose it will kill a man just as good as anything."

"Don't—don't shoot me," the agent said. "I have kids."

"Then you're in the wrong line of work," Gordon replied. "But don't worry. Answer my question and I won't shoot you."

The man nodded.

"Who requested I be brought in?"

The agent looked uncomfortable answering, but when Gordon gently tapped the man's knee with the gun barrel, he blurted out, "DHS!"

"Which office?"

"I—I don't know," the man cried. "It was a Fusion Center, but it didn't have a city designation. Just a P. Fusion Center – P!"

Gordon stared into the man's eyes. He'd seen the look before. The utter desperation. Plus, giving away the identity of the arresting agency wasn't exactly a breach in security. He believed the man. It meant that agent Hudson had survived the BioLance building's destruction. He would have to be dealt with, but not yet.

Gordon put the gun down on the concrete and smiled at the man, who looked relieved. Then he placed his thick hand over the man's neck and slowly increased the pressure. The agent fought, despite the severe pain it must have caused his leg. He punched, jabbed pressure points and kicked his good leg into Gordon's groin.

None of it fazed the general. He felt very little pain.

The agent's face turned deep red, and just before the man lost consciousness, something in the neck cracked. The flesh compressed quickly after that, and the man's body laid still.

A shifting sound took the general's attention away from the man. He looked back and found Endo dragging the man with the cratered chest to the open back hatch of the SUV where two bodies already waited.

"You are a marvel of efficiency, Endo," Gordon said as the man tossed the dead agent into the vehicle. Gordon picked up the agent with the crushed neck, lifting him with one hand. He carried the man to the SUV and put him in with the rest.

Endo closed the SUV's rear door and turned to the general. "You seem...well, sir."

Gordon grinned. "Better than that."

Endo nodded. "The heart?"

"There is no doubt about that," Gordon answered. "It would seem a little bit of our large Alaskan friend hitched a ride with my new organ."

"Is it safe?" Endo asked.

The question annoyed the general, but Endo had watched out for his safety for the past five years. It was his job to ask those kinds of questions. Gordon nodded. "I will let you know the second I feel anything but stellar."

Endo gave a nod, before turning away, climbing into the SUV and pulling away. He'd park it in a visitor spot where it wouldn't be discovered for days. Gordon looked around the garage.

Not a drop of blood or a sign of a struggle.

He bent down and picked up the lone discarded handgun and slid it beneath the driver's seat of his BMW before locking the doors and strutting away. If security was even watching the garage feeds, they would simply see Gordon's vehicle enter the dead zone and the SUV follow. Since both vehicles had tinted windows, they would never know Endo hadn't been driving the SUV all along.

Gordon opened the trunk, which contained his discarded hospital clothes, and opened a briefcase. Inside was a custom made, sound suppressed .50 caliber Desert Eagle handgun. It could punch a hole in a man's chest big enough to leap through without making much more sound than a cough. He chambered a round, tucked the weapon behind his back and headed for the elevator.

As the doors pinged open, Endo slid up next to the general and stepped inside. They both turned around to face the garage.

"Do you think security has been told to watch for us?" Endo asked.

Gordon looked at Endo. "Only one way to find out."

Both men smiled.

The doors slid closed and the elevator shot up toward the fiftieth floor of Boston's second tallest building.

28

As we descend over the staging area, I'm glad to see an array of armed men. Some are dressed in all black—police and SWAT. Others in camouflage military fatigues—the National Guard. I count at least a hundred men and can see transport vehicles arriving from the north and south.

Watson determined that Route 95 would make the best place to stage our assault. Troops could reach the location quickly and it was a wide open area. This specific stretch of highway is optimal, because on one side is a thickly wooded golf course that abuts the forest we believe the creature is traveling through. On the other side, to our backs, is a row of warehouses that have been emptied.

It's rush hour and the sun is heading for the horizon, so we've created the mother of all traffic jams, but if this thing shows up, it might decide to just follow 95 south and munch on every car it meets. If it doesn't show up, I'm going to be working at McDonald's by morning. Of course, that would actually be preferable to this thing laying waste to Portland. But I don't think we'll be that fortunate. I have no doubt that handing out Happy Meals is not in my future.

When I see Rod Cugliari, head of FC-Boston, storming toward my helicopter, I know my colleagues don't share the same opinion. Technically, Cugliari and I have the same position and rank. We're both directors of Fusion Centers and act as lead field investigators. We take orders from the same person, Deputy Director Stephens, or the people he takes orders from, but neither of us can give orders to the other. That doesn't stop him from feeling superior. It's no secret that FC-Boston views FC-P as a thorn in its side and as an embarrassment to the DHS as a whole. No one really knows that we exist, and Cugliari would like to keep it that way. So the fact that I have raised the threat level and mobilized a response has his face—what little of it can be see behind his Magnum P.I. mustache—turning beet red.

"He doesn't look too happy," Woodstock says, nodding at Cugliari, who is now waiting with his arms crossed.

"He rarely does," I say. "At least when I'm around."

"You sleep with his sister or something?"

Cugliari is a company man through and through. He has no other major devotion in his life. So he might very well see me the way a husband does his wife's ex-boyfriend. "Or something." I turn to Collins. "Stick with me, okay? Both of you."

They both nod.

"Let's go." I open my door and hop down on the highway pavement. The air is cooler and dryer here, and smells slightly of salt. We're not far from the ocean, which makes me feel a little more at home. Portland and Beverly, the home of FC-P, are both coastal cities with a lot of history, culture and arts. But Portland is twice the size and has a far denser population.

"You've got some nerve, Hudson," Cugliari shouts over the sounds of the winding-down helicopter, the prepping troops and the freshly arriving transports.

"Nice to see you, too, Rod." I say his name with the same sarcastic vitriol that one might use to address a schoolyard bully named Tad or Chaz. It's not intentional. That's just how I say his name.

"You looking to go out in a blaze of glory?" he asks.

"Not remotely," I say, not really in the mood for antagonistic banter.

He lets out an angry laugh that sounds like a long drawn out, "fffff," shakes his head quickly and says, "You do realize that this is the largest mobilization of U.S. military and emergency response forces since 9-11, right?"

I look around at all the men with guns.

Guns.

I see assault rifles, hand guns and a few SWAT guys with sniper rifles.

"Not big enough," I say. "Where are my heavy hitters?"

"Your heavy hitters?" Cugliari says. "I think you've misread the situation, Hudson. I am in charge here. Not you. And right now, my priority is saving the DHS some face. Best we can hope for is that the media will believe this was all an elaborate emergency-response training exercise for which the public could not be warned."

"What do you mean, 'could not be warned?'" Collins asks, beating me to the punch.

Cugliari regards Collins for the first time, then seems to notice Woodstock. "Who are they?"

I nod to each of them as I introduce them. "Sheriff Ashley Collins. Rich Woodall, Chief Warrant Officer Five, U.S. Marines." I leave off the retired bit. "They've been assisting me—"

"And now they can be done assisting you," Cugliari says. "We have all the personnel we need."

"Rod, this is a—" I can barely bring myself to say it, but shove the words out, "—paranormal threat. My office and my office alone has jurisdiction, whether the event is in your territory or Hawaii."

"Thanks for reminding me," Cugliari says. "You don't have a full team. Regulations say that each Fusion Center must have a minimum of three field team members and two office coordinators. You've been a three-man operation for years. Even if this was a paranormal threat, which it's not, you don't have the person—"

"That's why I've hired Collins and Woodall," I say, and am thrilled when neither of the two objects. They might later, but they no doubt understand that I'm up against a wall and that Cugliari is a dick.

He laughs in a way that makes me think he's going to wave his hand at me and say, "The very idea," but he just turns away and says,

"Just stay out of my way and I'll put in a good word. See if you can't be the janitor for FC-Boston."

"You want me to pop this guy?" Woodstock asks. He's just met the man, but his fists are clenched and his eyes are shooting lasers through the back of Cugliari's head.

Collins puts her hand on my arm. "You need to put jurisdiction aside. Focus on the big picture."

Right. The big picture is that all these people are going to die.

Collins's unanswered question hits me like a kick in the nuts. "Rod!" I shout it loud and angry enough that a good number of people turn and look, putting Rod on the spot. He turns around slowly. "Did you cancel my evacuation order?"

"You mean, did I save the City of Portland from widespread chaos that would result in the loss of life and property? You bet to hell I did." He gets in my face. "We're in the business of protecting lives, not endangering them."

I point to the city beyond the highway. "You need to get those people away from here." My eyes wander and I start looking for other requests that might have been canceled. There's no heavy ordinance. No tanks. No mortar. No anti-tank missile teams. The biggest guns I see are turret machine guns mounted to the top of five Humvees. They won't be any more use than Woodstock's helicopter-mounted weapon. I turn my right ear to the sky and ignore everything else. If there were jets circling the city, I would hear them.

"Everyone who dies here today," I say, "it's on you."

He cocks his head to the side, steps closer and twitches his mustache. "That a threat?"

I'm a millisecond away from pummeling Cugliari when a National Guard soldier approaches with a large handheld tablet like an iPad, but twice the size. "Sir, the satellite link is up."

Cugliari takes the tablet and looks at the image. It's a view of Portland, centered on the staging area. What I immediately notice is the number of cars moving on the streets behind us. Beyond the warehouses are blocks of residential neighborhoods, then the city proper and finally the ocean. The forest opposite the highway looks undisturbed, but that doesn't make me feel any better.

Cugliari, on the other hand, feels vindicated. "There's nothing there." Using the touch screen, he moves the image north. "Nothing at all."

"Can you point this thing somewhere else?" I ask the National Guardsman.

He nods. "Most anywhere in Maine and Northern New Hampshire."

"Bring up Ashton, Maine," I tell him.

"Showing me an empty town that was evacuated on your order isn't going to change any—"

"Evacuated?" I shout. "Have you even been paying attention?"

"You mean to your reports of an imaginary giant monster stomping its way through Maine? You've been marshaling forces based on your word alone. You lied about a biological threat, Hudson. You're in serious—"

The Guardsman saves Cugliari from a beat down. "Oh my God."

Cugliari looks at the satellite image. The town of Ashton looks like a scar on the face of the planet. "What is that?"

"That is Ashton," I tell him. "What's left of it."

I can see flashing lights of emergency vehicles on the fringes of downtown, but they probably have no idea what to do. "Zoom in," I say. "Center of town."

When Cugliari doesn't move, the Guardsman does it for him.

As the images of death and destruction come into focus, I watch all of Cugliari's anger and resolve melt away. "What happened?"

"That would be the imaginary giant monster," Woodstock answers.

"Ashton never got my evacuation order," I say. "If they had, all those people might still be alive. Instead, the town is a graveyard. Rod." When he doesn't look at me, I raise my voice. "Rod!" His head snaps toward me. I point to the warehouses behind us. "There are sixty-two thousand more people on the other side of these buildings than there were in Ashton. Their lives are at risk, because of you. Order the evacuation. Get me my heavy hitters. And call back the God-damned jets."

He's about to nod when Collins speaks up. "Jon..."

The worry in her voice tenses my back into a steel plate. I look at her and she taps her nose. I take a sniff.

Vinegar.

"What is it?" Cugliari asks.

I ignore him and speak to the Guardsman. "Can we get infrared on that thing?"

He nods.

"Do it. And center on us," I order.

Five seconds later, the screen becomes a rainbow of colors. We're looking at a city, so there are a lot of hotspots, but I'm not looking for car, home or people sized hotspots. The Guardsman points to the center of the screen where a large number of small, bright pink dots can be seen. "That's us, but, something is wrong with the image."

"What?"

He turns the screen toward me and points to a large, solid hotspot.

"Where is that?" I ask.

He points across the highway, to the trees. "Right there."

"Aww shit," Woodstock says.

"What?" Cugliari says. "What's wrong?"

"It's already here," Collins says.

29

Cugliari looks at the woods lining the far side of the highway. The trees are mostly maples, standing fifty to seventy-five feet tall, mixed with new growth pines that are nearly as big. "I don't see any—"

A loud crack cuts him off. Then another. The woods on the other side of the highway shake and sway. Trees fall, swooshing to the ground. And then rising above it all, standing on its hind legs and towering over the tree line, is the creature. It turns its head toward the sky and lets out a roar that shakes the pavement beneath our feet.

I take Cugliari's arm in my hands and squeeze until the pain draws his eyes away from the monster and back to me. "Get me those Air Force jets. Get them now!"

He stumbles away, but fishes into his pocket for a phone. As he quickly speaks, he walks backward, toward the warehouses without taking his eyes off the creature.

I turn to Woodstock and motion to his chopper. "Get her ready!" Then to Collins, "Come with me or stay here, it's up to you. I'm not sure either will do any good."

Then I'm running toward the collection of Humvees, and though I don't show it, I'm thrilled to find Collins keeping pace. As I pass by lines of soldiers, who have taken aim, but wisely held their fire, I shout, "Wait for it to clear the trees! Aim for the legs!" I have zero faith in this force's ability to actually kill the creature, but if we can immo-bilize it long enough for an air strike, that might do the trick. At the very least, we might be able to wound its legs, giving it a limp or the equivalent of monster hangnail.

"Cougar!" A man yells to me. I recognize him as one of the FC-Boston investigators under Cugliari. His name is David Price. He's clearly mista-ken me for his boss, probably because I'm shouting orders. When he sees my face, he stops short. "Hudson? Where's Coug—Cugliari?"

I look back for the FC-Boston director and spot him far off, retreat-ing toward the warehouses. "The cougar has become a cowardly lion."

The man sees his boss running. "The fuck!"

"You're under my command now," I say.

Price nods.

"Make sure these men aim for the legs and hold their fire until I give the order, understood?"

"Yes sir!"

I hear him barking orders as I sprint away and continue to shout my own, repeating the message to aim low and hold. When I reach the Humvees I'm fairly out of breath, but I repeat the orders to the five men manning the machine guns mounted to the top of the vehicles.

A second roar spins me around and the volume of it nearly drops me to my knees. Trees crack as the giant takes a single step forward.

"Hold your fire!" I scream.

"Hey!" A hand on my shoulder spins me around. I come face-to-face with a third FC-Boston agent whose name I either never learned or forgot outright. But he clearly knows who I am. An older National Guardsman with an arm patch that reveals he's a Sergeant Major—likely in charge of this unit—and whose name tag reads Humm, stands behind him looking equal parts terrified by the monster and confused by the confrontation. "You're not giving the orders here, Hudson!"

"We don't have time for this," Collins says, pushing me aside and driving her fist into the agent's stomach. The man folds over her fist with an expulsion of air and falls to the ground.

Sergeant Major Humm looks a little shocked, but when I step over the fallen man and say, "I'm DHS Fusion Center-P, Director Hudson. I've taken command," the man just nods.

"You have anything with more punch?" I ask.

More trees fall, many of them into the far side of the highway. Behind me, I hear Price shouting for the men to hold their fire.

"Humm!" I shout, regaining the man's attention.

"Uh," he says, coming to his senses. "More punch than the .50 cals?"

"A lot more," I say.

He shakes his head slowly, but then his eyes widen. "We've got an M-32 grenade launcher!" He leads us to the back of the second Humvee and opens the hatch. Inside is what looks like an oversized black briefcase. He punches in a combination and lifts the lid to reveal a grenade launcher with six barrels, like an oversized revolver. He lifts it out and hands it to me. I have no idea how to fire the weapon, but he says, "She's fully loaded and the safety is off."

Just aim and shoot, I think.

Collins reaches into the back of the vehicle and takes out an MP5 assault rifle. She checks the magazine, stuffs it back in and slaps the cocking lever forward.

"Here it comes!" someone shouts.

I turn and see a tree-sized leg step out of the shaded woods. The taloned, four-toed foot drops down on the far side of the highway, pulverizing the blacktop. On its hind legs, the monster now stands a colossal eighty feet tall. It leans forward and looks down at the throng of men, bravely holding their ground. Its large, human eyes scan back and forth, perhaps a little confused by all the action, or just indecisive about who to eat first. The membranes on its neck flare bright orange, and I see a few men adjust their aim.

A flash of understanding strikes. The creature glowed hot white in the infrared. It's not cold or warm blooded, it's hot blooded. And when that orange blood hits the open air, it combusts! When Collins was shooting the creature from the helicopter, a single round struck and pierced that membrane. The resulting spray of blood must have ignited. That's what caused the explosion. "Aim for the legs!" I shout as loud as I can.

The men adjust their aim down again. Thank God.

The monster brings its second leg out of the woods and takes a step forward.

Close enough, I think.

"Fire!" I shout.

A hundred men with assault rifles open fire on the creature's legs. The sound is like thunder. The bright orange tracer fire glows hot, like a fireworks finale. Then the five heavy machine guns open fire, their roar drowning out the hundred other firing weapons.

The creature roars with surprise, or pain, I'm not sure. But it stumbles back.

The trees behind the creature are shredded by missed rounds, but I think most are finding their mark. With a higher-pitched roar, the monster snaps at the air, biting nothing. Its arms flail, striking at invisible targets.

Collins steps up next to me and opens fire. That's when I pull the trigger. With a dull poonk that's quieter than any weapon currently being fired, the grenade launcher sends a single round sailing across the four lanes of highway. The grenade strikes the giant knee and explodes.

The monster shrieks and stumbles.

Men cheer.

I fire again.

And again. Striking the same leg two more times.

The monster raises its head to the sky. Its chest expands. Then it leans down, landing on its forelimbs. It opens its mouth and lets out a blast of sound that drops me to my knees—me and everyone else. My eyes clench shut. My hands go to my ears. And my insides quiver from the intensity of the sonic blast.

When I open my eyes again, just a second later, the monster has recovered. It rears back up onto two legs, steps forward and twists. The knowledge of what it's doing is the only thing that saves my life. I shout, "Get down!" and tackle Collins and Humm to the ground.

There's a crash, and I look up to see a Humvee pass by overhead. Then three more, pirouetting through the air like Ice Capades skaters. The long black tail, tipped with what looks like a six-foot-long, three-pronged blade, flashes over the roof of the fifth Humvee, cutting the gunner in half at the waist. The tail continues its deadly swipe, passing over the spot where we had been standing and continuing through the ranks of soldiers.

Those who are struck by the tail's tip are simply cut down, their top halves flipping away with a spray of blood. The rest of the men caught in the tail's path, struck by the meat of the thing, are sent flying—rag dolls with pulverized insides. The number of men suddenly dead is impossible to count, but since there are only three of us on this side of the fire line and maybe twenty on the far end, I'd guess the monster killed upwards of eighty men with the single strike.

I look to Collins, making sure she's okay. "Collins."

She groans and opens her eyes, which suddenly go wide.

Poonk!

I turn to find Humm firing the grenade launcher.

Up.

At the creature's glowing neck.

Poonk!

Poonk!

At that same moment, I hear the distinctive high pitched whine of an A-10 Thunderbolt, renowned for its ability to decimate tanks. It comes in low behind the creature and opens fire with its powerful chain gun. Hot tracer rounds ricochet off the monster's carapace.

And then, everything happens at once.

The first grenade strikes the creature's leg, pitching it forward. This action causes the A-10 gunfire to strike the back of the monster's head, which would have been great if it hadn't then twisted away, allowing the bullets to streak past and reduce Humm to sludge. The deadly barrage of bullets streaks past Collins and me, triggering our flight. We stand together and run for the side of the highway where a guard rail protects drivers from a fifteen foot gulley.

The second grenade strikes the creature's gut, pitching it forward and dropping its head and neck into the trajectory of the final explosive round.

Collins leaps over the guard rail without slowing.

I follow, diving on the grassy slope and rolling onto my back as I slide down the hill.

There's a whump, like the Earth itself has become a sub-woofer.

Then a shockwave that throws bodies, limbs, weapons and Humvees into the warehouses beyond the highway.

A ball of fire follows, roiling out, bright orange in all directions. It passes over our position, but its heat singes the hair on my arms.

A secondary explosion follows and a high pitched wail streaks past. It's the A-10. On fire.

Boom!

Its gas tank bursts and explodes, sending the plane down into some unsuspecting neighborhood.

All of that is followed by an agonizing, rage-filled roar.

As pain fills my head, I see the creature again, this time from below, as it steps over the gulley. Seeing it up close, from beneath, is beyond comprehension. As the tail sweeps past, I feel queasy. Then light head-ed. I put a hand to my head and it comes away warm and slick with blood.

Something...something...

I'm unable to complete the thought.

As my vision fades to black, I hear a repetitive booming, like fading thunder. And then nothing.

30

Katsu Endo believed in loyalty, perhaps to a fault, but he was at least aware of this personality flaw. So he made it a habit to scrutinize every order he followed and determine whether it fell within the range of what he believed was acceptable. So far, the seven people he had killed, starting with Master Sergeant Lenny Wilson, had been at the command of General Gordon. He had no real reason to kill any of his victims other than the fact that Gordon had asked him to. But each and every one of those deaths were acceptable because they kept Endo close to the one thing in his life that gave him a sense of purpose.

And it wasn't Gordon.

It was the creature unearthed from the frozen cave in Alaska. He needed to know what it was, where it came from and why. Those were the questions that drove him since laying eyes on the behe-moth. As a child in Japan, Endo had spent a good portion of every day watching cartoons and movies that were filled with giant monsters called "kaiju." Godzilla, Gamera, Mothra and so many more filled his imagination, and when his parents died, they kept him company. The

giant monsters of his youth were remembered with the same fond-
ness as his parents, but like them, the monsters would always be
intangible.

But then he saw the giant creature in Alaska, and he knew he was
wrong. Kaiju did exist, they'd just been killed, or were hiding in the
ocean or were simply waiting to be created on a secret island somewhere. The possibilities were endless, and his desire to uncover the
truth about kaiju drove him like a religious zealot.

But in five years he hadn't learned very much at all. Then,
somehow, the General told him he had acquired a sample of the
creature, and suddenly all of their work at BioLance came into
focus. Gordon had no real interest in micro-biology, transplantation
technology or organ growth—he simply wanted to build a lab
capable of studying the creature. That's what Endo had believed,
anyway. Then he found out about the General's heart and how he
intended to use an organ grown using the creature's DNA to save
his own life.

Endo had never experienced anger so primal before, and he had
nearly acted on it. But killing the General fell outside his range of
what was acceptable. If Gordon died, Zoomb would have no need for
Endo. It would mean never getting his answers. Keeping Gordon
alive had been and would continue to be his first priority. The man
was his only avenue to the knowledge he sought.

Despite that, Gordon had just gone outside what Endo felt was
acceptable. When the elevator doors opened, the pair had walked up
to the receptionist's desk and asked to see Paul Stanton, CEO of the
Boston-based tech company. When she gave an earnest smile and
said that Stanton was on the phone and would be available shortly,
Gordon took her head and smashed it down on the desktop.

"She's dead," Endo said, his hand on the girl's wrist. He fought
against his anger at Gordon. On the way up, Gordon had explained that
he would be demanding any and all information the company had on
the creature recovered from Alaska. This fell directly in line with Endo's
own goals. What the General hadn't explained was that he would make

these demands under the threat of extreme violence, severing all ties with the company and all access to any future discoveries.

But it was too late. The girl was dead and the act was caught on at least two different security cameras.

But maybe there is a way to—

Security guards burst through the door leading to Zoomb's offices. Three of them entered the sparsely decorated lobby while one remained next to the door, propping it open with his foot.

Amateurs.

"Don't move!" the chubbier of the guards shouted. "Don't fucking move." His hands shook while he kept the weapon leveled on Gordon. In fact, all four men were all but ignoring Endo.

It would be so easy, he thought, but he just slowly raised his hands. As long as he kept his hands clear here, he might find a way to secure a position in the company. Until then, he would aid Gordon, but not in a way that could incriminate him. He had arrived with the General, but he had yet to commit a crime on camera.

Besides, Gordon didn't really need Endo's help with the dirty work.

"She's dead!" a skinny guard said, checking for a pulse on the girl's neck.

"Hands on the back of your head!" chubby yelled. "Now!"

Endo complied.

Gordon did not.

"Do you know who I am?" Gordon asked, taking a step closer.

"Doesn't matter who you are," the chubby guard said. "Hands on your head or I will—"

Gordon lunged forward and punched the man's neck. The man toppled to the ground gasping for air through a shattered windpipe. His death would be slow and agonizing. While the guard dropped to the floor, Gordon reached around to his back and drew his silenced pistol. The man behind the desk died first as a .50-caliber round ripped through his nose and removed the entire back of his head, splattering it against the Zoomb logo mounted to the wall.

Before the other two guards could react, Gordon twisted, ducked and fired two more times, coating the ceiling with gore. It all happened in a blur. Gordon had been a strong man before, but not exactly spry. Now he moved as fast as Endo. Maybe faster.

Gordon caught the now headless man in the doorway and tossed him into the lobby, where his blood pooled on the white marble floor. He then caught the door before it closed and turned to Endo, whose hands were still raised.

"Impressed?" Gordon asked.

Endo lowered his hands.

"Let's go," Gordon said.

Endo stepped over the expanding pools of blood and the bodies that created them. He took hold of the door when he reached it and motioned for Gordon to go inside. "After you, sir," he said, but it came out quiet.

"Had to be done," Gordon said, perhaps sensing Endo's disapproval.

Endo gave a nod, but knew Gordon was wrong. Not one of these people needed to die. They could have waited for Stanton and spoke to him without drawing too much attention. Hell, they could have tortured Stanton for the information and Endo wouldn't have cared, but this just didn't make sense.

It was bloodlust.

And although the General had never shied away from violence, it always served a purpose. Their purpose. But now... Is he coming unhinged? Did the DNA bonded to his heart change his personality? He had heard that people who received organs sometimes took on the hobbies and food preferences of the donor. Some people woke up craving food they'd never had before. Could the General's new penchant for killing be like that? If so, it didn't come from the girl— Maigo—whose heart he now had in his chest. But the heart also held traces of the creature's DNA. He remembered how Maigo had changed back at the BioLance facility. At first, he had admired her— marveled at her. She was a living kaiju. But then he had seen her kill.

And feast.

She took pleasure in it.

Maigo had changed from a human girl into a monstrous killing machine. *It's the creature*, he thought. *Whatever the giant they discovered was, the world was better off with it dead. For every Gamera protecting the planet, there was a Ghidorah, Megalon or Gigan to destroy all things.*

Is that what Maigo became?

Is that what Gordon is becoming?

The rest of the fiftieth floor seemed to be empty. Large spaces lining the glassed-in hallway they walked through were filled with endless rows of cubicles, but not a single person. Endo looked at his watch. 7:15.

Apparently, Stanton had stayed late and the receptionist along with him. Because an alarm had yet to be sounded and no more guards encountered, Endo assumed the now dead guards were a skeleton crew nightshift. Their bodies, and the receptionist's, might not be found until the next morning. If they could find the security suite, deleting the footage of the killing should be easy.

But did Gordon know all of this before he went on a killing spree, or was it just dumb luck? In either case, there was a chance they could walk away without being implicated in the murders. *No, that's not true*, Endo thought. *The elevator camera would show them getting off on the 50th floor and that footage would go to the building's security feed, not Zoomb's.*

"Jenny, is that you?" the man's voice snapped Endo back to the here and now.

"Sorry to disappoint you, Paul," Gordon replied, pushing through the unlocked wooden door. They entered the large, but sparsely decorated office together, but Endo hung back and put on a confused and fearful expression. The far wall of the office was all glass and looked out over Boston and the harbor beyond.

Paul Stanton looked confused—his forehead furrowed deeply, forming wrinkles nearly to the top of his gleaming bald head. He held an open bottle of wine, which now hovered over two glasses. His coat was off and his tie was on the solid wood desk, next to the glasses.

Jenny, it seemed, was a little more than a receptionist. And since Stanton was married and had three children, this knowledge could have gotten them anything they wanted to know. But Endo didn't think that's how things were going to work out.

"Gordon?" Stanton said, sounding as confused as he should be. "What are you doing here?" His eyes locked on the gun. "Where's Jenny?"

"Dead," Gordon says.

Endo had never once been shocked by the General's usually blunt way of speaking to people, but this bold admission made him stumble. Gordon didn't notice. "Helluva view. Endo, get the blinds."

Endo didn't see any blinds, but found a light switch by the window that tinted the whole window black.

Stanton picked up the phone and hammered his finger down on a single button.

"Your security team is dead, too," Gordon said, slowly walking toward Stanton.

The CEO of Zoomb hung up the phone and then started redialing. No doubt 911. But Gordon raised the pistol and fired. It was an expert shot, far above the skill level the General normally exhibited at the range. It wasn't just his speed and strength that were changing, it was everything. The bullet struck the phone and tore it to pieces.

Stanton shouted in surprise and jumped back. "What do you want?"

"Everything you have about the creature."

"B—but why?" Stanton asked. "Why now?"

"I gave it to you, but it belongs to me. It always has. And now I want to know everything about it. Where is it? What is it? Where is it from?"

"B—but we haven't learned much," Stanton said. "It's unlike anything else on Earth. Our best people can't make any sense of it."

"Lies," Gordon said, raising the pistol toward Stanton's head.

The man screamed and fell back, cowering with his hands over his face, like it would protect him from a .50-caliber round.

There's no way he is lying, Endo thought. With Jenny and the security team dead, his only hope of surviving is telling the truth. He must realize that.

"We've only determined two things with certainty!" Stanton shouted.

"Go on," Gordon said, keeping the pistol leveled at the man's head.

"It's alien," Stanton said.

"From where?"

"We don't know!"

"And the second thing?"

"We were able to analyze its stomach contents," Stanton said. "It— it ate people. Exclusively."

Upon hearing this, Gordon lowered the gun and laughed like it was the funniest thing he'd ever heard.

"It's true!" Stanton said, misreading Gordon's humor as disbelief. He pointed to his PC. "Everything I have is on the computer. See for yourself!"

When Gordon finally controlled his laughter, he wiped a tear from his eye, raised the pistol in the air and put his finger on the trigger. "I believe you, Paul, I just don't like you."

When Endo saw the muscles in Gordon's arms flex, he acted on instinct, knowing that he couldn't allow Stanton to die. While Zoomb might have only had a limited knowledge of the creature then, someday they would uncover the rest.

Paul Stanton's death now fell into Endo's unacceptable range, while Gordon had just made his own life forfeit. Endo stepped forward and kicked up hard, striking Gordon's hand. The strong General didn't drop the weapon, but his shot went high, punching a large hole in the wall above Stanton's head.

Endo followed the kick with a second strike to the back of the General's leg that dropped the man to one knee.

With a growl of frustration, Gordon struck out hard with his club-like arm, but Endo had already leapt back and drawn his weapon.

"Arms up, General."

Gordon didn't move. He just looked back and stared at Endo. Through grinding teeth he said, "I should have known you would betray me eventually."

"Drop the weapon," Endo said.

When Gordon didn't comply, Endo added, "I know you're fast now, but you also know how fast I am. I will kill you before you can get a shot off. Now drop the weapon!"

Stanton got to his feet, his face full of fear and anger. "Forget that! Shoot him!"

Gordon must have known that Endo would obey his new master because he dove to the side. Endo fired, striking Gordon's shoulder. But he didn't have to fire again. Gordon struck the large window with enough force to shatter it. He and a thousand shards of glass fell from the 50th story.

Endo and Stanton dashed to the window and looked down.

A second crash of glass sounded from below. Ten stories down, the General began pulling himself back into the building, though a second shattered window.

"How is that possible?" Stanton asked.

"He has the alien's DNA inside him," Endo said, telling the truth. "He is no longer fully human." Endo turned to Stanton. "Make me your personal body guard."

"W—what?"

"Hire me," Endo said. "And give me access to everything you have on the alien. It is the only way you will survive."

Stanton seemed to be considering the request. "You can protect me from him?"

"I am the only one who can protect you from him," Endo said.

Stanton thought on it for just a second longer and then nodded. "Done."

"From now on, I go where you go," Endo said.

"Yes!" Stanton shouted.

"Is there another way out of the building?" Endo asked.

"There's a helicopter on the roof," Stanton said, "but the pilot isn't here."

"I can fly it," Endo said, and then led the Zoomb CEO on a pell mell sprint to the nearest stairwell and charged up two flights to the roof. He got the chopper started and lifted off without incident, but he couldn't help feeling the General would suddenly leap out and crush his skull. Once they were fifty feet above the Prudential Tower, Endo's fears faded some, but as they flew away, he saw Gordon standing in Stanton's office, watching them.

He knew at that moment that neither of them would be safe until General Lance Gordon was dead. He also suspected the same would be true for anyone who looked at the man the wrong way. Endo always knew that Gordon was cold and remorseless—maybe even a sociopath, but the man was now part something else.

Something not human.

Something that ate people. Exclusively.

And that, Endo thought, is unacceptable.

31

The rhythmic chop of helicopter blades reaches into the darkness and pulls my eyes open. The sky above is the most beautiful shade of orange—sunset on smoke. My head lolls to the side. I see grass. And blood. And Collins. She crawls toward me, her orange curls bouncing, her eyes blazing with a radiance that brings a smile to my face. She's shouting something, but I can't hear her. And then, I can't see her, either.

I wake, once again, to the sound of a helicopter. But the sunset is gone, which I find disappointing. I look up and see a window. The sun is just a streak of dull purple on the horizon. Night has fallen and I'm in the helicopter. Motion draws my eyes down, and I see Collins again. She's sitting in the seat next to me, eyes closed. I'm lying down, I realize, when I see my legs over her lap. Feeling safe, I close my eyes and give in to the exhaustion and pain.

The third time I wake up, it's in response to something wet on my cheek. A kiss? "Collins?" I ask sounding a little confused, but equally hopeful. I groggily push myself up and open my eyes.

The black, brown and white face peering at me isn't even human. On the bright side, it was a kiss. "Hey, Buddy."

The Australian sheep dog wags his stumpy tail. I'm not sure what happened to the rest of the tail, but I've never asked. Buddy Boy—Buddy or Bud for short—belongs to Watson and has been our unofficial mascot for the past five years. He has full reign of the house and the walled-in grounds that serve as home base for FC-P, including my bedroom.

I sit up in bed and Buddy joins me, lying down next to me so his paws hang off the side. He's not normally known to initiate a snuggle, but I think he senses my injuries, which I am now sensing as well. A groan escapes my lips as a pounding headache grows in my skull and sends roots down into my spine. Muscles ache in places I didn't know I had. And a sharp sting draws my hand to my forehead. There's a bandage there, beneath which I can feel a few small lumps. Stitches.

"You caught a piece of shrapnel when the plane exploded above us."

I look up and find Collins standing in the doorway. Her tan uniform, which had become a torn, dirty mess, has been replaced by a pair of jeans and a form-fitting black tank top. Both must belong to Cooper, because while the two women are nearly the same height, Collins has a lot more curve and these clothes are snug. Her hair has been pulled back into a wavy orange ponytail that looks a little like dragon fire.

"It's nothing major," she adds, "but an inch to the left..."

Buddy jumps up, stubby tail wagging, and greets Collins. He licks her hand then gets his forehead under it. Like a well trained human, Collins starts scratching.

"Knocked you out cold," she says.

"Why am I here?" I ask, but then I clarify, "Why am I not at a hospital?"

"That's where we were headed," she says, "When Ted called. He insisted we bring you here. Said you would want to be brought up to speed as soon as you were awake."

She looks worried that this was wrong, so I speak quickly. "He was right. And, for the record, I'm glad you came with."

"You're my boss now, right?" she says, but I can't tell if she's being sarcastic.

She strikes me as the kind of person I can be straight with, so I ask, "Are you joking?"

She looks confused, bumbles over her reply for a second, and then asks, "Weren't you joking? I mean, you were—serious?"

"I'm not really sure what you just asked me," I say, "so let me make the whole thing official. I need a partner. Someone I can trust. Someone with brains and guts, and someone who can put up with my personality flaws, which in your case might include gawking, drooling and the installation of a webcam in the bathroom."

When she laughs, I do too, and man does it hurt.

"The point is, while I have never really needed a partner before now, I have also never met someone who compliments me as much as you do—and I don't mean that in a webcammy way—"

"I know what you mean," she says.

"Good," I say. "So yes. I was serious. And once we defeat the giant man-eating monster, we can do something quiet like search for a Yeti in Colorado or something."

She steps forward and extends her hand. "In that case, I accept."

I take her hand and shake it, but I note that Buddy has left her skin wet with slobber. "Might want to wash your hands. That dog licks his balls like he's training for puppy porn." It's actually not true. The poor dog is neutered. But I like to see Collins smile.

We both laugh and it must have been loud, because a second later, the door opens and Watson leans in. His pudgy face is a sight for sore eyes. While Cooper is a trusted co-worker, Watson is a good friend, perhaps my only real friend, though I think the number of names on that list is growing.

"Good! You're awake." He leans back out. "He's awake!" Then he leans back in and points to my dresser. "Water and painkillers over there. Come out soon, there's a lot to catch you up on."

"How long was I unconscious?" I ask.

"Two hours," he says.

"And there's a lot to catch me up on?" I shake my head, and more quietly say, "What could have happened in two hours?"

It wasn't a real question—I have a very good idea of what could happen in two hours—but Watson answers it anyway. "For starters, Portland got leveled."

Then he's gone and he takes Collins's and my smiles with him. He gives a whistle and Buddy leaps from the bed, following his master.

"I'll let you get dressed," she says.

I look down and find myself wearing just my boxers. My chest still has grass stains from my drunken romp in the woods. "Just like old times."

Collins manages one more smile before she leaves the room and closes the door.

I make them wait fifteen minutes, but when I finally do emerge, clean, shaven, dressed and freshly bandaged, I'm far more awake and useful than I would have been if I'd just stumbled back out to work. The headache is starting to subside thanks to the four ibuprofen I took, but I wouldn't be surprised if I had a concussion. I probably shouldn't be up at all, but Jack Bauer wouldn't stay in bed, so I won't either. Of course, Jack Bauer wouldn't have showered, peed or eaten, either.

FC-P is located in what was once the solitary home at the pinnacle of Beverly's tallest hill. It's a four-story brick mansion with about an acre of landscaped yard surrounded by a solid, four-foot stone wall that the neighborhood kids like to walk on top of. In the time since the mansion's construction, the rest of the hill was sold off and turned into residential neighborhoods. We occasionally get kids playing ding-dong-ditch, but we're mostly left alone except on Halloween, when the kids come in droves to see the house. We don't give out candy or anything, but I put on a wig, backlight myself in red and I rock in the third story window. I'm supposed to be a hunter of all things paranormal. If I don't make somebody believe in it, I'll be out of a job someday.

Course, job security for FC-P will likely never be a concern again, that is, if the creature doesn't end up wiping out mankind.

The main work area, what Cooper calls "the Crow's Nest", is on the fourth floor, which we've gutted so that it's a wide open space. It's actually quite striking, with its large windows, ocean view and shiny wood floors. But we've kind of dulled the beauty of the space by filling it with computer stations, work desks, wall maps and cork boards covered with reported sightings of the world's weird, none of which have amounted to anything—until now.

I take the grand staircase one step at a time, clutching the hard-wood banister. The old rug—a maroon and blue oriental affair—is still soft, which speaks to its quality. The same family owned the house for more than a hundred and fifty years before the final living member—a one-hundred-and-four year old woman whose grandfather built the place—died, and the government seized the property because of unpaid taxes. FC-P inherited the home a year later.

When I reach the top of the stairs, I see everyone standing around the flat-screen TV mounted on the far left wall of the Crow's Nest. Cooper, Watson, Collins and Woodstock. My team, new and old. I can hear the melodic voice of a news anchor, but can't make out the words. Either the news is engrossing or I'm a ninja, because no one seems to hear me coming. When I catch sight of what's on the screen, I know it's the former.

The scene on the TV is an aerial view of what I assume is Portland, recorded before the sun went down, perhaps just minutes after the highway confrontation. It looks like an asteroid struck, or a laser from outer space carved a path through the city. A path of destruction, miles long, stretches through residential neighborhoods, a business district and then through the downtown itself. Fires burn everywhere. Buildings are leveled. People swarm through the streets, fleeing the city. The shot pans up toward the bay just in time to see the creature slip into the ocean and disappear.

"Has it been seen since?" I ask, making everyone but Cooper jump.

Cooper turns around on her heels. Her jet black hair is still straight and perfect, hanging just above her shoulders. Her power suit, which I've told her she doesn't need to wear, is unwrinkled and as smooth as her face. She's an attractive woman, but I've never been interested. She is far too serious and doesn't find me funny. At all. Her piercing blue eyes lock onto mine and she says, "No one has seen it since. Not on land. Not at sea. And everyone is looking for it."

"Coast guard?" I ask.

"Everyone," she says. "Coast Guard. Air Force. Navy. Police. Fishermen. The whole world is watching the ocean off Maine, looking for signs of the...what are we calling it?"

"Nothing yet," I say.

"I have an idea on that," Watson says, but Cooper continues.

"Canada is also helping with the search, and many coastal European nations have put their militaries on alert in case it decides to cross the ocean."

"It won't," I say. "It will head south."

"How do you know?" she asks.

I think back to how General Gordon sensed the thing to the south. Called it Maigo. None of that will go over well with Cooper's logical mind, so I say, "A hunch," which isn't much better.

"South to where?" she asks.

I shrug. "But wherever it ends up, we need to be ready for it. Coop, I need you to get IDs for Collins—" I point to her and then to Woodstock, "and for Woodstock." I look at the man. "If you're on board, I mean."

"Hells yes," Woodstock says. "Me and my bird are all yours."

I give him a nod of thanks and say, "Then coordinate with the Navy and Air Force. The second I start making requests, they better respond like I'm the damn President."

Cooper nodded. "We briefed Stephens on everything, including Cugliari's failure to respond to the crisis in Portland. He's also seen the footage and there is no doubt that this crisis and its management falls under the purview of our office, and our office alone. He promised that all future requests would be fast-tracked and granted without question."

"Good," I say and turn to Watson. "Now, what have you found out?"

"I know who the creature is," he says.

"What do you mean, who?" Woodstock asks.

Watson starts cleaning his glasses with his T-shirt. It's a nervous habit that reveals he's about to say something he thinks we won't believe. "Well, it's more than one 'who' actually." He puts the glasses back on. "It—she—is two."

32

"You're saying our giant man-eating monster has multiple personalities?" I ask.

"Maybe," Watson says. "I suppose. But not really. Your DNA is a combination of your mother and father, but you aren't born with their personalities...though that might not be true in this case."

"Not making a ton of sense," I say.

Watson sits behind his three-screen computer station. He doesn't necessarily need it, but it's where he does his best thinking, or so he claims. I think it's more of a security-blanket type of thing. The glow of electronics puts him at ease. Makes him less nervous. Even if he wasn't overweight, his tech dependence would keep him out of the field.

"Let me backtrack for a minute," he says. "I think I know who Maigo was."

"Was?" Collins asks.

"She died about a week ago. And not well." He brings the report up on his computer screen and turns to it. I know he doesn't need to read it. He doesn't forget anything he reads. But turning away from the three sets of eyes locked on him probably adds another layer of social defense. "Maigo Tilly."

"Tilly?" Collins says. "The name is familiar."

"Her father is Alexander Tilly. The third. They're Boston elite. His wife was in the news a lot, for charity donations and because she was a babe."

"Again with the was," I say.

Watson nods. "Mrs. Tilly was murdered in the family's penthouse. Report says they think that Maigo walked in on the murder and was killed so she couldn't identify the killer. Mr. Tilly is officially a person of interest, but there is no physical evidence linking him to the crime—"

"Prints don't matter because it's his home," Collins says. "Unless they found them on the murder weapon."

"Which hasn't been found," Watson says. "Maigo fell into a coma. Might have survived if she had received a liver transplant."

"A transplant," I say, sensing a connection. "BioLance was working on rapid organ growth and transplantation. Could she have been a test subject?"

"There is no doubt about that," Watson says.

I'm not sure I want to ask, but I do. "Why?"

"Ashley gave us the samples you collected—I told you those Ziplocs would come in handy—and we had them tested in the FBI lab in Danvers."

"You can get returns that fast?" I ask.

"Not normally, but I had them test it against names that had come up. Since Maigo was deceased and the case was an open investigation, we were able to compare the samples." He frowns. "The...husk of human skin you found..."

"It was hers," I say for him. "It was Maigo's. They grew her."

"It would seem so, but..." He runs his hands through his hair and pulls it a little. "Okay. Let's switch gears for a minute so this makes sense. Remember Nemesis?"

"The Greek word written in blood," I say, tensing at the memory.

"Right," he says, "but it's not just a word, it's a name."

"What kinda name is Nemesis?" Woodstock asks.

"The Greek goddess kind," Watson says. "Nemesis was the personification of vengeance, retribution and cold, hard justice. Some legends depict her as being so consumed with avenging her subjects that she laid waste to everything and everyone in her path, including those who prayed to her in the first place, which some scholars view as a judgment on society."

"A society that allows for horrible things to happen is just as guilty as the individual who commits the act?" I say. It's a twisted way of thinking, but in a weird sort of way, it makes sense.

"Right," he says. "Nemesis is most often depicted as a beautiful woman with wings. She's occasionally holding the scales of justice, but more often a sword. And there are a few images, some of the oldest, that depict her wrath as a dark, destructive form closer to—"

"A monster," I say.

He nods.

"So you're saying that this creature is an ancient goddess come to judge humanity?" Woodstock says. "Kind of hard to swallow, don't you think?"

"I'm saying that this...creature, which we know for a fact is real, by the way, might have been the inspiration for the Nemesis myth. As the story was passed down verbally, the monster became a woman and once adopted into the Greek canon, the woman became the beautiful daughter of Zeus."

Woodstock grunts his approval and rubs his chin.

"But the creature, if it is Nemesis, it's also more than Nemesis." Watson looks at me. "The second sample. Collins said you collected it from some razor wire?"

I nod. "It came from the creature—Nemesis—when it was smaller."

"The results are inconclusive, but only because they can't make sense of the results." He opens the DNA analysis on the computer screen. It means nothing to me, so I just listen. "But I can. There are two distinct DNA strands."

"It's a hybrid," Collins says.

"Yup." Watson point at the DNA results. "The first half is the screwy part. It barely looks like DNA as we know it. It's just a mess. The lab says the sample was contaminated, but I don't think so. I think it's simply something they've never seen before. It's like nothing else on Earth." He looks back at me, pushing his glasses higher onto his face so that his eyes grow a little larger. "Jon, this thing either evolved long before life as we know it began, or it's alien. Like from another planet."

"But not completely," I say. I haven't forgotten that only half of the DNA is alien. "The other half is human, right?"

He nods. "It's Maigo. I think she probably shed her human skin as her non-human body grew. Like how bull moose molt their antlers as they grow larger."

Woodstock looks to the ceiling and walks away, clearly disgusted.

Collins looks about ready to tear someone's head off.

I must look similar because Watson cringes and says, "Don't blame the messenger."

"No one is mad at you, Ted," I tell him. "It's just..."

"Sick," Collins says, completing my thought. "Who would do that to a little girl? And why?"

Ted shrugs. "Best guess is that they were using the alien DNA to enhance organ growth somehow. Maybe speed it up. You mentioned the creature was growing quickly."

"Very quickly," I say. "So the creature that laid waste to Maine and killed thousands of people is one part Nemesis, one part human girl?"

Ted nods, "But given the creature's appearance and the shed human skin, I think the non-human DNA is becoming dominant, which helps when we get to the business of killing it, but it's also very bad news."

"How so?" I ask.

"It means she's becoming fully Nemesis, goddess of vengeance who strikes down men and women, not just for their crimes, but also for their hubris and even evil thoughts." He turns to the screen on his right, opens a new window and reads. "'To every mortal is thy influence known, and men beneath thy righteous bondage groan; for every thought within the mind concealed is to thy sight perspicuously revealed. The soul unwilling reason to obey, by lawless passion ruled, thine eyes survey. All to see, hear, and rule, O power divine, whose nature equity contains, is thine.' That's from a Greek hymn. And if it's true, if Nemesis will exact vengeance on the human race based on our thoughts—"

"Yeah," I say. "I get it. We're all fair game."

"Not just fair game," Watson says. "We're screwed."

"Unless we kill it," I say. It comes out sounding bold and confident, but then I remember what happened in Portland. A hundred soldiers, five heavy machine guns, a grenade launcher and a frikken missile strike had absolutely no effect, other than pissing the thing off. I'm not sure what it will take to kill Nemesis, but it's not going to be men on the ground. We're going to need the full power of America's armed forces against this thing. I just don't know where. Thinking of the military reminds me of General Gordon. "What about the General? And Endo? Anything new on them?"

"Nothing," Watson says. "But I think it's safe to say both are employed by some secret division of Zoomb, who somehow acquired a DNA sample of Nemesis. But I seriously doubt there is a paper or digital trail that would reveal as much. Besides, it might have all been legal."

"Trying to kill Collins and I, not to mention murdering the Johnsons, is very much against the law," I say.

When I see Watson frown deeply I realize that he probably knew the Johnsons. "Sorry," I say, and I should probably say more, but I'm struck with a thought. "Why would Zoomb hire an active duty U.S. general whose career wasn't at all technology-based?"

Watson's frown disappears as the question takes root. "That's a good question."

"Can you access Gordon's records?" When Watson nods, I say, "Check his last deployment. Where was he?"

After a few seconds of furious typing, Watson says, "Here's the brief. Looks like he was in Alaska. There was an accidental death at a training exercise involving U.S. Marines and Japanese Defense Forces. A Master Sergeant Lenny Wilson was shot and killed when a weapon was dropped and discharged despite it not being a live-fire exercise."

"Is there a name given for the soldier whose weapon discharged?" I ask.

"Yeah," he says. "Uh. Katsu. Katsu Endo." He looks up quickly. "That's him! Endo! He was there, too." He looks back to the screen. "The General flew in and shut down the exercise. A month later, he resigned and...hold on. The brief includes a location. Coordinates."

He brings up a second program, Zoomb Planet, which provides a satellite view of the planet without using government resources. He punches in the coordinates and the view of the planet zooms to Alaska, then closer, and closer, the image resolving slowly as the computer tries to show the ever-changing images. When it stops, we have a top view of white sludge.

"What's this?" I ask.

"Low res filler," he says. "It's what the software uses when there is no satellite coverage of a certain area. It's the middle of nowhere, but there should be something." He zooms out. "See, the surrounding terrain comes in clear enough."

"Any reason that might happen?"

He laughs at me, scoffs really. "Isn't it obvious? We're using Zoomb software. There's something there they don't want anyone to see. This is the connection. Gordon found something in Alaska, and then used it to secure a position with Zoomb, and probably a good chunk of change."

"Can we use an active satellite to take a look?" I ask.

His fingers fly over the keys. "Would normally take at least a day to get approval and retask, but we've got full access and a green light to use whatever resources we need. Should take just an hour to get the satellite into position."

"Do it," I say. "And find out who owns that land now. If Zoomb is ultimately responsible for this mess, we're taking them down, and Gordon with them."

"Just the five of us?" Collins asks, looking a little dubious.

I nod. "FC-P now represents the combined resources of every federal criminal agency and the U.S. military. Far as I know, Nemesis doesn't have a monopoly on vengeance."

33

She swam. And though she had no memory of doing so before, the act came naturally after just a few minutes. At first, she tried to push herself through the water with her arms and legs, but that was slow and clumsy. With a roar of frustration that sent a plume of bubbles roiling to the surface, she thrashed her tail and moved through the water. Learning quickly, she put her arms to her sides, streamlining her body, and used her tail to swim like a marine iguana.

She didn't feel as comfortable in the water as she did on land, but it was quiet in the abyss. And less painful.

The events that lead to her flight through the busy, noisy place were a jumbled mix of memories—a confusing mash of light and sound that she didn't quite understand. She'd fought against the pain at first. Her burning hunger commanded her, and there was so much food. But the heat, and sound, and chaos jolted her.

Her rage still burned, but a curtain of confusion had been thrown over it, so she ran and flattened everything in her path, eating when it was easy, but moving forward until she reached the water and slid beneath the surface.

The raw emotions blinding her instincts had faded during the long swim, focusing her thoughts on just one simple goal: eat.

Her sensitive ears picked up a deep, throaty drone not far away. The sound was closer to the coast than she wanted to be, but she could sense a large number of prey. She didn't understand how she could sense them, only that she was drawn to them...and angered by them. Her hunger was matched only by her rage. Despite her apprehension of returning to the shore, and the potential pain it might bring, she changed course and headed toward the slow-moving food source.

Her deep feeling of loathing for the creatures increased as she grew closer. She could feel them. Feel through them. She felt a cascade of emotions flow down through the water. Fear, loathing, anger, jealousy and pride.

As she slid beneath the ship, the fear spiked.

Then she felt something new. A sense of wrongness, like an opposing force, that needed to be destroyed—no matter what. She stopped moving, hovering in the hundred and fifty foot deep water, and listened.

"Stop! Please, stop!" The words were distant, muffled by water, drowned out by the roar of engines, and mixed with cheers and loud thrumming music, but she could hear them all the same. She sensed that this was a language, that information was being conveyed, but she couldn't understand.

But the emotions carried by the words—terror and desperation—came through clearly.

"Help!" came the voice. "Someone help!"

She twitched uncomfortably, feeling tight inside her own body. Hunger burned in her gut. But she couldn't ignore the voice. It captivated her, drew her up from the deep. As she neared the ship, a revelation brought clarity to her actions—her emotions and physical needs were aligned.

With a thrash of her tail, she rose through the dark, toward the flashing light and hundreds of unsuspecting prey above.

"Get off me, Shane!" Lori Brooks shouted. She shoved at the larger man, but it did as little good as her words. Shane Brown, her boss, was nearly twice her size and was off his ass drunk. She'd punched, scratched and kicked when he first locked her on the ship's back deck, but it was like he couldn't feel any of it.

At first, she felt a small sense of victory knowing that the physical evidence would guarantee he lost his company and family, and he would spend a long time in jail, but then it occurred to her that he could simply kill her and toss her overboard. No one would be the wiser. He could explain away bruises and hide scratches. These thoughts fueled her desperation and she cried out again.

But either no one cared, or more likely, no one could hear her over the thump of music or the roar of the engines, which were directly beneath the rear observation deck to which she was now pinned.

Shane could hear her, though. "This is what good assistants do, Lori. If you want to have a job in the morning, shut the fuck up."

He pinned her arms above her head with one of his and used his free hand to hike up her skirt. When she fought harder, he punched her in the stomach, taking the air, and the fight, out of her.

"You think this was cheap?" he said, motioning to the boat. The hundred foot, Victorian style steamship that sailed out of Portsmouth, NH, had three decks, three open bars and was filled to capacity with three hundred and fifty people—all employees of Shane. And not one of them had any interest in the musicless, noisy, back deck. That, or he had people watching the door for him, which was possible. A lot of the guys in the company viewed Shane like some kind of messiah, probably because he threw parties like this and gave them company perks that included under-the-table bonuses and prostitutes, many of whom were spending the night in the ship's six bathrooms, "servicing the head," Shane had joked.

And Lori knew about it all. Hell, she'd arranged some of it. She didn't approve, but she was being paid to look the other way, at least that's what she thought. When Shane called her to the back deck, to "discuss the schedule change," she should have realized her boss was too drunk to discuss anything, but the booze cruise had been cut short. Their return hadn't been scheduled for another hour, but the captain said something about an emergency in Maine and turned around early. The revelers had continued partying, unconcerned with whether or not the drinking continued while they were at sea or docked, or if someone screamed for help.

Clutched in pain, Lori couldn't keep the man from spreading her legs.

"Stop," she said. "Please stop."

He laughed and said, "Don't whine. Tomorrow you'll get a raise. Next time, a car. I'm a generous guy. Give me what I want, and you can have whatever you want. Fight me and I'm serious, you'll be jobless in the morning."

That Shane thought she cared about keeping her job revealed either how drunk he was, or that he was a monumental dolt, which was possible. He'd inherited the company from his father. Never had to really work. Just let the board handle most things and took care of his "boys". She'd been hired on as his assistant just a month ago, and had been fairly well harassed during that time, but she could handle flirtations from an older boss, even one as repulsive as Shane. The pay was good, but she now understood she should have quit after the first day. They weren't flirtations, she thought, they were promises.

As her boss undid his pants, there was no doubt he was going to make good on those promises.

She thought about her husband. He'd told her not to come. That it was a waste of time. They had kids to put to bed, after all.

Her kids.

What would she tell them? If she had Shane arrested, there would be a trial. Her kids would know everything. Would they look at her differently?

But that wasn't even the worst option.

What if he did kill her?

She would never see them again. They would never see her again!

She felt his hand on her inner thigh, reaching higher, fumbling to pull her underwear to the side. He let go of her hands and used his body to pin her down. Using both hands, he positioned himself above her.

She pounded on his broad back, but it was useless; her lack of leverage and his drunken state kept him from feeling any pain. "Help!" she screamed as loud as she could. "Someone help!"

She clenched her eyes shut, pushing tears over her cheeks. She had never felt such fear, desperation and loathing. She would kill him if she could. Her mind filled with thoughts of Shane beaten to a pulp, hanging by a rope and shot in the head. She'd wanted nothing more in her life. "I'll kill you!" she screamed.

A wave of nausea rolled through her body and she felt sure it was too late.

But it wasn't Shane.

The weight of his upper body lifted off her.

She opened her eyes and saw Shane sitting up above her, looking at the sky. She looked up and saw the ship rocking against the backdrop of stars. But something was off. Most of the sky was completely starless.

The music on deck paused between songs.

The next song, a booming hypnotic beat, was accompanied by a bright white strobe that flashed like rapid fire lighting. Through the blinking light, something large and black slipped through the air off the starboard side of the ship, trailing water.

Shane's eyes widened.

His chest expanded.

He opened his mouth to scream, despite the proven fact that no one would hear him.

And then, he was gone.

Half of him, at least.

The black blur had moved over the ship's rear deck, drenching it with salt water, and when it passed, the top half of Shane went with it. His legs flopped to the side, pouring blood onto the deck where it mixed with the sea water.

Lori leapt to her feet, looking up as the rest of something massive lowered into view. Lit by the strobe, she saw a huge, horrible head. Its lips curled up in a snarl, revealing long, curved teeth the size of whale ribs.

Then she saw its eyes. They were brown, and almost looked human, but they were larger than her Mini Cooper Coupe. But the worst thing about the eyes was they were looking right at her.

A flicker of light drew her eyes to the thing's massive neck. An oblong patch of skin blinked orange, like a fluorescent light fighting to turn on. Then, it glowed brightly and roiled with swirling yellow-orange. A second patch lit up, then a third, each lighting up faster than the rest. Finally, the water beneath the back of the ship glowed orange.

A scream rose up from the top deck of the ship, loud enough for her to hear over the music and engines. The party-goers had finally noticed the monster looming above them.

And now, it noticed them, too. The eyes looked up, toward the top deck. A massive, five-fingered hand slid out of the night and slapped the top of the ship, crushing its radio antenna and satellite dish. No calls for help would make it out. When the hand came back, it held the pummeled bodies of at least twenty people. Lori could see some of the still living shouting, though she couldn't hear them. Then they were gone, dropped into the monster's upturned, wide open maw.

Before the creature retuned its attention to the ship, and the waiting feast of humanity, Lori did the only thing she could think of—she dove into the water and swam for shore, nearly a mile away.

As her energy waned, Lori turned over and swam on her back, keeping the pace even. She couldn't see the monster or the ship anymore, but she could hear distant screams and cracking wood. It was killing them all.

And while Lori felt bad for her co-workers, she couldn't help but offer up a mental, "thank-you," to the giant that had saved her life. She took a moment to look for the shore, and found it just a few hundred yards away. I'm going to make it, she thought, but then she realized what the following day would bring. She was the only survivor of a disaster she couldn't even begin to describe. There would be an investigation. The police would do a back-ground check on everyone who attended, including Shane and Lori. They'd find out about the under-the-table payments she organized. They'd find out about the escorts she hired after making sure they were "full service". She might even go to jail! A powerful feeling of guilt washed over her, but then hope followed it. She could easily drive to the office and destroy or delete all the incriminating records. Even better, she could put Shane's name on them. It's not like he was around to deny it. As she plotted out her course of action, her head struck something solid. She stopped and spun around, expecting to find an anchored boat or marker buoy. Instead, she found a wall of black.

The shoreline was gone.

She spun around. Darkness surrounded her.

She looked up and saw the stars, but they were slowly winking out, one by one. Then she saw a dark shape silhouetted against the lighter night sky—long, pointed streaks, like teeth.

She was inside the monster's mouth!

The jaws closed over her just before she screamed. Then, as if she was stuck in a giant toilet, the water spun and flowed down. She shouted and grappled and reached for something to hold onto, but then the water pulled her down. Mercifully, she drowned before passing through the fifty-foot-long esophagus. Her body fell into the giant's acid filled stomach where the rest of the booze cruise's three hundred and forty-nine souls, and much of the ship, were already being turned into a slurry of human flesh, wood pulp and metal.

Despite the large number of prey consumed, her hunger not only continued, but expanded, like her body. She felt tight inside her own skin. Moving became harder work, which burned more calories, and fueled her hunger. She reached out with her senses, searching for more of her preferred food source, but the waters were empty. There were scores of them—humans, she thought—on land, but she still felt wary of the pain she'd felt and her tightening body would restrict her movement.

More than that, she had grown increasingly revolted by the thought of consuming humans. It wasn't the flavor—she couldn't really taste them—it was just the idea. Some part of her said that eating humans was wrong. It was an emotion she had never felt before, not since waking up, and not in the time before, which she was slowly starting to remember as hazy images. She didn't know what, but something about her was different. And it was that same something that drew her south. Whatever force pulled her in that direction was bigger than her budding craving for justice or her unceasing hunger.

So she swam, following the coast, rubbing her itching body along the ocean floor and searching for larger prey that might satiate her hunger.

34

My bedroom is directly beneath the Crow's Nest. It has the same distant ocean view as the massive workspace, just a few feet lower. But what it loses in height, it gains by having access to a stone deck fringed by a three-foot-tall, Romanesque wall complete with columns. Iambic or something. No, that's poetry. Doric? No, Ionic. That's it.

I shake my head and roll my eyes at myself. I'm dwelling on the stupid columns so I don't have to think about anything else. I've seen things I'll never be able to forget, despite how badly I would like to. People have died. Thousands of them. Because I failed. I know it's harsh, but it's true. Had I taken the mission statement of FC-P seriously and actively pursued cases instead of just waiting for Watson to hand me something, maybe I would have caught wind of this sooner?

No, I tell myself, Zoomb covered their tracks too well. And with the General's help, they managed to stay below everyone's radar. I wonder if he had to call in favors. When the dust settles how many people will I be putting in cuffs?

Maybe no one.

"You already look like shit," Collins says, somehow materializing next to me. "You can stop beating yourself up."

After flinching and nearly falling two stories to the brick patio below, I say, "Geeez."

She smiles and says, "You okay?"

She's probably referring to my apparently obvious mental whipping, but I don't feel like having a heart-to-heart about that. It's too fresh. The smell of blood and smoke lingers in my nose, complimenting the screams echoing in my head. I'd told Collins and Woodstock to get some sleep and left Cooper and Watson with orders to wake us if anything developed, but I'm clearly not the only one avoiding bed. Dodging the emotional bullet, I say, "I thought you were old Mrs. Rosen."

"Mrs. Rosen?"

"She was the last owner of this house," I say.

"And you thought I was her?"

"Her ghost," I say. "But I've never seen her. Watson seems to see her every time the wind blows, but even Cooper claims to have seen her once."

Collins climbs on top of the wall and sits next to me. It's dark out, but the full moon glows brightly on her freckled face. She waits for the rest of the story.

"Said she was sitting in a rocking chair," I point up at the large windows of the Crow's Nest. "Up there. Just looking out the window. When she spoke, the old woman disappeared. It's funny, I always thought that Cooper and Watson looked up the death report on Mrs. Rosen and were teasing me, but now... I'd say just about anything is possible, and I think I need to change my Halloween tradition."

She smiles widely at this, despite not knowing how disrespectful my Halloween tradition could be taken if Mrs. Rosen is indeed wandering the halls of this gigantic house. Of course, she hasn't haunted me yet, so maybe she appreciates someone keeping the vigil.

"What would they have found in her death report?" Collins asks.

I hitch my thumb at the windows above us. "That's where they found her, rocking chair and all."

"You're serious?"

"The worst part is that she sat there, baking in the summer heat for a month before neighbors noticed she never moved and called the police. I'm pretty sure that's why we got the place."

"Well, I think it's interesting," Collins says. She props her hands on the wall and looks up at the stars. "Not as many as I'm used to."

I look up. Beverly's city lights drown out all but the brightest stars, blocking out about sixty percent of what can be seen from the backwoods of Maine.

"The ocean view makes up for it," I say, and then take a deep breath. Despite the heat, the night breeze is cool and smells of the sea.

"So," she says, still looking up. "Where do you think this is headed?"

"I have no idea," I say. "I'm kind of hoping Nemesis will drown or at least swim to Japan."

"I wasn't talking about that," she says.

"Oh," I say, and then figure out what she is talking about. "Oh! I, uh, where do you think it's headed?"

"Well, you're my boss now, right?" she asks.

Damnit.

"And I'm willing to bet the DHS has a policy about inter-office fraternization."

"They do," I say. "But I see it more like an insurance policy. Doesn't cover pre-existing conditions."

She laughs in a way that makes me think I'll fire her if her joining the team screws things up on a personal level.

"Be serious," she says.

"Okay. Serious." I take a moment to collect my thoughts, and I have to admit, it's a nice distraction from what I was thinking about before. "Sure, technically, I'm your superior now. But I would prefer to treat our professional relationship as more of a partnership."

"I'm not sure I've earned that yet," she says.

"In the past five years, I've basically sat on my ass and traveled around the country, taking mini-vacations while looking for various mythical creatures. The action we saw today constitutes the sum of my genuine experience dealing with the paranormal, and you were by my side for every second of it. So you're just as qualified as me."

"Which is to say neither of us is qualified."

I laugh and say, "Exactly. But don't tell anyone else." I let out a breath, unsure of what to say next, but decide I can be upfront with her, which is one of the things I like best about her. "The truth is, I think that we should take it slow. We do need to work together now, and I don't want to lose you—from the team, I mean. And...maybe I'm wrong, but I think you've got some...issues to take care of." I raise my hands when she looks at me with serious eyes. "You don't need to talk about it. Unless it affects your work here, it's none of my business...until you decide to make it my business." I'm not sure she gets what I'm saying, but then she replies.

"I was married," she says, and then sighs. "The short version is that my husband was psychotic. Like actually psychotic. He nearly killed the mailman when he found the guy in the house. Thought I was screwing him. And before you ask, no, I wasn't. The poor guy was sixty-two. He was in the house because it was hot and he looked close to passing out. I offered him a lemonade. My ex went to jail for aggravated assault. Got five years. He's been out for two."

"Wasn't just the mailman, though," I say, "was it?"

She shakes her head. "I was in the hospital for three days. Lots of damage. Nothing permanent. I wanted to be ready if he came to find me, so I became a cop and learned how to fight."

I remember the way she handled the highly trained soldiers, and her brawl with Endo. "I think you're more than ready."

"Please," she says, waving her hand like it's no big deal. "I've faced a giant fucking monster. I'm not afraid of my ex anymore."

We both smile a little, but then I get serious. I'm an observant guy, so I'm pretty sure I understand what's just happened, but I need to be sure. "So...did you just make it my business?"

She puts her hand on mine. "I did, but we'll still take it slow."

Her hand feels like an electric charge on top of mine, and all of my pent up stress and fear and anger is transmogrified into desire. Screw taking it slow, I think, but then a window on the floor above opens and I say, "That better be Mrs. Rosen."

"We've got something," Cooper says.

"Be right up," I say.

"Don't come here," she says. "Get to the roof instead. I'll give you the details in the air."

I hear the helicopter's engine warming up above us and wonder how long it will be before we get complaints from the neighbors. I hop down from the wall. "Where are we headed?"

"West Beach," Cooper says.

I freeze with my hand on the sliding door to my room. I turn my head up. "That's—"

"—Beverly Farms," she says. "You can be there in ten minutes."

35

Woodstock flies low and fast, performing the equivalent of a cross-town sprint that takes us in a straight line over the older neighborhoods fringing downtown Beverly, past "the Cove" and finally to the less densely populated but far higher tax bracket of Beverly Farms.

Woodstock marvels at the mansions as we fly past. While FC-P's all-brick megalithic home is nothing to complain about, it's surrounded by an average American neighborhood, doesn't have a garage and is one of the oldest large buildings in town. The homes in Beverly Farms have horse stables, fifteen car garages, half-mile driveways and guest houses the size of the Rosen estate. We live in the home of Beverly's old rich, whereas Beverly Farms houses the summer homes of the modern ultra-rich, though there are some normal neighborhoods scattered around the area's wealthy.

We descend quickly, circling close to a home with ocean views, and land in the West Beach parking lot. The bumpy dirt and gravel surface isn't ideal for a chopper landing, but Woodstock keeps us hovering right over the ground.

I look at my new pilot and give him a knowing grin. The low flight, the rapid landing and the residential fly-by aren't exactly legal. Given the circumstances, no one is going to give us a hard time, but most pilots would follow the regulations out of force of habit.

He shrugs. "What's the point of having the authority to fly however the hell you want if you don't do it? Besides, I need to keep up my skills if I'm going to avoid being chewed or blowed up."

"Good point," I say and pat his arm. "Keep up the good work."

He smiles and says, "I'll give you some light from the sky."

"Don't go far," I tell him. "In case, you know, something tries to eat us."

He gives a salute, and I exit to find Collins already out and headed toward the beach. We're both armed with Springfield Armory .45 ACP handguns, which can drop a person or a rhino with a single shot, but the weapons are useless against our foe and do nothing to ease my trepidation as I step onto the sand.

As my shoes sink in the sand, my instinct is to kick them off, but I'm not here for surfing. I scuff through the darkness, filling my shoes with sand, catching up with Collins.

Boats in the water and SUVs in the sand illuminate a large, dark shape just off shore. When Woodstock brings the helicopter overhead and casts his bright spotlight down on the thing, Collins and I stop. The dark skin is instantly recognizable.

"We need to get everyone the hell away from here!" I say, and take a breath to shout a warning.

"Wait," Collins says. "How deep is the water here?"

I'd been swimming at the beach just once, but I went out pretty far and don't remember it being deep where the boats are. "Thirty feet, tops," I say and understand her point. It's far too shallow for the goliath creature to stay submerged in. We'd see much more of it. "So what the hell is this?"

We head for the water where a line of police officers have gathered. Some are crouching. Some are standing. But all are looking down at what's in the water, which has apparently reached land.

"Hey," I say in greeting, not wanting to spook the officers more than they already must be.

The group turns around. The oldest of the bunch, a man with stark white hair and a suit jacket rather than a uniform, says, "Get off the beach, now! This is a—"

I hold out my ID. "DHS. I'm Special Investigator Jon Hudson. " I motion to Collins. "This is Special Investigator Ashley Collins."

"Detective Zandri," the older man says, "and I'm not sure you being here makes me feel much better. You were in charge up in Portland, yeah?"

"The Boston office," I say, not feeling guilty for placing the blame for that debacle where it belongs, squarely on FC-Boston's shoulders. That said, I'm not sure the outcome would have been much different if we had all the heavy arms I asked for.

"And what office are you?" Zandri asks.

"The one that deals with gigantic monsters," I say.

"That what we got here?" he asks, motioning to the black mass bobbing up and down with the waves. "A giant monster? 'Cause this looks like a big floating sack of rotten shit to me. Smells like it too."

He was right about that. The odor of raw meat and vinegar erased all traces of the ocean's salty scent. "Mind if I have a look?"

"Knock yourself out," Zandri says.

The officers part.

I flick on my flashlight and crouch by what looks like a black, textured comforter made of rubber.

"For the record," Collins says, crouching next to me, "Cops hate it when federal agencies refer to themselves as special."

I poke the black surface with my bare finger. It's rough, like shark skin, but has zero give. I push harder and feel just the slightest bend, but maybe that's the meat on the tip of my finger. "That's my title," I say.

"Doesn't matter," she says, handing me a knife and a Ziploc bag. "It sounds egotistical and creates tension."

"Huh," I say, both to Collins's observations and the fact that the knife is barely scratching the surface. "What should I call myself?"

"If you have to, use 'investigator'," she says, "but if they've already seen your ID, just use your last name."

I get a tiny flake of what I believe to be Nemesis's skin into the bag and seal it up. I don't think it's going to be pertinent to our investigation, but we'll learn what we can from it. There's more than enough to go around, but I don't know if continued exposure to salt water will degrade the sample. I look up, out to sea, and I can see a Coast Guard cutter illuminating a patch of black nearly a hundred and fifty feet from shore. Given the size and current toughness, I don't think the rest of it will be going anywhere soon.

I stand and head toward the detective. "Zandri."

"Yes, special investigator," he says.

Holy crap, she's right, I think, and say, "Call me Hudson."

He looks a little surprised and slightly placated, then seems to remember I'm looking at him and says, "What do you need?"

"Just inform your men that I'm going to discharge my firearm."

He looks at the black thing. "I think its dead."

I nod. "Yeah, it's a husk."

"A husk?"

"The creature that attacked Portland is growing," I say. "It molts."

"Like how a snake sheds its skin," Zandri says. "But the reports I hear put the thing at seventy-five feet tall."

"Taller," I say.

"And it's still growing?"

I look at the massive sack of skin floating in the water. "Apparently." I draw my .45 and he gets the message. While he informs all teams present that I'm going to fire my gun, I walk back to the water and aim the weapon.

"See how much better that went?" Collins says.

"Watch it," I say, "or I'll make Zandri my new partner."

"He wouldn't look as good in body armor," she says.

I look down the sight of the gun. For the purpose of my test, I'll need to keep my grouping tight. I'm firing at close to point blank range, but the .45 has a good amount of kick. "There isn't a single situation in which that man would look better than you."

"I could be a Zombie," she says. I can't see her, but I can sense her smile. I let out a breath, allowing her presence to calm me.

I pull the trigger. The single shots rolls out over the ocean. I look around the gun, see the damage, and then pull the trigger nine more times, emptying the clip. As the last thunderous report rings out, I look around and see lights coming on in the bedrooms of homes lining the beach. I turn to Zandri and point at the houses. "Have someone tell them that was kids with fireworks."

"They'll see it in the morning," Zandri says.

"Yeah, but at least they'll be well rested when they see the monster skin covering their beach."

He sends an officer running down the beach and then joins me beside the black fold of monster skin I just shot the shit out of. He adds his flashlight to mine.

"Holy mother," he says.

"Yeah," I say. It's all I've got. I bend down and pick up one of the mushroomed bullets. It crumbles in my fingers. All ten rounds simply rest atop the skin in small divots created by the force of their impacts. Not one of them penetrated the skin. While a higher caliber might, it definitely wouldn't get far.

"Detective!" The shout is distant and shaky.

I look toward the voice and see a flashlight bobbing madly. The man Zandri sent away is running back.

"Detective!" he screams again, sounding shaken.

Zandri steps forward to greet the officer as he stumbles out of the dark.

"Is it here?" Zandri asks.

The officer shakes his head, no, as he leans forward and tries to catch his breath. He points behind him. "Down the beach. By the old wharf."

"What is it?" Collins asks.

"I—I'm not sure," he says and points to the flotilla of skin. "It's like this, but...bloodier. I didn't see much. I just ran."

When I take off in the direction the officer came from, Collins, Zandri and a few officers follow closely. Woodstock's spotlight follows us for half the run, but then he must figure out there is something ahead of us because he takes the lead, following the surf line until he lands on a mass of bloody pulp.

I stop short when I see it.

"What is that?" Zandri asks.

I walk closer. It's a body. A large body. And it's been bitten in half. I can see the tooth marks lining the meat.

"Looks like a giant took a bite out of a king-sized apple," Zandri says.

"A bloody apple," I say.

"It's a whale," Collins says. "A fin whale. It's the second largest whale after the blue. Grow up to ninety feet."

"Ninety feet!" Zandri says and I understand that his outrage has nothing to do with how large the whales grow and everything to do with how much is missing.

Only about twenty feet of the whale rolls in the surf, which means it wasn't bitten in half, "It was bitten in two tenths."

"That doesn't even make sense," Collins says, but it's just a whisper. She's fixated, as I am, on the helicopter's spotlight as it pans farther down the beach, illuminating three more partially consumed whale carcasses, lined up like a plate of sausages big enough for a god.

Nemesis.

"I think you were right about the creature," Zandri says.

"It's growing bigger," Collins says, finishing the detective's thought.

I nod. "A lot bigger."

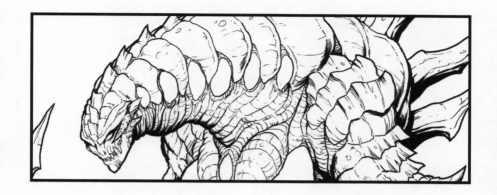

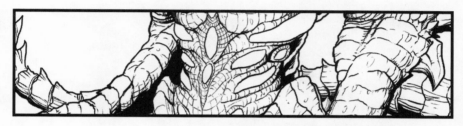

STAGE 3

36

By the time we get back to FC-P, it's two in the morning, and after the last couple of days, my eyes are hanging heavy. I sit at my desk while retelling the details of what we found at the beach. I ask Cooper to put the Coast Guard and Navy in the area on a higher alert, and ask that those sweeping the waters to the north, work their way south. My last request is a pot of coffee.

When Cooper leaves, Watson confirms that the land in Alaska is owned by a series of shell companies leading back to Zoomb. As he explains how he uncovered this information, I lean my head back and close my eyes. I hear him saying something about showing me satellite photos of the site.

And then, the coffee is there, tickling at my nose.

I open my eyes to what feels like a spotlight. "Turn the lights down," I say, covering my face with my hands.

"Hard to turn off the sun," Cooper says.

The sun?

I open my eyes again, moving out of the light by rolling my chair to the side, and I find the early morning sun pouring through the fourth story windows, the way they do every morning.

Cooper stands next to me, still looking impeccable in her power suit, but there are bags under her eyes. She stayed up all night. She's holding a large, steaming coffee mug.

"You shouldn't have let me sleep," I say.

"I would have woken you if anything new developed," she says.

I take the mug, and take a blissful sip. My body relaxes from the heat, familiar flavor and the knowledge that caffeine will soon hit my bloodstream. I blink my eyes and sit up straighter. Watson is at his computer, typing away. He doesn't like to use the same cup twice, so there's a collection of empty coffee mugs next to his workstation.

"What time is it?" I ask.

"Six in the morning," Cooper replies.

Six is hardly my typical wake-up time. Cooper's words sink in—I would have woken you if anything new developed. My heartbeat doubles its pace. "What happened? Do we need to leave?"

"Nothing that requires immediate action," she says.

As my racing heart slows, I notice that Collins and Woodstock aren't present. "Where are the others?"

"I assigned them rooms on the second floor," Cooper says. "They decided to sleep when they saw their fearless leader passed out in his chair."

I look up at her in time to see a small smile before she can hide it. "Coop, was that a joke? And a smile? We're going to have to keep you up all night more often."

"I'd rather not," she says, returning to her normal straight-faced self. For a moment, I wonder if she'd be a fun drunk, but then I remember seeing her drink half a bottle of wine one Christmas while we three loners, with no place to go, watched the snow fall, and later, kids sledding in a neighboring backyard. The alcohol seemed to have no effect, but that might have simply been a result of whatever Christmas memories she was trying to ignore. That, or she just needs something stronger. An experiment for another day.

"Do you want me to wake them?" she asks.

"Get Collins," I say. "Woodstock needs as much sleep as possible."

She nods in agreement. "Tired pilots are never a good thing."

"And he's old," I say, looking for a smile. Nothing. "Tell me what happened."

"Last night, sometime before you were called out to see the whales, a booze cruise steamship out of Portsmouth disappeared."

"Disappeared?"

"Last known contact was with the harbor master, who ordered all ships dock after the creature took to the ocean in Portland."

I nod. I'm the one who made the request that all ships return to port.

She continues. "But the ship never returned. There was no mayday sent. No GPS locator activated. This morning, the Coast Guard spotted debris that could have come from the steamship, but there was no way to identify it. However, based on the circumstances, I think it's safe to say that the ship was destroyed and everyone on board killed."

I cringe. "How many on board?"

"Manifest shows three hundred, but it was a private party, so whoever showed up was let on board. The person running the ticket booth at the time said he stopped letting people on board once it reached capacity."

"Which is?"

"Three fifty," she replies. "Apparently, many of the last to board were...entertainment."

"You mean hookers," I say.

She nods.

"Which is going to make identifying them a little harder." I say.

"With all due respect to the dead, that's not our problem," she says. "Local police and FBI can handle those details. We need to focus on the big picture."

The emphasis she puts on, "big," makes me think she's being funny again, but her face is like solid stone.

"Which is?" I ask.

Watson stops typing, sits back from his computer and picks up a couple of manila folders. He rolls across the hardwood floor and stops next to me. He hands the folders to me and says, "Open the top folder."

All of Watson's normal joviality is gone. "You sound like her," I say, motioning to Cooper.

"Not all of us got to sleep last night," he says, sounding genuinely irritated, but then he softens. "Sorry. That was stupid. I was sitting at a desk while you were getting shot at and almost eaten." He looks at me, waiting.

"Don't sweat it," I say, freeing his mind to get back on task.

I open the top folder to an 8x10 print of a satellite photo. It's a big brown patch of land lacking any trees or any other kind of growth. There's a large tunnel at the center of the picture, reinforced with a concrete archway. The rest is scoured earth, either dug out by heavy machinery or blown to bits with precision explosives. Scattered around the image are tractors, dump trucks and people in hardhats. "This is the land in Alaska? Looks like a mining operation."

"Yes, and it's very similar to a mining operation," he says. "They definitely took something out of the ground, but the site is no longer active. No machinery. No people."

"I see plenty of people in this image," I say.

"That's an archived image from eleven months ago," Watson says. "It was taken by a mapping satellite on a routine flyby. Turn to the next image."

I flip the photo over. The next 8x10 doesn't look anything like the first. It's just a mass of brown earth. I compare the two, noting the color of the soil. "It's the same place. When was the second image taken?"

"Three months ago. I don't have a live image yet because it's still dark in Alaska, but I expect it to look just like that." He points to the second image. "Whatever they were doing up there, they're done, and I doubt they left anything behind."

"Still," I say. "Someone up there should take a look."

"I'll take care of it," Cooper says.

"What's in the second folder?" I ask.

When the question brings a frown to both Cooper and Watson's faces, I know it's not good.

"It just came in ten minutes ago," Watson said. "It's why we woke you up."

"Is it Nemesis?" I ask. "Did it come back?"

"It's General Gordon," Cooper says.

I flip open the second folder. I'm greeted by an image no one should see just a few minutes after waking up. Four dead men, piled in the back of a black SUV. The vehicle and suits scream "agency". The mental leap to their identities isn't hard to make. "FBI?"

"These are the men we had watching Zoomb headquarters at the Prudential Tower in Boston. Their bodies were discovered two hours ago after a cleaning crew discovered the bodies of four security guards and a receptionist on the fiftieth floor."

I turn the page and see the bloody carnage.

Nemesis wasn't the only monster on the loose last night.

I turn to the next image. It's of one of the FBI agents. He's been laid out on the pavement, half concealed by a body bag, but his shirt has been opened to reveal his chest, which has been caved in.

"The coroner hasn't examined the bodies yet," Cooper says. "But based on the size and depth of the impact wound, he thinks a steel beam fell on the man's chest."

I shake my head, no, remembering Gordon's strength. "He was punched."

"Punched?" Cooper actually sounds surprised.

"I don't think Gordon is fully human anymore," I say. "What was he after."

"Looks like he was there for Paul Stanton, Zoomb's CEO. There were signs of a struggle in the office, and a broken window, along with a second ten floors below. Witnesses recall a helicopter taking off from the building late last night. We thought that Gordon had kidnapped Stanton, but he turned up in Martha's Vineyard and claimed to have been there all night."

"Any sign of Gordon since?" I ask.

"None," she replies.

The sound of approaching footsteps turns us all around. Collins pads into the Crow's Nest wearing one of my T-shirts...and that's it, as far as I can see, anyway. Her wavy, orange hair is in a tussle. Her eyes are half closed. Totally unaware of her powers, she pauses to stretch, lifting her arms, and the shirt, arching her back and pushing out her chest.

"Whoa," Watson says.

"This will just not do," Cooper says.

I mentally take my "let's take it slow," decree to an imaginary firing range, shoot the shit out of it and then light it on fire.

As she walks closer to us, we watch her in silence. The light dims as a cloud moves in front of the morning sun and Collins opens her eyes a bit wider.

"Hey," she says, sleepily. "What's going—holy shit!"

Her eyes pop open, locked on the wall of windows.

I spin around and nearly fall out of my chair.

We're a mile from the ocean. Powder Hill, the tallest in the area, is two hundred feet at its peak, which is the land the Rosen residence was built upon. Being on the fourth floor adds another forty feet. We're pretty used to looking down at the rest of the world from the Crow's Nest, which I think was the intent of Mrs. Rosen's grandfather, but the object blotting out the sun stands just as tall.

Nemesis wades through Beverly Harbor like a kid walking out of the surf a foot from shore—the water coming up to its knees.

I stumble to the window and rest my hands on the glass, frozen in amazement. It's over two hundred and forty feet tall. Pushing three hundred at least. While still lithe for a towering monster, its body has some extra bulk where, what were once bumps on the elbows, knees and high ankles, have grown into horrible looking spikes. Plates of thick armor cover much of its body, along with twisting coils of thick flesh. The thing's hands are now massive and while the thumb appears to have grown in a way I'd expect, the index and middle fingers have fused into a single, double tipped digit, while the ring and pinkie fingers have receded. The pinkie isn't much more than a claw protruding from the side of the hand. The tail looks even more deadly as each of the three pronged blades looks to be the size of a 747 wing. Its facial features have lost all traces of humanity—except for the eyes. Those remain deep brown. Its thickly plated black brow is furrowed, and its lips are upturned in a permanent sneer that reveals its mammoth tusk-sized teeth. Overall, Nemesis is still recognizable as the same creature it was before, it's just a shitload bigger, and exaggerated in dangerous looking ways.

The membranes on its neck flare to life, glowing orange. It steps forward, and I feel a light rumble. Then it turns its head, looking straight at me, and roars. The glass under my hands vibrates from the sound, which is hard to describe. It still sounds like a mix of different pitches, but it's so loud and powerful, that I'm sure there is nothing on the planet that can match it. Which I think can be said about every aspect of the creature...alien...god, or whatever she is.

When Nemesis looks away and stops roaring, my mind is freed. Every citizen in Beverly and Salem is now wide awake. Panic is going to spread quickly.

I turn to Cooper. "Coast Guard. Navy. Air Force. Go!" I turn to Collins. "Get some clothes on!" As Collins, now fully awake, dashes out of the Crow's Nest, I turn to Watson. "I don't think Nemesis is stupid. She's here for a reason. Find out what it is."

Before he can reply, I run out of the room to give Woodstock the worst rude awakening of his life.

37

General Gordon felt like a man possessed as he was guided—compelled really—down a path to which he did not know the end. It would end. He felt sure of it. He just didn't know when, or where, or how. Only that it was a road he had to travel alone—without delay or mercy.

His first stop had been his private locker at the Zoomb offices. He had a small cache of weapons and explosives hidden away. Endo had questioned him when he stuffed the backpack full of C4 explosives into the locker—not out of judgment, but out of curiosity. Gordon had explained that there might come a day when any evidence leading to them might need to be erased. If it became necessary, they would have everything they needed to destroy the fiftieth floor of the Prudential Tower. A drastic measure perhaps, but in addition to destroying physical evidence, it would send a message to anyone else who might have anything incriminating— don't screw with General Lance Gordon.

Fully armed, Gordon stole a car and drove.

He didn't know where he was going, he just worked his way through Boston's winding streets, following the speed limit, stopping for lights and letting the occasional pedestrian cross in front of him without laying on the horn.

After nearly five hours of driving around the city, he'd almost drained the economy car's gas tank, but he pulled over and parallel parked near the corner of Clarendon and Stuart streets.

He blinked as he got out of the car and looked up at the bright blue morning sky.

I drove through the night, he realized. What's happening to me? But as soon as he had the thought, it was gone. He looked to his right and then up. The building he'd parked in front of was constructed of stylized concrete, gray for four stories, then all glass, then classic red Boston brick to the top, nearly thirty stories higher. He felt drawn to this building. He didn't know what this building was, but he recognized the monstrous structure rising from the opposite corner of the intersection as the John Hancock Tower, a wall of reflective glass that seemed to disappear into the sky it reflected.

He turned back to the much smaller building he'd been drawn to. What's here? he wondered, looking at the sign above the entryway that read: One Back Bay – Rentals – Floors 3, 14, 25 & 26 and then listed a phone number.

It's an apartment building, he thought, which means the question was not what was there, but who?

It didn't matter, of course. He had no choice but to go inside and find out. He opened the back door, took out his backpack of C4, hand grenades and smaller weapons, and headed for the door.

When he got to the door, he found it locked. A doorman appeared and opened it. The doorman, who was elderly yet impeccably maintained like beloved china, looked Gordon up and down and said, "No solicitations."

Gordon got his foot in the door before it could close and said, "I'm here to see a friend."

The doorman grimaced down at the foot, but remained composed. "And who might you be here to see, at such an early hour?"

Gordon opened his mind, hoping a name would come to him.

None did, so he drew his sound suppressed weapon and shot the old man in the head. He tore the door open, stepped inside and caught the falling body before it hit the polished marble floor. Before he could be seen, he rushed the man to the service desk, threw him on the floor and pushed him under the counter.

Just then, the elevator pinged and the doors opened. Three men dressed for work in Boston's financial district strolled out, their shiny shoes clacking against the floor. They joked with each other, their words muffled, but their tone condescending. One of them looked to Gordon, saying, "Hey Mitch—" His forehead scrunched when he saw Gordon. "Where's Mitch?"

"Out sick," Gordon said. "I'm a temp."

The man paused and turned to Gordon, looking him over. "Well, temp, you look like shit. Maybe if you put in a little more effort you'd be retiring instead of temping."

Gordon raised an eyebrow at the man.

"You think this is funny?" the man said. "When you stand behind that counter, you represent this building and everyone in it. If you look like shit, we look like shit, and I don't spend thirty-five grand a month for a twentieth floor apartment in a tower...of...shit!"

Gordon raised his handgun beneath the countertop, aiming it at the man's gut. He wanted to shoot the man. Few things would bring him greater pleasure. But he couldn't pull the trigger.

For starters, the man's two buddies were close to the front door. He wasn't sure if he could shoot all three before one of them escaped.

He had a higher purpose here, one that could not involve outside interference. He didn't know what the purpose was, but he committed to it. He removed his finger from the trigger and said, "I'll try to do better next time."

"There won't be a next time," the man said, thrusting a finger in Gordon's face. "You can bet on that."

You can kill him when you're done, Gordon told himself, and remained silent as the man waggled his finger one more time and strode off to rejoin his cohorts, who burst out laughing. He watched them leave and then headed for the elevator. The doors slid open immediately and he stepped inside.

He turned around and faced the numbers. This is crazy, he thought, staring at an array of numbered white circles. When the doors shut, he closed and rubbed his eyes with his left hand. When he opened his eyes again, he found his right hand extended and his index finger pushing the button for the thirty-third floor.

"Penthouse it is," he said.

As the elevator rose, his sense of a higher purpose increased with each floor. By the time he reached the thirty-third floor, he was jittery with nervous energy. The doors slid open and Gordon charged into the hallway, gun in hand, backpack over his shoulder.

He strode to the door at the end and kicked. The doorframe cracked like thunder and the deadbolt tore away. The apartment was a spacious den for Boston's ultra-rich, with marble floors, sparse, but expensive looking décor and a view of the city that could make anyone feel important. He swung the weapon back and forth, looking for a target, but found none.

He lowered the weapon, looking for hints as to why he was here. The only thing that stuck out was the smell of fresh paint and harsh cleaning chemicals. The place had either been recently remodeled or some kind of mess cleaned up.

Stepping closer to the window, a new sound reached his ear. Three squeaks. Though Gordon had never been in the apartment before, he recognized the sound of a bathtub faucet being turned.

Someone's in the bathroom.

Moving slowly, he headed toward the bathroom door, which was open a crack. As he got nearer, he could hear humming. It was a man's voice. The song was Ave Maria.

As the humming reached a crescendo, Gordon kicked the door open. He pointed his gun at a fat, pasty white man wearing a pair of black knee-high socks and white boxers. As the man shouted in surprise and fell backwards, wedging himself between the tub and the toilet, Gordon finished the song, letting out a vibrato-filled, "Aaaaave Mariiiia," that would make Pavarotti proud.

When Gordon took a bow, the fat man said, "W—who are you?"

"Doesn't matter," Gordon said.

"What do you want?"

Gordon shrugged. "I have no idea."

The man's balding head went from white to pink as his confusion slowly transformed into righteous indignation. He gripped the side of the toilet bowl, which had the seat up, and pushed himself up onto his knees. "Do you have any idea who I am?"

It was a question, but Gordon heard the threat in the man's tone. Whoever he was, he believed Gordon should be afraid of him, not the other way around. Gordon looked into the man's eyes and saw the glare of a predator. He grinned and matched the stare, which unnerved the man.

Gordon pointed to the sink. "Wash your hands."

"What?" the man said. "Why?"

"Because that wasn't sanitary," Gordon said, motioning to the toilet bowl. "And I want you to get used to obeying orders."

When the man just stared at him, Gordon lowered the gun toward the man's leg and started counting down from five. "Five, four, three."

The man turned on the sink's faucet and quickly scrubbed his hands.

"Soap, too," Gordon said.

The man obeyed, picking up a bar of soap and rubbing it between his hands. When the man finished, Gordon tossed a hand towel to him and said, "Let's go."

"Can I finish getting dressed?" the man asked.

Gordon twisted his lips. He didn't like the man's belligerent tone. In fact, he detested everything about him, though he didn't understand why. "No. You can't."

The man grumbled, but followed Gordon out of the bathroom.

"Do you want money?" the man asked. When Gordon didn't answer, he added, "Women? I can buy you one. Or three."

"Turn around," Gordon said, and the man complied.

"Just tell me what you want and—oof!" The man crumbled to the floor as Gordon pistol-whipped the back of his head. Gordon rolled the man over and quickly bound his arms and legs with plastic zip-tie cuffs.

"Actually," Gordon said to the unconscious man, "Just stay here. I'll be back in a few minutes." With that, he opened his backpack and took out several bricks of C4, detonators and a half dozen grenades. "I'll be right back."

38

We're in the air five minutes later, but Collins is still tucking in her shirt as we lift off, and half of Woodstock's gray hair resembles a pom-pom. At least no one can see us up in the helicopter. I don't think anyone would feel at ease knowing we're the frontline of defense against the colossal monster stomping its way through the harbor.

As we turn toward the ocean, I look out the cockpit and find that we're at eye level with Nemesis.

"Higher," I say, "Must get higher."

But Woodstock is already ascending, taking us to a thousand feet—out of leaping reach—before bringing us closer horizontally.

"How come it's not destroying anything?" Collins asks, looking out the side window as we circle high above.

Nemesis is still in the harbor, following the water's path. If she wanted to eat people, she could. I can see the streets below filling with people on foot. I count at least three accidents on Cabot Street alone, bringing fleeing traffic to a standstill. But the giant is still in the water.

What do you want? I wonder.

"Maybe it's never been just about eating people?" I say. "She's been moving steadily south. I think all of her victims just happened to be in the way."

"Not steadily south," Collins says. "We're only a few miles from West Beach, right?"

She's right. "She shed her skin last night. And ate at least six whales. Maybe she slept?"

"And grew," Woodstock said.

I nod. "Yeah, that, too. So does anyone know where we can find a giant robot or flying submarine?"

"I've got a normal submarine," Cooper says. Before we left, Watson and Woodstock got the helicopter radios tuned into the Crow's Nest via a satellite uplink that connects directly into FC-P's computers. It's like a fancy, encrypted, government version of Skype. But without the video.

"How far out?" I ask.

"Twenty minutes," Cooper says.

"Too long."

"There's a Coast Guard cutter five minutes out. And a Navy Destroyer ten minutes out."

"Turn the cutter back," I say. The ship is big, but the mounted machine gun will be useless again Nemesis. "Bring the Destroyer into visual range, but instruct them to engage from a distance, and only if I give the order." From sea level, the average person can see three miles to the horizon. But Nemesis is so tall that they should be able to see it from twice as far. I know the ship's Tomahawk missiles could probably be deployed from the ship's current position, but I don't feel remotely comfortable shooting long range missiles, which sometimes miss, toward my city. "Air Force?"

"Hold on. Just hearing now." The line goes quiet for a few seconds, then she's back. "On the way. Two F-22 Raptors. ETA five minutes."

"Thanks, Coop," I say.

"Hudson," she says, sounding more serious than usual. "Is that going to be enough?"

It's a good question, but the answer is an easy one. "Not remotely."

"We've got a fleet between you and Boston," she says. "Three Destroyers, two subs, two cruisers and an aircraft carrier. I can have all of them sent your way."

"Have them on standby," I say, watching Nemesis through the window. The monster has stopped short of Essex Bridge. "What's she looking at?"

"I can't see from here," Cooper says.

"Sorry," I say. "Wasn't talking to you. Just keep everyone ready. I'm not sure what's happening here, and I'd like to avoid blowing up the neighborhood if possible. Best if we engage out at sea if we can."

"Agreed," she says. I hear a click and she's gone, no doubt already relaying my requests. Can't really call them orders, but at this point they might as well be.

"I think it's interested in that building," Collins says, pointing down. "What is that?"

I recognize the location. "It's a luxury condo."

"It's just staring at it," Collins says.

"Watson, you there?" I ask.

"Yeah," he says. "I can see you out the window. You guys look like a fly."

"That makes me feel so much more confident, Ted, thanks," I say. "Listen, do you know the condo between Dane Street Beach and the yacht club?"

"By the bridge?"

"Yeah."

I hear computer keys clacking. "Seaside Condos," he says. "Big bucks with full access to the docks."

"See if there is anything interesting about them," I say. "Nemesis can't take her eyes off of them."

"On it," he says, and then he's gone.

"What now?" Woodstock says. "We could distract it. Get it to chase us back out to sea? Might remember us."

It's a horrible plan that could very well end in our deaths. I'm about to agree when the membranes over the creature's ribcage flare to life.

"Something's happening!" Collins says.

"Take us down," I say to Woodstock, and then to Collins, "Get ready to remind it who we are."

She nods and opens the side door, letting in a whoosh of morning air. But before she's done readying the weapon, Nemesis raises her long, black arm. A sense of dread fills me as I realize she is about to level the condo. My eyes scan the streets behind the building. They're empty. Anyone living in the building would have fled already.

I feel a little better knowing the damage will only be structural, but this feels like the opening shot of a battle. A lot of people are going to die.

Nemesis roars, and swings.

And then stops.

Her giant hand must be just feet from the side of the building, but hasn't destroyed it. The hell?

We watch in silence as Nemesis continues to just stare.

"What's it doing?" Collins asks.

Nemesis takes a step back.

Then another.

"F-22s are two minutes out," Cooper says, making me jump. "But they can fire now."

"Tell them to hold their fire!" I shout, far louder than necessary. "I think she's leaving."

When Nemesis turns around, she looks slow because of her size, but I know she's actually moving quite quickly. As the massive tail spins around behind her, it kicks up a thirty foot wave that rolls upstream, heading up the three rivers—Bass, Danvers and North—that converge in the harbor. It flows under the Essex Bridge, but will no doubt destroy a good number of homes and small bridges. Still, it's a mercy compared to what could have happened.

"Stay with her," I tell Woodstock. "I don't want to lose sight of her."

Nemesis is moving fast now, trudging through the harbor, back out toward the open ocean. As she pushes through the water, pressure waves rise up ahead of her. There are several islands on the outskirts of the harbor. Some with homes. I'm about to contact Cooper and request emergency services for the islands and the areas around the rivers, but she beats me to the punch.

"Hudson!" Cooper says quickly. Her raised voice and tone are very unusual, bordering on unheard of, and instantly get my attention. "Get away from Nemesis!"

"What? Why?"

"You have incoming! Four Tomahawk missiles from the Destroyer and twelve AMRAAMs from the F-22. ETA, thirty seconds!"

"Get us the fuck out of here," I say to Woodstock.

The chopper banks hard toward land and we pick up speed.

"The harbor is surrounded by dense civilian population!" I shout. "What idiot superseded my orders? Get whoever it is on the line, now!"

"I can't," Cooper says, sounding defeated. "The President gave the order. This is no longer a DHS operation."

"No longer a—then what the hell is it?"

"War," she says.

"Meaning collateral damage is acceptable," I say and look back at Nemesis. The orange glowing membranes catch my attention. "It's going to be far worse than they know. Cooper, you need to tell—"

A loud roar rockets past the helicopter.

"Holy mother of Cthulu!" Woodstock shouts.

The roar is repeated eleven more times. My head spins, watching the AIM-120D AMRAAM "fire and forget" missiles rocket past, closing the distance to Nemesis's plated back.

It's too late.

Streaks in the sky above Nemesis catch my attention. It's the Tomahawks. Their trajectory shifts, heading downward toward the colossal target. Each Tomahawk packs the equivalent punch of twenty AMRAAMs and are designed to level buildings.

A plume of orange fire, which looks tiny in comparison to Nemesis, appears on the monster's protected back. I don't think any real damage was done, but the creature turns in the direction from which the attack came, spinning her back toward the Tomahawks, which strike next. The resulting explosion is massive and the fire ball it creates silhouettes Nemesis as she pitches forward from the force, raising her arms and roaring—not in pain, but in anger.

The shockwave strikes in time with the boom that rivals the volume of Nemesis's roar earlier this morning. The chopper shakes for a moment, but Woodstock levels us out, and I see that we're back over HQ, heading for the roof.

That's when I see what's going to happen. Nemesis's midsection is exposed. The orange membranes flare brightly in response to the monster's anger. Five of the remaining AMRAAM missiles strike a tall, spiked plate angling out from her back, doing no damage. Two more strike her arm with a similar lack of effect. Three strike between the patches of glowing skin. But the final missile hits one of the more fragile membranes over her ribs, and explodes.

I feel the helicopter skids hit the landing pad on the mansion's roof.

But then there's a flash of light so bright that I can still see it through my clenched eyes. Before the light dissipates, a shockwave strikes. It's so powerful that I only register its existence for a fraction of a second. Then I'm unconscious along with everyone else within a three mile radius.

39

The pain was intense, but brief, flaring out from her chest and then away. When the light faded, the world around her had changed. The life she had sensed all around her no longer existed.

And it felt wrong.

She didn't know why. The humans were prey.

Though the whales she'd eaten, while not psychologically satisfying, avoided upsetting her growing emotional side. They also satiated her physical hunger long enough to stay focused on the force driving her since she opened her eyes.

Justice.

Retribution.

Vengeance.

In the silence that followed the explosion, her thoughts cleared. There was nothing for her here, which meant her journey was not yet over. Sloshing through the now boiling ocean, she turned south. From her three-hundred-twenty-foot height, she could see the towering skyscrapers of Boston, many far taller than her. Despite their size, she sensed they were nothing more than man-made mountains and posed no threat.

What she saw between her and the city, which called to her with every beat of her tank-sized heart, were a number of objects that made her pause. She had felt the sting of their weapons, and though she survived, the pain was still fresh in her mind. She thought about avoiding the jets in the sky and ships in the sea, but they would just be waiting for her when she surfaced.

Her competing traits—mind, body and soul—fought for the best course of action. Her mind, which was fueled by thoughts of destruction, violence and unbridled revenge for the wrongs done to her, both past and present, wanted to charge forward and crush everything in her path. It's what she'd always done. What she'd been sent here for. But her emotions riled against such thoughts, tempering the rage with...mercy.

The mind revolted at the thought.

She hadn't found what she was looking for in the condo build-ing, but she could sense guilty humans all around. There were innocents, too, but their deaths had once been acceptable. Now... If not for the explosion, which was not her doing, she would have left the harbor without laying waste to it. Her pursuit for justice took her somewhere else, and when she found the object of her rage, which her intellect did not yet understand, nothing would stand in her way.

Her body was a driving force when hunger struck, the need for sustenance superseding all thought or feelings. Right now, the body sent warnings of imminent pain, but continued to grow and change in ways that supplied the mind unceasing confidence.

A wave of energy suddenly passed through her, drawing her eyes to the tall buildings. She could feel...something. A signal. A beacon. Then it came clear and for the first time she knew. She remembered.

Her emotions welled up, and for the first time since they emerged, they were in concert with her intellect and body, screaming for vengeance. Functioning as a whole, she opened her mouth and let out a roar that every person in Boston, every jet in the sky and every ship on the sea, would hear. They would know she was coming.

If they were smart, they would flee.

If they weren't, they would die.

She lunged forward into the water, casting up waves that crashed to shore, pulverizing charred homes. She flattened her arms and legs against her body and with a thrash of her tail swam out to sea.

She made no effort to hide her approach or avoid a fight.

Adrenaline fueled her body.

Rage filled her thoughts.

Bloodlust drew her forward—not on a straight line for her target, but on a path that would bring her into direct contact with each and every human that wished to do her harm. That was something she would not stand for. Not ever again.

Seeing in the ocean lacked the clarity that being in the open pro-vided, but her powerful eyes amplified light when needed, and as the images viewed by the eyes were processed by the brain, the distor-tions created by currents, waves and pollutants were compensated for. The result was a fairly clear image of a submarine three miles away and closing.

Doubling the submarine's speed, she plowed through the ocean, slipping beneath the surface when it became deep enough to accommodate her size, which was still expanding, and once again growing tight and itchy.

Two small cylinders shot out of the front of the submarine while it was still a mile off. Then two more, two more and two more. The way they were fired, in quick succession felt like the panicked kicks of a zebra being chased by a lion. She knew the cylinders were weapons. They might cause her great pain. But she also knew they would not kill, stop or slow her down.

She closed her eyes, lowered her carapace and took all eight torpedoes head-on. They stung, like bees, she thought, but she had only a hazy memory of what that meant. The sound of the explosions rang loud in her ears. In response, she let out a roar. The powerful sound carried perfectly through the water and reached the subma-rine at full strength, filling the metal tube with an echoing rage.

She could hear the men inside screaming in pain, ears shattered by the force of her roar. The sound drew her closer, fueling her thirst for destruction.

The 377-foot-long submarine was about the same size as her body if measured snout to tail, but it lacked her bulk, maneuverabili-ty and ferocity. Before it could fire another salvo, she swam alongside the massive sub, gripped the front of it in one clawed hand and the back in another, freezing it in place.

The modern killing machine was now nothing more than an oversized banana in the hands of a hungry child. Opening her massive maw, Nemesis wrapped her mouth around the sub's midsec-tion and bit down. Exerting an unimaginable amount of pressure to the diamond hard tips of her teeth, she bit through the hull, filling it with dozens of puncture wounds, each several feet in diameter. When she withdrew her teeth, fountains of bubbles exploded from the sub's interior. She flexed her arms and the weakened hull snapped in half. Air exploded into the water and rose up as a shimmering cloud. It was followed by the bodies of sailors, some still living, sucked out into the ocean.

She was about to eat the men, but a distant thrum, thrum, thrum turned her south toward Boston. Vengeance was near.

The cleaved halves of the sub sank to the bottom, the ballasts ruptured. Thirty-two sailors remained behind, free floating in the ocean's depths.

She left the scene, swimming fast again, cresting the surface where she found two large ships, six helicopters and four circling jets waiting. Brow furrowed, eyes narrowed, jaws snapping, she let out a war cry that made the hearts of the men standing in her path quake with fright.

Then, she charged.

40

I wake with a groan, confused by where I am and my spinning view of the world around me. When I start to feel nauseous, I close my eyes and focus on what I can hear—nothing but a high pitched whine—and what I can smell. The odor is familiar. A mix of mechanical and human scents, one of which is Collins. I hadn't realized she had a distinct smell before, but I know she's here. I reach my hand out, and I feel something solid and curved. I then register the tightness across my chest.

A seatbelt.

Then I remember. Nemesis. The attack. The explosion.

I'm in the helicopter.

I open my eyes again. I'm less dizzy, but everything is still shifting left to right. I fight it long enough to look to my left. Woodstock is in the pilot's seat, slumped forward. His chest rises and falls with a steady rhythm. I look back for Collins. She's sprawled across the two back seats, but breathing.

When I look forward again, the world twists around me, but I notice another reason for my disorientation. The helicopter landed askew. One skid is on the foot-high landing pad. The other isn't.

I push open my door, but it slams shut again. Stupid gravity, I think, and then shove it open again with enough power to open it all the way. I can see it's balanced precariously between "it's safe to exit," and "I'm going to smash your face in," so I unbuckle and pull myself out slowly and carefully.

My legs feel weak when I hit the concrete landing pad, so I take a moment to steady myself. After several deep breaths, I stand up straight and open my eyes. The world is no longer spinning, but I wish to God it was.

I stumble toward the ocean-facing side of the mansion's roof, taking in a scene of destruction straight out of an apocalyptic movie.

A ring of black covering the land in Beverly and Salem, segmented by the ocean, is the first thing I see. Portions of both cities fringing the coast line for at least a quarter mile inland have been incinerated. I don't see any fires burning. Everything is just charred to the core—burnt so hot and fast that there isn't even smoke, though I can smell the burn on wind.

How many people were left in those buildings? How many more people have died?

I clench my fists. If the President was here, I would kick him in the nuts.

A curtain of rising white mist, like a giant ghost, pulls my eyes to the harbor. It's steam, I realize. The ocean is hot.

Sunlight cuts through the steam, shimmering off the water's surface and thousands of small reflective objects.

Dead fish.

Everything within a quarter mile of the blast's epicenter has been superheated—land and sea.

"Oh my God," Collins says, stepping up next to me. I'm surprised by her arrival, but too shocked to react in any way other than to just look in her direction. "Where is it? Where is Nemesis?"

In my dazed state, I forgot to look for the creature. I focus on the part of the harbor where I last saw the behemoth.

Nothing.

I search farther out to sea.

"There's no sign of her," I say.

"I can't imagine anything surviving an explosion like that," she says. "Maybe it was destroyed?"

I look for signs of Nemesis's body. She was massive, so there should be chunks of her everywhere, scattered around the city, maybe farther, but I don't see anything. Maybe she was vaporized? Is such a thing even possible?

"God damn," Woodstock says.

I turn around to find him climbing out of the chopper. He gives the helicopter a quick once over, more concerned for it than himself or us, which means he's fine.

"Any damage?" I ask him.

"She'll fly," he says. "Our next take-off is going to be a might wonky, but she'll fly."

A shouting woman draws my eyes to a neighboring house. All of the ocean-facing windows have been blown out. I look down the street and see the same thing. I turn around, looking at the houses on the backside of the hill. The same. Stepping to the edge of the mansion, I look down. The Crow's Nest has no windows, which means all that glass is now inside.

Shifting glass from below is followed by a grunt, then I hear Watson say, "Cooper? Cooper!"

I'm running for the roof door before he's done shouting her name. I thunder down the single flight of steps and burst into the Crow's Nest, which is now a kaleidoscope of glass shards. Most of it litters the floor, but several large triangles protrude from the walls like a clan of glass-flinging ninjas rode through.

Watson is on the left, by Cooper's station. He's bleeding from a wound on his forehead, but it doesn't look too bad, and not nearly as bad as Cooper. She's lying on the floor with a five inch shard of glass rising from her chest. I rush over and fall to my knees beside Watson.

When I look at Cooper's chest, I'm both horrified and relieved. The shard is large and there's no way to tell how deep it is without yanking it out, and I'm sure as hell not going to do that. She'd bleed out in less than a minute. My relief comes from the wound's placement, far to the side of her lungs and heart. If she can get to a hospital, and soon, she'll make it.

I turn to Woodstock, who followed me down with Collins. "Warm up the chopper. You need to—"

A hand grips my wrist. It's Cooper. "Is it dead?"

I think for just a second and answer truthfully. "I doubt it."

"Then you need the chopper," she says.

"Horseshit," I say. "You're—"

"Hudson!" she says, her voice surprisingly commanding despite the grave wound. "Everything bad that has happened so far has mostly been because people are not listening to you. They're going to wage a war on U.S. soil and I'm not sure we can win. Millions could die. Entire cities might be destroyed. If they can't kill it, you need to stop it. It's why we're here. It's your job." She looks at the others. "And it's your job, too."

As I listen to Cooper's passionate plea and see the way she's fighting against the pain, I realize how much I have come to respect and admire her. More than that, I now know she is a dear friend. She notices the wetness forming around my eyes and takes my hand. "I'll be fine, but you need to stop it."

I nod. I have no idea how such a thing will be possible, but she's right. Stopping threats like Nemesis is why FC-P was formed. I'd never taken it seriously before, but I now understand the reason for our agency's existence. Paranormal threats do exist and it's our job to stop them, even if it is just once every five years. And I can't ignore that responsibility because Cooper is injured, or even if she dies.

"You're still going to the hospital, though." I turn to Watson. "Drive her to the hospital. It's just five minutes by car. Make sure they know who she is and see her immediately. Go now. They're going to be very busy, very soon."

"Wait," Cooper says, then to Watson. "Did you tell him?"

"Tell me what?"

"General Gordon surfaced," Watson says.

"Where?"

"In Boston," Watson says. "He's on the roof of the Clarendon Back Bay building. Has a hostage."

"Who?" I ask, continuing the game of twenty questions.

"News choppers got some pictures, which is how Gordon was ID'd, but the hostage is wearing a hood. Police tried to breach the roof, but the stairwells are all booby trapped. Two officers died."

"What the hell is he doing?" I ask, and I'm sure no one has an answer for that, but then Collins says, "Hold on. When did Gordon show up on the roof? While we were in the chopper?"

Watson nods, and I think I know what Collins is thinking.

"Around the same time Nemesis was about to put the smack down on that condo?" I ask.

"Actually," Watson says, "Yeah. The bulletin went out around the same time, maybe thirty seconds before. I was going to tell you when I saw Nemesis raising its arm. But...it has to be a coincidence, right? Gordon is in Boston."

"And Nemesis has been heading south," I say. "Once you have Cooper admitted, find out if there is a connection between the condo and something in Boston."

"Think you also have to consider that this Gordon guy is some-how controlling the creature," Woodstock says. "He was there when it was made, right?"

"Actually," I say, "he had her made...and I'm pretty sure he has part of her inside him." That Woodstock made this connection means I made the right call asking him to be on the team. It also means I need to sharpen my intellect. I don't know if he's right, but I should have thought of it. "Find out if Gordon has a connection to the condo, too."

Watson nods, runs to his station and picks up a laptop bag, which he throws over his shoulder. "Our power is out, which means we have no network access, but the hospital is far enough away from the blast zone that they still might have connectivity, and even if they don't, they'll have backup power. I'll be in touch." He bends down and scoops Cooper into his arms. I have always thought of Watson as pure pudge, but the way he lifts Cooper up reveals he's got some serious muscle hiding beneath his chubby exterior.

As Cooper is carried toward the stairs, she points to her workstation. "Hudson, on my desk." Then they're gone, moving down the three flights of stairs to the cars parked outside.

I move to the desk, expecting to find some kind of report or folder full of information. Instead, I find a maroon beanie cap. With a smile, I brush off the broken glass and place the cap on my head. I know Cooper didn't have time to go out and buy me a new cap, so she must have already had this one on hand, just in case.

Take care of her, I think in my head, and I realize I've just said a prayer for the first time since I was a kid. If there can be three-hundred-foot tall giant alien monsters, why not God? And if there is a God, we're going to need him, or her, or whatever, on our side.

I head for the stairs leading to the third floor and my bedroom. "I need to get something. Anything you need to do to get that chopper ready, do it."

"Boston?" Woodstock asks.

"Boston."

41

When we rise from the mansion's roof once again, and turn south, we're greeted by a wall of white steam rising from the heated harbor. Our view of Boston is blocked, but I have no doubt that's where the creature is headed. Gordon is somehow connected to her, and is drawing the creature to him. I have no real proof of this, but the timing is hard to ignore and really, what good is the P in FC-P if we need concrete proof for things? The paranormal, by definition, defies explanation.

We tilt forward and hit 150mph in just a few seconds.

When my phone rings, I look around for it and realize it's in my pants pocket, buried inside the suit I recovered from my closet and put on before leaving. Working fast, I peel up the Velcro straps across the front of the vest, then yank down the zipper underneath, careful to avoid the button on my chest that will activate the suit's primary function, which would really suck, even though I'm currently seated in the back of the chopper and Collins is riding shotgun.

I'm sure the caller is going to hang up, but ten rings in, I reach the phone in my pocket, pull it out and answer. "Hudson."

"What the hell happened out there?" Deputy Director Stephens shouts in my ears.

"The U.S. Military blew up a good portion of my city, that's what," I reply, voice oozing vitriol. "Why the fuck did they fire missiles over a civilian population?"

Silence for a beat, then, "It wasn't my call," Stephens says. All of his own anger has faded away. "What's the damage?"

I want to keep yelling, tell him he's an idiot and cuss him out until I'm out of breath, but I know it wasn't his call. When the Military comes in guns-a-blazing, there isn't much the DHS or any other federal law enforcement agency can do about, especially when the orders come from the Commander-in-Dickhead. After a deep breath, I answer. "High millions in structural damage. The harbor coastlines of two cities got incinerated. I don't know how many dead. People were evacuating, but it's the coast and heavily populated. Best guess, one to ten thousand dead in the immediate blast, but FC-P is a mile from the blast and the windows were blown out. Agent Cooper took some glass to the chest and is en route to the hospital."

"I'm sorry to hear that, is she—"

"Cooper is an illustration, sir," I say. "The point is that the number of injured and dead will be much higher because of shrapnel, accidents and panic. Ten thousand might be on the low end."

"God..." I hear him sigh, long and deep. I almost think he's exaggerating so I'll know just how sympathetic he is. We've never really got along. He's part of the mustache brigade after all, but I never really thought he was a bad person. Just a douche bag. There's a difference. But he does a lot to change my opinion when he adds, "Look, the President is all in with this action. I'm not going to be able to change his mind. But they might give me a minute to speak my mind. I can't guarantee they'll listen, but is there anything I can tell the President that will help them not kill any more civilians?"

"Actually, yeah," I say. "Tell them to stop using fire-and-forget missiles. They need to avoid striking the glowing orange membranes on the sides of the creature's neck and ribcage. That is what caused the explosion."

"How the hell does that work?" he says.

"We think the fluid inside those membranes reacts to the gases in the air and combusts. The bigger the wound, the bigger the explosion. But the flames seal the wound and Nemesis remains unharmed."

"Nemesis?"

I have no idea how to explain the name to this man over the phone, and I don't have time either, so I settle for, "That's what we're calling it, but that's not important. Tell them to aim for the legs. If they can immobilize it, they might be able to hit it in the head with something powerful enough to kill it. If they shoot more of those orange spots, there will be many more civilian casualties."

"What about the military?" he asks. "Think they have a chance?"

"Short of dropping a nuke on a U.S. city, they don't stand a chance. They hit this thing with twelve AMRAAMs and four Tomahawks, which is enough to take out an aircraft carrier, and it barely flinched. Our best bet is to lead it out to sea and hit it with something heavy."

"You mean nuke it," he says.

The idea of dropping a nuke anywhere in the world repulses me, but I don't see how conventional weapons are going to help. "That would be one option."

"Understood. I'm going to get on with the President now, let him know what you recommend."

His words, "let him know what you recommend," resonate quickly and I open my mouth to clarify that dropping a nuke is not my recommendation, but he's hung up. I could call back, but I know he won't answer. If things go south based on "my recommendations", his scapegoat is in place. He started the conversation with promise, but landed himself right back on my douche bag list.

A gentle hiss pulls my eyes forward and I find the chopper is enshrouded in white. A moment later, it clears and we get our first view of Boston, and the water between.

The three of us stare in silence, too stunned to offer a surprised curse. The ocean is a path of destruction. We're only five hundred feet up, so I can see the bodies littering the water, which shimmers with a rainbow oil slick. Beyond the bodies is the remains of a Navy vessel. I can't tell what it was—a Destroyer maybe—because it's torn in half, on fire and sinking fast. A second Navy ship, once again unidentifiable, looks like a giant torch. Every inch of the vessel is ablaze.

Someone must have shot the orange membrane, I think. The luminous orange flesh is like a brightly colored snake, advertising its deadly poison so that predators will keep their distance. It's a lesson I hope the military will soon learn.

Beyond the destroyed ships is Nemesis, standing tall in hip-deep ocean, plowing ahead toward Boston. A squadron of Apache helicopters circles the monster like angry bees.

"We need to get to Boston before Nemesis does," I say.

Woodstock gives a nod and says, "She's moving pretty fast. Only way to beat her to the punch is to go straight through. Circling too far around might get us there at the same time."

"Do it," I say.

A streak of tracer rounds create a glowing line, like a laser beam, from the nose of an attack helicopter's mini-gun. Nemesis twists with the attack and lifts an arm, allowing the bullets to strike the orange flesh. This is the first time I've seen it from a distance, but I see what I expect to. A column of orange flame that's nearly white hot at its core, jets out of Nemesis's body, covering two hundred feet. The helicopter is momentarily blanketed in fire.

Then it's gone, extinguished as the wound seals. Nemesis roars, perhaps in pain, perhaps in celebration. The helicopter, now a fireball, plummets into the ocean. The five remaining helicopters back off and circle at a distance.

It's clear that my advice has not made it down the chain of command, if it even made it up to begin with.

"Woodstock," I say. "Get me in touch with those choppers!"

I see him quickly work the radio switches. "All right, we're on all VHF frequencies...now." He flips a switch.

"All military aircraft currently engaging the creature, this is Jon Hudson of the DHS—"

"Someone get this asshole off the air!" someone shouts. I think it's one of the pilots because whoever it is, he sounds rattled.

Ignoring radio protocols, I shout, "Shut-up and listen! Up until ten minutes ago when you idiots blew up two cities and killed a shit-ton of civilians, I was organizing the response to the crisis, and I have intel that might save your damn lives."

I take their silence as my cue to deliver said intel. "Do not engage with any armaments that you cannot manually control. That means no fire-and-forget missiles."

"That means most of what I've got," says a much cooler voice, probably one of the fighter jet pilots who are high above the action.

"Doesn't matter," I say. "You need to avoid hitting the orange membranes at all costs."

"That's what took down Cougar Three," someone agrees.

"If you strike one of the membranes with a missile, you'll destroy everything in a quarter mile radius. That's pretty much all of you."

"Copy that," someone says.

"Yeah, copy," says the cooler voice. "Switching to the 20 mil."

A few more pilots join in, confirming they've heard the news.

"Anything else?" someone says.

"Yeah," I say, "aim for the legs. See if you can't slow it down."

"Slow it down?" comes an aghast voice. "We need to kill this thing. We're not in a race."

"Actually, I am." I have no idea if these guys are going to take me seriously, but they've been listening so far, probably because they've seen several Navy ships get torn apart and just lost a chopper. "This thing took four Tomahawks and walked away. You won't be able to stop it." Every one of the men listening knows what a Tomahawk can do. I have their attention. "There is something in Boston. Something it wants, bad. And I think I can lead it away. I just need to get there first."

Several seconds pass before the cool jet pilot says, "Copy that. Will do what we can."

"I'm coming in from the north. Red civilian helicopter. Try not to shoot me."

"Will do," says one pilot.

"Copy that," says the jet pilot, and a few more join the affirmative chorus.

"Godspeed," I say. "Out."

Woodstock flips the switch again and we're back to internal communications.

Collins looks back at me. "Do you really think it's heading for Gordon?"

I shake my head, "Not Gordon. The hostage."

"The hostage?"

"Gordon has been out and about from the beginning. She wouldn't have headed for the ocean if she was following him. She wouldn't have made the pit stop in Beverly, either. She wasn't interested in Gordon until he showed up on the roof with a hostage."

"But it's still a guess," Collins says.

"I thought you cops called it a hunch?"

"Not a cop anymore," she says. "But it's a good guess."

Actually, I think, it's my only guess. And if I'm wrong, the Boston skyline looming ahead might not be there a few hours from now.

We're just two miles out and Nemesis fills a lot of the windshield. In a minute, we're going to be flying right through the action. For a moment, I think we're going to look like a bright red treat to Nemesis as we fly past, especially if she recognizes the chopper from our previous engagements.

The Apache helicopters take up stationary positions around Nemesis, each facing her. Nemesis swings out with her hands, but comes up short. The choppers maintain a safe distance, two hundred feet above sea level. That's when they open fire, all five of them, aiming for the creature's knees. A roar draws my eyes to the left and I see three F-22s cruising in, side-by-side, just a hundred feet above the water. Once they're in range, all three planes open fire with their 20-millimeter cannons. The combined firepower shreds the monster's thick hide.

My eyes widen when I see chunks of flesh go flying.

Fluid sprays.

Nemesis stumbles and roars.

This might actually work, I think.

That's when the giant's tail explodes from the water and thrashes through the air like a monstrous whip, catching two of the choppers off guard and reducing them to metal confetti. As Nemesis spins toward the fast approaching F-22s, I see one of her giant eyes rotate and land right on us.

Crap.

42

The tail finishes its arc through the air and slams into the water, sending a massive wave toward the shore. I shift to the right side of the chopper and look out the side window, watching the water rise up the beach and engulf entire neighborhoods.

An explosion draws me back to the left window. Nemesis has reached down and caught one of the F-22s. The collision must have been like slamming into a wall of steel. She crushes the burning heap in her hand.

Then, she looks back up.

At us.

I look down, out the side window, as we pass a few hundred feet above her. Something looks off. "Are we ascending?"

"Nope," Woodstock says. "Straight and steady. We'll be through this mess in thirty more seconds."

Collins looks out her window, craning her head to get a view of Nemesis below. "Is it sinking?"

It looks like it, but I don't think so. Then I see it. Her knees are bending.

She's crouching.

Getting ready to jump!

"Holy shit!" I shout. "Woodstock, look o—"

He figures out what I'm in the middle of saying, and with a twitch of his hand, the helicopter pitches to the side, fast and hard. I'm thrown around the back like a Mexican jumping bean. We level out for just a moment, but it's long enough for me to see Nemesis's open jaws snap shut just twenty feet away.

"Look out!" Collins shouts, looking up.

I'm tossed in the other direction as the chopper banks hard to the left, circling around Nemesis's head. As I land on the side door, I look up through the opposite window and see a giant black, clawed hand dropping toward us.

"Faster!" I shout. "And down!"

The helicopter dives forward, and I manage to catch myself on the big mounted gun. Below, the ocean waves grow larger. And still, we pick up speed. Then I'm thrown back, into a seat as the chopped strains to level out, just ten feet above the waves.

We quickly ascend back to a hundred feet, and while still moving forward, Woodstock spins us around so we can see Nemesis. All three of us shout with surprise when the giant winds up and tosses the crushed F-22 at us like Roger Clemens, after the 'roids. I'm crushed into the seat as Woodstock pulls us up and the hundred-and-forty-three million dollar ball of scrap metal spins past beneath us.

Nemesis follows the throw with an angry roar.

"I think it remembers us," Collins says.

I point past her. "You think?"

The giant monster has taken what appears to be a sprinter's stance. Her muscles coil. I thought she was moving fast already, but I'm starting to get the feeling Nemesis was just pacing herself.

"Higher," I say. "Higher!"

We're shaken by twin roars as F-22s heading toward Nemesis open fire with their cannons, once again aiming for the monster's knees. The distraction breaks the giant's focus on us, turning it back on the attacking planes.

One of the F-22 pilots makes a bold decision, firing an AMRAAM missile from close range—so close that it can't hit anywhere above the waist. The missile strike homes in on Nemesis's thigh, blowing off chunks of flesh and gore. The plane rolls beneath the debris and hooks away for another run. The three remaining choppers return as well, keeping a healthier distance and firing their collective mini-guns.

When more chunks fly away, I say, "Something isn't right. Those guns are pebbles compared to the Tomahawk missiles, but they seem to be doing more damage. That missile looked like it did serious damage, where the twelve that hit her before did nothing."

"Maybe it's the continuous fire?" Collins says. "Or a chink in its armor. Maybe the knees are a weak spot."

I don't think so, but I don't mention it. For now, we can put Nemesis in the rear view and focus on reaching Gordon. I see the monster shrug off the gunfire and continue her charge toward the city. We're only going to have a few minutes to deal with Gordon before Nemesis makes landfall.

"Turn us around," I say. "Get me to that building."

The next few minutes are smooth flying. I can hear the thunder of battle behind us coupled with Nemesis's angry roar, but we're on course, and for now, we're safe. We pass over Nahant Bay and Broad Sound, finally reaching land, turning over Logan Airport—where flights have been grounded or diverted—so that we're headed downtown. I'm pretty sure it's the same path Nemesis will take, so I'm not exactly pleased to see all the traffic below.

"What's that?" Collins says, pointing out the front window.

I look at the sky above downtown and see what looks like a cloud of locusts—very large, heavily armed locusts. The array of gray military jets and helicopters flying directly toward us is astounding—enough to invade a small country. Maybe even a large one. My mind races to identify the jets. Off to the left, closer to the ocean are F/A-18 Hornets and Super Hornets mixed in with some F-35 Lightnings. Those are the Navy fighters, probably from the nearby aircraft carrier. To the right I see several F-22s Raptors, F-16 Fighting Falcons, F-15 Eagles, A-10 Thunderbolts and even a few jet-black F-117 Nighthawks, which is strange because they were retired in 2008.

They scrambled every nearby fighter they could find, I realize.

The helicopters fly lower and are closer. A mix of Apache, Little Bird, Viper and SuperCobra attack helicopters. The combined might of this air force could level a mountain. For a moment, I feel a surge of hope. That much firepower might be able to blow Nemesis's legs right out from under her.

Then, a Thunderbolt fires a missile.

Someone didn't get the memo.

"Woodstock! Military channel n—"

Twenty more missiles follow it. And they're headed right for us.

I sit back and buckle my seatbelt, which it turns out was a wise idea because we're suddenly pitching to the side and rolling. For a split second my view of the city flips, and I feel a distinct sense of plummeting to the ground, but then we're righted again and the jets are roaring past us. Finally, somehow in one piece, we reach the northern edge of Boston.

"Did—did we just fly upside down?" Collins asks. "In a helicopter?"

I'd like the answer to that, too, but I haven't forgotten those missiles, and I'm pretty sure I know what's going to happen next. "Get behind the nearest building!"

We drop down as we pass over the Charles River and loop around one of the many squat, solid-looking brick buildings that line the fringe between water and skyscraper. As we turn perpendicular with the water, I see Nemesis in the distance, but closer than expected. Somewhere in the middle of Broad Sound, I see a series of explosions slamming Nemesis's body. Arms, legs, head, and then, as the monster takes in a breath and lets out an aggravated roar that vibrates all the windows in the city, it happens.

I don't see the missile, or where it hits, I just catch a glimpse of the blooming light, but that's it, we're behind the building a moment later, hovering ten feet off the ground. We touch down a moment later and I think to complain, but then remember what happened to us last time. Losing consciousness while piloting a helicopter even ten feet from the ground could be a very bad thing. My mind flashes to all the helicopter pilots facing down Nemesis.

They're all dead, I think, and then the earsplitting boom and shockwave arrive. I have my ears blocked, but the sound still makes me shout in pain. The chopper shakes, but it's not too bad, we're more than a mile from the blast and most of the impact has been absorbed by the brick building. The city is still standing, for now, but it's taken its first real hit.

Collins looks up and says, "Glass," like it's a common, everyday thing to say. I peer out of the side window, craning my head up. I see a shimmering in the air, like clear snow falling from the cloudless sky. I look forward and see all of the skyscrapers on the northeastern side of town shedding shards of glass like a leprous man with a bad case of dandruff.

We pull up fast and then back out over the Charles River where we ascend. But we're not moving forward, through the city. "What are you doing?"

"Can't fly through this shit," Woodstock says. "Need to go over it."

I don't like it. Feels like a waste of time, but I know he's right. When we hit an elevation of one thousand feet, we're higher than anything in the city, and we start forward again. "Give us a quick look back," I say.

We spin around. Nemesis looks like she's right behind us, but she's a mile off, stomping her way across Logan Airport, crushing 747s beneath her massive feet like they're balsa wood airplanes. Behind her, Revere Beach and a giant swatch of land are a smoldering ruin. When a glint of sunlight sparkles off the beach, I realize it's been melted into a sheet of glass. I don't see a single helicopter, though a large number of jets are circling high above, probably trying to figure out what happened.

"Good?" Woodstock asks.

"Not at all," I say, realizing that the train-wreck of destruction is about a minute away from reaching the city. We spin forward again, cruising over Boston's North End, then Beacon Hill and then to Back Bay, where the Clarendon building is located.

"There it is," Collins says, pointing to a tall brick tower with three distinct levels, each wider than the other.

Woodstock begins to descend, but I stop him. "Don't. Fly past."

He nods and maintains our altitude, flying high above the building. Using a pair of binoculars, I look out the side window. It's hard to get a clear image, but I see two people on the roof of the building, one with a hood over his head. "They're still there." I scan the other buildings, expecting to see police and snipers. But there's nobody. They've all left. I look down to the streets and see gridlock. People are running between the cars, trampling each other, but no one really seems to know where to go. They can hear the battle, I realize, but they can't yet see it.

"This is good," I say. "Level out here."

Collins looks back. "What do you mean, this is good?"

I take the side door handle and pull, yanking the door open. The cabin fills with churning air and the sound of rotor blades booming.

Collins shakes her head and gives me a stern look. "You said we were partners! What am I supposed to do from up here?"

"Woodstock," I shout over the wind and chop, "Drop Collins off at the front door." I look at Collins. Her eyes look as bright orange as Nemesis's glowing membranes, and for a second, I think she's going to burst into flames. I reach out and squeeze her hand. "You can take the normal elevator." I offer her an apologetic smile and add. "I'm taking the express elevator."

Then I let go of her hand, and jump.

43

The helicopter wash throws me down, propelling me to terminal velocity and launching me farther—straight down. In seconds, I'll be a smear on the pavement below, adding even more panic to the throngs of fleeing civilians. But I came prepared for this moment.

Years ago, I had a girlfriend, Jenn, who wasn't a pick-up truck. She was a fiery little thing with a wicked sense of humor and a junkie-like habit for adrenaline. She was also a designer for an extreme-sports equipment company and was always testing her new products. Somehow, she managed to get me to bungee jump, white-water kayak and sky dive, all using gear she designed. I really had no interest in all these things, but her extreme lifestyle balanced my calm and we had a lot of fun. Things went south when I found her going south on the tall, blond Swedish man instructing us how to use our new retractable wingsuits. The plan was to jump off a mountain, glide like a bird for several miles and then deploy parachutes.

Jenn made the leap with her new, far more extreme, ten years younger, boy toy, but I kept my suit. I had no intention of using it, I just didn't want Sven or whatever the hell his name was, to have it.

I never heard how well the suit worked, or if it did at all, but Jenn's designs always seemed to get the job done. Not all of them went into production, but they never resulted in my death. So, I'm kind of putting my life in my ex-girlfriend's hands when I reach up and slap the button on my chest.

My arms and legs suddenly snap open as the suit pressurizes and the wings stretching from my wrists to my hips, and between my legs, unfurl and catch the air.

I'm still falling, but I've been slowed to a much more manageable 50 mph and am no longer dropping straight down. Instead, I'm like a human-sized flying squirrel, capable of maneuvering and controlling my speed to a point.

The Clarendon building is eight hundred feet below and about a quarter mile away. I spin to face it head on, and dip my head toward the roof. Descending at a 45 degree angle, I pick up speed.

When I cut the distance in half, I spot Gordon on the roof. The hooded man is on his knees, pitched forward in a posture of defeat. Gordon stands stock-still, looking toward the skyscrapers of Boston's South End district, otherwise known as downtown.

He's waiting for her, I think. For Nemesis. But is he controlling her?

Doesn't matter, I decide, my course is set. I angle toward his back, descending like a missile.

I heard about a guy in England who landed in a wingsuit without deploying a parachute, but I'm pretty sure he finished the flight by crashing into a runway full of boxes. As much as I would like to careen into Gordon's back at 50 mph and break his spine, the collision would kill us both.

When I'm 200 feet from the top of the building, it's time to deploy Jenn's second design—a parachute that deploys fast enough for short jumps, or in my case, low opens. I fight against the air pulling my arm out and push the button on my chest one more time.

150 feet.

The pressure around my body snaps away, the wings retract, and for a fraction of a second, I'm free falling.

100 feet.

But then, with a burst of compressed air, the chute deploys and snaps open.

50 feet.

I'm jolted as the parachute slows my decent from 50mph to 18mph, which is still pretty quick.

10 feet.

Gordon turns around, alerted to my presence by the loud crack of the parachute unfurling and filling with air. But his shocked expression reveals he had no idea how close the sound was, or even what made it. I can't help but let out a small smile when I pull my legs up and drive them forward like pistons, striking the confused General square in the chest and sending him flying.

As Gordon falls to his back with a loud, "oof!" I land and slap the button on my chest one last time, freeing the chute and resetting the system. The bright red and white parachute is caught by the wind and carried off the side of the building. As it flutters away, I see Woodstock's bright red chopper drop past the top of the building. Collins is in the window, looking relieved, but is motioning for me to turn around.

I spin and find Gordon on his feet, facing me with a big smile on his face. His eyes are predatory. Hungry.

I note that the gun he was holding is no longer in his hand and see it some twenty feet behind him. My gun is buried beneath the Velcro and zippers of the wingsuit. I don't tell him, but I think Gordon could get to his weapon before I could retrieve mine.

But he doesn't seem interested in his weapon. His clenched fists reveal he intends to pummel me. When I remember what it felt like to punch his chest, and the way he kicked in that door, I think I'd prefer a gun fight.

"I'm impressed," he says. His voice is deeper than I remember, rougher, too. "But you're wasting your time. You can't stop her."

"I'm aware," I say.

"Then why come for him?" His eyes flare with understanding. "You want to lead her away from the city."

"And I'm not exactly keen on sacrificing innocent people to appease an ancient goddess of revenge."

"Is that what she is?" he asks, and I don't hear a trace of sarcasm in his voice.

I answer truthfully, biding time for Collins's arrival. She won't have any trouble getting to her gun. "Her name is Nemesis. Greek goddess of vengeance."

"And here I thought she was an alien," he says.

"That, too, maybe," I confess. It's the one explanation that makes any kind of sense to me.

"But that's not her name," he says.

My big internal, "Huh?", must reveal itself on my face, because he laughs and points at the hooded man on his knees. "You don't even know who this is, do you?"

"Help," the hooded man says, his rolls of pale-white, flabby skin jiggling. "He's crazy!"

Gordon backhands the man's head, knocking him to the roof.

"You're in way over your head, DHS-man," Gordon says. "She'll be here in a minute. If you leave now, you might actually survive the day."

That he wants me to leave, and is willing to let me go without a fight means that there is a chance I could undo things, maybe even stop it. "I'm not going anywhere."

If life came with a redo moment, this would be mine. I would have found something less definite and confrontational to say, because the moment I reveal that I'm here to the end, his tack changes.

He leaps—leaps—across the fifteen feet between us, slamming his fists down. If I hadn't dove to the side, I would be dead. The indented roof is proof of that.

Back on my feet, I do the only thing I can think to do.

I run.

The roof is covered with large air conditioning units, electrical utility boxes, satellite dishes and three mobile home sized units with doors that probably lead to stairwells or elevator service access. I weave my way through the maze, trying to put distance between Gordon and me, but he keeps pace, a smile on his face.

Then I'm out in the open again, my back to an air conditioning unit the size of truck-Betty. Gordon steps out, slows to a stroll and then, in a blink, charges. He lowers his shoulder and covers the distance in a flash. I barely have time to dodge, and I'm struck a glancing blow that spins me around and throws me to the roof.

A sound like a car accident fills the air, and I spin around to find Gordon pulling himself from the ruins of the air-conditioning unit. This guy is like a frikken tank now, I think before scrambling to my feet and running once more.

Gordon's laugh pursues me before he does, but as I round a stairwell, I can hear and feel his feet thundering over the roof.

After leaping out of the hovering helicopter onto the roof of a stationary UPS truck and climbing down into a panicked mob, Ashley Collins found the abandoned lobby of the Clarendon building a welcome relief. The thick glass blocked out the screaming and the air was cool and—

—rank. Collins drew her weapon and scanned the lobby. Nothing. She worked her way to the reception desk and saw no one, but when she moved around it, she discovered the scent's source—a dead doorman, shot in the head.

Gordon's work, she thought, and then she headed for the elevators.

The ride up was the longest forty seconds of her life. She was in a rush, and despite the elevator ascending far faster than she could climb stairs, standing still just felt wrong. But the ride was also nerve-wracking because the power had begun to flicker, and she thought she might get trapped inside while the giant she-beast moved in, to flatten the building.

But then the doors opened with a ding and she stepped into the hallway of the thirty-third floor. She saw a sign for the stairwell at the end of the hall, not far from a door that had been kicked in. She drew her weapon and moved toward both doors. Inside the open door was a nice, but bland apartment for someone who clearly had money to burn. But nothing else. When she turned toward the stairwell door, it was already open.

She froze, frowning deeply.

A gun was leveled at her face.

"What are you doing here?" a man said from the dark stairwell. She recognized the Japanese accent.

"Kind of a stupid question, don't you think?" she said. "I'm here to stop you. How about you put the gun down and we finish the fight you ran away from?"

Endo stepped into the hallway light, forcing Collins back. Then he did something unexpected—he lowered his gun. Collins instantly brought her weapon up. Despite the sudden role reversal, she felt unnerved. Something weird was going on. She looked around the hall as much as she dared, searching for signs of hidden danger.

"We are no longer enemies," Endo said.

"How's that?" she asked. "You would have killed us before."

He nods his affirmation. "But the General is no longer my employer."

"Zoomb?" she asks.

He ignores the question, but says, "Our goals are currently aligned. I am here to stop General Gordon."

Collins read between the lines. Endo wasn't here to stop Gordon, he was here to kill Gordon. She was sure there was some kind of corporate endgame being played out, with Endo a willing pawn, but she wasn't sure what it was. And she didn't actually care. "Why should I believe you?"

Endo looked down at his gun. "If it were not the truth, I would have killed you...but the General is different now. Altered. I know how you fight. I have seen your spirit. And strength."

"Now you're trying to get me into bed," Collins said.

"Actually, I could use your help."

Collins squinted at him. He sounded sincere and he had lowered his weapon. But could she trust him? She didn't think so. But then he said, "And I'm certain agent Hudson could use help—from both of us."

As though to punctuate the point, the roof shook from an impact.

Collins lowered her weapon. "Fine, but when this is done, I'm taking you in for murder."

Endo didn't reply to that, he just turned and headed up the stairs.

Collins followed.

STAGE 4

44

For the second time today, I'm flying, or at least that's what it feels like, except that this second flight lasts just a second and ends without a parachute. I slam into the hard roof and slide across its rough surface. The wingsuit is thick and helps absorb much of the impact, and it prevents my skin from being sandpapered away, but my body is still reeling from the previous day's pummeling. I struggle to regain my footing as Gordon, who caught and flung me as easily as a cat taunting a mouse, closes in.

It could be worse, I know. If he'd punched me instead of thrown me, I'd be dead. I'm certain that's what he did to the FBI agent with the caved-in chest. He's got his fists clenched now, so I'm pretty certain that's what's about to happen to me too.

I scramble away backwards on my hands and feet, but there's no way I can outrun the man. The best I can manage, as he cocks back a fist, is to squint in fright.

But his punch never falls. Instead, a heavy haymaker slams into the side of his face. His head snaps to the side, but he doesn't lose footing, stumble or even grunt. He swings a backhand at his unseen attacker, but finds only a few strands of red hair as Collins ducks beneath the blow.

"Don't let him hit you!" I shout. "Not once, he's—"

My shouts bring Gordon's attention back to me, but his attack is once again interrupted by a black-shoed foot that kicks up and catches him in the face, not once, but three times. And this time, Gordon stumbles back, a hand to his nose.

I look to the new attacker and I'm shocked to find Endo standing next to me, offering his hand. I'm not sure what to make of this turn of events, but there's no question that he arrived with Collins, which means we have some kind of truce. Endo, for some reason, is now working against the General. I take his hand and get back to my feet.

Gordon chuckles. "The prodigal son, returned to die." He waves his hand to Endo, egging him on. "Come on, boy."

But Endo is unfazed. "You know that's not how I operate."

Gordon's face morphs from confident to confused to understanding in the exact same time it takes Endo to draw a sound-suppressed 9mm handgun and pull the trigger—about half a second. The first bullet catches Gordon dead center in his chest. The big man stumbles back, looking down at the hole in his shirt.

Endo pulls the trigger until the clip runs dry. Gordon, who remained standing throughout the barrage, is still looking down with a look of shock on his face.

But not pain.

He smiles and then laughs, standing up straight and gripping his hole-filled shirt in both hands. With a yank, he tears the shirt apart, revealing an inhuman black torso that looks very much like Nemesis's. All thirteen bullets are embedded in the thick flesh, and when Gordon puffs out his chest, many of them simply fall away.

Her body itched more than hurt, but the warplanes continually bombarding her body with cannon fire and missiles had begun to annoy Nemesis to the point where she could no longer ignore them. But she could not reach them either. Her fury was reaching a breaking point. To make matters worse, she had reached the edge of the city and found her way blocked by a thick patch of skyscrapers that dwarfed her.

She tried to push her way through, but the streets were too narrow for her bulk, and the tall buildings were built solidly. In anger, she struck out at the nearest building, a five-hundred-foot column with thousands of windows but no glass. Her massive hand and thick finger-tips tore through steel and concrete easily, and she struck out again and again. Then there was a crack and a rumble, and the top half of the building collapsed, tipping like a falling tree and dropping toward her.

Nemesis leaned forward, shifting the protective carapace on her back to deflect the falling debris, but the weight of the massive structure bent her legs and nearly forced her to the ground. Seeing this as a sign of weakness, the jets pressed their attack, blowing more flesh from her body and increasing the persistent itch.

She could sense her goal nearby. The beacon shrieked at her from beyond the towering buildings, beckoning her to move faster.

But she was stuck. It would take hours to force her way through this forest of metal and stone.

Unless... Her intellect provided an idea that her emotions em-braced. Her physical instincts riled against it, but the closer she got to the beacon, the more power her emotion wielded.

She turned her back to the sea, letting the incoming missiles explode harmlessly against her carapace. Then, with a shriek of pain, she dug her fingertips, each the thickness of Boston's Bunker Hill Monument, into the glowing orange flesh beneath her ribs—

—and yanked them out.

Gordon charges Collins, who is closest to him and drawing her .45. He strikes the gun from her hand and reaches out with both arms, no doubt intending to crush the life of out her. She ducks beneath his embracing arms and rolls to the side, as Endo leaps in the air and drives his foot into the General's back, knocking him head-first into a stairwell wall. I follow Endo's strike with a kick of my own, driving my foot into the back of Gordon's knee. But it's like kicking a tree trunk.

All three of us are forced back when Gordon spins around, swing-ing wildly. He's not hurt. Not at all. He's just really, really pissed off.

And maybe a little bit insane.

"Righteousness will fall from the sky," he shouts. "She will judge the living and purify the land."

Gordon steps toward the three of us, and we all take a step back.

"Do you know what he's talking about?" I ask, stepping back again.

Endo shakes his head. "No idea, but the heart in his chest came from the creature, and it's clearly consuming his body. Maybe it's in his mind, too."

"You're saying he's remembering something?" Collins says, aghast at the idea.

Endo shrugs.

Gordon lunges.

Collins and I dive to the sides. Endo is like living lightning, but he's not fast enough to avoid Gordon's outstretched hand. Endo's feet leave the ground as Gordon lifts him up by one arm.

"And you have been judged—" Gordon looks up at Endo's face with a sick grin. "—guilty." He draws back his fist.

A gun fires, its unsilenced report booming across the roof. Gordon's head snaps forward from the impact. But he doesn't fall. Collins fires her weapon again, but the effect is the same. The thick flesh protecting Gordon's torso is beneath his human skin, which I'm now sure he will eventually shed, like Nemesis.

But not all of him is protected.

"Collins!" I shout, reaching out to her.

She understands my request and tosses the gun to me. It breaks a few dozen safety rules, but I manage to snatch the weapon from the air without shooting myself and turn the gun around on Gordon, just as he whips Endo aside. I hear a pop, and a scream as Endo's shoulder comes out of its socket, but I ignore it along with Nemesis's distant roars, the sounds of explosions, and the pain wracking my body. I pull the trigger.

The .45 caliber round sails through the air, faster than even Gordon can move, and finds what might be the only soft spot left on his body—the center of his eye. The bullet penetrates the orb, turning it to jelly.

Gordon's head snaps back.

He stumbles.

But doesn't fall.

I fire again. And again. Each round strikes his head, pushing him back farther and farther. I run at him, still firing, still moving until the back of his legs hit the short safety wall at the edge of the building. After firing my last round I leap up, do my best Endo impression, and kick Gordon's chest.

The impact stops me in my tracks and I fall to the concrete roof. Gordon is off balance, leaning back. His hands twirl in circles as he fights to stay on the rooftop. But he's dazed. And blood pours from his wounded eye.

Still, he's far from dead, and I suspect, thanks to his strength, he's about to regain his balance.

But I'm not about to let that happen. I grab hold of his ankles and pull. It's not much, but the top-heavy General is suddenly ass over tea kettle. He disappears over the edge, falling thirty-four stories to the pavement below. I grab onto the ledge and look over in time to see him pancake the roof of a school bus.

I'm about to stand and offer up a one-liner that would make a young Bruce Willis envious, but a bright glow filtering through the skyscrapers of the South End is followed by a BOOM that sucks the air from my lungs and knocks me to the Clarendon's roof.

45

Despite the pain wracking my body and exploding in my ears, I hit the roof like a thirteen year old gymnast, springing back to my feet in time to see my worst fears realized.

Downtown is crumbling.

The core of the city is now a black husk of its former self.

Skyscrapers crumble and fall, one after another, dropping in on themselves like God is lowering a finger and pushing them into the Earth.

Not God, I think, Nemesis.

As the buildings fall, filling the air with a low rumble and roiling plumes of dust that roll over the much smaller buildings of Beacon Hill, sunlight cuts through the haze, revealing the silhouette of Nemesis. The monster thunders through the now clear path through the city, framed on either side by the skyscrapers that are still standing.

A loud tinkling sound turns me around. Glimmering shards of glass descend from above. I look up and see the John Hancock Tower, one of Boston's tallest buildings, shedding its all-glass exterior. As the reflective shards fall into the street at the corner of the Clarendon building, they form a hazy, moving mirror, through which I see Nemesis looming larger and larger.

Screams rise up from below. The panicked people who weren't sure which way to go, now have a solid direction—away from Nemesis. But in their panic, they're trampling each other, adding more numbers to the death toll. I want to shout at them to stop, but they wouldn't hear me over their own screams, the thirty-four stories between us, and the Air Force, which has taken the destruction of the South End as permission to unleash hell on Earth.

Missiles rain down from the sky, striking Nemesis hard, knocking the monster around and tearing off heaps of dark flesh.

"Jon, look!" Collins shouts, stepping up next to me and pointing at Nemesis.

I'm not sure what she's talking about at first. Nemesis is hard to miss. But then I see it. The orange membranes...are black. Whatever was in them got used up when downtown was incinerated.

My attitude toward the Air Force one-eighties and I grip the side of the building, saying, "C'mon... C'mon..."

Nemesis falls forward, landing on her forelimbs. But she's not seriously hurt, just allowing her armor-plated back to take the hits. In fact, now on all fours, she's moving faster, trampling through Beacon Hill and into Boston's Back Bay area, where the John Hancock building and the few towers around it are the only skyscrapers around.

But the monster doesn't appear to notice us. In fact, she seems to be wandering around aimlessly.

It's Gordon, I think. Gordon was leading her to us. Without him, she's confused, unsure of where to go, and she's leveling the city as a result. This isn't like Portland where she just wanted to get from one side of town to the other. Without Gordon guiding her, Nemesis is going to flatten every last bit of Boston looking for what? Some guy?

I look back at the underwear-clad man. He's still hooded, but bound and struggling.

Could this really all be about him?

If so, we need to get him out of here, but I'm not sure if Nemesis will follow us without Gordon drawing her in, but maybe if she sees the man. Of course, if she sees the man, she's likely to just smash the chopper out of the sky. Still, it has to be done.

"Get Woodstock here," I say to Collins.

She pulls a radio from her belt and starts talking. I head for the fat man and am about to call out to Endo for help, when I remember his arm was dislocated. Not that it matters. He's gone. The man is a killer and should be locked up, but he's pretty close to the bottom of my list of concerns right now.

I turn back to Collins. "Knife!"

She takes a folding knife from her belt and tosses it to me. I catch it, pull the blade out and make short work of the man's plastic bonds. He cowers and yelps as I free him. "You're safe," I tell him. "I'm with the DHS."

"Thank God," he says, his voice trembling. "Get me the hell out of here!"

"Gladly," I say, and I yank off the hood.

The man blinks several times, eyes adjusting to the brightness of day. Then he sees the smoldering ruin that is Boston and the three-hundred-foot plus freakshow that is Nemesis slowly working her way toward us. He lets out a shrill scream that's so loud I'm almost certain the monster will hear him. I slap the man hard across the face, point my finger at him and let my glaring eyes do the talking.

He clamps his mouth shut. Collins arrives and together, we help the man to his feet.

Just then, the heavy bass beat of a helicopter rises up next to the building. Woodstock brings the chopper over the roof, finds a clearing free of obstructions and lands. The side door slides open. Collins hops in first and turns around to help the stranger on board, but he's dazed, terrified and looks weakened by his ordeal. It's going to take both of us to get him in, and my phone has just started ringing.

I would normally ignore the phone, but something tells me this call is likely time-sensitive. I tear through the Velcro and zippers of my suit, pull out the phone and shout a, "hello!" over the chopping rotor blades.

"Hudson?" shouts Watson in reply. "I can barely hear you!"

"Just tell me what you have!" I yell.

"The condo," he shouts. "One of the units was owned by someone who rents an apartment in the Clarendon building. The penthouse. His name is Alexander Tilly!"

Tilly?

Then it registers. Alexander Tilly was the father of Maigo Tilly, the girl who was murdered.

The girl whose DNA was used to grow organs.

The girl who became Nemesis.

I turn to the fat man. "Alexander Tilly?"

He looks at me. "Help me up!"

"Are you Alexander Tilly?"

"Yeah," he shouts, "Which is why you better damn well—"

I take the man's shoulder and yank him back away from the chopper.

"What are you doing?" Collins shouts.

"You wouldn't like it if I told you," I reply. "You're going to have to trust me." When she doesn't move or reply, I add, "Partners have to do that sometimes."

She purses her lips for a moment and then nods.

I slide the door closed and then open Woodstock's door. "Take her up. Stay close. Be ready."

"For what?" he asks.

"Anything," I tell him. Then I slam the door and step back. The chopper lifts off and banks away from the building, leaving me with a very confused, very angry man.

"What the hell do you think you're doing?" he screams.

I've still got Collins's gun so I point it at him. It doesn't have a single round left, but he doesn't know that. I motion toward the roof edge nearest Nemesis, who is still a half mile off and still on all fours.

The man looks like he's about to argue, but he's had a rough day and concedes without incident.

As we walk toward the edge of the roof, closer to Nemesis, his legs start to quake. I'm tempted to feel pity for the man, but before I can change my mind, I ask, "Did you do it?"

"W—what?" he says.

"Did you kill your wife?" I ask. "And your daughter."

His legs give out and he falls to his knees. "Just shoot me."

Not exactly the words of an innocent man.

"Why?" I ask.

"Because she was a cheating bitch," he says, growing angry. "And the stupid kid came home early! That the answer you wanted?"

"I had a girlfriend who cheated on me," I say. "I'm pretty sure I loved her, too. She gave a hummer to a guy named Sven, if you can believe it. I didn't kill anyone, though. Didn't even cross my mind. I did keep this cool suit, but she never asked for it back, either."

Tilly looks up at me like I'm nuts.

"Look at the city, Mr. Tilly."

He does.

"All of this is because of you. The thousands of people that died over the last few days are because of you. And even though I believe in the laws of this country and the system that puts people like you in jail—" I point to Nemesis. "—she does not. Here is the simple fact."

"What do you intend to do?" he asks, a bit of fear creeping into his voice.

"I'm going to invite her over," I say, and then shout, as loud as I can, "Nemesis!"

Nothing.

The monster is still heading toward us, but shows no reaction to me calling her name.

A missile catches her in the side, blowing off a chunk of her skin and revealing a patch of white beneath it. Is that bone? She rears up on her hind legs and roars. I nearly fall to my knees beside Tilly, but manage to stay standing and shout her name again. "Nemesis!"

Still no reaction.

I watch the jet that fired the missile turn and fly away, its ammunition apparently exhausted. That's when I notice that the skies are now empty, save for a few daring news choppers hovering a mile away.

I'm on my own.

With a single giant step, she's nearly reached the building, but she's paying no attention to it.

I'm really struggling to not run in fright, because I'm now standing at eye level with Nemesis. But my fright turns to confusion as a chunk of the monster's shoulder falls away to reveal white flesh beneath.

Not bone.

The white flesh is brilliant, almost reflective, and makes me squint until I look away from it.

"Nemesis!" I scream, and am ignored once more.

Then I remember Gordon's words, "That's not her name." Then what is her name? I look down at Tilly and suck in a gasp. I shake my head against the idea, but it's the only thing that makes some kind of ridiculous sense. As the monster starts turning away to trample some other part of the city, I fill my lungs and scream, "Maigo!"

The eyes shift first. Then the head. Then all at once, I'm standing face-to-face with a city-destroying monster who somehow believes that she is a thirteen-year-old girl who was murdered by the man now quaking behind me.

This isn't going to end well, I think.

46

Despite me being on the roof of a thirty-three story building, Nemesis, or rather, Maigo, looks down at me. It's not by much, maybe ten feet, but she is still massive and horrifying. Her dark face is etched with fresh wounds, through which I can see glimmers of white. Tall spikes jut off the sides of her carapace, which extends down from the back of her skull to the start of her tail. Her jaws hang open, revealing giant, but needle-sharp teeth—a promise of things to come. I can hear her breath rumbling as deeply as the still-falling buildings around the city, as her chest heaves in and out.

She's tired, I think. Or stressed.

Maybe neither, some other part of my brain argues. I can't assume anything about this creature.

Her forehead scrunches as she looks down at me and her eyes squint the way a teenage girl's might if you had upset her. She knows me. I can feel it. The angry growl that rises in her throat and shakes the building confirms it. But she hasn't killed me.

Maybe it's because I used her real name.

Or she's somehow judging me right now.

I don't know what it is that keeps her from smearing me across the roof, but I'm thankful for it.

"Maigo," I say, more gently.

She flinches back at the sound of the name, then lets out a huff that smells vile and nearly knocks me off my feet. When I steady myself, I find her eyes focused on me, intense and angry. She flexes her body, and I see and hear bits of her flesh tear.

She's molting again, I realize. But into what?

I decide it doesn't matter and get on with it.

I step to the side.

Maigo's eyes track me for half the step, then flick back, noticing the man cowering behind me.

Her reaction this time is more telling than anything so far. She reels back, sucking in a breath that is something close to a gasp.

I take a step back.

She ignores me, so I take five more. And then ten.

Her forehead furrows so deeply that the flesh above her eyes cracks. When she sneers, revealing her teeth, the same thing happens. Then she lets out that gasped-in air as a roar, leveling it straight at Tilly. If he screams, I can't hear it, but I can tell by the way his body shakes that he's sobbing.

Maybe apologizing, but probably begging for mercy, which I know he will not find from this creature. Part of her might be Maigo Tilly, but there is little doubt that just as much of her is Nemesis.

To my surprise, Maigo takes a step back, but I don't think she's going anywhere. She hunches forward, flexing her back, and I hear something pop. It sounds like Endo's shoulder, but much louder. Then she leans up and back. Massive slabs of her thick, black hide fall away to reveal a smoother, white skin beneath. She sheds the older flesh quickly, scraping at her body with her massive claws, peeling like a giant rotten banana until all of the black has been removed.

I stumble back, squinting at the now gleaming white monster, which is still horrible, but in many ways, beautiful. With a hand over my eyes, I stop walking backwards and just marvel at the thing.

Another loud pop sounds and the carapace on the monster's back shifts.

Then it splits.

I'm frozen in place as Maigo's transformation continues. The carapace lifts away from the back and opens, each side lifting up, its tall spines pointed skyward. And then, from within each side of the carapace, wings unfurl. I only catch a glimpse of their brilliant surface. As soon as the sun hits them, I have to turn away.

I look down toward the roof. Little rainbows dance around me. The wings aren't just reflecting light, they're bending it. The rainbows swirl around me, but they slowly move away, converging toward Alexander Tilly. I look at the man. He's on his feet now, facing the giant monster. There's nowhere to run and he knows it.

When the rainbows have all moved away, I turn my head up and find I'm able to look at the wings. But they're not wings. Not really. It's clear that they're not meant for flight. They're far too delicate looking to lift Maigo's bulk off the ground, and this isn't a Japanese monster movie where having wings means you can just float through the air while emitting a high pitched whistle.

Some of the details resolve and I see hundreds of thousands— maybe millions—of diamond-shaped feathers. But they're not really feathers. They look solid, like scales, but not. One thing is for certain, the feathers—for lack of a better word—are shifting, each of them moving a bit of sunlight.

"Maigo!" Tilly shouts.

I see a reflection of the sun shift across the wings.

"Maigo!" he shouts again. "Ple—"

The giant shifts, just slightly, but the subtle motion causes the sun to reflect off each and every feather, focusing the sun across what is essentially a six hundred foot mirror and directing it straight down at Alexander Tilly, the man who murdered his wife and daughter just two weeks ago.

Tilly bursts into flame and is swept away as a cloud of white dust a moment later.

The building shakes.

The roof catches on fire.

I rush the rest of the way to the far side and look down. The beam of light has pierced all the way through the building and is burrowing a hole in the ground. It hits what must be a gas line, because the street lifts and explodes. The underground eruption follows the street, bursting manholes around the city and billowing balls of fire into the sky.

A roar turns my head to the sky.

A fresh squadron of jets is en route, an F-22 leading the way.

Missiles fire, striking Maigo's massive shoulder, sending flesh and blood—actual blood—arcing through the air.

She can be hurt in this form, I realize, though part of me no longer wants her to be. Tragedy created her. It doesn't seem right to kill her again.

My moral debate is cut short when Maigo roars in pain and twists.

The beam of focused light cuts through the Clarendon building like a laser beam, cleaving it cleanly at an angle. The building shifts.

I sprint for the edge.

As I reach the side of the roof, I see the beam of light slide to the right, cutting through the bases of several buildings that are shorter than the Clarendon, and then through the John Hancock Tower. The building drops, jolts to a stop and then pitches to the side, falling like a 790-foot-tall tree.

I'm a dead man, I think, but I'm committed to at least trying to survive. I leap from the roof of the Clarendon just as it folds in on itself and collapses. As my fall begins, I see a flash of red to my left, but can't look to see what it is. I reach up and slap my chest. A burst of air pressure expands the wingsuit into position, and I'm gliding once again, though this time I think I would prefer a jet pack.

I can't look up, but I can see the base of the John Hancock Tower crumbling, as the rest of the tower falls above me. I shoot past the front of the tower, just one hundred fifty feet from the ground, moving at 50 mph.

Suddenly, a desk falls past me.

Then a chair.

Reams of paper flutter in front of me, and I crash through them.

A thunderous roar sounds out behind me, but I can't tell if its Maigo, or the lowest part of the falling tower striking the ground. Then, I'm out of the tower's shadow and in the glow of the sun.

But I'm also still falling from the sky. I look for someplace soft to land. If I lean back, I can slow my decent to 40 mph, maybe a little less, and that might be survivable if I don't smack into the side of a building. Or a car. Or just about anything else. All I see ahead is a very solid looking, spiky church, a line of parked cars, running people and a few small trees that I think might hurt more than the pavement.

Then the red blur returns and this time I look.

It's Woodstock!

The red chopper descends alongside me, matching my angle and pace.

The side door slides open and Collins waves me over.

I tilt my body in their direction, but as soon as I get close, I can feel the rotor wash pushing me down.

I glance forward.

I have seconds before I hit the ground like a very soft meteorite.

I widen my wings and lean back for just a moment, bringing me right next to the chopping blades. If a breeze hits the side of the chopper right now, or me, I'll be hacked to bits. Before that can happen, I lean forward, bringing me just below rotor level. I tilt hard to the left. I fly under the blades and am quickly flung down, but I'm ready for it and reach out. When I slam into the chopper's right skid, I clasp onto it like a giant sloth. When I feel my legs slipping off, I reach over the skid, and slap the button on my chest twice. The pressure fades and the wings retract.

As we level out, Collins reaches down and helps me up into the chopper. Once inside, I collapse into her arms, exhausted and out of breath. As she holds me tight in a way that says, "I'm not letting you go," I feel safe, but I'm not yet sure we are.

I slip on a headset. "Take us up. I want to see."

We rise up to five hundred feet, which is far higher than any building remaining in Boston, and I catch sight of Maigo.

Her new, white body is less bulky than her previous form, but also less protected. The first thing I notice are several splotches of red blood. The second thing is that this new form is also much more agile. As missiles rain down from the sky, she runs through the ruins of the city like a giant cat. Her thrashing tail takes out any buildings still standing as she follows her path of destruction back toward the South End and the ocean beyond.

I hear her roar in pain as a missile strikes one of the wings, which is folded against her back. A cloud of sparkling white erupts from the blow, fluttering back down to Earth. Then she's in the ruins of the South End, sheltered somewhat by the buildings still standing on either side.

Missiles give chase, striking her back and the surrounding buildings. I don't think anyone is worried about collateral damage any more.

When she reaches the water with a massive splash, I find myself mentally urging her on. I know I shouldn't. She's killed a lot of people. But somewhere in there is an innocent girl who was merged with an ancient goddess, or alien, and given the chance to exact vengeance, or justice as the case may be. With Tilly dead, we might not ever see her again.

Maigo lopes through the ocean, leaping up and forward, paying no attention to the jets now chasing her. Then, with one last leap, she dips her head forward and slides beneath the water of Boston Harbor. Her glowing white form looks turquoise in the shallows, then dark blue, then nearly a mile out to sea, she slides into the dark depths of the ocean and disappears.

I look down at the smoldering ruin of a city.

Boston has been destroyed.

But has the part of the monster that is Nemesis been satiated?

I think back to the moment when Maigo first laid eyes on Alexander Tilly. She was filled with anger and fury, but also horror. She remembered what had been done to her. She had to. It's what drove her to that exact point in time. Her charge south, all the dead, her growth and transformation all lead to that single moment in time when she opened her beautiful wings and sentenced her father to death...by sunlight. For that one moment, when the rays of the sun caught on her wings and focused on the man who had caused her so much pain, she was a being of purity, which is something the world could use a little more of.

I look at Collins and see a little bit of Maigo in her fiery eyes. Despite waves of bodily pain from injuries and tension, I manage a small smile. "You're not an alien, are you?"

EPILOGUE I

I'm lying behind a tree, concealed by large ferns and a full-body ghillie suit—the kind that snipers wear to blend in with their sur-roundings. I'm trying to stay as quiet as I possibly can, but that's hard to do when 1) you've been lying in the same damn place for three hours, 2) have a beautiful woman lying next to you, and 3) really, really have to pee.

"I can't take this anymore," I whisper.

Collins shushes me, but then asks, "What happened to taking the 'P' in FC-P seriously?"

"The 'P' is the problem," I say. "I gotta take a leak."

"You know if you go here, it will smell you and the last two days will be a waste."

Collins and I are on our first official FC-P mission since Maigo leveled Boston. We've been camped out in the deep woods of Oregon scouring the forest by day and bunking together in a tent by night.

I grin and say, "Not a total waste." She sees my grin through the ghillie suit's dangling tendrils and elbows me in the ribs.

As it turns out, we did take it slow.

For a week.

While our bodies healed.

We've been healing our minds since. Turns out seeing scores of people crushed, eaten, burned and torn apart leaves a mark on the psyche. Luckily, we found each other at the right time, and unlike

Mulder and Scully, we didn't feel like dragging things out for a few years before finally getting together.

Under different circumstances, we might have let things play out longer, maybe a few months, but we really needed the distraction. It's hard to do anything or go anywhere without being reminded about what happened. The Crow's Nest has new windows, as do the houses in the surrounding neighborhoods. But the view isn't quite as beautiful, because we can see the circle of destruction left around the fringe of Beverly Harbor.

The country, and the rest of the world, really came together in support of cities and towns that got ravaged. But it's only been a month and they're still finding bodies. Boston is completely shut down, but will eventually be rebuilt. The President has promised as much, and the nation is rallying behind him, despite much of the destruction being his fault—a fact cut from my reports by Deputy Director Stephens. A large part of me really wants to expose the President's failures, and those of my co-workers, but I understand the need to not upset the status quo or cause any more strife. The nation needs to heal first. Although Maine, New Hampshire and Massachusetts took the brunt of the damage, all those dead had friends and family across the country, if not around the world.

Most of Boston's suburbs are still intact, and many area high schools are housing refugees from the downtown area who are more accustomed to living in high-rise luxury, not that any of them are complaining. Most of them know people or had family who were killed by Maigo. If they're alive, they're counting their blessings. I know I am.

I feel the greatest sting when I think about the dead, all of the 13,532 (and climbing) of them. I actually rooted for Maigo at the end. Not to kill, but to escape. Sure, she might have some part of that little girl in her, but she is not Maigo. I've come to call her that instead of Nemesis, I think because that's the personality I hope becomes dominant before she surfaces again.

And I believe she will. Something that big can't stay hidden forever.

That is, if she's alive.

There's no body, but millions of her shimmering scales have washed up on the shores of Massachusetts, from Rockport to the Cape. People are collecting them and selling them on eBay. I saw a chandelier made from them, which cast beautiful light, and I hear the Chinese have a growing demand for "feather dust" which is supposed to make men more "virile" and women more likely to have boys. I think it's more likely to cause them to grow claws and go on a vengeful killing spree, but who am I to stand between a man and his "monster" boner?

Although most of the public attention has been on Maigo, a lot of people have been working behind the scenes to locate the body of General Lance Gordon, with no luck. My hope is that Endo or some other Zoomb employee snuck away with the body to cover up their involvement, which they have done quite well, but my fear is that he got up and walked away. As for Endo, I know exactly where he is. In the few public appearances Paul Stanton has made, Endo can be seen standing in the background, watching for danger. Despite his efforts to stop Gordon and the fact that he might have saved my life, I would love to bring the man in and lock him up. But there's no evidence against him, Gordon or Zoomb that hasn't disappeared, including anything conclusive from the fake Nike site in Maine, which was completely incinerated when Gordon destroyed the building. While this lack of evidence has kept us from making arrests, we've opened files on everyone we believe is involved. We're watching them all closely, with cooperation from other agencies...which is what the DHS does best. If Endo is up to something, we'll figure it out eventually.

There's been plenty of speculation about what the monster is, what she wanted and where she'll go next, but no one, myself included, has any idea. At first, most people didn't believe a little girl could be part of something so massive and horrific, but after seeing the photos or videos of Nemesis, or what was left of Boston, even the most skeptical were willing to believe just about anything. Thankfully, TV audiences found the idea of a little girl being bonded to a city-destroying behemoth to be disturbing and stopped watching. In response, the news channels focused on the Nemesis angle—that a god-monster laid waste to several cities and killed thousands just to avenge a single murder. And that's what people really need to hear. Somewhere in the world, lurking in the depths of the ocean, is a being capable of obliterating a large city. But she's not just a mindless creature or hungry predator, she is the judge, jury and executioner for the entire human race, and if she finds you guilty, well, the images of Boston are impossible to forget.

Several wars came to an abrupt end.

Crime is down. Globally.

Again, this might be messed up, and my fellow New Englanders might lynch me for saying it (which is why I keep it to myself), but in the long run, I think Maigo might have done the world a favor. The wrath of God, who not everyone believes in, only goes so far into scaring people into peace, especially when several different religions heap wrath upon each other, and Jesus technically heaps wrath upon himself. From a global perspective, lives and money will have been saved as a result of Boston's destruction. I wouldn't be surprised if the numbers of saved surpasses the number of dead within a few months, and dwarfs it within a few years...if we can keep the human race on track.

If we can't, she'll be back faster than Arnold Schwarzenegger.

And the FC-P will be waiting for her with a bigger budget, direct access to military resources and four of the best people I've ever worked with. Woodstock enthusiastically declared his allegiance to the team when I asked him if he'd like to stay on permanently. He even agreed to name the chopper Betty in honor of my truck, which as it turns out, took a bullet for me, something I'm pretty sure girlfriend-Betty would never have done.

Girlfriend-Ashley Collins on the other hand—she'd take a bullet for me. And I'd do the same for her. Her response to staying on long-term was more thought out than Woodstock's, mostly because of our relationship, but in the end she couldn't deny we made a good team.

Watson stayed with Cooper through her surgery and several days of recovery. It was a display of affection and camaraderie that made me, and Cooper very happy. There was nothing romantic between them, but it really revealed that our past five years chasing shadows wasn't a complete waste of time. We were all loners in our own ways, but not really anymore—we have each other now. After three weeks off, we met in the refurbished Crow's Nest and got back to work, which led Collins and me to this lush, lime-green redwood forest.

"Fine," she says, "I'm pretty sure this is a bust, anyway."

"Get used to it," I say. "Not every mission results in mass destruction, helicopter acrobatics and new girlfriends."

I stand, and then freeze.

"What?" she says. "You're not going right here, are you?"

"Shh," I say gently. "Smell something."

I crouch slowly, and lie back down, picking up the air rifle lying next to me.

Collins brushes away the ghillie suit tendrils hanging in front of her face and gives me a, "don't screw with me" face.

I give her a wide eyed, "I'm serious!" look and face forward.

A loud crack makes us tense.

When it steps out from behind a redwood, not thirty feet away, I have to stifle a gasp. Its fur is thick like a husky's, and a mix of light and dark brown that would let it blend in with the forest as well as our ghillie suits. It stands at least nine feet tall and has arms as thick as my legs. Not something you'd want to piss off. But when a deer slowly steps out behind it, munching casually on some ferns before wandering past and beyond our target, I realize that this giant is actually gentle. As I watch, I nearly forget what I'm there to do.

A rash of sightings brought us to the area, but there were no reports of attacks or even close encounters, so we're not here to pick a fight. It's more of an intelligence gathering mission, though I honestly thought it was going to just be a "quality time with the new girlfriend" kind of mission. While Collins takes video of the creature, I take aim with the air rifle. When it squats to pick some blueberries, there's no mistaking that this is a male. He also provides me with a nice, wide target.

I pull the trigger and a gentle puff shoots the dart into the big guy's right ass cheek. He flinches at the sting and stands to his feet. He takes a long, slow look around and then wanders off, disappearing into the forest. When he's gone, I stand up and put my fist in the air. "Terrorist fist jab for shooting Sasquatch in the ass."

Collins grins wide, bumps my fist and says, "That was amazing." She looks at the camera, which now has definitive proof of Sasquatch on it.

"We'll keep that to ourselves," I say. "If people knew he was really here, he'd be a dead-squatch inside a week."

"You don't think he's dangerous?" she asks.

"Hasn't been so far," I say. "But that's why he's got a tracker in his butt. We can keep tabs on him without getting him killed. The way I see it, our job is to protect all Americans, and that includes our very distant, very hairy cousins who have probably been living on this continent long before we crossed over from Mother Russia."

"Does that include Maigo?" she asks.

She is the only person who knows about my mixed feelings for the creature. I didn't want to tell her, or anyone, but it was eating at me and she was one of few people who knew the truth about the Tilly family. So I told her the truth, and while she didn't share my mixed feelings, she understood them.

After thinking on it for a moment, I say, "No, I'm not even sure she's from this planet, and whatever part of her was that little girl...she had her revenge. If Maigo comes back, and threatens people in any part of the world, the gloves are coming off."

EPILOGUE II

Being an FBI agent out of the Anchorage, Alaska office meant you could be assigned one of two different kinds of investigations: a short case or a shit case. Cases were often short because to qualify for FBI jurisdiction, the crime had to involve multiple U.S. states, which was a problem for Alaska. Most crimes were local, and those that did cross borders (Canadian mostly—not many people fled to Russia) fell under the purview of the CIA, who seemed to never have enough to do. There was the occasional case involving a criminal who fled from the contiguous forty-eight to the wilds of Alaska, but searching the endless expanse of rugged, mostly cold, frequently dark territory fell into the second, shit-case category.

When Special Agent Kevin Jones's foot sunk into an ankle deep puddle of wet sand and came back up missing a shoe, there was no doubt that he'd landed his third shit case that month. Of course, it also looked like it would be a short case, too, so that was something. The site looked like an old dig or a failed mine. Not that old, though, maybe a year or two. The forest hadn't reclaimed it yet, just a few pine sprouts here and there.

"Damnit," he said, fishing his shoe out of the muck and shaking it off.

"Told ya, you should'a worn boots," Darrin Donovan said. He was a heavyset helicopter pilot that most of the division called Double D, on account of his name, though his size didn't help. Truth was, everyone was jealous of the man because of all of them, he saw the most action. The quickest way to get anywhere in Alaska—sometimes the only way—was by air, and Double D could fly helicopters and planes. So he was always busy.

Jones flicked the mud from his shoe and slipped it back on, fighting to ignore the grit beneath his toes. "And I told you to go on a diet."

"I'm not the one with mud in his shoe...or on high blood-pressure meds." Double D grinned when Jones looked surprised, but didn't say anything.

Jones wanted to argue, but he knew it was a losing fight. Double D seemed to know everything about everyone, and getting into it with the man really wouldn't be good for his heart. So he focused on the reason for their visit—the DHS had flagged the sight and wanted someone to take a look. For what, they wouldn't say, which is probably why it sat on a desk for a few weeks. Everyone was pretty well distracted by what had happened in Boston. When work had resumed in earnest, they discovered that crime had taken a nose dive. Cable news argued it had something to do with the Nemesis creature, that people were afraid it would judge them. Jones didn't think that would last, but for now, it seemed they were stuck working old cases. When he rediscovered the order to explore an area of empty terrain, he'd jumped at it. It wasn't much, but it was something.

"You going to start investigating?" Donovan said. "Or do I need to point out the obvious."

Still distracted by his wet foot, Jones asked, "Which is?"

"Ain't no roads," Donovan said.

He was right about that, too. The map of the area revealed no official roads, but he thought they'd see something from the air. Other than a few trails that circled back to the old dig site there wasn't a single road connecting the site to the outside world. "So they flew everything in."

"This site wasn't made by hand," Donovan said, motioning to the sloping dirt, piled rocks and the sealed mineshaft. "This took some heavy machinery. If they flew it in, and out, and took whatever was in the mine with them, it would have cost a fortune."

Right again, Jones thought. Something big had gone on here, but not recently.

"What does the search request say?" Donovan asked.

Jones dug the folded-up piece of paper out of his pocket. Donovan wasn't an investigator, but he'd been on more investigations than anyone and was pretty smart, to boot. He also knew the land better than most agents who preferred to stay in the city and beg for reassignment. While agents came and went, Donovan had been around for twenty years. He was an easy target for teasing, but he was also a valuable resource. Though he came with a price. "How many?"

"If this turns out to be nothing, we'll make it a twelve-pack." He shrugs. "If it's interesting, my help is on the house. Haven't seen anything worth my while in a few weeks now."

"Tell me about it," Jones said, as he unfolded the paper and handed it to Donovan.

The large man took the paper and dropped a pair of reading glasses onto his nose. "Huh, kind of vague."

"I know," Jones said, looking at the caved-in tunnel. "Looks like they blew the tunnel entrance, but it's nothing a backhoe couldn't get through."

"If you could get a backhoe out here."

"Right."

As they got nearer, the size of the excavation revealed itself. "Must be twenty five feet tall," Jones said. "Nearly as wide."

"Bigger," Donovan said. He pushed his booted foot into the loose ground. "I think they filled in this whole area. He pointed to the caved-in tunnel. "That's just the top."

"But it would have been huge," Jones said.

Donovan suddenly gasped and thrust his finger toward the top of the caved-in tunnel. "I think I saw someone."

Jones's hand went to his holster. "Where?"

"Up at the top."

Jones looked to where Donovan was pointing and saw a tunnel through the rubble. "Have a flashlight?"

Donovan produced one and handed it to Jones, who scrambled up the mound of rocky debris. Near the top, Jones drew his weapon, flicked on the flashlight and aimed both into the hole. It was roughly three feet around and at least twenty deep before opening up into a larger chamber.

"This is FBI, special investigator Jones," Jones shouted into the hole. "Come out now. Hands on your—ahh!" Something large and black, like an arm, or a python, shot out of the tunnel, wrapped around Jones's waist and turned him around before yanking him inside and folding him in half—backwards.

If not for the loud crack of Jones's spine, Donovan might have remained rooted in place like a shocked deer. But that sound and the death it signified sent him running.

The chopper was just fifty yards away. The distance could be covered in seconds by a man in decent shape, but Double D was far from in shape and by the twenty-fifth yard, he was wheezing for air. He slowed and glanced back. There was no sign of Jones, or a pursuer, so he stood still for a moment and pitched forward, catching his breath. When he was sure that whatever took Jones wasn't coming, he turned forward and stepped into a wall that sent him sprawling.

When he recovered from the fall and looked up, he found the silhouette of a man standing above him. But there was something off about the man. Not only was he large, but he was also oddly shaped...like he was wearing armor.

Was this the person who killed Jones?

"Who—who are you?" he managed to ask.

The stranger leaned in close revealing that he wasn't wearing armor, or anything else—the armor was part of his body, which wasn't silhouetted so much as it was solid black. Donovan was quickly convinced that this wasn't a man at all.

But then, it spoke.

"General Lance Gordon," the monster said. "At your service."

With glaring, very human eyes, Gordon looked Donovan up and down. He grinned, revealing his new, sharp teeth. "You're a bigun, aren't you. The kids are going to love you."

"K—kids?"

Gordon drew back his three scaled fingers, clenched a fist and drove it into Donovan's skull, shattering it like an ostrich egg beneath a sledge hammer. He looked at the thick armored flesh of his hand, now covered with gore and dollops of brain matter. "Mmm," he said, and slurped some off. Then he cupped a hand to his mouth and said, "Chow time!"

EPILOGUE III

Two thousand feet of frigid water covered her like a blanket, providing darkness to sleep, pressure for comfort and nutrients to heal. Her body ached all over, in part from the wounds received during battle, but also from her violent growth. Her joints throbbed now, as did the muscles pulling the carapace back down over her back. The protective covering, more for the fragile wings hidden beneath than for her body, would fuse together in a few days. Until then, it had to be held in place.

In the days after leaving Boston and entering the depths, she shed the reflective plates covering her wings. Many had been damaged in battle, but they also itched like a burning fire. Her gleaming white skin dulled and clumps of black, hard flesh had begun to form. In a month, she would be back to her more bulky, impervious form.

Soon after that, she would be ready.

She could feel them.

All of them.

Humans.

All their hate and anger, jealousy and loathing. It pulsed across the globe like radio waves, drawing her attention to the strongest signals. The ocean helped muffle the call to action, but there was no escaping it. Right now, her attention was torn in several different directions. She wasn't sure how, but she had names for the places: Syria, North Korea, Moscow, Iran, Washington, D.C.

The call from these locations felt strongest, but there were flaring tensions all around the world, and she wanted to stomp them out of existence with all of her heart and soul. The silence would be bliss. She longed for it. Craved it. But it would not come until justice was served, vengeance was had...or every last human being was dead.

Her gut twisted uncomfortably. Her mind burned with a fury that would exact retribution without concern for what lay between her and her target, but another part of her, which felt foreign, tempered her bloodlust with conscience...and a sense that allowed her to detect a second signal. The pulse was weaker, but always there, fighting for her attention.

Her mind called it a distraction.

Her conscience called it love.

When the mind gave love any thought, an image would emerge. A woman with light brown skin, dark almond eyes and a smile that said everything would be okay. Weary from her endless indignation, she focused on the woman's face—and slept.

For months.

And then, somewhere in the world, someone murdered a little girl.

A drone dropped a bomb, killing a family.

A man was robbed, and then shot.

A woman, bound and gagged, was sold.

The list of offenses struck with such force and frequency that the lingering image of the woman's face was forgotten. The ocean flickered orange and then glowed brightly for a half mile in every direction, bringing light to that area of the deep for the first time in millions of years. Panicked fish scattered or twitched in shock. But the light soon faded.

Nemesis was rising.

NEMESIS SKETCHES

The following pages include the original creature concept designs for Nemesis (Maigo) by illustrator, Matt Frank. While they were based on descriptions provided by Jeremy Robinson, the concepts took on a life of their own, influencing and inspiring the story in progress.

Nemesis Close-up – Stage 2

Nemesis – Stage 1

Nemesis – Stage 3

ABOUT THE AUTHOR

JEREMY ROBINSON is the author of over twenty novels including the highly praised, *SecondWorld*, as well as *Pulse*, *Instinct*, and *Threshold*, the first three books in his exciting Jack Sigler series. His novels have been translated into ten languages. He lives in New Hampshire with his wife and three children.

Visit him online at: www.jeremyrobinsononline.com

ABOUT THE ARTIST

MATT FRANK is a comic book illustrator and cover artist who has worked on well known titles such as *Transformers* and *Ray Harryhausen Presents*, but he is perhaps most well known for his contributions to multiple *Godzilla* comic books. He lives in Texas and enjoys pineapple juice.

Visit him online at: www.mattfrankart.com

ρ

Made in the USA
San Bernardino, CA
10 March 2013